If anyone finds this letter, then it's probably too late . . .

My name is Nate. Me and my best friend Cat are inventors, and a few months ago we entered a competition to win a year's scholarship with Ebenezer Saint — the richest, cleverest and most charismatic inventor in the world.

It started off like a dream — we and twenty-three other kids won the competition and began our year-long stay in Saint Solutions, a massive industrial complex in the heart of the city. We could invent anything that we wanted to, and we did — including a pint-sized robot called Clint (who ended up as a holograph inside my watch, long story).

But soon things started to go wrong. Saint's assistants turned out to be killer robots, and we discovered that Saint Solutions was actually deep underground where nobody would ever find it. Eventually we realised that Saint wanted to destroy the world, wipe it clean so he could start it all again. It would have meant the death of every single living thing on the planet. He was crazy, and we were the only ones who could stop him.

Me, Cat, Clint and a boy called David Barley managed to defeat Saint. David carried the other inventors to safety in a rocket ship while Cat and I blew up the master inventor's bombs, turning his headquarters to dust and killing him. You have to believe us when we say we didn't have a choice.

We escaped from Saint's underground lair, but instead of finding ourselves back in the city we are in the middle of nowhere. There's snow everywhere and it's freezing! I don't know if David and the other inventors made it out before the explosion, and I don't know how long we can survive out here. By the way my teeth are chattering, I'd say not long. If we don't make it, then I just wanted you to know that we saved the world and deserve heaps of medals and things.

But like I said, if anyone finds this letter, then we're already dead.

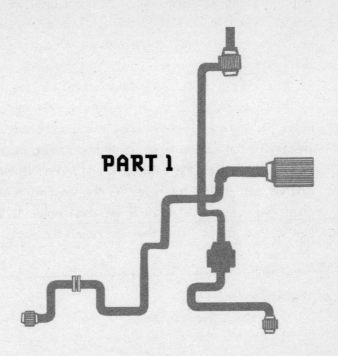

PART 1

1

Into the Freezer

'Talk about out of the frying pan and into the fire.'

Nate and Cat had been walking for half an hour since hurtling from the air vents of Saint Solutions, and this was the first time either of them had spoken. It had been a difficult trek, through bitterly cold wind and seemingly endless snow showers, but now the two young inventors had made their way to the top of a steep, rocky hill, and Cat's words floated down towards the most amazing view imaginable.

'Don't you mean "Out of the frying pan and into the freezer"?' Nate replied in little more than a whisper.

Ahead of them lay a vista of snow and ice that seemed to go on for ever. At the bottom of the slope was a lake which glittered in the cold, bright sun. Rising from the black water, like a family of snow monsters, were hundreds of enormous icebergs. Each was unique – some were the size of a house and shaped like hippos or giant crocodiles, others were at least a hundred metres tall, towering over the landscape like cathedrals of crystal.

'Are we there yet?' came a small voice from the vicinity of Nate's arm. The two inventors looked down to see the holographic image of Clint emerging from Nate's watch. He had poked his see-through head up from the dial and was gazing around with a confused expression. 'We're not there yet, are we?'

'Cat,' Nate said tentatively, ignoring the robot. 'Where on earth are we?'

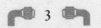

Cat shivered in the bitter cold and turned to face Nate, pulling her overalls around her neck. Her teeth were chattering, and when she spoke clouds of breath billowed from between her lips.

'Remember when Saint told us that the air was being piped straight from Greenland?'

'Yeah.'

'Well, I don't think it was a very long pipe.'

Nate scanned the icy world before them and frowned. It certainly didn't look very green out there, but from what he remembered of Mrs Pommelrind's geography lessons Greenland was actually smack-bang in the middle of the Arctic Circle. For all he knew, they might actually be standing on the North Pole.

'Well, thank you very much, Ebenezer,' Nate muttered. The skin on his face and arms tightened the way it did when he had to pull something out from the back of the freezer, and he thrust his hands into his pockets to try to warm his numb fingers. 'So what now?'

'We have to try and find a town or a camp or something,' Cat said without hesitation. 'If we stay out here too long we'll end up like a couple of snowmen.'

'You mean *cool* dudes?' said Nate, trying to force his frozen face into a smile.

'Nope, I mean cold, lumpy and dead.'

'I'm already cold, lumpy and dead!' shouted Clint from the watch, frowning at the two inventors. 'When are we going to get back to civilisation so you two blethers can build me a new body?'

Cat glanced up at the sun, shielding her eyes from the glare, then stared off towards the lake.

'We have to head south,' she said, 'if there are any towns at all then they'll be in that direction.'

 4

Nate was about to respond, but was beaten to it by a deafening screech which cut through the air and made him stagger backwards. He tripped on a rock and landed squarely on his backside. Terrified, Clint disappeared back inside Nate's watch with a yelp.

'What the bloody hell was that?' Nate yelled, expecting to see a dragon swoop down over the ice and snatch them both in its talons. The noise came again, this time accompanied by a series of cracks which echoed off the ice like gunshots. Oh, great, he thought, a dragon with a machine gun.

'Pick yourself up, you great ninny,' said Cat, offering him a hand. 'It's just the icebergs. They're calving.'

Nate grabbed Cat's arm and hoisted himself up with a grunt. He had no idea what she was talking about, but looking out over the lake he saw an enormous berg directly ahead of them split down the middle. Jagged fissures appeared along its side, each producing another ear splitting crack, until eventually the strain proved too much and the top half of the icy mountain broke off. It toppled downwards, almost in slow motion, and hit the black lake, creating a tidal wave that crashed and spat its way across the water.

'So,' Nate said when the spectacle had finished, 'let's head south.'

He turned and started making his way down the hill, back the way they'd come, but Cat stopped him with a nervous cough.

'Actually,' she said, pointing out towards the black lake and its fleet of deadly icebergs, '*that* way is south.'

For the next ten minutes Nate protested loudly at having to cross the lake, until Cat rolled up the biggest snowball she could and hurled it at him. It hit Nate square in the face, and he immediately fell into a shocked silence.

'Right then, Snow White,' said Cat, doing her best not to laugh. The only features of Nate's face that were visible were his nose, which had turned bright red, and one eye which glared at her furiously. 'We're tired and by the look of those clouds it's going to get even colder, so I suggest we make a shelter and try and get some rest while we come up with a plan.'

As Nate wiped the snow from his face Cat scanned the horizon. To their right, the lake curved round and disappeared behind a range of imposing mountains that cut into the clouds like alligator teeth. In the distance to their left, barely visible in the darkening sky, a small copse of sad-looking trees stood firm against the bitter wind, separated from the lake by a stretch of icy ground. Cat grabbed Nate by his sleeve and began dragging him in that direction, ignoring his complaints.

'Those trees look like the best place to camp out until we know what we're doing,' she said when Nate finally stopped grumbling. 'You get a fire going and I'll make a shelter, then when we're warm and toasty we'll sort out a plan.'

'Fires and shelters, eh?' Nate replied. His nose had gone completely numb, and he felt it to make sure it was still there. Unfortunately, his fingers were senseless too so he had no way of telling. 'Shall I whip up a Sunday roast and a television while I'm at it?'

Cat turned and scowled at him.

'Come on, Nate, we've just outwitted the world's greatest inventor, saved the planet and narrowly escaped being reduced to dust. I'm sure we can survive a bit of cold weather and a hike!'

Despite his aching feet Nate managed a smile, and they continued towards the copse in silence – apart from Clint popping his holographic head up every now and again to ask 'Are we there yet?' Nate had done his best not to think about Saint since they escaped his underground headquarters, but talk of the master inventor sent his thoughts spiralling back over the previous few months.

It was almost impossible to believe – only that morning he and Cat had been inside Saint Solutions, desperately planning their escape. Everything since seemed distant, as though it had happened years ago, not a couple of hours – getting all the young inventors into the rocket, the chaos as David tried to take off, the standoff between Saint, Cat and himself and the terrifying chase as they tried to escape the master inventor's fury on Leonardo da Vinci's ancient wooden flying machine.

The image that stuck in Nate's head, that would *always* stick in his head, however, was that of Saint as he tumbled down the lift shaft, swallowed by the almighty power of his own bombs – an explosion so powerful that it reduced the entire complex to nothing but purple ashes.

The thought of their escape made Nate realise how tired he was, and he stumbled as his wobbly legs gave way. Cat caught his arm to stop him hitting the ground, and practically dragged him across the last stretch of icy rock to the battered copse. The trees looked ancient and withered, but they kept out the worst of the wind and the ground beneath them was dry. Collapsing, Nate and Cat spent several minutes in silence staring up at the black clouds through finger-like branches.

Eventually, Cat scrambled to her feet and began prodding Nate with her foot.

'Come on, lazy bones,' she said. 'If we don't get warm and dry soon then we'll never leave these trees. Get to work on the fire – you know how to do it, don't you?'

'Of course I do!' he answered, sitting up. 'It's the most basic invention in the book.'

Every muscle in Nate's body was screaming with pain after

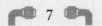

their escape, and the cold had made him stiffer than one of the surrounding trees. Yet he knew Cat was right – if they didn't get a fire started then they could die. The truth was, though, that he couldn't quite remember how to use sticks to make a spark. But there was no way he was going to admit that to Cat. How hard could it be?

'Off you go then,' she went on. 'I'm going to make up our own private Hilton.'

'Make mine an en-suite room,' Nate replied as he struggled to his feet. Sighing, he walked to a nearby patch of ground that was shielded from the wind by a cluster of thick bushes and began collecting loose twigs and branches, leaning them upright against each other until they formed a small tepee.

As he worked he watched Cat make a start on their shelter. She must have been as tired as him, but she ran to and fro between the trees and her campsite as though she'd just woken from a week's sleep. She heaved enormous branches over to the area of ground next to Nate to make the walls of the shelter, stripping long strands of bark from them to act as twine. She even climbed a couple of trees and hung from their long branches, jiggling herself wildly until they snapped off.

Just the sight of Cat working exhausted Nate, so he turned his attention back to the fire. Or rather to the pathetic heap of twigs and leaves that he hoped would become a fire very soon. He found a flat piece of wood and laid it next to the pile, covering it with a few dry leaves. Then he picked up a long, round twig and began rubbing it up and down the flat piece as fast as he could. It was hard work, especially with his aching arms, but after a couple of minutes a sliver of smoke appeared from beneath the leaves.

'Woo hoo!' Nate yelled. 'There's no smoke without fire!'

Cat stopped what she was doing and hunched over Nate as he continued to rub the sticks together. The wisp of smoke had all but vanished, and there was no sign of a flame beneath the leaves. He stopped when he heard her tutting in his ear.

'What?' he asked, panting for breath. Despite the cold he felt boiling, and was sweating from all the hard work. 'It's going to light any minute now!'

'Not like that it isn't,' Cat answered. She nudged him out of the way, kneeling down and picking up his stick. Tying a strip of stringy bark around each end she made a crude bow, then connected the bow string to another piece of wood. When she moved the bow from side to side, the twig spun around like a drill. Placing the tip against the flat bit of wood, Cat began gently easing the bow back and forth, and after a few seconds a pillar of smoke emerged from the pile of leaves.

'Well I was about to do that,' Nate snapped, irritated at Cat's success. He glanced at her shelter to see that it was actually a little like the Hilton – with solid wood walls, a comfy single room and a leafy roof to keep the snow out. It even had a little flag of twigs and leaves hanging above the door. Frowning, he bumped Cat out of the way and grabbed the bow, determined to be useful. 'I'll finish off here.'

Twisting the bow back and forth as fast as he could, Nate managed to keep the trail of smoke going, and after a couple more minutes the little pile of leaves erupted into flame. He whooped with joy, and picked up the flat piece of wood with the fire on top to show Cat.

'Look!' he yelled in as manly a voice as he could muster. 'I made fire!'

'Put that down!' Cat shouted, her expression one of alarm. Nate turned to place the flat piece of wood under the pile of twigs, but before he could the fire spread, devouring the dry wood and threatening to set his fingers alight. Yelping with pain, Nate threw the burning torch to one side and plunged his hand into a nearby pile of snow.

 9

It was only when he heard Cat yelling, and looked up again, that he realised what he'd done. Her cabin was on fire, the wooden walls burning fiercely and the leafy roof smouldering.

'You bloody great big gibbering idiot!' she yelled as she jumped around, trying to blow out the flames. Nate ran over and waved his arms in front of the blaze but it was no use, and in less than a minute the cabin was lost in a wall of fire.

Cat turned and glared at Nate, and he backed off nervously, concerned that she might try and make a cabin out of *him*.

'It's not all bad,' said a tinny voice from his wrist as Clint popped up to see what was happening. 'At least we're warm!'

2

Stranger in the Night

Two hours later, Nate and Cat were sitting in a newly built cabin warming their fingers on the heat of the old one, which was still burning. Nate had gathered all the branches for their second home, with Cat standing like a furious foreman, tapping her foot against the hard ground as she barked orders at him.

'Technically, this means I built the fire *and* the cabin,' said Nate, feeling the warmth creep back into his frozen body, 'while you just stood around talking.'

He soon wished his arms were still numb as Cat punched him playfully on the shoulder, but it was a light-hearted jab and judging by the smile on her lips she was in a much better mood. Through the trees, the dark clouds were still brooding and a dusting of snow had begun to appear on the ground around the copse. The sound of the wind screaming past the battered trees made the young inventors shiver despite the heat of the fire.

'I suggest we camp here for a night,' said Cat after a moment's silence, leaning out of the cabin door and throwing a log on the fire to keep it burning. 'We have to head south, and if we can do it on water then it will save us a lot of time and energy. I think I can probably build a boat from some of these old trees, then we just need some supplies.'

'Supplies?' asked the holographic figure of Clint, who was trying in vain to warm his fingers on the fire. 'I didn't see a shop round here.'

'Me neither,' Cat answered. 'So who knows how to fish?'

Despite the fact that Nate had absolutely no idea how to fish, he soon found himself traipsing across the stretch of ice towards the black lake. In one hand he held a sharpened stick which, according to Cat, he could use as a spear. In the other he held a small net that he had woven from leftover pieces of stringy bark. Staring out across the vast expanse of water, Nate realised that the two pieces of equipment looked about as useful as a toothpick and a tissue.

'You know, I don't think you could even catch a cold, let alone a fish,' came Clint's robotic voice. Nate raised his watch to eye level and scowled at the little robot's holographic grin.

'How about I chuck you in and see how well you do?' he hissed. Clint raised his hands apologetically and sank back into the watch face until only his eyes were visible. They stared out across the water.

'Careful, there might be monsters in there,' he whispered.

Nate ignored him and walked right to the lake's edge, careful not to slip on the ice. Looking down he saw vague shapes darting through the crystal-clear water – ghosts which swam back and forth between the marble-like blocks of ice. He had no way of telling how deep the fish were, or how big. For all he knew, they could be hundreds of metres down and the size of double-decker buses.

The idea brought back the memory of David Barley. Nate had tried not to think about the boy since he'd last seen him – steering his silver ship out of Saint's headquarters and breaking free via the elevator shaft. With any luck they had flown out of the tunnel and blasted off to freedom, but the odds against them succeeding were so high. Maybe the ship had crashed before it hit the air vents, and was a crumpled mess at the bottom of the shaft when the bombs went off. Or maybe they had made it out into the fresh air only to plummet into the black lake.

He shuddered. It wasn't just David's life at stake, it was twenty-one other young inventors who could be suffocating in a tin can in the freezing depths.

Nate shook the thought from his head, getting down on to his knees and lowering his face until it was centimetres above the rippling water. Life with Saint had been terrible, but at least there had been as much food as you could eat. Surely the future of the world was less important than his rumbling stomach. Clint strained his body out of the watch and peered downwards as well.

'There's one!' the little robot shouted, pointing at a dark object which swam past just beneath the surface. Around three seconds later, Nate's tired reflexes sprang into action and he jabbed his stick into the dark lake. The fish had long gone – scared off either by the attack or by Clint's metallic laughter which echoed across the ice. 'Wow, those fish must be trembling in their scales at the sight of you!'

Nate jabbed again at a second shape that darted through the water, coming away empty-handed once again.

'Don't swim away from me, fish!' he shouted angrily, waving his stick above his head. The black shapes below the surface were increasing in number, almost as if the creatures were gathering to laugh at Nate's poor display of survival skills. Two or three even had the cheek to jump right out of the water, flapping their tails and showering him with ice-cold droplets. Nate swiped at them but they were far too quick for his frozen movements.

He was about to try again when another deafening groan cut

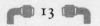

through the air. A jagged, skyscraper-sized iceberg was calving, one entire side of it splitting loose with an almighty crack. Nate felt the ground beneath him tremble as the enormous chunk of ice smashed into the water, and watched in horror as the calm surface erupted into a wave which thundered towards him.

'Oh, pants,' said Nate, scrabbling to his feet and backing away. Needless to say, Clint had vanished as soon as the wave had appeared, with not even his antennae showing. Nate ran for it, making his way up a small rocky hill seconds before the wave crashed into the shore. The foaming water slammed into the side of the lake and gushed across the ground, hard enough to gouge giant cracks in the ice and rip through the rock.

Only when the noise had subsided did Nate dare peer out from behind his trembling fingers. But when he did his face instantly broke into a smile. Flapping around on the cracked ice were three fat fish which had been thrown ashore by the wave. Nate leaped off the hill and ran to the closest one, spearing it with his stick.

'Ha!' he exclaimed as he collected the others on the end of his spear. 'Not so tough now, are we!'

Stuffing the wriggling creatures into the net he turned and started walking back to their makeshift camp. As he neared the copse, however, something on the ridge of steep hills behind the trees caught his eye. Although it was getting dark, and the snow was gathering strength, he was sure he could see a lone figure standing on a peak, a black silhouette against the moody sky. But it was a fleeting vision, and the moment he blinked the figure vanished into the swirling snow.

Nate ran across the smooth ice and crashed through the trees into their camp, panting. Cat was standing by the fire, staring off into the distance, and she turned and hushed Nate as soon as he started to tell her about the mysterious shape.

'It might be a rescue team,' Nate whispered, walking to Cat's side and trying to get a glimpse of the figure. 'They might have detected the explosion when we blew up Saint Tower and come to find out what caused it.'

'I don't know, Nate,' Cat replied, her low voice barely audible over the howling wind. 'It looked like there was only one person. What if it's a psychopath?'

Nate raised an eyebrow.

'How many psychos do you know that live in the Arctic Circle?'

She didn't answer, not taking her eyes off the distant hills.

'It might be a bear,' added Clint, who had emerged from the watch again.

'You're not helping.' Nate scowled down at the little holographic robot. 'I say we risk it, build another fire out there on the ice so he can see our smoke and hope that he's somebody friendly.'

This time it was Cat's turn to raise an eyebrow.

'Do you not recall whose company we've been keeping for the last few months?' she said. 'And the last person we thought was somebody friendly?'

'Fair point,' he replied, thinking about how they had both looked up to Saint, even seen him as a father figure, before discovering his horrific plans to destroy the world. 'But I still think it's probably a rescue team.'

Cat hushed him again, pointing up towards the hill with one hand and grabbing his arm firmly with her other. Nate followed her finger to the distant peak and saw that the figure had reappeared, standing motionlessly on the highest rock as if it was scanning the valley below for any sign of life. Or for them.

'Whoever he is,' Cat hissed, 'he probably knows we're here.'

'Exactly, a rescue squad,' said Nate. But something about the way the figure looked was making him uneasy. Although he was too far away to see in any detail, it was obvious that the man was almost skeletal in shape, and hardly wearing any protective clothing. From here he looked like a scrawny tree poking out of the rock and hunched against the fierce wind.

'Maybe it's another survivor?' Nate said.

'Maybe you're an idiot,' Cat replied. 'Doesn't anything about that guy seem a little weird to you?'

Nate screwed up his eyes, straining to get a clearer view. The storm clouds were still gathering overhead, plunging the freezing world into darkness, but every now and again a silver ray of sunlight would break through the blanket of grey, making the ice appear to glow in the dark. As he watched, another beam of light escaped the overcast sky and struck the hills where the man was standing, presenting a sight that made Nate's heart freeze harder than the surrounding landscape.

'How many rescue teams do you know that are metal?' Cat asked, her finger still pointing to the figure on the hill, whose entire body glinted as though it was made of steel.

3

The Ark

Neither Nate nor Cat said a word for the next few minutes. Nate's mind was racing as he tried to find a reason why the figure on the hill was glinting in the sunlight. Maybe he was wearing special cold-weather gear made from foil, or a protective metal suit as a defence against polar bears? Maybe it was just a hallucination brought on by the cold?

But his mind already knew the answer even if his mouth was too scared to say it out loud. It was a robot, obviously one which had survived the destruction of Saint Solutions. And like all loyal robots it was probably seeking them out to avenge the death of its creator.

'We've got to get that boat finished,' Cat whispered eventually, not taking her eyes from the gleaming figure until it had once again disappeared. 'If that's what I think it is then we're not going to want to be here when it comes down the hill.'

'How can it be, though?' Nate replied. 'That explosion destroyed everything, not even Saint's robots could have survived. They're all purple ashes now, surely.'

'Maybe it was outside,' said Cat, turning her attention back to their camp. Her tapping feet let Nate know she was furiously thinking of a plan even as she was replying to him. 'On a recon mission or something.'

'Well, then it probably doesn't know what happened,' Nate went on hopefully. 'It's probably just looking for company because it can't find its way home.'

Cat turned to stare at him.

'Fine, Nate,' she said, her face expressionless. 'You stay here and comfort the poor robot and keep your fingers crossed that it doesn't tear you limb from limb. I, on the other hand, am going to make a raft and skedaddle faster than I've ever skedaddled before.'

'Okay,' he said, imagining himself being chased around the campfire by a robot bent on destruction. 'I'll skedaddle too.'

Cat nodded her approval and walked over to the far side of the tiny copse, where she had already cut down a few long branches and laid them across the cold ground. Picking up a bundle of stripped bark she began to wind it up into a rope.

'I can handle the boat,' she said to Nate. 'Try and do something with those fish so we've got grub to eat along the way.'

Nate realised he was still holding the makeshift net full of fish, and made his way over to the fire. Sticking his spear into the hard soil, he skewered the miserable creatures on to the end and angled them so that they were close to the flames. Within minutes a smell like burning rubber wafted up to his nostrils and he pulled a face. He was hungry, but not that hungry.

Not wanting to disturb Cat, he scanned the copse and tried to think of other ways to make himself useful. All he wanted to do was curl up in their shelter and fall asleep next to the warmth of the fire, but he knew that if he did he'd be woken up by a furious Cat – probably with a giant snowball stuck down his trousers. Instead, he decided to try and create some booby traps just in case the robot did decide to pay them a visit.

Picking up a long strand of stripped bark that Cat had woven, he searched the copse until he found a couple of young trees side by side. The saplings were almost four times as tall as him, but bendy enough to be pulled down so that their tops touched the ground. He climbed the first, his weight dragging it down until it was low enough to be tied to an exposed root. He did the same to the second, creating two crude catapults.

Returning to the fire, he found his fishing net and carried it back to the trees, stretching it out as he walked until it was the size of a badminton net. He laid it along the ground between the saplings and tied one end to the top of each tree, covering it up with dry leaves and soil. He used his last piece of rope as a tripwire – one which would release the trees if it was triggered, hopefully launching any intruders into the grey sky.

'Now that's what I call a con-*trap*-tion,' he said proudly as Clint popped up to check on his progress.

'Tasty!' exclaimed the little holographic robot, nodding his head in appreciation. 'Do we have a boat yet?'

In the excitement of building his booby trap, Nate had completely forgotten about Cat and the boat. Jogging through the trees he found her on the other side of the small copse putting the finishing touches to their vessel. It was a boat roughly the size of a small car, constructed from long branches and held together by strands of stripped bark. The most remarkable thing, however, was the spring mechanism she had somehow managed to construct using another bendy tree and some spare branches.

'Nice of you to join me,' she said, not looking up from the knot she was tying. 'This little thing will give us a quick getaway if we need it,' she patted the spring and looked at Nate, beaming. 'All we have to do to escape is pull this lever and the spring will fire us out across the ice towards the lake.'

'Very, very tasty!' shouted Clint.

They spent the next couple of hours perfecting their inventions while the world outside the copse became increasingly hostile. Eventually, when their fingers were too frozen to move, and the shadows had plunged the copse into darkness, they retreated to the roaring fire.

'We leave first thing,' said Cat when they had both settled inside their makeshift shelter. They sat side by side, pressed together for warmth and their hands held out to the comforting flames. 'Whatever is up there, it will take it a while to find us in the dark, especially as it's got to get down that hill. But we should sleep in shifts, just in case.'

Nate shivered, making his teeth chatter, but it was less to do with the cold than the thought of a killer robot on the loose.

'Okay,' he replied eventually, struggling against the tiredness that seemed to have taken over his whole body. 'You can sleep first, if you like. Even though I've done most of the work.'

Cat attempted to punch him playfully, but her exhausted limbs had none of their usual strength, and instead she simply rested her hand on his arm. Nate placed his hand on top of it, squeezing gently and shuffling so that he was pressed even more tightly against her. He had never seen Cat look this weak, and for the first time he wondered what would happen if they couldn't find a way home. They would be like the Babes in the Wood, cowering in a hollow until they froze to death.

The image brought a lump to his throat, and for a terrible moment he thought he was about to blubber helplessly in front of his friend.

'We have to get home, Cat,' he said, fighting the tears. 'For our mums, for our friends, for us. I don't want some future explorers discovering us inside giant ice cubes and bringing us back to life in the year 4000.' He paused, realising that the idea actually seemed quite cool. 'I don't want to lose everything because of some loony who thought it was a good idea to move his base to the coldest place in the northern hemisphere.'

'I know,' Cat replied, 'we have to get home. But it's got nothing to do with any of that.' She looked up at him, her expression distorted by the flickering firelight and ever so slightly mad. 'We have to get home so I can have a cup of tea!'

Nate burst out laughing, and Cat soon joined in, the sound echoing off the trees and filling the cold copse with warmth. It felt like they hadn't laughed like this for weeks – months – and their helpless giggling went on for a good ten minutes. By the time they settled down, the stress of the day seemed to have vanished, and both young inventors were feeling positive about the long journey ahead.

'Come on, Cat,' said Nate, still grinning. 'I'll take the first watch and wake you in a couple of hours. The sooner you get to sleep, the sooner you get that tea.'

'Don't you think we should eat something first?' she asked, her words slurred from tiredness. Nate looked across at the fish which Cat had pulled from their skewers and laid along the ground to cool. Thoroughly burned, with their tiny black eyes staring out accusingly at Nate, they looked about as appetising as a dog turd. He'd have to be on the edge of death before he'd stick one of them in his mouth.

'I think we're probably okay for tonight,' he whispered. 'Sleep tight, Cat, don't let the polar bears bite.'

Cat whispered something that sounded like 'you too', but before the words were even out she was fast asleep and snoring gently. Nate carefully laid her down on the ground, tucking her overalls around her neck to keep the chill out and throwing another log on the fire. He looked at the orange flames, mesmerised by the way they danced and snaked over the crumbling wood, and tried not to think about the fact that they had to cross the lake of death in the morning.

'Gotta stay awake,' he whispered to himself as he felt his eyelids droop. 'Gotta guard the camp.'

But with the warmth of the fire on his face, and the weight of the world on his shoulders, he was soon curled up beside Cat, his sleeping mind filled with dreams of steaming hot mugs of tea.

4

Leg It!

Nate woke to the sound of a branch snapping.

He sat bolt upright, still half dreaming that he had been locked inside a freezer by Santa for not being a good boy. It took him a second to remember where he was, but a quick scan of the copse – bathed in blinding silver light and bitterly cold – brought the memory back with a painful jolt. It was morning, and their once impressive fire was now little more than a couple of smouldering twigs.

Rubbing his numb limbs, Nate looked down to see Cat still fast asleep beside him, a strand of drool hanging out of her open mouth. Nate smiled, wishing he had a camera, but he was distracted by the sound of another crack – the unmistakable noise of a twig being broken underfoot.

He got to his feet, ignoring his aching limbs, and gave Cat a gentle nudge with his shoe. He couldn't see anybody else in the small copse, but that didn't mean there wasn't someone behind one of the trees, waiting for the right moment to pounce. He prodded Cat with a little more strength and she began to stir, muttering something as she returned to the waking world.

'Turn the heating up, Mum,' she said, her voice muffled through the drool. 'And be a darling and bring me some tea.'

'Cat!' Nate hissed, not taking his eyes off the trees. 'Cat, wake up. It's definitely time we skedaddled.'

Very slowly, one of Cat's eyes opened, closely followed by the other, and for a few seconds she lay on the ground looking at her surroundings.

'Oh yeah,' she said eventually as the reality of the situation sunk in. 'I forgot we were here.'

'And I don't think we're alone,' Nate whispered. She grabbed his hand and struggled to her feet. They stood in silence for a moment, listening to the wind which still howled through the trees. Then it came again, two snaps this time, and closer than before.

'Is the boat ready to go?' asked Nate. Cat nodded, backing away towards the wooden raft. The sound of her feet disturbing the undergrowth was deafening in the silence of the copse, and almost as soon as she started moving several more snaps came from behind the trees. Whatever was here now knew they were awake, and didn't appear to be bothering with tact any more.

Nate saw something move in the corner of his eye. He wrenched his head round in time to see a dark shadow flicker between two ancient trunks and vanish behind a bush.

'Did you see that?' Cat hissed. He heard her start moving again, quicker this time, and he was about to turn and follow when the shadow moved again, darting out from cover and swooping across the copse to another tree. It disappeared with frightening speed, but not before Nate got a good look at it. It was a huge metal man, but not like any of the robots they'd seen at Saint Solutions.

'Nate, run,' came Clint's voice from his watch. But Nate was frozen to the spot – half from sheer terror and half from a morbid curiosity to know what was chasing them.

'Have you got a death wish? Come on!' yelled Cat as she turned and sprinted towards the boat, stumbling on the uneven ground. Nate jogged after her, not looking over his shoulder until he reached the raft. Clambering on board he scanned the copse, but the metal man had disappeared.

'What the hell was that?' he asked Cat, who was on board and prepping the boat's spring mechanism.

'A robot,' she answered, her brow furrowed in concentration as she struggled with the wooden lever. 'One of Saint's.'

'No, it wasn't,' Nate said, turning his attention back to the copse. 'No way. It didn't look anything like one of his robots, apart from the fact it was metal. This one was thin and spindly.'

'Like the Tin Man,' added Clint, who had his hands raised to his eyes like binoculars.

Cat looked up at Nate, an eyebrow raised.

'Do you think there are other crazy scientists out here with the ability to make robots? No? Right, henceforth that thing belongs to the master inventor.' She returned to the spring, tugging the rope which tied the bent sapling to the ground. 'Dammit, this is supposed to be foolproof.'

Nate shuffled across the deck to see if he could help. Cat had basically used the same crude mechanism for the boat as he had for his booby trap – a bent tree designed to act like a catapult and launch them across the stretch of icy ground towards the lake. But for some reason the rope had become jammed, preventing the tree from pinging upright.

'I'll get down and untie it,' Nate said. 'But for god's sake don't let go until I'm back in.'

'Roger that,' Cat replied, bracing the rope against the side of the boat to prevent it launching.

Nate jumped over the side, and ran across to the bent tree. The rope that acted as a tripwire was caught on something, and getting down on his hands and knees Nate saw that it was metallic – a sliver of steel which had been placed there deliberately. He reached out and tugged at the obstruction, the cold metal burning his skin, and stood up to show it to Cat. He stopped when he saw her expression.

 25

She was staring over his shoulder, her face deathly white and her eyes wide in horror.

'Please don't say it's right behind me,' he whispered, but before Cat could respond he whirled round to find himself face to face with the most terrifying sight he had ever witnessed.

The metal man didn't have a muzzle like Saint's robots, or the giant arms which could squish a young inventor like he was made of butter. In fact, its face was almost human, and under any other circumstances could have looked quite friendly.

But the eyes – the eyes were long and narrow and glared at Nate with undisguised hatred, a look which burned into his soul, which threatened to turn his legs to jelly and his heart to stone. And Nate knew that expression, he'd seen it before, less than twenty-four hours ago – a golden glare which could only ever belong to one man.

'Saint,' Nate hissed.

The metal monster didn't respond. This time there were no words, no showing off. The robot wanted only one thing – to crush the young inventors who had destroyed its dreams. It raised one of its thin arms and brought it down like a sword, striking Nate on the shoulder and sending him flying.

Nate felt as though he'd been hit by a car. He spun across the rough ground, hitting the side of the boat and collapsing to the floor. For a second the world went black, and he struggled to stay conscious. *This can't be happening again*, he thought, watching the creature pound towards him. *Saint's dead, we saw him die*.

The sound of screams brought him back, and he checked to see if Cat was okay. She was scanning the boat for anything she could use as a weapon, but it wasn't her making the noise. Looking down, he saw Clint cowering on the watch face, head in his hands and screeching in an ear-piercing falsetto.

The giant robot crashed towards him, raising a metal foot to bring down on his head. Nate rolled just in time, feeling the ground shake as the creature stamped. He scrabbled upwards, ducking as the beast swiped its glinting arm towards his head and running round it to try and get to the boat.

'Come on!' cried Cat, her hand on the spring lever, ready to propel them to safety. Nate jumped on to the side of the boat but the robotic Saint was too quick, grabbing the back of his overalls and pulling. Nate clutched the wood with all his strength and Cat took hold of his arms, struggling to keep him on board.

'Just hang on,' she said, tears of anger rolling down her cheeks. Nate looked her in the eye, knowing that he couldn't keep his grip on the boat for more than a few seconds. The robot's strength was incredible – it felt like a fleet of trucks was trying to pull him back. If he didn't let go now, then they'd both die.

'Go,' he said to Cat. She shook her head, tightening her grip on his arms.

'I'm not leaving you, Nate.'

'You don't have a choice,' he replied. 'Goodbye, Cat.'

Feeling like his heart was about to explode, Nate let go of the wood with his left hand and slapped the lever for the spring mechanism.

'Nate, no!' Cat screamed. For a second, nothing happened, then the bent sapling snapped back with a deafening crack, propelling the boat out of the copse and across the ice. With nothing to hang on to, Nate and the robot flew backwards, sprawling across the hard ground. Nate leapt to his feet, watching as the robot rolled over and stood, its golden eyes even more ferocious than before.

But despite the danger, Nate turned his back on the beast, staring out at the lonely figure of his best friend. She gazed back, her arm held out as if she could still grab him as she hurtled towards the lake, as if she could change the fact that this might be the last time they would ever see each other.

5

Trapped

Nate kept his eyes on Cat until the tiny boat had skidded across the ice, sending a plume of icy water jetting into the sky as it hit the distant lake. Then, with a shuddering sigh, he resigned himself to his fate and turned to face his killer.

The robot was standing several metres away, watching him with its cold eyes and saying nothing. It didn't appear to be in any hurry to finish its murderous business – with Cat and the boat gone, it knew it had all the time in the world to make its young nemesis pay.

Nate studied the creature. It was tall but extremely skinny, like a man who had been starved for a month, with long limbs little thicker than Nate's arms and spindly fingers that moved continuously as though playing an invisible piano. Every now and again the robot would tremble, as though it was having a fit – its whole body spasming uncontrollably for a few seconds.

At one time, less than a year ago, Nate would have run screaming from the sight of the metallic creature before him, or just collapsed into a quivering ball of terrified jelly. But he was a different person now – stronger, braver – and taking a deep breath he strode confidently towards the beast.

'Saint,' he said, his voice little more than a whisper but carrying easily across the hard ground. 'I didn't think I'd ever see you again.'

The robot's eyes narrowed another notch and its mouth

opened as if to reply, but all that came out of it was a pitiful coughing sound. It tried again, this time producing a noise not unlike a jammed CD, almost as if it was trying to speak but didn't know how. Nate wondered if it really was Saint inside the creature's head, if somehow the master inventor had managed to download his personality to the machine as he was dying. It seemed impossible, but then looking back *everything* they had seen and done in the last few months seemed impossible.

The robot tried to speak again, stamping its foot in frustration when it failed. Instead, it pointed one of its bony fingers at Nate before drawing it across his throat – a threat that didn't need words.

Then the creature pounced, its spindly legs propelling it across the ground with awful speed. Nate wanted to dive out of the way but his tired body couldn't react in time, and in the blink of an eye the creature's metal fist was round his throat and he was hoisted into the air. Trying to ignore the sense of déjà-vu, he lashed out at the robot with his hands and feet, but it was like trying to attack a tank with a marshmallow, and the beast simply pulled Nate towards it, gloating in its victory.

'D-d-d-d-d-d-d-d-d-d-d,' it said, its golden eyes never leaving Nate's, 'i-i-i-i-i-i-i-i-i-i-i-i-i-e!'

Nate felt the grip around his throat tighten, struggled to breathe in. His vision darkened, and once again he found himself thinking that Saint's face was going to be the last thing he ever saw. He turned his thoughts to Cat – pictured her making her way across the lake, finding help and ending up back at home, wrapped in a blanket and drinking tea with her mum – and despite the pain he found himself smiling. The robot could do what it liked with him, Cat was too far away to hurt.

At least, she was for now. Despite the pain Nate twisted his head around towards the lake, hoping to see Cat sailing off into the distance. Instead, to his horror, he saw a tiny figure running back towards the copse.

Bloody typical! He thought to himself. But inside he was grinning.

The robot was also watching Cat's return. Its face broke into a malicious grin, and it began to emit a noise that sounded like nails being dragged across a terracotta pot – a screeching laugh that made Nate squirm.

For a second, Nate felt the fingers tighten even further, and thought his throat was about to be crushed. But then the robot began to spasm once again – its entire body juddering and shaking as the human mind inside struggled to control the mechanical frame. Its grip weakened, and Nate wrenched the fingers free, dropping to the ground and gasping for air.

Rolling to one side, he jumped to his feet, almost falling again before his legs found strength. The robot was still convulsing – vibrating and jerking like a mechanical pony – but it would only be seconds before it recovered.

'Oh lordy,' came a voice from his wrist. Clint's head had popped up from the watch face and was looking at the robot. 'Without Cat we're toast.'

'Thank you very much!' shouted Nate, scanning the trees for an escape route. 'I don't need Cat to save my hide!'

But the truth was his brain was desperately trying to work out what Cat would do in this situation. The robot stopped shaking, twitched a couple of times and shook like a dog drying itself after a swim. Then it targeted Nate with its eyes and charged again.

'Run, you great dolt!' came Clint's voice.

Nate sprinted towards the nearest tree, scowling at his little holographic friend. Clint had obviously been spending too much time around Cat, and was becoming increasingly cheeky. Nate ducked behind the trunk, his panic evident from the short bursts of clouded breath that emerged from his mouth. The sound of pistons and heavy feet was getting louder, and he knew he only had seconds to act.

'Hide!' whispered Clint. 'You great –'

Nate shut the little robot up by swiping his hand through the holograph, then darted out from behind the tree, sprinting further into the copse. The creature screamed when it saw him moving, doubling its speed and charging. He ducked behind another tree, feeling the wood splinter as the robot struck it from the other side. Hiding was out of the question – sooner or later every tree in the copse would be reduced to splinters.

'We're trapped!' screamed Clint, popping up again. 'Oh woe is me!'

'Trapped, that's it!' Nate pushed himself away from the tree just as a metal hand shot round, aiming for his throat. He looped round a bush then doubled back, heading towards the area he'd been working in the day before. The part of the copse where he'd built the trap.

'Nate, what are you thinking?' asked a nervous Clint, eyeing the booby trap in front of them. 'The trap won't work, the robot is too heavy!'

Nate cast a look over his shoulder to see Saint bearing down on him, and dived to one side just as a metal limb sliced the air where he had been standing. His foot struck a rock and he stumbled, rolling across the ground. The beast on his tail was too close to stop, tripping over Nate's splayed body and tumbling forwards. Nate felt as though he'd been trampled by a dinosaur, but he leapt to his feet and ran towards the trap.

'I wasn't thinking about pinging the robot,' Nate hissed as he leapt on to the rope net, careful not to hit the tripwire too early. The mechanical Saint was struggling to its feet, rubbing its head and glaring at him. Then it hurtled forwards again, bent on destruction.

'Nate, whatever you're thinking, don't,' said Clint.

'Just trust me,' Nate replied, smiling. 'This will either be great fun or it will kill us. Or maybe both.'

The robot was metres away, hurtling towards him like a steam train. Instants before it reached the net, however, Nate triggered the trap's tripwire. The effect was instantaneous, loosening the ropes that held down the trees and causing them to spring upright. The net, which was connected to their topmost branches, sprang upwards as well, launching Nate into the air.

He felt as though his stomach had been pulled out of his bottom, and his head spun as the ground was ripped away from him. The wind roared past his ears, but behind this he heard screaming; he looked down to see another impressive display of bravery from Clint. Nate briefly considered joining in, but instead he whooped with delight as the world flew past beneath him.

Cat was still running towards the copse, but she stopped when she saw Nate in mid-flight. Even from this distance Nate could see her open mouth, gobsmacked, as she watched him soar towards her.

But what goes up has to come down, and within seconds Nate was dropping to the hard ground below. He hadn't given any thought to the landing, and braced himself for impact, hoping that he wouldn't break any bones when he hit the ice. Luck was on his side. He sped past Cat's head – so close that she had to duck – and slammed into a snowdrift, sending a wave of powder floating into the air.

Nate felt giddy, but the freezing snow snapped him to attention. He jumped to his feet wiping the dust from his eyes, and grinned at Cat who had run over to see if he had survived. Her face was a mask of concern, and she gave him a hug worthy of a bear before letting him go and slapping him round the face.

'That's for making me leave you!' she shouted, before hugging him with even more force. 'Never do that again. Whatever we face, we do it together, right?'

'Right,' he started to answer, before feeling Cat slap him across the other cheek.

'And that's for the stunt you just pulled,' she yelled. 'You could have killed yourself!'

'Not as quickly as that could have,' he answered, rubbing his cold, stinging cheeks and pointing in the direction he had just come. They both looked back at the distant copse to see the robot emerge from the trees, its body glinting in the fractured sunlight and its eyes two yellow pinpricks of hate. It was running towards them, but it had a lot of ground to cover.

'Where's the boat?' Nate asked, turning his attention to the black lake.

'I pulled it on to the ice before I started running,' Cat answered, grabbing Nate's arm and leading him towards the lake. They ran at full pelt across the slippery surface, skidding to a halt when they reached the boat. It was wedged on the ice, its tail end in the lake and bobbing gently up and down. Cat clambered in, grabbing one of the oars and preparing to launch.

'Come on,' she said. Nate turned to see that the robot was gaining on them again, running so fast that each step made the ice crack – a sound not unlike a fireworks display. It would reach them in less than a minute. He looked back, staring at the giant icebergs that stood in their path.

'Talk about being stuck between a robot and a cold place,' he muttered as he climbed into the boat, feeling it rock unsteadily with his weight.

'That was rubbish!' said Cat, using the oar to push them off the ice. The little wooden raft wobbled slightly, threatening to turn over and plunge them to a freezing death. But with a couple of gentle strokes Cat steadied it, guiding them away from the white shore.

As Cat paddled, Nate watched the glinting figure of Saint. The robot hurtled towards the lake, looking as though it was going to launch itself into the water in pursuit. Nate thought about the previous day, when Saint had risked life and limb to chase them up the elevator shaft. Was the robot really going to plunge into the water after them? Follow them to the ends of the earth?

'I hope that thing can't swim,' Cat said, echoing his fears. But the metal monster stopped when it reached the lake shore, raising its head and screaming in frustration. Nate felt relief flood his body and he got to his feet, blowing a giant raspberry at the robot.

'See you later, Saint!' He shouted, sitting down again when Cat scowled at him. Picking up the spare oar and plunging it into the water, he doubled their speed as they floated into the icy gauntlet ahead.

6

The Black Lake

'You know, this really isn't so bad,' said Cat, several minutes after they had pushed themselves away from the shore. She was sitting at one end of the craft, leisurely steering them across the black lake. Despite her attempt at reassurance her face had turned an odd shade of green from the steady rocking of the boat.

Nate had dropped his paddle and flattened himself to the deck of rough wood with his head in his hands as soon as he'd heard an iceberg screech, and hadn't opened his eyes since.

'Let's hear you say that when one of those bergs comes crashing down on our heads,' he muttered. He scrunched his eyes up even tighter, trying to imagine that he was on a leisurely cruise along the small river in Heaton, on a glorious summer's day.

'Nate, these icebergs aren't doing anything,' Cat continued, her words punctuated by the soothing sound of the paddle sweeping through the water. 'And this view is to die for.'

Nate decided not to point out the irony in her words.

'Come on,' said Clint, who was straining his little holographic body to try and take in the vista beyond the side of the boat. 'I can't see anything from down here.'

'Fine,' he replied, gently pushing himself up into a seated position and trying not to rock the boat. 'If you want me to look into the face of my own death then so be it.'

He was planning to say more, but suddenly found himself speechless. In every direction lay the black lake, its still water reflecting the brilliant blue sky so perfectly it seemed they were one and the same – the icebergs appearing to float weightlessly in midair. They were motionless, and for a moment Nate thought he was inside a photograph. But looking down into the dark water he saw schools of fish sweeping beneath the boat, occasionally leaping above the water and playfully flicking their tails as though wishing them a pleasant voyage. Nate smiled as they splashed back down, trying not to think about their dead relatives that he had tucked into his pocket as they were preparing to flee the approaching robot.

'Wow,' said Clint, his eyes glued on the breathtaking scene. 'It just goes on for ever.'

Despite the looming towers of ice on every side, Nate found himself breathing deeply through a wide smile. The feeling of being trapped inside Saint Solutions, far beneath the ground, had been unbearable. This place, wherever they were, was the complete opposite – a land of snow and ice which seemed to have no end.

'Not quite,' said Cat, taking one hand off the oar to point across the lake. Nate followed her finger, and saw that in the distance the lake ended with a small wooden jetty. Beyond it, dwarfed by the mountains that stood to either side, were what looked like a number of huts.

'Civilisation!' Nate yelled, leaping to his feet and almost tumbling into the water before Cat pulled him back down. 'We're saved!'

'Maybe,' she answered. She turned her attention from the distant jetty to the side of the lake. 'Maybe not.'

Nate turned and felt his heart sink. The ground that ran alongside the black water was made up of giant rocks, and clambering over them like some kind of mechanical spider was the robot. It was moving fast – overtaking the boat and heading straight for the end of the lake.

'Let's just hope his batteries run out before he gets there,' Cat said, trying to force a smile. Nate laughed weakly before taking hold of his oar and helping her guide the boat through the water. The temperature seemed to be dropping steadily, the wind whipping across the water like icy fingers, penetrating their thin overalls and making them both shiver.

On top of that, Nate was hungrier than he had ever been in his entire life. He pulled out the fish from his pocket and looked at them forlornly. If they hadn't been looking back at him even more forlornly then he might have taken a bite. Instead he put them back, deciding he could wait a while longer.

With Nate and Cat working together, the boat picked up speed. Every now and again one of the bergs would creak and crack as they passed it – the tower-block-sized slabs of ice threatening to collapse down on them and send them plunging to the bottom of the lake. But the two young inventors managed to steer their craft safely between them without incident.

Saint too seemed to have disappeared, with no sign of his metal body in between the giant rocks that lined the lake. Nate hoped he'd tumbled into a ravine, or slipped into the lake, but knew the master inventor wouldn't be that clumsy – not when he had a vendetta to carry out.

Clint kept the time as they rowed, announcing each half-hour as it passed. By the time he had called out the sixth, the sun was drooping back towards the horizon and the little boat had almost reached its destination. Nate felt as though he'd been paddling through treacle for the last hour, but he gave his oar another couple of flicks to draw them level with the jetty.

Waiting until the boat had settled, he jumped on to the dock. Cat hopped across after him, still looking slightly queasy but happy to be back on solid ground.

'Do you think *he's* here?' she asked, lowering her voice to a whisper. Nate scanned the ground ahead – a gentle slope which led up to a circle of wooden huts, each no bigger than a garden shed. At first glance, the place looked deserted. But Nate's eyes fell on a cluster of three figures standing in the shadows between two of the huts. They were completely motionless, but Nate could tell that they were human – two children and an adult by the looks of things.

'Why don't we ask them?' he said, pointing to the collective. 'They might be able to tell us where we are.'

'They might have some food,' Cat exclaimed, setting off at a trot. 'They might have some tea!'

Nate followed her up the slope, keeping his eyes on the figures. There was no doubt that the trio would have seen them, but they made no effort to come forward or retreat. Nate started to get an unpleasant feeling in his gut – one that had nothing to do with his hunger. Something very strange was going on, and he didn't like it one little bit.

'Hello?' Cat called out as they reached the huts. The figures stared at them out of the shadows, silent and still. 'We're lost, and we need food and shelter.'

'Er, Cat,' Nate said. They were close enough now to see that the figures were white all over, as if they were frozen. In fact, it soon became clear that they *were* frozen – sculptures immaculately carved from blocks of ice.

But neither Nate nor Cat was appreciating the craftsmanship. Both inventors were standing in horror as it dawned on them what they were looking at. The three people in the sculpture were terribly familiar. The largest was Ebenezer Saint as he was before he died, complete with long coat, wild hair and hate-filled glare. And he had his hands wrapped around the necks of the two smaller ice figures – who bore an uncanny resemblance to Nate and Cat.

For several minutes, neither of the young inventors could move – feeling as frozen as the statues before them. Then Nate reached out to touch the sculpted ice, running his fingers across the polished surface until the cold was too much to bear.

'These have just been made,' he said, realising the implications of this at the same time Cat spoke them out aloud.

'That means Saint's here,' she said. She screwed up her fists and squared up to the white figure of the master inventor, who seemed to study them with a look that was half hatred, half smug humour. 'Why won't he just leave us alone?'

'Well, we did destroy his empire,' Nate replied matter-of-factly. 'And there was the small matter of us killing him.'

Cat lowered her fists in frustration, then set off towards the hut to their right. Nate held out a hand to stop her but before he could she had kicked open the door and disappeared into the dark interior.

'Cat!' Nate hissed. 'Don't go in there! Saint might be in one of these sheds!'

But Cat wasn't listening to him. From the hut came the sound of crashing metal as she rummaged through the equipment inside. Several minutes passed and there was no sign of their robotic nemesis, so Nate walked away from the eerie ice statues and sat down on a nearby snowdrift.

His hunger was painful now, each time his stomach rumbled it felt as though he had a load of spiked ball bearings in his gut. Reaching into his pocket he pulled out the dead fish and studied them, trying not to notice the burned scales and the accusing eyes. But there was nothing else for it – if he didn't eat something soon then he'd waste away.

'You sure you don't want one of these fish?' he shouted in to Cat, who was still rummaging through boxes and making a racket that could probably be heard on the other side of the lake.

'No way, they're all yours,' she replied.

Nate picked the least disgusting-looking fish and closed his eyes. Trying not to think about what he was doing, he opened his mouth and bit down on the charred creature. It was like eating a brillo pad that had been left in the sink for a week, and the sensation caused him to gag. But he persevered, chewing the tough, cold skin and doing his best to imagine that he was eating a steaming-hot plate of macaroni cheese.

'Nice?' came Cat's voice from the hut door. Nate nodded, not opening his eyes in case he saw the insides of his dinner. 'You know, if I was you I'd much rather be eating one of these.'

Nate snapped his eyes open to see Cat wrapped in a bright red Arctic survival coat munching happily on a chocolate bar. In her other hand she held a veritable feast of chocolates, sweets and energy bars. Nate spat out his mouthful of fish flesh and threw the rest to the floor, leaping off the drift and snatching a packet of candy from her. Ripping it open, he tilted back his head and poured the purple sweets into his mouth, barely even bothering to chew them before swallowing noisily.

The sugar rush was almost instant, and he found himself beaming at Cat as he stuffed chocolate bar after chocolate bar into his gob. She smiled back, reaching into the hut and handing Nate another jacket. Slipping it on was like stepping into a hot bath, and he soon found the sensation returning to his arms and legs.

After a few minutes of frenzied chomping, the young inventors threw the rubbish into the hut, stuffed their pockets with supplies and set off to explore.

'It's probably a fishing town,' Cat explained as they started to walk between the huts, squeezing past the creepy ice figures and trying not to think about Saint. 'Some of that stuff in there looked quite new, so there must be people around here somewhere.'

Nate didn't reply as they emerged from the huts into a large, empty space beyond. Well, not quite empty. Dotted around the clearing, just visible in the weak red light of the setting sun, were several more remarkable ice sculptures. Each depicted the same three figures but in different poses – one showed Saint lifting the inventors above the ground, another showed him feeding them to a polar bear, a third gruesomely depicted Nate and Cat in pieces at the master inventor's feet. The polished ice reflected the shimmering evening light in a way that made each one seem alive.

'Oh,' was all Nate could manage. He had never really felt his blood run cold before, but he was pretty sure that's what was happening now.

'Well, that's a bloody cheek, isn't it!' came Clint's voice from his wrist. 'All those ice sculptures and am I in any of them? No.'

'Shush, Clint,' Cat hissed, grabbing Nate's arm and leading him around the outside of the clearing. 'I think we definitely need to get out of here, right now.'

Nate nodded, running his eyes across the clearing in search of movement. But everything was deathly still. Saint was nowhere to be seen. They jogged past two of the statues, heading for a path that led out of the tiny town and up towards the low hills which lay further south.

It was as they were approaching the last sculpture that Nate noticed something strange about it. The figures of himself and Cat were buried head first in the ground, with only their icy legs visible. But it was the statue of Saint that was odd.

Although it showed the master inventor in vivid detail, as he was before he died, the proportions seemed wrong. It was too long, too thin.

'Cat, stop,' he said, coming to a halt. Cat was still running, turning to usher him on as she moved towards the edge of the clearing.

It was as she passed the statue that Nate's nightmares became reality. Inside the ice two golden lights appeared behind Saint's eyes, narrowing into slits and focusing on the figure of Cat. Then the statue moved, the ice splintering and flying outwards like daggers as the robot inside pounced.

7

A Last Stand

Cat screamed, slipping on the snow just as Saint lashed out at her head. She tumbled under his fist, rolling clumsily and clambering back to her feet. The robot lifted a leg, shattering the rest of the ice that covered it, and lunged towards her.

'To the hut!' she shouted, running back the way they had come. Nate didn't think it was a great plan, but he couldn't for the life of him think of anything else to do. Turning, he fled back to the hut with the sound of pistons and stomping metal right behind him. They dashed down one side and spun through the door, tangling themselves up and collapsing to the floor in a pile of sweets and chocolate.

'This is no time to eat!' Cat shouted at Nate as he tried to stand, slipping on a bag of Ebenezer's Teasers. The sound of footsteps on the other side of the wooden wall grew louder, and then stopped, plunging the world into silence. Then a scrawny metal arm burst through the panels, showering them with splinters and narrowly missing Cat's head. The arm withdrew, then came crashing in a second time, this time causing half of the wall to collapse.

There was nowhere to run – the hut was too small, and Saint's robotic arms could easily reach from one side to the other. One fist closed around Cat's jacket, hoisting her effortlessly into the air. Nate tried to bat away the robot's other hand with a Twix but it was useless, and seconds later he found himself yanked painfully through the wood and out once again into the cold air.

He had faced death so many times in the last few days that it was almost as if he had forgotten how to be afraid. Now, held above the ground by his throat, all he found himself thinking was that they were in exactly the same pose as the ice sculpture next to them, and that it would make a nice postcard. *I must be delirious*, he thought to himself, struggling against the iron grip.

Saint leant in towards them, his eyes boring into their souls, his steel mouth twisted into a terrifying grin. He tried to speak again, emitting the horrible stutter of a jammed CD. At least that was one thing, thought Nate, Saint couldn't go on and on about how he was going to kill them like he did when he was alive.

Saint snapped open the fingers that were clamped around Cat's jacket, and she fell to the hard ground. Before she could get up, the robot placed its foot on her chest and started to press. She struggled against the weight that was crushing her lungs but she was powerless against the beast of solid steel. Saint never took his eyes off Nate, making sure that he was watching as his friend died. Nate punched the arm that held him, but he knew it would do no good.

'Sorry, Cat,' he whispered. 'I'm so sorry.'

But from nowhere a gunshot rang out. At first Nate thought it was one of the icebergs on the lake, but a second followed almost instantly, this one causing Saint's head to jerk back. The robot stumbled, taking its foot off Cat as it tried to remain upright. It wrenched its head forwards and Nate saw a huge dent in its forehead. Nestled in the middle of the crater, crumpled almost beyond recognition, was a bullet.

A third shot rang out across the snow, and this time Saint's shoulder spun round. The metal monster began to spasm again, shuddering and vibrating with such force that Nate was thrown to the ground. He scrabbled backwards, watching as the robot righted itself, its hands reaching for a second dent that had appeared in the silver metal of its torso.

Nate heard shouting behind him and turned to see a group of men running into the clearing, one of whom was armed with an impressive-looking rifle. The man got down on one knee, took aim and fired again, the bullet smashing into Saint's leg with enough force to tear a hole in the metal. The robot narrowed its eyes and uttered a scream of pure rage, grabbing at the wound. Then it cast one more look at Nate and Cat and leapt behind the ruined hut, limping as fast as it could into the darkness.

Nate ran over to Cat, who was struggling to sit up. She rubbed her chest, looking at the group of men with a smile that stretched from ear to ear.

'We're saved!' she shouted, letting Nate pull her to her feet. The men approached, each tall and burly and unshaven, wearing huge winter jackets, goggles and hats.

'Hvem er du?' shouted the man with the gun, lowering it on to the snow and walking up to Nate and Cat. 'Hvem var det uhyre?'

Nate didn't have a clue what the man was saying, but it didn't matter – he was a real person, not a robot or a psychotic maniac. Unable to control himself, he threw himself at him, wrapping his arms around his coat and squeezing so hard that he heard the man wheeze.

'You're real!' he shouted. 'You're real!'

The man gave him a gentle hug, then pushed him away, obviously embarrassed.

'Det ser ud til du trænger til noget te,' he said, turning his attention to Cat who he obviously felt was slightly less insane. Although she didn't speak his language, she understood the last word.

46

'Tea?' she shouted, bounding towards him and squeezing him even harder than Nate had done. 'You have tea!' This time the man laughed, taking off his hat and pulling it down over Cat's head. He turned to his friends, wiggling his finger round his ear and pulling an insane face.

'Engelsk,' he said, returning his attention to Nate and Cat. 'You both crazy,' he went on in broken English. 'But you like tea. Come with us.'

And with that he took Cat's hand, slung his arm over Nate and started walking up the hill.

Despite the fact that both Nate and Cat were more exhausted than they had even been before, they were soon skipping with glee up the slope alongside their rescuers. Nate was waltzing in clumsy circles pretending to hold Clint's holographic arms while humming an out-of-tune version of *The Blue Danube*. Cat was dancing around the man who had shot Saint, giving a breathless summary of what had happened in the last few months. By the look on his face, however, he didn't understand a word.

The men, who each had a Danish flag stitched on to the back of their thick winter coats, talked among themselves as they walked. Every now and again they stared down at Nate and Cat with bemused expressions, which wasn't really surprising – after all it wasn't every day that you stumbled upon a pair of kids in the Arctic Circle being attacked by an eight-foot-tall metal monster.

The unusual group crested the top of the hill and Nate was delighted to see a modern cabin ahead of them, with satellite dishes and radio antennae bristling on the roof and smoke idly drifting from the chimney. A number of snowmobiles sat outside, dusted with powder from a recent trip, and beyond them was a small plane equipped with skis instead of wheels.

One of the men pushed open the door and ushered them inside, and both young inventors made straight for the roaring fire. Collapsing to the wooden floor, they leant on each other as they warmed their numb fingers on the fierce flames.

Minutes later the man who had saved them returned holding two steaming mugs of tea. Cat's eyes practically leaped out of their sockets when she saw the drink, and she snatched it from his hands, gulping it noisily as tears of joy spilled down her cheeks. Nate sipped the scalding liquid more slowly, but as he felt the warmth spread through him he discovered that he had tears in his own eyes. He wiped them away, not wanting to look like a wimp in front of their big, bearded hosts.

The man pulled a chair out from a nearby table and sat down, ruffling a hand through his hair and looking at Nate and Cat. His friends were clustered by the door, talking agitatedly to each other, but he called out to them and they fell silent.

'I am Mikkel,' he said, turning back to Nate and Cat. 'We are scientists from Denmark, here for conducting experiments on the ice.'

'I'm Cat.'

'I'm Nate.'

'And I'm Clint,' said the little robot from Nate's watch. The man stared at the holograph for a second in amazement, then continued slowly, thinking hard about each word.

'What are you doing here?'

Both Nate and Cat started speaking at once, blurting out everything about Saint Solutions and the explosion and Saint's reincarnation as a robot. Mikkel held out his hands and told them to slow down.

'That robot was going to kill us,' Cat said, pointing out of the window in the direction of the huts. 'His name is Ebenezer

Saint, he's an inventor. We're inventors too, we were staying with him.'

'Inventors?' Mikkel repeated, confused.

'Scientists,' Nate chipped in, feeling the heat from the fire burning through his jacket and shuffling away from it. 'Like you.'

The man started nodding, then sighed and shook his head. He was about to speak again when one of the men by the front door shouted out an alarm, pointing to the slope they had just climbed. Mikkel leapt to his feet, snatching his rifle and racing outside. Nate and Cat struggled up and hobbled to the window to get a better look at the shadowy vista.

'There,' said Cat, nodding at a large boulder at the top of the hill, less than twenty metres from the cabin. Nate squinted into the darkness and made out a pair of golden eyes peering from behind the rock, glaring at the men as they sped out of the door. Mikkel wasn't the only one who was armed. Two more of the men pulled pistols from holsters on their belts while the rest nervously held knives. Saint may have been full of rage, but it was obvious that his senses hadn't completely deserted him as he ducked back behind the boulder.

'We've got to get out of here, Cat,' Nate whispered. 'Saint won't hold back for long, you know what he's like. He'd fight his way through a herd of angry elephants to get hold of us.'

Fortunately, Mikkel dashed back through the door and called to the inventors, beckoning them outside.

'We go now,' he shouted, slinging his rifle over his shoulders and pulling a set of keys from his pocket. 'Fast!'

They followed him out, pulling their coats around their necks to keep out the freezing wind. Mikkel sprinted across the ground towards the plane, wrenching open the door and ushering Nate and Cat inside. They clambered in, pressing themselves against the far wall as one by one the Danes squeezed themselves inside.

49

'Hurtigt!' shouted Mikkel, pushing the last man in before slamming the door shut and sprinting round to the other side. He paused before climbing into the pilot's seat, letting off a couple of rounds from his rifle at the glints of silver just visible behind the rock. Then he was in, firing up the plane's engine and opening the throttle.

Nate felt himself squished against a very fishy Danish man as the powerful propellers pushed the aircraft across the ice. He risked a backward glance as it lifted and saw Saint bound out from behind the boulder. But even with his long legs there was no way he could keep up. That didn't stop his cry of rage chasing them, chilling Nate to the bone as they set off into the dark sky.

There was a moment of silence in the cramped plane before the Danes all remembered to breathe and started chattering loudly to each other about what they had just seen. Nate did his best to ignore them, but he was cramped between two hairy giants who waved their arms wildly as they talked.

'Now I know how sardines feel,' he muttered to Clint as the plane wheezed its way higher.

'Try living in a watch,' was his only reply.

He peered through the flailing limbs to check how Cat was doing, but was surprised to see her eyes closed, the colour returning to her cheeks as she settled into sleep. She clasped a shred of paper in her hand, the remains of the photo of her dad which Saint had torn to pieces. Mr Gardner's eye twinkled out at them and Nate hoped Cat was with him as she slept.

He thought about his own parents, about how glad they'd be to see him, how relieved they'd be that he was okay. He wondered if they'd be getting a medal for saving the world, or if not then at least a whopping great big cheque from the government in recognition of their heroism. He felt his own mind start to cloud as he pictured the award ceremonies, the interviews, the television appearances. Maybe, just maybe, all the fear and pain had been worth it.

He stared through the window, the great icy mass of Greenland appearing grey in the dusky light below – like a vast whale which had just breached the black ocean. His ears popped as they continued to gain height, and before long the world below, and all the horrors it contained, was lost and forgotten beneath a shield of cloud.

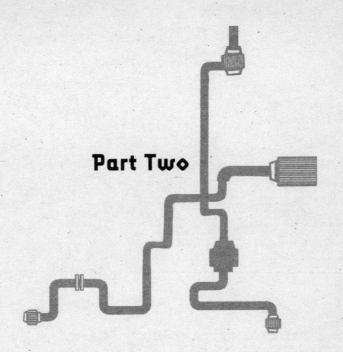

Part Two

Home Sweet Home

'Don't you know what bloody time it is?'

Nate let his tired shoulders slump. It wasn't the greeting he'd been expecting from his dad, but then ever since they'd touched down in the small local airport he had experienced disappointment after disappointment.

For a start, there had been no press or television crews there to greet them, no army generals ready to take their statements and hang medals around their necks. There had only been one rather rotund policeman in the tiny airport, and he'd been so busy telling them about how he'd once tried to build a flying truncheon that he didn't seem to hear a word they were saying about Saint. After uninterestedly taking a statement from the Danes as they refuelled the plane the policeman had reluctantly put Nate and Cat in his ancient car and driven them home.

As soon as Nate saw the familiar streets of Heaton, gently brushed by the orange glow of the rising sun, he felt the relief surge through him like hot milk on a cold day. They drove to Cat's house first. Saying goodbye to her had been more difficult than Nate had expected – they had spent so much time together, been through so much, that he wondered whether he could cope without her. He soon forgot about it as the battered car pulled up outside his house and he practically ran up the path in his excitement to see his parents again.

His dad didn't seem to share the emotion. Peter Wright was standing in the doorway now, dressed in nothing but his Y-fronts and blinking heavily to clear the sleep from his eyes.

'I'll tell you what time it is,' came a grumbled answer to his own question. 'It's the middle of the bloody night.'

'Hi, Dad,' Nate replied in a whisper.

'Mr Wright?' interrupted the policeman. 'My name is Constable Spence and I'm just returning your son. He was dropped off at Brickwell Airport last night after flying in from Greenland.'

'Greenland?' exclaimed Peter, hoisting up his pants. His voice was heavy and Nate realised he was still half asleep. 'What on earth were you doing over there? One of Saint's mad experiments, I assume.'

'He tried to kill us,' Nate answered. 'He was going to blow up the planet.'

He realised that neither of the men was listening to him. The policeman was giving his dad a lecture about wasting police time and Peter was giving the policeman a lecture about waking him up when he could have just asked Nate to wait outside until seven. They were both speaking at the same time, and seemed to have forgotten that he existed.

Slipping past the noise, he walked into the kitchen, flicked on the kettle and crashed on to a stool. As he waited for it to boil he noticed something horribly familiar pinned on the notice board above the counter – the flier he had received the day he and Cat had entered the competition. He grabbed it, tearing the picture of Saint to pieces as Clint poked his head from the watch and stared at him.

'So,' said the little robot. 'This is where the expression "home sweet home" comes from.'

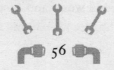

The next few minutes were a time of profound confusion. Having been woken at such an early hour, Peter – who was like a zombie in the morning at the best of times – left the policeman at the door and started wandering round the ground floor in circles. Nate made him a strong cup of tea to help wake him up, but in his confused state his dad went round watering the plants with it, then placed the Noddy mug in the cabinet with all the good china, coming very close to knocking over the entire display.

The sound of expensive plates rattling drew his mother out of bed, and she went straight to the cabinet and gave it a hug before turning to Peter and demanding to know what on earth he was doing. Nate's dad only seemed able to answer her every question with 'marmalade', and Wendy became so irate that she tweaked Peter's nose, causing him to yelp. It was at that point that she noticed Constable Spence still standing at the door.

The colour drained from her face and she started saying Nate's name, as if something bad had happened to him. The bemused policeman pointed at Nate and Wendy turned, seeing her son sipping tea quietly in the kitchen. Overburdened with the morning's events, she put her hand to her forehead and promptly fainted.

A short while later Wendy was reclining on the sofa, Peter had thankfully put some trousers on and was eating toast, Constable Spence had made his excuses and left and Nate was standing by the window trying to explain what had happened during the last few months.

'So Cat and I stayed behind and tried to stop Saint from sending out his bombs,' he finished, gesticulating wildly with his hands. 'We nearly got killed by his robots, but Cat stopped them with an electromagnetic pulse, and she built another one to destroy the bombs, and we escaped on a 500-year-old flying machine.'

'Is this the normal marmalade we get?' Nate's dad said, poking the toast with his finger. 'It's just I remember there being less peel before.'

Wendy tutted at her husband and looked sympathetically at Nate.

'Well that sounds very dramatic, dear,' she said. 'And very dangerous. I don't know what Saint was thinking exposing you to all of those bombs and robots and things, you might have been hurt! No wonder your scholarship was ended.'

'Ended?' asked Nate, frowning. 'What do you mean?'

'Now where did I put that letter?' Wendy smoothed back her hair and looked around the room, then muttered an exclamation of some kind or other as she spotted what she was looking for. She got up and slid a large piece of paper out from beneath a stack of bills on the windowsill, handing it to Nate.

His mouth dropped open as he examined the letter. Beneath the large Saint Solutions logo were several lines of printed text claiming that because several of the students had been conducting unauthorised experiments that placed lives in danger the scholarships had all been cancelled.

'We hope your child isn't too disappointed with this decision,' Nate read aloud in hushed tones. 'But in the interests of safety Ebenezer Saint feels that this is the right thing to do. He has greatly enjoyed his time with the students, and hopes they have all benefited from their brief internship at Saint Solutions. Your child will be returning to you in the next two days.'

The date on the letter was from two days ago, the day of the explosion. There was no way that Saint could have sent it – apart from anything there were no post boxes in the arctic wastes of Greenland. He dropped the letter to the floor, feeling the room dissolve around him.

'Mum, this letter isn't real,' he tried to explain. 'That isn't what happened.'

'You would say that,' Peter mumbled. 'From what we know of your experiments you were probably one of the troublemakers.'

'Besides,' added his mum. 'You always seemed happy enough when we talked to you on the videoscreen.'

'That wasn't me,' Nate spat back. 'It was all an illusion.'

He tried to explain but his dad was busy prodding his breakfast. 'I always think too much peel ruins marmalade. It gets stuck in your teeth.'

'For god's sake, Peter,' Wendy said. 'There are more important things to worry about right now than your marmalade. And no, it isn't the usual kind. My mother made it.'

Peter pulled a face and began nibbling the outside of the toast while his wife continued.

'You'd think, with all those dangerous pieces of equipment, that Saint would have warned us. As parents we should know if our children are in harm's way.'

'No, Mum, you don't understand—'

'There was a form warning us that there may be injuries,' Peter said, putting his unfinished breakfast on the floor. 'I remember signing it. It said we couldn't blame Saint if something went wrong.'

'And you agreed?' Wendy said, outraged. 'Why didn't you say anything?'

'Well, you were here,' he went on. 'You were signing the form that told them about any food allergies, and I had this waiver. I didn't think it was worth mentioning. I mean Nate knows what he's doing.'

'Mum, Dad, the form isn't important —'

But his parents had launched into an argument and were snapping at each other about the importance of communication in a marriage. Wendy couldn't believe that Peter hadn't told her about the form, and his spurious counterargument was that Wendy hadn't informed him she would be ordering inferior marmalade from her mother. The debate raged for a few minutes before Nate lost his temper and stamped his foot down on the carpet.

'The master inventor tried to kill us!' he yelled. There was silence for a few seconds. Eventually his dad coughed and spoke in a hushed tone.

'So does this mean you won't be going back?'

After several more fruitless attempts to explain the gravity of the situation to his parents, Nate gave up and said he was going for a shower. His mum gave him a giant hug, telling him she was glad he was back, and not to worry that things hadn't worked out with Saint. His dad complained about how he thought they'd be having the house to themselves for a bit longer, but did squeeze Nate's shoulder and said it was nice that he'd decided to come home early.

Nate finished his cold tea and tramped upstairs to his bedroom. Flinging open the door, he found himself face to face with one of Saint's dogs. He tumbled backwards, tripping on his feet and falling back against the hall wall. But the dog didn't move, it didn't even pant. Its eyes were black and expressionless, the spark of life the vicious creature had once possessed obviously extinguished when Saint Tower was destroyed.

Even so, the creature sent chills up Nate's spine. He remembered all too well what Saint's dogs were capable of, how they had mutated into mechanical killing machines, how they had stripped David's parents to the bone in seconds. He shuddered as he stood, grabbing the monster by the ears and dragging it out into the hallway.

'I'm going to take that thing apart later,' he said quietly as he closed the door.

'Definitely,' replied Clint, looking around the room with a curious expression. 'So this is your house then?'

'Yup,' Nate replied. It felt so strange to be back in his old room. Nothing had changed: the immaculate plasterwork, the Wallace and Gromit wallpaper, the postcard-sized picture of Lara Croft and his elemental tables and star charts. Even his wardrobe was the same, the mechanical arms from his dressing machine hanging limply down each side. But at the same time the room was like a stranger's. After everything that had happened, he felt about as at home here as a fish at the top of a tree. It was as though he had stepped into somebody else's life.

'What do you think?' he asked Clint, trying to change the subject. The little robot put all four hands to his chin and looked thoughtful.

'Well, it's a bit disappointing, to be honest. I mean, Saint Tower was huge, the rooms were like palaces and that chalet you had was packed with state-of-the-art equipment. This place is just . . .' he paused, his metal brow frowning. 'Well, it's a bit poky.'

Nate laughed, unstrapping the watch and laying it down on the bed before pulling off the Arctic coat and his overalls and grabbing his dressing gown from the back of the door.

'Yeah,' he said. 'I guess it's a bit less impressive than the place you were born.'

'Still,' said Clint, his eyes twinkling. 'At least it hasn't been blown to a billion pieces in a purple crater in Greenland.'

Nate spent almost an hour in the shower, turning the heat up as far as he could stand it and letting the water flow over him until he had completely forgotten what it was like to be cold. He emerged from a very steamy bathroom to find his dad prowling up and down the corridor, desperate for the toilet and late for work.

'Did you take another trip to Greenland while you were in there?' he spluttered as he ran through the door.

Nate returned to his bedroom to see Clint curled up on the watch face, his processor whirring gently and letting Nate know that the little robot was asleep.

'Not a bad idea,' he whispered under his breath, collapsing on to the bed in his dressing gown. In seconds he was unconscious, walking through a landscape of purple snow and golden lakes where the trees had metal arms that tried to snatch him from the ground.

Several hours and umpteen versions of the same dream later, he woke to the sound of growling in his ear, and once again found himself staring into the eyes of Saint's gruesome killer mutt. He yelped, diving under the duvet and screaming for his mum, only to hear a familiar giggle. Pulling off the quilt, he saw Cat laughing uncontrollably by his bed, holding the severed dog head with both hands.

'Cat!' he shouted. 'After everything we've been through, how could you? I'm still extremely sensitive!'

'I can see that, duvet boy,' she replied, dropping the heavy head on to the carpet and plopping down on to the bed. 'Sorry, I couldn't resist it. I knew you'd be asleep.'

'Shouldn't you be too?' he asked, noticing the dark bags under her eyes. She shrugged, kicking the dog head gently.

'I tried, but I couldn't knowing that thing was still in the house. I've just spent the last few hours taking it apart. I saw yours out in the hallway, we should dismantle that one too, just in case it decides to come back to life.'

Nate climbed out of bed and tightened his dressing gown. Lifting the watch, he caused the holographic image of Clint to stir.

'Good plan,' he said, watching as the little robot yawned and stretched. 'And I know just what to do with the parts.'

There was a familiar glint in Cat's eye as she guessed what he meant. She pulled her Swiss army knife from her belt and brandished it like a sword.

'Then let's get inventing!'

Back to Normal

After the technological wonders of Saint Solutions, Nate and Cat struggled to get to grips with their old workspace. Nate's bedroom didn't have any of the state-of-the-art equipment or endless mechanical parts that they had come to take for granted while working for the master inventor, and his junior welding kit and clunky old laptop seemed like they belonged in Victorian times. The lack of giant robot assistants stomping around, however, meant that the young inventors set to work with grins plastered across their faces.

'It seems like donkeys' years ago that we were last here,' said Cat as she hauled in the robotic dog from the hallway. 'It's like another lifetime.'

Nate nodded, delicately unscrewing the back of his watch to expose the complex circuitry inside. Clint was watching his every move with a worried expression, waving his four arms around every time Nate's screwdriver came too close to his central processor.

'Please be careful,' said his metallic voice for the fourteenth time in three minutes. 'One wrong move and I'll be rendered less intelligent than a toaster.'

Nate hushed him, placing the last of the tiny screws on the desk and studying the watch.

'Nice joints,' he said to Cat, admiring the welds that held the various components of Clint's temporary body together. 'It seems a shame to take them apart.'

'No, it isn't a shame,' came Clint's reply. 'Do you have any idea what it's like to live in a watch? Or to have no body, for that matter. Trying to scratch an itch when your arms pass straight through your butt is one of the most frustrating things imaginable!'

Nate and Cat laughed as the holographic robot demonstrated his problem.

'It will be very nice to have a real body again,' he went on. 'Something shiny and posh.'

'Yes sir,' replied Nate. 'Anything else?'

'A top hat. And a cummerbund. I've always wanted a cummerbund.'

'Okay.'

'And no cans! I suffered the humiliation of being dressed in a can for months and I can't go through it again.'

'Better than being naked,' said Cat, turning the dog on to its side and running her hands over its smooth flank.

'Trust me, it isn't,' Clint said, clambering over the watch face until he was facing Cat. 'At least when you're naked you don't have any sharp edges wedged in your –'

Nate unclipped the central processor from the holographic display unit before the robot could go any further. With a soft beep the image of Clint vanished from the screen to be replaced by a glowing set of digital numbers. They read 2:37.

'Wow, was I out for that long?' he asked Cat.

'Yeah, your mum said you were zonked but that I should go and wake you anyway or you'd never get to sleep tonight.'

'So, she does care,' muttered Nate as he knelt down on the floor next to Cat. She looked up at him, frowning. 'It's just that she didn't really believe me about Saint,' he explained. 'Neither did Dad. They thought I was exaggerating.'

'Tell me about it,' Cat replied, pulling an Allen key from her pocket and inserting it into a tiny hole in the dog's belly. 'My

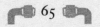

mum was so pleased to see me that she refused to hear anything about it. She had a letter telling her that the scholarship had been cancelled because we all broke the rules or some nonsense.'

'Mine too,' said Nate, nodding thoughtfully. 'I don't get how Saint could have sent them so quickly. I mean everything was destroyed.'

'There's plenty of stuff I don't get,' said Cat, fiddling with the dog. With a pop a panel on the creature's underside came away, exposing an impressive network of wires, circuit boards and other high-tech gadgetry underneath. Nate whistled – the device in front of him would be worth a small fortune on the open market.

'Like what?' Nate asked, still not taking his eyes from the dog's mechanical guts.

'Like, there are no reports of any explosions in Greenland,' Cat went on. 'Nothing about Saint having died and currently clanking around in a robotic body murdering polar bears. Saint Solutions is operating the way it always has, as far as I can see. It's like nothing has happened.'

'Or nobody has noticed,' suggested Nate, dejectedly prodding some of the components inside the dog. 'It's just our bloody luck. We saved the world and nobody was paying any attention.' He was suddenly furious, something dark and unpleasant rising up from his gut as he thought about everything they had gone through, everything they had lost. 'What's it going to take? Saint turning up in Heaton and tearing our heads off in front of our parents?'

Cat raised her Swiss army knife at exactly the same angle as her eyebrow.

'Come on,' she said, chewing over her words as if unsure about what she was saying. 'Saint wouldn't risk coming here. He may be crazy but he's not stupid. He'll go somewhere safe, probably back to the capital, back to what's left of Saint Solutions. I mean think about it, can you imagine Ebenezer Lucian Saint, the master inventor, in Heaton?'

Nate was halfway through a laugh when he heard his mum's voice drifting up the stairs.

'I wouldn't be so sure,' she bellowed, demonstrating her remarkable, and unsettling, sense of hearing. 'He's on telly now and it looks like he's got plans for our little town.'

The shock of what he'd just heard turned Nate's limbs to stone and his brain to mud. He felt like a computer that had just crashed, and by the time he had figured out a way to reboot himself almost a minute had passed. He looked at Cat, who had gone so pale that she looked like a cut-out from a black and white photograph against the colourful wallpaper.

'Please tell me I imagined that,' she said eventually. 'Did your mum just say Saint was on telly?'

'Maybe she said Saint was smelly,' he replied. 'Because he can't be on telly, that's impossible.'

They pushed themselves from the floor and walked out of Nate's room as slowly as they could, neither wanting to find out the truth. They were only halfway down the stairs when they heard his voice, floating from the living room like a toxic cloud, its deep, musical lilt seeming to mock them as they plodded across the hallway.

'Look,' said Wendy as she saw them enter. 'There he is, as handsome as ever. It's so weird that you both know him personally! And you'll never believe what he's up to.'

'Global destruction?' muttered Nate, opting to stare at the carpet rather than look at the small screen in the corner of the room. He heard Cat gasp, felt her body press against his as if she needed his support to stop her tumbling to the ground. With a shuddering sigh he looked up, found himself staring right into the golden eyes of the master inventor.

For a moment the room spun, everything seeming to peel away and disappear except for the man on television. He looked exactly the same as he had before the explosion, his messy blond hair in perfect contrast with his immaculate white suit. His mouth opened like a shark's as he continued to speak.

'It's the greatest event since the dawn of humankind.' The voice winged its way from the television with all the charm and humour that Nate remembered. 'No, since the earth formed from the mass of molten rock floating aimlessly round our solar system. Believe me, you've seen shopping malls before, but you've never seen anything like this.' The master inventor took a couple of steps towards the camera, pointing at the screen. 'Do you like shopping?'

'Yes!' exclaimed Wendy, so loudly that it made Nate jump.

'But do you think normal shops just rip you off with their high prices and poor service?'

'Definitely!' Wendy shrieked again.

'And would you like a shopping mall packed with everything you could possibly ever want, all for a fraction of the price of a normal retailer?'

'Of course!'

'No, not just one shopping mall, but four? One in each corner of every town and city?'

'I would,' said Wendy as if she was talking to Saint himself. 'I'd like that very much!'

'Then consider it done,' the master inventor went on, taking another step towards the camera so that just his face was visible. His golden eyes seemed to look right at Nate as if they were fingers picking inside his brain, the gaze so intense that he was forced to take a step back. 'The Saint Supershoppers are on their way. And the first lucky place to have them will be . . .' There was a drum roll from somewhere. 'Heaton!'

Saint performed an elaborate bow then blew a kiss to the camera.

'I'll be seeing you, real soon,' he said, then his golden eyes flashed and he was gone. A local newsreader appeared in his place, her cheeks flushed as she excitedly discussed Saint's plans for his new malls. But Nate wasn't listening. He replayed the video in his head, picturing the way that it had shifted and distorted every few seconds as if it had been viewed underwater.

He knew the effect well, remembered it from the artificial conversations he'd had with his computer-generated parents, and the way the window had wobbled then blanked out in Saint Tower when David's jetpack had collided with it, disclosing the fact that it was actually a computer screen.

Whoever it was on television, it wasn't Saint. Not his flesh and blood version anyway. It was an illusion.

10

A Brand New Clint

'*I'll be seeing you, real soon.*'

For the next week those six words echoed through Nate's mind like the relentless clangs of a church bell, reverberating with such strength that he couldn't think about anything clearly. Too exhausted to try and work out Saint's plan, he did his best to put the master inventor out of his head. But it was like trying not to think about a plane crash when you're flying – every time he managed to focus on something else he realised that Saint was still there, lurking behind the thoughts just waiting to pounce.

Having been apart from her daughter for months, Mrs Gardner wasn't overly keen on letting her out of the house. But the few times that Cat did manage to escape she made her way to Nate's so they could try and make sense of things.

'It must be him,' she said the day after they'd seen Saint on television. 'He's using the same technology that he did to convince us we were talking to our parents, so the world thinks he's still human.'

'But why is he building shopping malls?' said Nate. 'I mean what's he planning to do, kill everyone by giving them too much free ice cream? And why is he starting in Heaton? Don't you think that's a bit of a coincidence?'

Every time they met up the same questions reared their ugly heads, and every time they failed to think of any answers. From the occasional news reports he caught, and the frequent excited accounts from his parents, Nate realised that the malls were being planned at record speed, and it was only three days after the announcement that he heard the rumble of trucks entering the town. From his bedroom window he could see the heavy machinery rolling in, but he just pulled his curtains closed and refused to go outside, doing his best to pretend that nothing out of the ordinary was happening. Far better to hide away and tinker with some old inventions than face up to reality.

It was exactly a week later, on a freezing cold afternoon in early December, that Cat stormed into his room, practically ripped open his curtains and stood facing him like a mother scolding her child.

'Are you planning to sulk the rest of your life away in this flea pit?' she demanded, hands on hips and foot tapping. Nate thought she'd been spending too much time with her mum and just pouted at her.

'Well, I'm not going outside if that's what you mean,' he replied. 'Saint could be anywhere.'

'He's not,' Cat said. 'It's perfectly safe. There are just loads of builders in town working on the malls. Anyway, that's not why I'm here. I miss Clint.'

Nate nodded. He'd been missing the little robot too, but with Cat spending so much time at home and him being as miserable as hell they hadn't done any more work on his body.

'He's probably stuck inside that watch thinking we've forgotten about him,' Cat went on, sitting on the end of Nate's bed. 'Come on, let's finish him up so at least we'll have one cheery soul.'

The thought of doing something other than moping cheered Nate up, and with renewed enthusiasm they both set to work. Nate was too nervous to risk poking around inside the dog's circuitry so Cat set about the delicate task with a pair of tweezers and a screwdriver, pulling out enough mother boards and wires and battery packs to power an aircraft carrier.

While she sorted them into several piles – useful, useless and 'no-idea-what-this-is' – Nate used a small saw to slice open the dog's metal exterior. The steel skin was tough, but he didn't need too much of the black metal for what he was planning. He stopped when he'd removed a piece the size of a napkin, wiping his sweating brow on his sleeve and rummaging around in his tool box for a hammer.

After several minutes of pounding the metal Nate was even sweatier, but held in his hands a small object which looked vaguely like a top hat. He placed it on his head and gave a clumsy bow.

'M'lady,' he addressed Cat. 'Would you like to accompany myself to the ball?'

'Only if you find a hat that fits,' Cat laughed, flicking the tiny hat off Nate's head. 'Nice job, though. Clint will be chuffed to bits with that.'

'You're not going to try and make him a dress or something are you?' Nate asked, looking at the mounds of electronics Cat had piled up on his carpet. 'I think he's still scarred from the last time you tried to change his gender.'

'No, no,' she replied. 'I accepted his masculinity a long time ago. I was going to give him a suit to match his top hat. There are enough gears and rotors here for his body – he could have forty arms and legs.'

'I don't think turning him into a centipede will help,' Nate replied. 'Let's stick with four arms and two legs.'

'Gotcha.'

They returned their attention to work, Cat starting to piece together various pistons and joints and Nate adding some finishing touches to the hat. He realised that if he didn't do something a little more complex than fashioning a trendy top hat then Cat would claim she had built the little robot singlehandedly, so he started fishing around in the piles of mechanical dog-guts for something else to do.

It didn't take him long to find inspiration. Amidst the odds and ends that Cat had pushed to one side were a number of small, finger-like metal rods which had obviously made up the creature's ribcage. They were like telescopic radio antennae in that they could slide into themselves to shrink or grow – morphing from friendly toys into vast, slavering beasts intent on disembowelling anyone in sight.

Shaking his head to dislodge the memory, Nate picked up one of the metal ribs and set to work on it with his pliers. He bent the tip of the first, shaping it into a grabber and adding some wires to operate it. He twisted another then, when Cat wasn't looking, he pinched one of her Swiss army knives and welded it to the tip, adding more wires to each of the tools. As an afterthought he found his junior welding torch and added it to a third of the arms.

Blowing the last of the metal ashes away he placed all three inside the top hat, fastening the bases to the sides and pulling the lid closed. Flipping the modified accessory over he ran the extra wires through the bottom and held it up for Cat to see.

'Ta-da!' he exclaimed. 'The world's very first Swiss army hat!'

Cat looked unimpressed, and Nate had to open up the lid and show her the tools inside before she finally raised her eyebrows.

'Isn't that my knife?' was all she could say.

'Yeah, but now it's Clint's,' he replied. 'Once I've rewritten part of his internal programming he'll be able to use all of these tools like they were extra arms. He'll be like our own personal robotic toolbox!'

Cat just nodded then turned her attention back to the metal

framework that was gradually taking shape on the carpet. It looked very similar to the one they'd made together on their very first day at Saint Solutions, the robot that had won them their scholarship. Once again Nate tried to stop the memories flooding back and once again he failed. They hit him like a speeding train – each thought accompanied by an emotion so powerful he felt the room spin. The happiness of winning, the excitement of meeting Saint, the horror of discovering what he was planning.

He looked up at his window to see that the sun had managed to break through the heavy clouds that sat above Heaton. Cat had noticed too, and her joints did a good imitation of somebody popping bubble wrap as she got to her feet.

'I don't know about you but I could do with some fresh air,' she said. 'What do you say to actually leaving the house?'

It had been so long since Nate had stepped out of his front door that the suggestion awoke a sense of panic in his gut.

'Come on,' Cat went on. 'At this rate you're going to spend the rest of your life in this room and turn into a scary old man who throws his false teeth at children outside the window.'

Nate reluctantly put down his spanner and flashed Cat a weary smile that soon turned into a yawn which then became a nod.

'Yeah, you're right,' he reluctantly admitted. 'I have spent too much time inside. And I do need a break.'

'Well, I don't know about that,' Cat said through a cheeky grin. 'I've already constructed half of Clint's extremely complicated body, you've just made him a hat.'

Laughing, she bolted from the room in time to avoid the collection of screws that Nate threw after her.

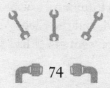

After travelling to the Arctic Circle and back, Nate was relieved to see that, on the surface, Heaton was exactly the same place it had always been. He and Cat made their way into town along the High Street, staring at the familiar sights as if they were the most riveting scenes imaginable – crowds of old ladies sitting outside Madame du Pompador's tea shop, Mr Croll armed with a piece of plywood guarding the entrance of his hardware store against stray teenagers, the crazy busker who stood in the middle of the street waving puppets around to the sound of Abba.

For the first few streets Nate did his best to hide behind parked cars and keep to the shadows just in case Saint was lurking in an alleyway somewhere. But by the time they reached the town centre he had started to relax.

'God it's good to be back,' he said. 'I never thought I'd say it but I missed this place.'

'When faced with your own death you'd probably miss living in a pigsty populated by man-eating porkers,' muttered Cat. 'But you're right, it's nice to be back.'

They strolled past the newsagents, then took a right by the Nag's Noggin public house in order to make their way down to the cemetery only to see that the road was cut off by a wire fence. Beyond was a massive pit in the ground, as if an asteroid had thumped its way into the earth.

'Whoa!' shouted Nate, peering through the wire to get a better look at the bizarre scene. The hole was easily the size of a football pitch, and was six or seven storeys deep. Scampering about on the dirt floor below were hundreds of men in bright red hard hats avoiding the bulldozers which tore up the ground.

'Wasn't this Wilberforce Road?' came a stunned whisper from Cat. 'And that golf warehouse?'

'Yeah, and Wacky's Fun Barn,' said Nate with a scowl.

'And the Solar Bowl, and the Clocktower cinema.'

'And Wacky's,' Nate went on. 'I had so many good times in

there as a kid and now look at it.'

'Stop blubbering, you were too big for Wacky's six years ago,' Cat said, walking up to a billboard fixed a little further down the fence. It had a picture of a shopping mall, all futuristic glass and steel. On one wall was a giant picture of Saint with a huge grin and upturned thumbs. Nate felt himself go pale at the sight, and turned his attention to the text that ran below the picture.

COMING SOON

THE NORTH CORNER SAINT
SUPERSHOPPER MALL!

Complete with hundreds of shops, cafés, restaurants and cinemas, all with prices you won't believe!

Opening on 15 December for all your Christmas shopping needs!

Workers needed

'Two weeks!' Nate exclaimed, looking at the giant hole in front of him. 'They're never going to finish that in two weeks. No way.'

'This is Saint, Nate,' Cat said. 'Anything's possible, remember?'

'It isn't Saint,' Nate hissed, stamping his foot on the concrete in frustration. 'How can it be? Even if he was a robot and still pulling the strings, how can he have thought of a plan this quickly and put it into motion when he's still in Greenland and when all his robots were destroyed?'

'Maybe this was his backup plan, if the bombs didn't go off,' Cat suggested. Nate just laughed without humour.

'Yeah, I can just see that board meeting. "So, what if we can't destroy the world? Oh, I don't know, how about we set up a retail park and sell underwear and stuff."'

He was cut off by an air horn behind him. Nate jumped before scrambling on to the pavement, while Cat strolled after him, letting a massive yellow truck pull up to the fence. Two men in red hard hats climbed out of the cab and walked over to the gate, grunting as they swung it open. Nate and Cat jogged forward to get a better look at the chaotic building site ahead.

'Now you better mind out, kids,' said one of the men as he walked back to the truck. 'It's dangerous in there. Stay away.'

Nate took a step back but Cat didn't budge.

'How long have they been working down there?' she asked. 'I've been away, just got back last week. I can't believe how much it's changed!'

The man took off his hat and wiped his brow, leaving a trail of dust along his forehead.

'You won't believe it,' he answered, looking out over the pit. 'Only started work five days ago. It's my first day on site, they've been recruiting guys from all over the place. I've never seen so many people working on one project, and the money's crazy too – we're getting five hundred quid a day. But it is Saint, and he knows how to get things done.'

'Five days!' Cat said, whistling. 'That's insane.'

'You should see the other malls,' the man continued. 'Just passed West Corner and they've already started building. Got the foundations down and everything.'

'West Corner?' Cat asked.

'Yeah, four malls in each corner of the town,' the man went on. 'God only knows why a place like Heaton needs four shopping malls, but Saint must have his reasons.' He plopped his hat back on and returned to the truck. 'Anyhoo, better not stand around talking all day, not when there's five big ones to collect. Remember what I said now, it's dangerous in there.'

He clambered back inside and slammed the door behind him. The truck started with a splutter and trundled through the gate, which was being held open by the second guy. When the vehicle was clear the man pushed the gate closed and padlocked the chain. Then he looked up at Nate and Cat and smiled – a perfect, emotionless grin that remained imprinted in Nate's mind long after the man had disappeared.

11

Four Corners

'It's just your imagination, Nate,' said Cat for the fifth time as they walked back down the High Street towards the west end of the town. This had long been the dodgier side of the tracks, with the kind of shops Nate's mum detested but Nate's dad always seemed to find himself drawn to whenever they were passing through. 'It wasn't a robot, just a smiley man, okay?'

'Okay,' Nate gave in, but he wasn't convinced. He recognised that smile, those perfect teeth and friendly gaze. He'd seen it on all of Saint's robotic assistants, right before they'd ripped themselves out of their artificial skin and become metal monsters. Maybe it was just his imagination, but what if it wasn't?

Bethel Street was the same as it had always been, but as soon as they reached the junction that led on to Church Road Nate and Cat's senses were assaulted by what could have been the end of the world. Clouds of dust billowed out over the street, accompanied by the deafening symphony of a million trucks and lorries and cranes and men with sledgehammers. Heat radiated from the construction site ahead as if somebody had opened a gateway to hell itself.

Somewhere beyond the dust and smoke and frenzied activity Nate thought he could make out a framework of metal stretching out from the ground – a vast skeletal hand that looked like it was poking up from a grave. It was probably just the wall, but it made him shudder.

'Cat!' came a voice from nearby. Nate squinted into the dust to make out a little huddle of people standing by the metal fence holding signs. Their placards, much like their clothes and skin, were covered in dust and debris, making them illegible. But Nate could tell by their chants of 'no more malls' that they were protesters. One of the crew ran towards them, and it took Nate a minute to realise that the filthy female was actually Cat's mum.

'I'm so glad you could join us, darling,' she shouted above the noise, coughing wildly for a couple of minutes before continuing. 'Grab a banner and do some shouting. Can you believe what they're doing to our beautiful town?'

'How did Saint get permission?' Cat shouted.

'A tissue?' replied her mum, reaching into her jacket. 'Yes, somewhere I do, hang on.'

'No, Mum, how did Saint get *permission* to build all this, to knock everything down?'

'Oh, sorry, dear, it's just so loud,' she took a couple of steps closer before continuing. 'I don't know. Nobody does. He just paid the storeowners so much money that they sold on the spot, then his crews moved in to start work. None of us got a say, not even the town council got a word in. He just paid them all off. It's just like when he bought all that land by the river in the capital. When he wants to do something he's unstoppable.'

'Have you seen him?' Nate bellowed, spitting out the tonne of dust which had accumulated in his gob in the seconds it had been open.

'Who, Saint? No, no sign of him. He just leaves all the dirty work to these poor souls.'

As if on cue an ancient bus rattled around the corner, pulling to a halt beside the gate. It shook wildly as the thirty or so burly men inside ran out, barging past each other to get to the site office which lay just beyond the gates.

'Hundreds of workers arrive here every day,' Mrs Gardner went on, watching them queue up for work. 'They're pulling Heaton apart.' She returned her attention to Cat. 'So, are you going to help fight Saint?'

Cat laughed humourlessly and started to walk away, shouting back to her mum over her shoulder.

'We've done quite enough of that, thank you!'

Forty minutes later Nate and Cat had done a tour of the whole town and were back on the High Street sharing a chocolate milkshake at Madame du Pompador's. They had visited the South Corner Mall, getting a good look at the underground car parks as they were being constructed, and the East Corner too – although that was the least developed of the four mammoth projects, the pit still being dug.

Neither could quite believe what they were seeing, and from the conversations they heard around them nobody else could either. Most of the pensioners in the tea shop were chattering excitedly about the prospect of a mall just for them – according to reports the South Corner facility would cater especially for the discerning tastes of people of fifty and upwards.

Cat was engrossed in the local newspaper, which had pictures of Saint plastered all over it.

'Listen to this,' she muttered, slurping some shake from the glass. '"Heaton is now the focus of the entire country as everybody eagerly awaits the opening of Saint's first Supershopper malls . . ." Dah de dah de dah. "The town was picked because of its proximity to several main cities . . ." Blah de blah de blah. "If the project is a success then malls just like Heaton's Four Corners will open up across the country . . ." Piffle, dribble, rubbish. "Saint plans to reduce prices in his outlets to make everything affordable no matter what your income, for example a brand-new plasma television is rumoured to cost less than one hundred pounds, rather than the thousands you would expect from other retailers . . ." God, would you listen to this.'

'Sounds all right to me,' replied Nate. 'I'd love to be able to afford a new plasma telly.'

He yelped as Cat kicked him under the table. She flicked through another couple of pages before seeing something that made her unleash a flood of chocolate shake from her nose.

'Oh my god, look at this!' She slammed the paper down and swivelled it towards Nate. It took him a moment to identify the grainy black and white picture he was looking at, then he cheered so loudly that everyone in the café turned to look at him. The snap showed a silver craft soaring through the sky above a city, and the headline read 'UFO Sighting Still Mystifies Ministry of Defence'.

'That's David's ship!' cried Nate, feeling the relief well up from his chest and reach his throat with such force that he felt like screaming. 'They made it!'

Cat was grinning too as she read from the article.

'"The rocket was sighted two nights ago, giving off trails of green light as it blazed across the countryside. Experts in extraterrestrial technology claim that the sighting is related to a bizarre purple light spotted in the Arctic Circle on Wednesday morning – possibly a mother ship which landed somewhere in Greenland – but the MOD still refuses to comment on a possible invasion."'

'Invasion?' Nate giggled. 'Can you imagine anyone less likely to invade than David?'

'At least we know they survived,' Cat replied, wiping away her chocolate moustache. 'Maybe once a few more reports of Saint's activities have come in people will start to believe us.

And David's got proof.'

'Proof?' Nate asked. Cat just stared at the table, and suddenly Nate realised what she meant. Poor David would have to return home to the house that Saint destroyed, and the parents that the master inventor killed. Nate felt his bottom lip tremble and his throat close up at the thought, and for a moment he had to stare at Cat through two pools of tears. Then he regained control, wiping a hand across his eyes and coughing to conceal his embarrassment.

'We should try and contact him,' Cat went on. 'Come up with a plan. If we all go to the police together they can't ignore us.'

The bell above the door rang and Nate turned to see two of the builders walk into the teashop. There was a chorus of tuts and sighs from the old ladies as the workers clomped across the floor in their dirty boots, but Madame du Pompador was happy enough to serve them with a wink and a smile.

The men sat down two tables over from Nate and Cat, staring silently at each other like they were madly in love. Nate eyed them suspiciously, then yelped again as Cat's shoe made contact with his shin.

'Are you paying attention?' she hissed.

'Of course,' he answered, rubbing his throbbing leg.

She started talking again, but Nate was drawn back to the builders sitting across the room. They hadn't said a word to each other, but every now and again they'd both stare across the tables at Nate and Cat. Nate caught them looking and they smiled at him before glancing down at their menus.

'Nate!' shouted Cat. 'I swear I'm going to slap you in a minute. What's wrong with you, have you developed attention deficit disorder or something?'

Nate nodded subtly to his left but Cat just frowned. He shook his head more frantically and she finally took the hint, looking at the two builders.

'What?' she asked, holding her hands up. 'Do you want me to ask one out for you?'

'No,' he whispered, blushing slightly as a few of the old ladies laughed at Cat's comment. 'Don't you think they seem a little weird?'

'What, like they haven't washed in a day or two?' she replied.

'No!' Nate repeated. He leant over the table and mouthed under his breath. 'Their smiles.'

Cat looked over at the men, who smiled and nodded at her, then she returned her attention to Nate, one eyebrow firmly raised.

'Look, I know we've been through a lot,' she said calmly, tapping Nate gently on the arm. 'But if you think you might be going cuckoo then you should go see a doctor.'

Nate scrunched up his face into an expression that he thought was disapproval, then he pushed back his chair and stood up.

'Humph,' was about all he could manage. Cat rolled her eyes and got to her feet, folding up the paper and tucking it under her arm.

'I guess we should get back to Clint,' she said, leading the way out of the café. 'If he spends much more time in that watch then I'll have two crazy people to look after.'

They said goodbye to Madame du Pompador, who was delivering two pots of tea to the workers, and made their way out of the door. It was just as it was swinging shut behind them that Nate heard the sound of gasps from inside, and turned to see what the fuss was about.

'Come on,' said Cat, pulling his arm. Nate relented, but as he walked away he peered over his shoulder and through the glass panels in the door he caught a glimpse of something very odd. He couldn't be sure, but it looked as if one of the workers was pouring scalding hot tea right into his mouth from the pot.

'Maybe I am going mad,' he said to Cat as they left the High Street and headed home.

12

Hard at Work

It was getting dark by the time they returned to Nate's house, the entire town masked by a veil of shadows except for beams of artificial orange light that broke through the four corners of Heaton like steeples from some ghostly church. The dusk was accompanied by a steady supply of rain, but despite the down-pour the work went on – the distant rumble of Saint's con-struction sites detectable more as a vibration in the floor than as a sound.

Even though it was after five Nate's parents weren't back from work. Nate offered to make the tea, heading upstairs with two steaming mugs five minutes later to see Cat hard at work on Clint's metal skeleton. Nate passed her the drink, managing to spill some on the delicate mechanical framework. Cat just shook her head, placing the mug on the carpet and using one of Nate's T-shirts to mop up the mess.

'It's a good job all this stuff is state-of-the-art,' she said. 'Which includes being waterproof!'

'I just thought Clint would like a drink too,' Nate muttered, sitting down next to Cat and fiddling bashfully with the modi-fied top hat. Cat ignored him, using her wire cutters to trim down a component of the robot dog until it was the right size for one of Clint's forearms. She did the same with several other metal pieces, leaving the outline of the little robot on the carpet.

'You know, you could be doing something useful instead of ogling me,' she said, looking up at Nate.

'I'm sure you never used to be this mean,' he replied as he struggled to his feet. He was joking, but only partly. To be honest the comment had hurt his feelings, and he was glad he was facing away from Cat as he sat down to boot up his laptop. He heard her drop her tool on the carpet and sigh loudly.

'Sorry, Nate,' she said. 'I guess I have been cranky. It's just . . .' She paused, and he turned to face her. 'It's just after everything we've been through. None of this feels the same, you know, inventing stuff. It's like it's all been tainted.'

Nate nodded, unsure what to say.

'And Saint was really going to do it, he really was going to destroy the world. I mean, how can we ever relax knowing that this could all end at any minute? Especially with him building his bloody malls right next door.'

'Come on, Cat,' Nate said. 'You can't start thinking like that. It could all end at any minute anyway. An asteroid could hit the earth and flash-boil the oceans, global warming could fry us all, aliens could attack – you could walk out of the front door tonight and be squished by a tractor.'

'Gee thanks, that's cheered me up.'

'No, that's not the point,' Nate struggled to remember what he was trying to say, but his message seemed to have deserted him. 'Anyway, Saint didn't win last time, he didn't win because of us. So even if he tries again then who's to say someone won't stop him again?'

'Well, as long as it isn't us, Nate,' Cat replied. 'Let it be someone else this time.'

'I hear that,' he said. 'Besides, we're not doing this for fun are we? We're helping out Clint.'

'Yeah, you're right,' she said, returning her attention to the mechanical parts scattered over the carpet. 'So stop preaching and let's get on with it.'

Nate rose above the comment and turned his attention back to the computer. Taking Clint's main processor he jammed a USB cable into the access port and linked it to the laptop. Cat was in the kind of foul mood that could last for hours, so Nate prised Clint's holographic projector and vocal synthesiser free from the watch and laid them on the desk, running another cable from it to the laptop. After jiggling the connections to make sure they were all secure, he flicked on the processor and watched as the little transparent robot emerged from the projector.

'Trendy new suit and hat, here I come! And it better be the best suit in the world after being stuck in there for a week,' came the metallic voice, followed swiftly by a disgruntled choke. 'Hang on, this isn't a new suit, I'm still a holograph! Oh woe is me!'

'Calm down, Clint,' said Nate, trying not to laugh as the robot waved its four hands frantically in the air. 'We're working on it. I'm just going to fiddle with your program a little bit.'

'Fiddle?' Clint exclaimed. 'Is that a technical term?'

'Yup,' said Nate, opening up Clint's code on screen. The home computer groaned as it struggled to cope with the huge amounts of information it was trying to process, but by some miracle it didn't crash.

'Be careful, Nate,' said Clint. 'Editing my software on that thing is like trying to operate on a human with a crowbar and a meat mallet.'

'Don't worry, this old gal is as reliable a piece of kit as you're ever likely to find.' The machine whined a little then popped before reverting to its doleful groan. 'Outside of Saint Solutions, that is.'

Nate scrolled through the code until he found the section dealing with the robot's motor skills. There were six large chunks of information relating to his arms and legs, and Nate began to add another series of mathematical strings designed to allow the robot to operate the tools in his new hat. He stopped when he realised that Clint was being unusually quiet.

'Everything okay?' he asked.

'Never better,' came the squeaky reply. 'Don't mind me, I'm just looking through your old files.'

'You can do that?' Nate spluttered.

'Looks like it,' the robot said. 'I can read everything on this machine. School essays dating back three years, blueprints for some inventions, even personal files, like this letter to Mandy Middleton.'

'Don't read that, it's private!' Nate shouted, feeling his cheeks burn. He heard a noise from behind him as Cat got up.

'No, go on, what does it say?' she said.

'"Dear Mandy,"' Clint said, his voice lowered so that he sounded like the presenter on a cheesy dating show. '"You're a popular girl so you've probably heard all of this before."'

'Clint, I'm warning you,' Nate shouted. Cat punched him on the shoulder, her face a giant grin.

'No, I have to hear this,' she said.

'"But I just wanted to tell you that I think you're the most beautiful girl in school. In fact, I think you're the most beautiful girl in the world."'

'I was ten when I wrote that,' Nate protested, his words lost beneath Cat's hysterical laughter. She had collapsed to her knees and was holding her stomach like she had a stitch.

'"When I look at the stars, I see your face. When I look at the squirrels in the trees, I think of your grace. The warmth of the sun is like your touch. I like you very, very, very much."'

Cat was now howling.

'I never knew you were a poet,' she gasped, hardly able to speak because of the strength of her guffaws. 'What else?'

Clint took a deep breath and spoke with even more bravado, like an actor on stage.

'"I've watched you from afar and I'd like to get closer, so please listen because I'm not a loser. I'd really love you to go out with me, so meet me tomorrow by the chestnut tree. At three."'

'That's enough!' Nate yelled, but nobody was listening. Tears were streaming down Cat's cheeks and Clint was sloppily snogging the back of one of his hands. Nate tried to fight his own amusement but he was powerless as it bubbled up inside him and broke free as a quiet laugh.

'Okay, robospy, you've had your fun,' he told Clint as he returned to his work.

'I didn't even know you liked Mandy Middleton,' Cat said as she slowly pulled herself back on to her knees, staring at the screen past Nate's elbow.

'Every boy in our year liked Mandy Middleton,' he replied.

'Did you ever give her that note?' she asked.

'What do you think?'

'Well, she hasn't spoken to you for our entire time at school, so I'd say yes, you did.'

'Shut up!' Nate said. 'At least my heartthrob didn't turn out to be a crazed megalomaniac with a passion for atomic weapons.'

'Touché,' Cat replied. 'If a little close to the bone.'

'Come on, you gasbags,' said Clint, breaking up what was sure to be an awkward silence. 'Every moment you spend chin-wagging is a moment I don't have a new body.'

'Yes sir,' said Nate and Cat together. Cat returned to the carpet, but not before whispering into Nate's ear.

'Any chance you can make him a little less bolshy?'

'I heard that!'

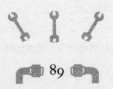

The next couple of hours were dedicated solely to fixing Clint. Nate barely said a word to Cat as he hammered the keyboard, while Cat responded with an equally rigorous silence as she welded Clint's limbs and joints together and ran the wires between them.

Cat was right in that the simple act of inventing no longer seemed as innocent and as fun as it once had, but Nate revelled in the comfort and familiarity of an old home and an old way of life. If he tried hard enough, if he immersed himself in his work, he could forget that anything bad had ever happened.

It didn't take him long to finish the code for Clint's hat. He gave the robot operational directions on how to work the implements inside the accessory, then he uploaded the new information to the little robot's main processor.

'Are you telling me I'll have arms in my head?' Clint asked when he'd accessed the new data.

'Yes,' Nate replied.

'Cool.'

Nate's parents came home at half past six, explaining that they'd been to a council meeting about the new malls. Both Peter and Wendy were trying to appear outraged at Saint's building plans, but after a couple of token comments about ruining the town's aesthetic beauty and preserving areas of historic importance they both started chatting about the kind of things they'd be able to buy there.

'East Corner is going to be the woman's mall,' Wendy explained, not really caring that neither Nate nor Cat were listening. 'Thirty shoe shops, a Betty's boutique, a makeup warehouse and a store where you can design and make your own clothes!'

'West Corner is for the men,' Peter added. 'One shoe shop, but loads of gadgets.'

'That's not at all stereotyped then, is it,' muttered Cat without looking up from her work.

'Well, it might interest you to know that North Corner is for the kids,' Wendy responded. 'More toys and fun stuff than you can shake a stick at.'

They praised the new development so much that Nate started to think they were being paid to advertise it. Eventually they ran out of things to say and disappeared back downstairs. Cat sighed with relief as soon as they'd gone, holding up the metal ragdoll that was Clint's framework and shaking it gently. The little robot looked it up and down and whistled.

'Nice work!' he said. 'Although it's weird having your insides dangled in front of you like this. Any chance of something to cover them up soon?'

'It's the next job on the list,' Cat replied.

'But it will have to wait,' came Wendy's voice, bellowed from the hallway below. 'It's getting late and you've both got a big day tomorrow.'

Nate and Cat looked at each other in confusion.

'Big day?' asked Nate tentatively.

'Yes, we've spoken with Mr Green and it's all agreed. You're going back to school.'

13

Back to School

School. The thought of going back hadn't even occurred to Nate. For some reason he'd just assumed that saving the world and coming within millimetres of several painful deaths would be justification for a few weeks' absence.

He thought about stepping back inside his classroom. In all honestly he'd rather be back in Saint Solutions fighting giant robots. At least there was something heroic and noble about that. What was heroic and noble about sitting at his desk learning French while Allan fired soggy paper balls at the back of his neck? He shuddered at the thought of returning, but he had no choice.

As soon as his mum had mentioned the dreaded S word he'd sunk back into a state of utter misery. It hadn't helped that his parents had barely even acknowledged him when he went to bed. His mum had been engrossed in a documentary about household hygiene and had inadvertently said 'see you in the waste bin' instead of 'see you in the morning'. His dad had been obsessively picking out pieces of peel from the marmalade jar with a toothpick. He had muttered something that could have been 'sleep well' or 'sweet dreams' or 'stupid peel' but Nate wasn't sure which.

Nate was just as grumpy when he woke the next morning. Groaning, he pulled himself out of bed, spending a good ten minutes trying to remember where he'd left his uniform before getting dressed and traipsing downstairs. It was as though nothing had changed. His mum was cooking eggs and bacon and his dad was sitting at the breakfast table impatiently drumming his knife and fork on his plate.

'Come on, woman, I don't have all day,' he said, then spotted Nate shuffling into the kitchen. 'Ah, good lad. I thought I was going to have to come and prise you out of bed. Saint may have let you sleep in till eleven but it's back to the real world now.'

Nate was too tired to argue. He went to the fridge and poured himself a glass of juice then practically collapsed on to a chair only to jump up again three seconds later when a pile of congealed fried breakfast appeared before his nose.

'Thanks, Mum,' he said, feeling like throwing up. 'But I think I'll pass. I'll grab something on the way.'

'Okay, son,' said Wendy as Nate made his way towards the front door. 'Have a good day.'

Nate couldn't think of anywhere he was less likely to have a good day than Heaton School. He walked down to the High Street, throwing his bag over the wall that led to the park before leaping it himself and making his way across the grass to the chestnut tree in the middle. Cat was nowhere to be seen, so he leant against the rough bark to wait for her.

Dozens of people were traipsing up and down the path on their way to work, all with expressions as sour as Nate's. With each miserable soul that passed Nate felt his heart grow heavier. Was this what lay in store for him now? Five more years of dismal school then an equally gloomy job in a Heaton office.

'Oh woe is me,' he said under his breath.

He was distracted from his self-pity by what sounded like a

herd of elephants making their way along the path. He peered around the tree to see a group of workers running through the park. No, not running, skipping. There were five of them, all daintily prancing along like a bunch of schoolgirls on their way to a performance.

As they passed Nate they all turned their heads to stare at him, not missing a beat or tripping up despite the fact they weren't looking where they were going. Each wore an identical smile, one that froze Nate to the spot until the strange group had disappeared through the park gates.

'If your mouth was any wider people would be potholing in it,' came a voice from his side. He jumped, spinning round to see Cat approaching.

'Did you see that?' he asked, closing his gaping mouth and pointing at the gate.

'What?'

'The builders. They were skipping. In time. And watching me.'

'Nate,' she replied, pulling a concerned expression. 'Is there something you're not telling me? I mean you're developing a bit of an unhealthy obsession with builders.'

'It's not an obsession,' he snapped back. 'There's just something weird going on.'

Cat tutted and started walking towards the path.

'Come on, Mr Paranoid, we'll be late.'

Walking into his classroom was, without a doubt, more stressful than anything Nate had experienced in his life – and that included trying to escape Saint Tower on an ancient wooden flying machine. As soon as he appeared in the doorway Nate was greeted by a chorus of jeers and catcalls as the form realised he was back.

'Aw, did Saint throw you out?'

'Poor thing, were your inventions not good enough?'

'Is Saint not your boyfriend any more?'

All of the insults were directed at Nate (even the last one), as everybody knew Cat's violent mood swings well enough to give her a wide berth. Nate did his best to let the taunts slide off him like water from a duck's back, but unfortunately he was so busy holding his head up high and pretending not to notice that he missed his seat entirely and ended up collapsing to the floor. Cat helped him up amidst the laughter and applause and he sat down next to her, trying not to cry.

Things didn't improve when Mrs Truelove arrived, spending form period asking Nate and Cat how they'd got on and what sort of things they'd built. Infuriated by the one-word answers she was getting she eventually said it would be best if they gave a report during assembly tomorrow, and refused to listen to their protests.

First period was English, and Nate struggled to keep up with discussions on a Shakespeare play that he hadn't read. To make matters worse, for the rest of the lesson – and the chemistry class that followed – he was teased with Romeo and Juliet jokes usually involving either him and Cat or him and Saint.

By lunchtime Nate was in the worst mood of his life, and with a banging headache to boot. He met Cat by the canteen to discover that she wasn't faring much better, and after buying some food they made their way to a quiet spot on the school field to eat in peace.

An hour later they were both preparing to endure a double dose of Religious Education, but fortunately the topic was something they knew a little bit about.

'Today we'll be looking at the myths, legends and religious stories involving the end of the world,' said Mrs Allen. 'Armageddon.'

Things went fine for the first hour as Nate and Cat studied the Four Horsemen of the Apocalypse and learned about the End of Days, but then Cat launched into a furious argument with the teacher about the fact that the end of the world was just a religious allegory. She ended up blurting out a summary of everything that had happened at Saint Solutions, and how close the world had come to a real Armageddon, until a red-faced Mrs Allen screamed for her to go and stand in the hallway until she stopped making things up.

After the last bell they made their way out of the school gates past Mr Green the headmaster, who had entered them into Saint's competition in the first place. He looked at them sympathetically.

'I'm sorry things didn't work out for you, kids,' he said. 'But there's always next time.'

They took a detour through the Bluebell Woods, heading for Cat's house. Her mood had turned from furious to demonic. She picked up a stick and tore through the trees and the bushes like a machete-wielding loony, screaming incoherent words at the top of her voice. Nate remembered the last time he had seen her like this, a lifetime ago when they thought they hadn't got through to the finals.

'We should have just let him destroy the world,' Cat said when she finally calmed down. Every animal in the vicinity appeared to have fled – Cat's rage had even sent a man and his dog running for their lives – and now the woods were strangely quiet. 'Then they would have believed us. I mean how can they be so stupid? Why won't they listen to what happened?'

'Because they don't want to hear it,' Nate answered, kicking at a loose stone by his feet. It turned out to be less loose than he thought, and he stubbed his toe and almost tripped before continuing. 'They don't want to believe that their world is in danger, so they refuse to even consider that what we're saying is true.'

Cat just grunted and kicked out at another innocent bush, creating a fountain of leaves which rained down on them as they walked.

'I can't go back to this,' she said. The anger had left her voice, with only sadness and futility remaining. 'After everything we've been through, Nate, how can we return to an ordinary world? I feel like my life is over.'

'Come on, Cat,' Nate said. He reached out for her hand then pulled back, then swallowed hard and grabbed it. She protested but only weakly, and eventually laced her fingers through his, squeezing them gently. 'We escaped Saint by working together, and we can get through this too. Things will start to feel normal again soon, I promise.'

'That's the problem,' she replied. 'I don't know if I can do normal any more. I feel like I want Armageddon to come, I want this world to end.'

Nate opened his mouth to reply but not before hearing a noise in the trees above. He glanced up through the dense leaves to see a flash of red in the branches far above their heads. There was someone up there, a builder, his hard hat and a half moon of bright, white teeth grinning down at them.

'Well, just be careful what you wish for,' was all he could think of to say.

After all the talk of doomsday and the end of the world Nate and Cat were in desperate need of something to cheer themselves up. Nate suggested cutting through the woods to the aerial slide and using it to head back to his house, and the mere mention of their old mode of transportation brought a smile back to Cat's face.

'I'd forgotten all about that,' she said, beaming. 'Come on, slow poke, last one there is a faulty crank shaft.'

They set off along a barely visible path that led through a patch of elderflower bushes, almost tripping over themselves in a bid to arrive first. They dashed round a willow tree, scanning the branches above for the thick metal wire, only to discover to their horror that it wasn't there. In fact, there was nothing there – no trees, no plants, no wildlife. Just a barren patch of ground torn in two by a steel fence.

It took them a minute to process what they were seeing, but there was no denying it. Half of the Bluebell Woods had been stripped clear, replaced by what looked like the ugly rear end of Saint's South Corner Mall.

Cat tried to speak but all that came out was a choked sob. She walked up to the fence and peered through at the construction work visible in the distance. The stretch of ground ahead reminded Nate of pictures he'd seen of First World War trenches – all mud and despair. Gone was the haven where he and Cat had retreated when they needed time to think, to heal.

'My mum said they'd started building in the woods,' Cat whispered after a lengthy silence. 'I just didn't think . . .' She hesitated, her face ashen. 'I didn't really believe it.'

'Oh well,' Nate said, turning and heading back into what was left of the wood. 'It's just an aerial slide.'

'It's not just a slide,' she called out to his back. 'It's everything. He's taken everything from us. We beat him but he's winning, Nate.'

Nate didn't stop. He couldn't. He had a sudden fear that if he stopped moving he'd just sink into the ground, be buried alive. It was all too much, the entire weight of the world was pressing down on him and something was starting to break.

'Let's just get back to Clint,' he replied, too softly for Cat to hear. She followed him anyway, a pale figure as ghost-like and lifeless as the landscape of destruction behind her.

14

Stalked

'You two look more miserable than an atom that's lost its electron,' said Clint as they stomped back into Nate's room. 'More gloomy than a star which has lost its supply of hydrogen.'

Nate had dumped his bag on the bed and sat down at the desk before he realised he didn't have a clue what the robot was talking about.

'I've been browsing the Internet,' he said proudly. 'There's loads of really interesting information out there. Anyway, why the long faces?'

'Bad day,' replied Nate. Cat had slumped to the floor and was solemnly prodding Clint's metal frame. 'Very bad day.'

'Well, please don't let that stop you,' he hinted, waving his four arms in the direction of his skeleton and winking feverishly. 'If I have to spend one more day stuck inside this room by myself then it'll be me trying to destroy the planet. And thanks to the World Wide Web I now know how.'

'Okay, okay,' said Nate. 'Just let me get a brew on.'

While he waited for the kettle to boil in the kitchen he flicked through a pile of old newspapers lying in the recycling bin. There was nothing about the Heaton malls until a week ago, when the local *Gazette* praised a surprise new development in the town. The picture showed a stock press image of Saint waving his hands manically at a crowd of onlookers, and Nate's heart missed a beat when he realised the shot must have been taken on the day he, Cat and the other competitors arrived at Saint Solutions for the competition.

He looked at the date of the article and tried to count back the days in his head. The morning that this newspaper came out was the morning after they had escaped. It just wasn't possible.

Upstairs, Cat had a welding iron in full swing and was busy soldering the joints on Clint's new body. Nate set her mug down on the carpet then returned to the skin of the robotic dog, picking up the tin opener again and slicing off some more strips of the tough metal. Clamping one in a vice on his desk he hammered it with a mallet, slowly bending the black steel into a jacket and gluing three silver buttons to the front of the outfit.

For finishing touches he fished out a panel of brushed steel and cut out a tiny bowtie shape and a thick band to serve as the cummerbund, using the welding iron in Clint's hat to fix them into place. When the metal had cooled he held it up for Clint to see. It looked remarkably like a dinner jacket from a posh white-tie event.

'Wow,' said Clint, looking genuinely awestruck. 'I'll look like James Bond!'

'And here's the sexy body to put in those sexy clothes,' said Cat, standing up and stretching. She held out a finished metal skeleton, complete with tiny gears and pistons and wires immaculately fixed in place. It was the same size as Clint's old body, but the materials from the robotic dog made it a space-age achievement. Nate handed Cat the black dinner jacket and she carefully eased the skeleton inside, sealing it in place with a quick patch of solder.

She held the pint-sized robot up for Clint to see, and Nate was just about to put the top hat on to complete the master-piece when they realised what they'd left out.

'Oh,' said Nate.

'Oh,' said Cat. 'You don't appear to have a head.'

'Oh,' said Clint. 'Well, can I have one? It is quite important, after all.'

For the next couple of hours Nate and Cat worked together on Clint's head, beating another strip of brushed steel into a small cylinder, drilling out eyeholes and hinging the base into a mouth. Cat carefully inserted the robot's vocal synthesiser, adding telescopic lenses and optical circuits from the robotic dog.

A few decorative touches and a good polish later and the tiny head was ready.

'Clint, meet Clint,' said Cat, holding the head out for the transparent robot to see. He purred gently, his eyes lighting up.

'Well, aren't you a good-looking robot!' he exclaimed. 'Go on then, get me in there.'

'Okay, old buddy, see you on the other side,' said Nate, unplugging the robot's central processor. The holographic image vanished with a wave, and Nate handed the little black box to Cat who slid it inside the brand-new head. She connected the wires from the robot's skeleton to ports along the processor, adding the ones from the top hat as well. After a quick check to make sure everything was in place she picked up one of the dog's battery units and slid it underneath the back of Clint's jacket, running another wire between it and the processor. A few more blasts sealed it in place and fixed the top hat to Clint's head.

'Well, I think that's everything,' said Cat.

'Yup,' Nate added. 'It looks just like our old friend, only shinier and better dressed.'

'I just hope he likes it.' Cat held out the lifeless robot. 'Do you want to do the honours?'

'No way, José,' he replied. 'Please be my guest.'

Cat took a deep breath then reached inside the unit and flicked on the main processor. For a moment, nothing happened. Then there was the smallest of whines and the robot started to shake, quivering so hard that Cat had to place it on the carpet. It vibrated across the floor for a moment, then suddenly stopped.

With a low groan, Clint opened one eye and stared at the ceiling. His other eye followed suit, and the robot spent a few seconds scanning the room, eventually settling on Nate and Cat.

'Mein sauerkraut ist kranken,' he said.

'Pardon?' asked Cat, frowning.

'The South American chestnut monkey has a penchant for grasshopper manure,' he went on.

'Huh?' asked Nate. Clint shook his head, rubbing his temples.

'Sorry about that, my processor's just settling in. I think you put my eyes in the wrong way round,' he said. 'Everything's upside down.'

'You're lying on your back,' Cat explained, walking over to the robot and offering a hand. He stretched out two of his four arms and gripped Cat's finger, pulling himself up and tottering uneasily before finding his balance.

'Oh yeah, that's better.'

'So, how does it feel?' asked Nate.

'Wonderful,' the robot sang out, taking several steps across the carpet and growing more confident with each one. He danced a clumsy jig and spun round a few times, flexing each of his arms. Then without warning he crouched and sprang on to the desk, landing like a champion athlete. 'I feel like a brand-new robot. These parts you gave me are excellent!'

'Job well done, I'd say,' said Cat as they watched him do a few flips, sending papers and tools flying from the desk.

'Maybe a bit too well done,' Nate added as Clint propelled himself from a hole punch and grabbed the light, swinging round in circles going 'wheeeeeee!' He eventually let go, spinning uncontrollably and hitting the wall above Nate's bed like a fly splatting into a window. The little robot slid down the wallpaper on to the crumpled duvet, then clambered back to his feet and faced his audience.

'And I haven't even tried my hat yet!' he shouted in metallic tones of glee. 'Watch this.'

Straining as though he was on the toilet, Clint made the top of his hat flip open and the welding iron attachment fly out. It expanded to full size – almost thirty centimetres in length, and exploded into a fierce blue flame. Clint grinned as he folded the arm away, but it didn't go quite as planned, the tip of the iron flipping forwards and getting wedged in the little robot's ear. He struggled with it for a moment before using his hands to stuff the tool back in the hat.

'Okay, so I need a little practice,' he muttered. 'But the rest is great! And the best thing is, I can scratch all my itches.'

He demonstrated by scratching his rear, before looking at Nate and Cat suspiciously.

'I appear to have a battery up my butt.'

Nate and Cat spent what was left of the evening tidying up the loose joints in Clint's new body and tightening up any logical loops in his operating system. Whenever they took a break he would leap and cartwheel and bounce around the room as if every surface was made of hot coals, only coming to a halt when, exasperated, Nate or Cat lobbed a pillow at him.

It was only when Nate's alarm clock read a quarter to nine

that Wendy Wright dared knock on the door. Clint dived under the duvet while she informed them that it was bedtime.

'I was just about to leave, anyway,' Cat replied. 'I'll get my coat.'

'I'll walk you home,' said Nate. His mum looked like she was about to protest about him going out in the dark but she didn't say anything. *And just as well*, Nate thought, *I have saved the world, I can handle a walk through town.*

He followed Cat down the landing and was at the top of the stairs when his mum called out.

'Nathan, your duvet appears to be following you,' she said, a slight tremor in her voice. Nate looked along the landing to see his colourful quilt sliding along the carpet, a bulge in the centre revealing its pilot.

'Don't worry, it's just Clint,' he said. 'Okay, buddy, you can come too.'

The little robot leapt from under the heavy blanket and slid down the banister, leaving Nate and Cat to follow his 'wheeeeeeee' all the way to the front door.

It was freezing outside, the thin drizzle that fell quickly solidifying into an icy runway which several times left Nate doing an impression of his dad on roller skates.

'You sure you want to walk me home?' Cat asked as Nate slipped again at the end of the road, almost doing a back flip. 'It's very nice of you but I'd hate to be responsible for you breaking your neck.'

The icy patches meant that it took a little longer than usual to reach Cat's house, but fifteen minutes later Nate was standing outside her front gate shivering like a terrified kitten and waving goodbye. Clint had decided to stay with Cat for the night, but just as the door was closing the robot leapt to the floor and hugged Nate's leg.

'Thanks for the new body,' he said as he scampered back to Cat.

'No problem,' Nate answered through chattering teeth. 'See you both tomorrow.'

He set off back down Cat's road, pulling his collar around his neck to keep out the chill. Every now and then a car would drive past at low speed, the tyres struggling to grip the road, but other than that the streets were deserted. The streetlights reflected in the puddles along the pavement, casting weird flickering shadows on the bushes that lined the road, and Nate began to get gooseflesh on his arms that had nothing to do with the cold.

It was like being in a ghost town, and the thought inevitably drew Nate back to Saint's plan. If the master inventor had succeeded then the whole world might have been like this, only a little more purple. There would have been new people, new plants and new animals eventually, but the moment the bombs were detonated the world would have been an empty husk except for twenty-five inventors and their crazed mentor.

The sound of footsteps behind him made Nate feel a little more relaxed. He wasn't alone on the planet, there were seven billion other people here to keep him company. Everything was normal.

Except it wasn't. Peeking over his shoulder he saw two figures further down the road. The darkness and drizzle obscured them a little, but could do nothing to conceal the bright red hard hats that both men wore. They were walking in time – left, right, left, right, left, right – steps that seemed to increase in speed as soon as Nate turned away.

He started to walk more quickly, almost slipping over again on a frozen puddle. He was approaching the junction with

Tench Street, one of the busiest roads in town. If he could reach it there were bound to be more people there. The footsteps behind him echoed off the surrounding buildings with an even faster beat, and Nate risked another look over his shoulder to see the men were closer than ever.

They caught Nate looking and their mouths peeled open to display that same perfect grin, a smile which closed in too quickly – thirty yards, twenty yards, spitting distance.

By the time Nate reached the junction they were right behind him. Gritting his teeth he spun round to confront them only to find that they had crossed the road, heading in the opposite direction along Tench Street. Feeling like he was on the verge of a heart attack, Nate let his hands drop to his sides and turned right, but not before he saw two more figures emerge from a doorway on the other side of the street.

He didn't believe it. There were two different builders, each wearing a red hard hat and each flashing Nate a grin as they walked towards him.

Nate started to run, slipping on the pavement so leaping on to the empty road and sprinting back towards his house. The men behind him didn't follow, and he lost sight of them as he turned the corner on to the Galloway Estate. Cutting through an alleyway he found himself three roads away from his house, but he wasn't alone. Two more workers were making their steady way towards him, wearing the same outfits, the same grins, and stepping together with the same relentless beat.

'What the hell is going on?' Nate mouthed to himself as he raced along the street, suddenly wishing he had let Cat walk home alone. He bolted to the end of the road and turned left, looking back over his shoulder to see the men still in pursuit. Ignoring the stitch that gripped his side, he staggered the last few metres down Whitley Avenue then found himself back on his street.

He had his house in his sights when suddenly a figure stepped out of a driveway right in front of him. It was a worker, complete with red hat, and Nate careened right into him. The man's arms seemed to grab his head and he batted them away, giving his attacker a shove before leaping out into the road.

'Get away from me!' Nate shouted. 'Leave me alone!'

The man held up his hands, obviously shocked. Nate studied his face. There was no perfect grin, just a pair of tiny eyes perched above one of the biggest nose and chin combinations Nate had ever seen. He was rubbing his belly where Nate had shoved him.

'Jeez, kid,' the man said, wheezing. 'I was just off to start my new job. No need to attack me.'

Nate mumbled an apology, running past the last few houses until he was safely back at his front door. He took one more look down the dark street as he turned the handle. The man he had bumped into was gone, but right at the end of the road stood two figures, each watching Nate with eyes that seemed to glow in the cold, dark night.

15

School's Out

Nate couldn't sleep that night. Every time he dozed off he'd see the workers in their red hats running towards him and he'd sit bolt upright in bed, his heart racing and his skin cold with sweat. He lay under his duvet trying to work things out in his head, but he couldn't make sense of any of it. It was as though he was in some crazy dream – maybe he and Cat had crashed on their way out of Saint Solutions and were both lying in Greenland hallucinating all this.

He must have fallen asleep eventually as he woke to the sound of his alarm, the shrill whistle grating through his tired mind like nails on a blackboard. He lashed out and batted the clock off his bedside table, then clambered out of his duvet and circled his room like a zombie.

Once he had remembered how to get dressed he stomped downstairs, ignoring his parents' comments about how blood-shot his eyes looked and doing his best to work through a soggy slice of toast covered with rubbery eggs. Making his excuses, he grabbed his school bag and headed outside, hoping the fresh air would wake him up.

The cold, bright morning did the trick, and as Nate made his way down the road towards the High Street he soon found his foggy brain clearing. A layer of frost covered everything in sight, turning the town into a crystal ornament that sparkled in the fierce white sun.

Nate climbed the wall into the park to see Cat already waiting by the chestnut tree. The closer he got to her, the more stressed she appeared, and by the time he was close enough to say hello it was evident that something big was on her mind.

'Let me guess,' said Nate, clouds of breath billowing from his mouth. 'You were followed here by the men in red hats.'

Cat frowned and shook her head.

'No, why? Were you?'

Nate filled her in on the events of the previous night, changing the details ever so slightly so that instead of running for his life he stood his ground and confronted his pursuers.

'That is a little weird,' Cat said, pulling up the collar of her shirt to keep her neck warm. 'I have seen loads of builders around town this morning, but it isn't surprising really. I mean there are thousands of them working on the new malls. Anyway, that isn't what I'm worried about. It's the assembly this morning. We've got to do that presentation thing.'

Nate felt his legs go weak. He'd completely forgotten about the fact their form tutor had asked them to give a talk about their time with Saint. The thought of getting up in front of the entire school was terrifying – he'd rather be face to face with one of Saint's robot dogs.

'Bloody Nora,' he muttered. 'Do you know what you're going to say?'

Cat shrugged.

'The truth, I guess,' she replied. 'I know they won't believe it but we've got to keep trying.'

'Maybe we could show them Clint?' Nate asked. 'Where is he, by the way?'

'At home,' Cat said. 'He was totally hyperactive all night so I lost my temper and told him he couldn't come with me.'

Almost as soon as she had finished talking there was a tiny sneeze from behind the tree, followed by a soft metallic voice.

'Bless you,' it whispered.

Nate and Cat peeked round the trunk to see Clint on the other side. The little robot was shuffling his feet bashfully and looked up at his creators with big, round eyes.

'Clint,' said Cat. 'I told you to stay at home.'

'I got lonely,' he replied.

'Come on then,' Cat went on. She bent down and picked him up by his top hat, lowering him on to her shoulder. He immediately pounced off on to Nate's arm, scrabbling up until he was sitting on his head.

'You can only come with us if you promise to behave,' Cat scolded.

'I will, I will. It's just difficult not to jump around when you've got a body like this!' He flexed his four stick-like arms to demonstrate.

Clint's appearance cheered both young inventors up, and they walked the rest of the way to school with a spring in their step. Nate was still nervous about the presentation, but having Clint there provided a little reassurance. If he got stuck for words he could just ask the robot to do something funny.

As soon as they walked through the school gates Mr Green accosted them.

'Mrs Truelove tells me you're going to give an account of your scholarship in assembly,' he said, talking to them but not taking his wide eyes off Clint, who was attempting to do a hand stand on Nate's head. 'That's very good of you.'

'You know he tried to destroy the world,' Cat said. But her words were drowned out by the morning bell which echoed across the playground. The head teacher ogled Clint for a few moments longer before seeming to snap out of a trance, clapping both inventors on the back and wishing them good luck for their talk.

'Go and sit in the hall, if you like,' he told them as he walked away. 'It will give you some time to prepare.'

They made their way through reception and along the main corridor, pushing open the heavy hall doors and shuffling nervously into the giant space. Just being there turned Nate's spine to jelly, and he wobbled unsteadily across the wooden floor and collapsed on to a seat.

'I really don't want to be here,' he said, his voice echoing around the empty hall. 'I think I'm going to be sick.'

'It will be okay,' Cat replied, the tremble in her voice betraying her own fear. 'It's only the pupils and teachers, not the UN.'

'I'd rather it was the UN,' Nate replied. 'At least they don't pelt you with missiles and shout insults at you if they don't like what you're saying.'

Clint was sprinting up and down the hall like a toddler pumped full of E numbers, skidding across the smooth boards and using the chairs as hurdles. He stopped when he saw Nate and Cat's despondent faces, skipping over to them and leaping on to Nate's lap.

'You're both looking glum again,' he said. 'What's the matter?'

'It's okay, Clint,' said Cat. 'We just don't really want to have to talk to the whole school. It's a little scary.'

'Can I help?' he asked.

'Not unless you can close this place down in the next five minutes,' Nate replied.

Clint stood still for a moment, deep in thought, then suddenly sprang off Nate's knee and scampered across the floor.

'Clint?' Nate said, jumping to his feet. 'Where are you going?'

'Just leave it to me!' the robot cried, vanishing through the door into the corridor. Cat chased after him but was cut off by the reappearance of Mr Green, who waltzed into the hall oblivious to the tiny metal shape darting between his legs.

'I hope he's not going to do anything stupid,' she whispered as the head teacher approached. Both Nate and Cat grinned nervously at the man, who waited for the second bell of the morning to ring out before speaking.

'Right then, let's get you some seats at the front of the hall,' he said. 'How are you feeling?'

'Fine,' lied Nate and Cat together as they took a seat on the chairs that Mr Green laid out for them. There was a distant rumble of chatter from outside, which erupted into a cacophony of shouts and whoops and laughs as the pupils stampeded into the hall. Nate felt his stomach go a little funny at the sight of them and wished he'd gone to the loo that morning.

'Just ten minutes or so,' said the head teacher. 'Just tell us what the best bits were. Are you going to show us your little companion?'

'Definitely,' lied Nate again. 'He's just, er, having a rest.'

'Great stuff,' said Mr Green, raising his voice to speak to the crowd that was fighting over seats like hyenas over a corpse. 'Come on now, sit yourselves down. We've got a special talk today.'

The noise level ebbed away as the pupils settled down, and Nate found himself the object of several hundred pairs of eyes. His cheeks throbbed and he felt the sweat oozing from his brow. He did his best to smile at his audience – an expression he knew from experience was more like a grimace.

'Okay, good morning everyone,' said Mr Green. 'I hope you all got here safely despite the icy weather. I'll be giving out merit awards at the end of assembly, but first I thought it would be fun to hear from Nathan and Sophie, who of course have been working with the legendary Ebenezer Saint for the last few months.'

The head teacher stopped talking as a deep, farty noise bubbled up from somewhere behind him. It only lasted a second, but it was followed swiftly by a very suspicious smell. The pupils all burst into laughter, causing Mr Green's cheeks to turn such a vivid shade of red that it reminded Nate of the incident with the Bully Blow.

'I assure you that was not me,' said Mr Green. But nobody heard him because the noise came again – a trump so loud that it caused the floorboards in the hall to vibrate. This time it was followed by a worrying series of clanks and pops, like somebody was using the water pipes as a glockenspiel. The smell in the hall was becoming quite unbearable.

'Oh no,' whispered Nate. 'I hope that isn't Clint.'

'Anyway, please ignore that sound,' said Mr Green, who was obviously perturbed. 'It's just the pipes. They must be frozen. Please give Nathan and Sophie a round of applause.'

He stood to one side and motioned for Nate and Cat to stand up. They did, Cat walking to Mr Green's side while Nate did a clumsy bow that caused the seated children to laugh uproariously. Cat opened her mouth to introduce the talk, but she was cut off by another noise from beneath the floorboards, this one reminiscent of a dinosaur letting rip. An invisible, but extremely potent, wave of foul wind rippled across the hall, causing everyone to scrunch up their face or grab their nose.

'This stinks!' came a voice from the crowd, untethering another round of giggles.

'Now now,' croaked Mr Green, holding up a hand and obviously trying to not breathe in. 'Please let them speak.'

The noise was constant now, as though there was an earthquake taking place right below the hall floor. It was spreading, too, travelling up the copper pipes in one corner of the hall. With a screech one of the pipes exploded, spraying water out on to the assembly. There was a bang as a radiator on the far side of the room split in two, steam billowing into the room.

'Please remain calm,' said Mr Green, trying to make himself heard over the screams of the pupils. 'Let's just make our way slowly out of the hall on to the –'

He was cut short as the boards beneath him bulged, splitting with a crack as the dirty water beneath forced its way out. A disgusting brown fountain jetted upwards, eventually giving in to gravity and arching gracefully back down to earth, landing square on the head teacher's head. Mr Green stood for a moment while his brain processed what had happened, then he screamed in an impressive falsetto and started running round in circles.

'It's poo!' he squeaked. 'Get it off me! Get it off me!'

With a banshee-like wail he sprinted for the outside doors, barging through them on to the playground where he could be seen running back and forth pulling off his suit. The rest of the teachers calmly guided the pupils out of the hall, which was gradually filling up with unmentionable substances. The last one out flicked the fire alarm as she closed the door behind her, and a few minutes later everybody was safely out of the building.

From their vantage point on the playground Nate and Cat had a clear view of the chaos that was ensuing. Through the windows they could see that pretty much every pipe in the school was leaking – either water, steam or something far more unpleasant. The building was ruined.

'Oh. My. God,' whispered Nate. 'What did he do?'

'Returned the favour for my lovely new body,' came a metallic voice from his feet. Nate looked down to see Clint walking up to them, brushing his hands together as if he was celebrating a job well done. 'You didn't want to be there, and now you're not.'

'But,' Nate said, aghast. 'But . . .'

He stopped when he noticed Mr Green storming towards them, wearing nothing but his pants and some nasty stains. He came to a halt in front of Nate and Cat, his entire body shaking with rage. He tried to talk, but he was so angry all that came out was a series of squeaks and bubbles.

'This'd better not have had anything to do with your robot,' he said a few seconds later, when he had composed himself. Clint climbed up Nate's trousers and flipped himself on to his shoulder, pulling as innocent an expression as his metal features would allow.

'He never left our side,' Nate said, trying to conceal his lie with an innocent expression of his own. 'Besides, it's just a little water damage.'

No sooner had he spoken than a giant explosion rang out across the playground as the tower in the centre of the school blew its top – the century-old clock face replaced by a forty-foot jet of loo water that sent everybody running from the playground.

16

Life Goes On

It was announced later on that morning that the school would be closed until the beginning of the new year – at the very least. A police investigation revealed that several key pipes had been unbolted and connected to each other, reversing the flow and causing the entire system to erupt.

'It's amazing what you can do with a Swiss army knife and a welding iron in your hat,' said Clint when Nate and Cat questioned him about it.

The only evidence the police could find was a small piece of graffiti on the basement wall which read 'Clint rules', but as there were no pupils at Heaton High with that name, and nobody knew the name of Nate and Cat's little robot, the case was dropped.

Mr Green rang Nate's house late that afternoon to inform their parents about procedures for home education until after the Christmas break. He was calling every pupil in the school, but he talked at length to Peter Wright, who kept watching Nate and Cat suspiciously whilst muttering in conspiratorial tones.

'I'm sure they probably did, Mr Green,' he said. 'No, there never is any proof, I don't know how they do it. Yes, I'll be sure to ground them, don't you worry.'

But somewhere between saying goodbye and putting the phone down Mr Wright had forgotten all about his promise to the headmaster, and Nate and Cat spent the rest of the day roaming the town again watching Saint's new developments taking shape.

In each of Heaton's four corners massive spotlights picked out the vast malls as they sprouted from the charred ground – girders and support beams and concrete pillars soaring upwards like monstrous plants. Even for Saint, the speed of the building work was astonishing – in the space of a few days West Corner was two storeys high, while the enormous pits in North, East and South Corners were now bristling with their complex steel foundations.

Everywhere they looked Nate and Cat saw people hard at work. The building sites themselves were literally swarming with men and women in red hats, all working in what looked like complete harmony. Nate watched them closely from behind the wire fences, noticing each time a worker stepped out of the path of a falling brick that he couldn't have known about, or the way a group of builders with mallets ducked to avoid each others' swings – their perfect timing all that was stopping them getting their brains bashed out.

In contrast to this, every ten minutes another bus would pull into town, spilling a gutful of new employees out on to the pavement. They were all men, women and even some teenagers drawn to Heaton by Saint's promise of well-paid work, but aside from a handful of steely-eyed construction workers everyone else looked about as fit for the job as a penguin for a train driver. Despite this, they were all welcomed by a grinning manager, who led them one by one into an office nearly lost in the constant cloud of dust that hung over the site.

Maybe it was his imagination, but Nate thought he saw a flash of crimson light emanating from the concrete building each time someone entered. And when the men and women stepped out of the far door, masked by the dirty air, they marched right into the maelstrom as if they knew exactly what they were doing.

Despite repeated attempts to convince their parents of the truth about Saint's plan to take over the world, nobody was willing to believe them. Both Peter and Wendy pointed to the master inventor on screen and explained, with the kind of pompous authority that only an adult can use, that Saint couldn't have died and been reborn as a robot because there he was on television as large as life, and that even if by some horrific twist of fate he was trying to destroy the world, then why was he building malls in Heaton?

They also fished out the letter that they had received from Saint Solutions, once again pointing out that the scholarship had been cancelled for legitimate reasons.

'There's no need to be bitter,' said Wendy. 'Saint gave you almost three months of his time and I'm sure you learned a lot.'

If they couldn't convince their parents of the truth there was no way they could convince the police – especially with no means of contacting David or the other inventors. And they didn't even know what the truth was. It was pretty clear that Saint was up to something – who else could be behind all this? But was he still trying to destroy the world or was he planning something else? Nothing made any sense.

Even if they did manage to find out what was going on and bring it to the attention of the authorities there was absolutely no proof. The Saint Solutions complex still lay in the heart of the capital as if nothing had ever happened, and Saint's company was still pumping out its plethora of innovative products and had even announced some new ones.

If Nate didn't have such vivid memories of his time as

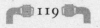

Saint's prisoner, and of freezing his butt off in Greenland, he would have assumed it was all a twisted fantasy concocted by his own disturbed mind.

With no school to worry about, and with their parents too busy to provide them with a home education, Nate and Cat decided to pass the time the way they loved best: inventing. The day after the 'great poop attack' – as the infamous incident at school was now known – they started work in Nate's bedroom laboratory, spending the entire morning arguing about what to create.

'We never got round to making X-ray specs,' said Nate with a mischievous grin. Cat rewarded his suggestion with a clip round the ear. 'I've had enough spy glasses and laser specs to last me a lifetime,' she replied.

'Okay, then a machine that converts poo to money,' he went on, inspired by the explosion at school.

'That's disgusting,' Cat replied with a fitting expression. 'How about a chip you can implant in your brain that provides you with all the things you need to learn. You'd never have to go to school again.'

'Boring,' said Nate. 'Anyway, since when have you been a brain surgeon?'

'Okay, fair point.'

'How about a system that refines poo into some kind of fuel?' Nate said. 'So we can drive poomobiles.'

'Nate!' Cat's face twisted into an even more convincing expression of disgust. 'Come on, be serious.'

'I am being serious. Nobody has harnessed the power of poo.'

'How about a pair of boots that heat the ice automatically, stopping you from slipping over,' Cat continued. 'I know you could benefit from a pair of those.'

'Forget cold fusion, poo could be the future,' Nate continued, oblivious. 'Imagine a world powered by our own waste.'

'Nate!' Cat shouted, louder this time. 'Just forget it, okay. I'm not playing with poop.'

'Fine,' said Nate, feeling a strop brewing.

'Fine,' echoed Cat, folding her arms.

'I've got an idea,' came a little voice from the corner of the room. Both inventors looked up to see Clint gazing dreamily out of the window at the crystallised world beyond.

'What?' asked Cat. The robot dropped from the sill on to the desk, sitting down and dangling his legs over the side.

'Well,' he said sheepishly. 'You know how you two are best friends, and spend all your time together . . .'

'Yeah,' said Nate and Cat together, drawing the word out.

'And how I'm just little old me with no one to play with . . .'

'Yeah.' Nate thought he knew where the conversation was going.

'And how I can get a bit lonely, you know, with nobody else around . . .'

'Yeah.'

'Maybe you could build me a friend?' the robot requested.

'A friend?' asked Cat. 'You mean another robot?'

'Yes!' exclaimed Clint. 'Just think of it, I'd have someone to have fun with when you two are off doing boring stuff like inventing and sleeping.'

'Two Clints?' asked Nate, shaking his head. 'Can you imagine the chaos?'

'Well, I wasn't thinking of another Clint . . .' the robot went on. 'More a Clintina.'

It took a few seconds for the information to sink in, then Nate and Cat burst out laughing. If Clint could blush then his cheeks would have been on fire. Instead, he did his best to scowl at his creators, folding all four arms across his chest in protest.

'You want a girlfriend!' shouted Nate, laughing. 'Well why didn't you just say?'

'It's not a girlfriend,' Clint argued. 'Yuk, who'd want a girlfriend? It's just another robot, someone to spend time with.'

'Kissy time,' teased Cat.

'No,' blustered Clint. 'No definitely not kissy time, just normal time, ordinary normal everyday time. Normal, not kissy. Just forget it, okay, I don't want another robot, I'm a one-machine team.'

After a few more minutes of gentle tormenting Nate and Cat finally agreed to the idea. They set to work straight away, interviewing Clint like a dating agency, trying to determine what kind of robot friend he'd like. They started with the name.

'You can't call her Clintina,' said Cat. 'That's just weird. How about Clarissa?'

'Yuk,' said Clint. 'Maybe Clara?'

'Clarice?' added Nate.

'Clover?'

'Camel?'

'Chamomile?'

'Crunchie?'

'Cauliflower?'

'This is getting silly,' said Cat after several rounds of names. 'How about just Camilla?'

There was a moment of silence as they all considered the name, then Clint nodded enthusiastically.

'Yes, Clint and Camilla, I like it,' he said, his eyes glowing.

Nate began a completely new programming code on the computer, doing his best to translate Clint's requests into logic strings and neural networks. Cat set to work on the body, once again salvaging the remains of Saint's metal dog in order to find components suitable for another mini robot.

Unlike the frantic day at Saint Solutions when they had

built Clint, there was no rush to complete Camilla. Both inventors took their time, checking each piece of code to make sure it was immaculate and cutting out strips of metal for the body with the greatest care. By the end of the first day they had made great progress with the project, an outline of Clint's new belle lying on the carpet and several gigabytes of Nate's computer taken up with her operating code.

Immersed in their work like this, the days flew by with the added bonus of being secure inside. Every now and again Nate would see a platoon of red-topped builders marching past the window, but they no longer seemed to be stalking him.

They were cocooned in Nate's room, the four walls like a barrier against the outside world and the difficult memories it inspired. Sloppy sandwiches courtesy of Nate for lunch, a cooked dinner courtesy of Mrs Wright, occasional calls from Cat's mum to check she was alive and to remind her to come home at night – it was just like old times.

Even Clint kept out of trouble, so excited about having a companion that he spent all his time helping Nate and Cat, fetching tools and drawing clumsy pictures of his dream girl on the back of the inventors' blueprints.

Three days passed, then five, then a week. All the while Saint's malls grew larger, dominating the landscape of Heaton like prison walls while the town's residents continued to fight each other over the new development. But Nate and Cat didn't care. They were inventing, they were happy, they were safe.

17

Clint and Camilla

'Clint, if you polish that bloody suit any more then you're going to wear a hole in it!'

It had been ten days since they'd started work on Camilla, the last five of which Clint had spent rigorously scrubbing his metal outfit with every kind of cleaning agent he could find in the house. Nate and Cat could both see their faces in the shiny metal of his coat, which wasn't great because neither of the young inventors had been outside for more than half an hour since starting the new project, and both were as pale as ghosts.

'Come on, you two,' said the little robot, throwing his chamois into the bin and impatiently poking Nate. 'I'll be collecting my robot pension by the time my friend is ready.'

Nate whooshed his hand in the air to shut the robot up, translating a string of neural networks into binary and filtering them into Camilla's operating code. The sound of a bleating goat floated round the room as he saved the file.

'Bingo,' he said, turning to look at Cat and Clint. Cat was sitting on the bed dangling a pint-sized robot body as if it was a marionette. She had done an incredible job of putting the skeleton together, crafting a framework of toughened steel bones made flexible by numerous silicon joints, all linked together by optical-fibre wiring. The impressive interior was now covered with a short black metal skirt and a silver blouse.

Camilla's face was more feminine than Clint's, and was

topped by a flowing fountain of silver metal curls made up from an old bike chain that Cat had stolen from her mum. All in all, she was a perfect model robot, and Nate was pretty sure that if he was made of metal he'd have a crush on her.

'Right, Clint,' he went on. 'Think hard: is there anything else you'd like in your new *friend*?' He emphasised the last word, winking.

'I told you, I'm not fussy,' he replied. 'Just as long as she's beautiful, intelligent, funny, caring, sensitive, brave and modest. Like me.'

'Well, I've done my best.' Nate pressed a button and the computer programme began flowing down an Ethernet cable into a second processor, which Cat had removed from her computer at home. It took a good ten minutes to transfer, during which time Clint dug the chamois from the bin and began furiously polishing his face again.

'I'm so nervous!' he shouted when he'd finished, hopping from foot to foot as he watched Nate unplug the processor and hand it to Cat. She pushed apart Camilla's curls and flipped open a panel in the metal scalp beneath, placing the processor inside and carefully welding in the optical fibres. When she was done she closed the panel, brushed the hair back into place and flicked the little robot's power switch.

'Don't worry, old buddy,' said Nate as Cat placed the robot on the carpet. 'She's going to love you.'

Camilla lay still and silent for a moment before all four arms suddenly jolted upwards as if she'd had an electric shock. Then she began to shake, spinning round like a break-dancer before leaping to her feet and opening her eyes. She studied Nate for several seconds, then Cat, and lastly Clint, who leapt down from the dresser and stood nervously in front of her.

'Hello,' he whispered. 'I'd take my hat off like a gentleman except it's welded to my head.'

Nate smiled fondly. The scene reminded him of his first day at school, trying to make friends with new people. Unfortunately, just like his first day of school, it didn't go very well. Camilla narrowed her eyes at Clint, then with a yell that could rival Bruce Lee she did a flip over the carpet, grabbed him by two of his arms and chucked him across the room. Clint landed headfirst by the bed, and barely had time to scream before Camilla had sprinted over and pinned him.

'Surrender!' the little female robot squeaked. 'Who's the daddy?'

'You!' squawked Clint. 'You're the daddy!'

Camilla leapt off the robot's back then stretched out a hand to him.

'Only kidding,' she said, pulling a dazed Clint to his feet before punching him on the shoulder. It was meant as a friendly gesture but it sent him flying across the carpet again. 'Whoops, sorry about that. I don't know my own strength. Come give me a hug.'

Clint glowered at Nate, rubbing his shoulder with three sets of metal fingers. Then he shuffled tentatively towards his new friend.

'Please don't hurt me,' he said.

'Don't be such a baby!' was her reply. She grabbed Clint and hugged him, then pushed him away and stretched out an arm. 'I'm Camilla, by the way.'

'Clint,' he replied, shaking her hand then taking a few steps backwards just to be safe. 'It's nice to meet you.'

'It's nice to *beat* you,' Camilla replied, feigning another punch and sending Clint skittering backwards. 'Relax, I'm only playing!'

Clint threw Nate another furious look but Nate just shrugged.

'It's not like building a flat-pack wardrobe,' he explained, picking Camilla up and sitting her on his shoulder. 'She's alive. Besides, you wanted her to be funny, and we're laughing!'

Both Nate and Camilla had to duck to avoid the chamois that hurtled towards them.

It was only when Camilla asked Nate and Cat when her birthday was that the young inventors realised the date.

'Oh my god, Nate,' said Cat, flipping through his calendar. 'It's 14 December.'

'Is that bad?' asked Camilla. She was sitting on the bed swinging her legs idly. Well, that wasn't strictly true – she was sitting on Clint, who was lying on the bed squirming to try and free himself.

'No, not at all,' said Nate, lifting the robot off her helpless victim and putting her down on his knee. Clint leapt to his feet and flexed his arms as menacingly as he could. 'It's just a big day for the town tomorrow. Saint's opening his new malls.' He turned to Cat, ignoring Clint and Camilla as they squared up for another wrestle. 'You want to go take a look? See if we can find anything fishy?'

She didn't respond, just stared out of the window at the frozen grey suburbia beyond.

'Cat?'

'He's planning something, Nate,' she said eventually, her hushed words appearing as foggy clouds on the glass. 'He has to be. I don't know if I want to be anywhere near it.'

'So you do believe me?' he asked. 'About the men in red hats.'

'What do you think?' she replied, turning to face him. 'Of course I believe you. I just didn't want to. It's not fair, Nate. I mean why won't he leave us alone? You think it's a coincidence that Saint's first Supershoppers are in Heaton? A small town with nothing special about it except for the fact that we live here – the kids who stopped his plans, who . . .'

'Who killed him,' Nate finished. He paused for a moment, unsure what to say, then got up off the bed and walked over to her, laying a hand on her arm. 'I don't know what he's doing or why he's building those malls,' he said quietly. 'But it's good that we're here. We know Saint better than anyone alive, if he's doing something then we can spot it, we can warn people.'

Cat just grunted, shrugging his arm off and striding to the bedroom door.

'You go take a look if you like,' she said as she plodded down the stairs without so much as a backwards glance. 'But it's getting late and I'm tired. I'm just going to head home.'

She opened the front door and Nate followed her out. It was pitch black outside. The moon was masked by a blanket of thick cloud and even the streetlights seemed to be hunkered down against the bitterly cold wind which scoured the pavements. It was a night for people to be inside, wrapped in their woollens and enjoying the warmth of a log fire and a good meal.

'Okay,' he said softly. 'But you'll be here in the morning, won't you? We need to work out what's going on, and I can't do it by myself.'

She reached the end of the drive before she turned around, her eyes dark in the tired night.

'Fine,' she said pulling her collar up around her neck. 'But I'm not being a hero again, Nate. We've saved the world once, that's enough for any lifetime.'

18

Let's Go Shopping!

That night Nate once again found his dream world invaded by the sinister figure of Ebenezer Saint. The master inventor was human again, parading around a landscape of purple ice shouting words that Nate couldn't hear, despite the fact there was no other noise.

Saint stopped when he spotted Nate, seeming to teleport across the colourful snow until he was right in front of him. Then his body started to tremble, the skin peeling apart to reveal a robot underneath, which stepped from the human suit as if it was undressing.

'I'm coming for you, Nate,' the metal monster said, rising up to full height and narrowing its golden eyes to hate-filled slits. 'I'm going to kill you.'

Then the figure stretched out a hand towards Nate's head. He tried to move, tried to turn and run, but his dreaming mind betrayed him, paralysing him. The master inventor was going to kill him, crush his head or snap his neck. But he didn't. Instead, he extended two bony metallic fingers, which glinted in the purple light, and rammed them up Nate's nose.

Nate woke with a gargled scream, quickly realising that the pain wasn't imaginary. Feeling his face he was shocked to discover two sharp pencils wedged up his nostrils. Grabbing them with one hand he pulled hard, tugging them free, then tried to focus his blurry eyes on the two hysterical little figures before him.

'Clint, I'm going to kill you!' he muttered, his words distorted by sleep drool.

'See, I told you he screamed like a monkey,' came the robot's voice.

'And you were right,' said Camilla between fits of laughter.

Nate rubbed his throbbing nostrils with one hand and wiped his eyes with the other, the blurriness in his vision dissolving to reveal Clint and Camilla rolling around on the duvet. Clint stopped when he saw Nate's expression, coughing and scratching the back of his head.

'Sorry about that,' he said. 'I was just teaching Camilla some old tricks.'

Exactly thirty seconds later Nate left the room, ignoring the cries of distress from the two little robots locked inside his wardrobe.

With all the nasal pain, Nate had completely forgotten about Saint's Grand Opening until he clumped downstairs to find his parents in full dinner party regalia straightening each other's collars.

'Better get your best gear on, boy,' said Peter, doing what looked like the Mexican Hat Dance around the table. 'It's time to go shopping.'

'I thought you two were against the new malls,' Nate said grumpily, pouring himself a bowl of Saint Crispies and trying not to look at the picture on the box. Both his parents looked a little uncomfortable at the reminder, but quickly perked up.

'Well, they're built now, so there's nothing more we can do,' said Mrs Wright defensively.

'Except spend some money,' added Peter. Nate raised his spoon to his mouth then paused.

'But you don't even like shopping, Dad. You're allergic to spending money.'

'Not when everything has a ninety-per-cent discount,' Peter explained. Nate couldn't be sure, but he thought this was the happiest he'd ever seen his dad, and that included the time Nate first learned to ride his bike without stabilisers.

'Come on, chop-chop,' said Nate's mum, clipping her fringe back with a hairpin and prodding Nate repeatedly in the arm. 'Let's go see what Saint's got in store.'

Fifteen minutes later, dressed in the Arctic survival coat he had found in Greenland, Nate reached the centre of town to discover it was absolutely chock-a-block.

Literally hundreds, if not thousands, of people had braved the freezing weather to see the opening of Saint's first four Supershoppers. Most of these were local punters desperate to see what all the recent fuss had been about. Some, evident by their posh suits and air of indifference, were obviously people from nearby cities who had made the trip in search of a bargain. Others, weighed down by cameras and microphones and other pieces of equipment, were reporters here to cover the new revolution in shopping.

A particularly large crowd was milling around anxiously halfway down the street, old ladies with placards and banners jostling for position with families counting out cash and checking their credit cards. The two camps were each shouting out their mantras, one side bellowing 'No more malls!' and the other 'Go for it, Ebenezer!' in a medley that sounded strangely like 'Gopher's Malteasers'.

The streets were lined with people in red overalls with Saint's face stitched in gold and ivory across their chests. Some were juggling, others were balancing in human pyramids at least six people high, more were handing out chocolate bars, tea and hot dogs, a few were blowing up balloons – filling metre-long, sausage shaped inflatables with what looked like a single breath.

Nate froze when he first saw them. Each of the red-suited entertainers wore the same perfect smile, the same penetrating gaze. They were all shapes and sizes, and only a few were as good looking as the assistants working in Saint Tower, but Nate had no doubt that there was more than flesh and blood beneath their skin.

Following his parents past one cluster of assistants, who were performing a barbershop quartet number about the goods available at Saint's Supershoppers, Nate swore he saw a familiar face. One of the singing men was the guy who had talked to Nate and Cat when they had first discovered the building site, the guy who had been driving the yellow truck. On the surface he looked exactly the same now as he did then, but there was something about his expression that wasn't right.

Nate couldn't describe it, but it was almost as if something had been stripped from him. He looked empty, as though his soul had been stolen.

'Stop being so bloody melodramatic,' he muttered to himself under his breath, snapping back to the real world and trailing after his parents to the section of the High Street that was now the entrance to the North Corner Mall.

As they had arranged on the phone, Cat was waiting for him outside Lorna's Shawl Shop, trying to stay upright in the surging crowds. She spotted Nate and barged her way through the jostling people until she was close enough to grumble.

'Hell's bells, Nate,' she shouted. 'The whole town's gone bonkers! Hi, Mr and Mrs Wright.'

Nate's parents were too engrossed by the sight before them to respond, and Nate couldn't blame them. Where only two weeks ago there had been a giant hole in the ground there now stood a glittering monument to shopping. The mall was a seven-storey artwork of glass and steel, shaped like a vast upside-down ark with a curving roof made of silver panels. Emerging from the top, like a colossus from the ancient world, was an immense statue of Saint himself, his arms held out by his sides as if saying 'what's mine is yours'.

'Well, some things never change,' muttered Cat as they plodded towards it. 'The master inventor still loves himself.'

Nate couldn't reply. He was staring through the glass wall that made up the front of the mall, his eyes glued to the shops that lined each of the seven levels.

'There's a Game Master,' he said. 'And a Movie Muncher store.'

'Nate,' said Cat. 'This is no time to be looking for bargains.'

'And a Bloodbath Horror Memorabilia outlet!' he exclaimed. 'I bet they've got all the *Furnace* action figures!'

'Nate!'

'And look, Cat, that's a Gears superstore. I've waited my whole life for one of them. We'll be able to get all our parts there instead of ordering online.'

This time Cat stopped to look, but she quickly dismissed the idea.

'It's Saint's mall, Nate,' she went on. 'Even if he isn't planning to take over the world again do you really want to give him any more money?'

'When in Rome,' Nate mumbled, drooling ever so slightly at the thought of visiting the Polka Dot Munchkin gaming centre. Grunting with frustration, Cat grabbed Nate's head and twisted it round until he was looking right at her.

'Oh my god, Nate, I know you're a boy but even so you

have the attention span of a gnat,' she hissed. 'Just because there aren't any spooky men in red hats running around any more doesn't mean there isn't something going on. One flash of cheap gears or action figures and you're away with the fairies.'

'Sorry,' he said, his voice muffled by the cold fingers on his cheeks. He was about to apologise again when he spotted something over her shoulder, a strange figure in the crowd. He snatched his head free, trying to peer through the constantly shifting clutter of excited people. There it was again, a tall, spindly man in a filthy overcoat standing towards the back of the large group.

A fat woman in a Hawaiian shirt blocked his view and he sprinted forward, squeezing between her and her equally large husband until the figure came back into sight. A battered fedora hat threw the man's face into shadow, but when he raised his head to get a better look at the mall Nate could make out something beneath that turned his blood to ice.

There were two dull yellow lights where his eyes should be, unblinking and unmoving in the darkness of his face.

'Nate? What is it?' Cat asked, following him through the crowd. He didn't answer, diverting all his attention to keeping his eye on the man. There were still dozens of people between them, but he had to find out, had to be sure.

'Nate!' Cat cried out, louder this time. Her voice obviously carried over the chants, as the man in the overcoat snapped his head round and his golden gaze struck Nate directly. They both froze, still and silent mirror images of each other on opposite sides of the swirling crowd. Then the man pulled his hat down over his eyes, turned tail and bolted. Nate followed, fighting against the tide of people until he had pushed through back on to the High Street.

But it was too late, Saint had gone.

By the time they had navigated their way back through the crowd and spotted Nate's parents there were only fifteen minutes or so left until the grand opening. There were already humungous queues lined up outside the massive doors – two vast gates which, Nate realised with a shudder, were identical to those that had led into Saint Tower. The people at the front were violently defending their position as the first in line, one woman even waving her umbrella around like a sword.

'We're going to join the queue,' said Wendy, speaking up to be heard over the constant drone of excited chatter and music. 'Are you coming?'

'We'll just have a wander round and meet you guys later,' Nate replied, backing off into the crowd. He turned, then thought twice and called out after his mum and dad. 'Be careful.'

'It's just a mall,' said his dad, baffled. 'A little shopping isn't going to kill us.'

Nate did his best to ignore the remark, leading the way towards the edge of the heaving throng. On their way they spotted a police officer being hassled by some Japanese tourists.

'We could always try and tell him that these people are in danger,' Nate suggested.

'Hmmm . . .' Cat replied. 'I can just see that. Excuse me, officer, but the Saint Supershoppers are actually death traps that will explode and turn the world to purple ash.' She put on a deep voice. 'Okay, kids, hang on while I close them down.'

'We could call in a bomb scare.'

'Nate, it's Saint. The authorities know well enough that even the most sophisticated terrorists wouldn't be able to sneak a bomb past his security.'

They sighed in unison, five minutes ticking by while they tried to think of a plan of action. At five to nine the entertainers all collected their things and made their way up towards the mall, disappearing through a side door where they could be seen on the other side of the glass taking up their positions inside each of the shops. They all flashed the waiting customers a flawless smile as they passed, and Nate cast Cat a knowing look. She nodded, turning pale as she studied the image of Saint stitched on their overalls.

When the last of the red-suited assistants had left, a fanfare sounded from the roof of the mall. Thousands of eyes turned upwards to the vast statue of Saint, clapping and cheering as the eyes of the monument glowed with a golden light. Nate felt Cat's hand grip his arm.

'Oh god, something's going to happen,' she said. 'That thing's gonna climb off there like Godzilla and kill us all.'

But the statue remained motionless as the fanfare ended and a familiar musical lilt emerged from speakers inside its mouth.

'I can't tell you how excited I am to welcome you all here today,' said Saint's voice, sending shivers down Nate's spine. 'All these years inventing and not once did I stop to think "Let's open a shop". What a dunce! So here I am, unveiling my first four Supershoppers for your delectation. Well, as you may have guessed I'm not doing this personally, as there are three more malls in Heaton opening at the same time and I can't be in so many places at one time! Two, maybe three, but not four! And, as most of you know, I am not a giant metal man stuck on the roof of a shopping centre.'

The crowd laughed at this, all except for Nate and Cat who shuddered at the comment.

'So, prepare for a short but sublime laser show, then my little corner shops are all yours. Happy shopping!'

The yellow eyes faded, but from Saint's outstretched hands

came another sound that made Nate tremble. It resembled a lightsabre igniting, and signalled the appearance of a holographic generator from each of Saint's palms. They fired a beam of red light into the sky, which fanned out into a twin rainbow which then began to shift and change colour to display a series of images – scenes from movies, from video games, famous paintings and book covers, models in designer dresses and even a brand-new Rolls-Royce – all bright enough to burn their images into Nate's retinas.

Most of the crowd were looking up, mouths gaping like prehistoric people watching a volcano, while others were pointing at three identical displays taking place in the overcast skies above the other corners of town. Just as the impressive show looked as though it was coming to a close the holographic projectors buzzed extra loudly and each sent out a beam of light – all four uniting above the centre of Heaton and expanding to form a criss-cross pattern that resembled a net. The crimson weave sank down towards the awestruck shoppers, then with a faint crackle faded and disappeared.

When the last of the beams had fizzled away there was another fanfare, then without so much as a click the giant golden gates swung open. Immediately the crowd started screaming as if there was a rock star present, then, as one, they stampeded through the doors into the mall. Nate and Cat stood firm against the torrent, gripping each other for support.

'What do you want to do?' shouted Cat. Nate didn't answer. He hated the thought of entering North Corner for fear of what might happen. But at the same time something inside him desperately wanted to know what Saint was up to – whether he really was trying to destroy the world again. He knew there was no way he could walk away, not when the truth was right before him. He clutched Cat's hand and led her forwards.

'Are you getting a feeling of déjà-vu?' he asked as they followed the crowd through the golden gates. Cat just looked at him, her face ashen.

'I hope not.'

19

North Corner

Nate had no idea what to expect as he shuffled into the main lobby of North Corner – an army of robots waiting to take them away, a laser gun that would reduce them to purple ashes, chains and handcuffs to imprison the people of Heaton. As he studied the view ahead of him, however, he realised things were far worse than he imagined.

'Oh my god, eighteen shoe shops, fourteen knicker shops and a makeup warehouse,' he muttered, aghast. 'I thought this mall was for kids, teenagers and young adults, not just girls.'

Cat opened her mouth to reply but she didn't seem able to get the words out. Her eyes were locked on a shop window down one of the massive avenues that led into the mall, where a beautiful black and crimson ball gown was displayed.

'Earth to Cat,' said Nate, prodding her when she didn't respond. Cat was hardly ever into girly things, but every now and again it was as if something in her head rebelled and made her wear beautiful dresses and makeup. It never lasted long, thankfully. 'Don't get sucked in. Maybe that's what Saint wants – hypnotised by sequins.'

'But look at the price, Nate,' she replied in a reverent whisper. 'I have to go and try it on.'

Nate grabbed Cat's arm and gave it a yank, dragging her across the lobby to one of several spiral golden escalators which wound their way to the upper floors. It took Nate a moment to recognise the fountain which the escalators circled – a twin stream that resembled a DNA double helix and which constantly shifted colour. It was exactly the same as the one that had been in Saint's penthouse. Seeing it made Cat forget all about fashion.

'This is really spooky,' she said, clambering on to the moving steps. As they rose they got a good view of the lobby beneath them and the hundreds of people who were running around desperate to spend their money. Some were already struggling to hold armfuls of bags while others, obviously too overwhelmed by the experience, were on their knees crying. The red-suited assistants were weaving their way through the shoppers doing their best to help these poor individuals out, picking them up and literally carrying them into the shops.

'Now this is more like it,' said Nate as they reached the first floor. Ahead lay a gauntlet of DVD shops – at least three Mega Movies, a Movie Muncher, a Massive Movie Megastore, a Movie Maestro and a Master Massive Movie Maker. Next to them was a vast home entertainment store with all the latest cinema projectors and Blu-ray players. 'I think I'm going to pass out.'

'Come on,' said Cat. It was her turn to yank his arm, and this she did with force, distracting him from the glorious sights ahead. 'We're looking for anything strange, remember?'

'Well Mega Movies is as good a place as any to start . . .' he hinted. Cat rolled her eyes but led the way into the shop, stalling as soon as the interior came into sight. It was vast, almost a hundred metres long and half as wide, each of the mammoth walls lined with every DVD imaginable, plus related merchandise like posters, action figures and even an entire booth devoted to popcorn. Nate was sure he'd had dreams about a shop like this, and felt his head start to spin the way it did on Christmas morning.

'Everything a pound,' he said, reading the posters positioned every two metres along the walls and trying not to drool. 'This is fantastic!'

'What are those?' Cat asked, ignoring him and pointing to a series of booths along the far wall, each of which had a heavy door labelled 'Viewing Station'.

'I'd guess they were viewing stations,' answered Nate. She batted him around the back of the head and started making her way towards them. Because of the size of the store, and the sheer number of shoppers inside, it took a good minute to get there. There must have been thirty stations in all, and when Nate prodded open one of the empty doors he saw a veritable cinema inside, with two comfortable lazyboy recliners and a sixty-inch screen.

'Nice,' he said. 'Fancy watching a film?'

'You'll have to get in line,' came a rough voice behind them. They turned to see a greasy teenager striding forwards with three bags of popcorn and a copy of the *Star Wars* box set, episodes four to six. 'I've bagged that station and I'm going to be in there a while.'

He – and his greasy smell, which was pungent enough to make Nate gag – wafted past and disappeared into the viewing station, locking the door behind him. Nate shrugged, walking back towards the front of the store.

'I hope he chokes on his popcorn,' growled Cat.

'All the shops have probably got booths like that,' Nate said. 'Pretty good idea if you ask me.'

They had only taken a few steps before they heard a noise behind them, coming from the booth they'd just been looking at. Turning, Nate saw a strange crimson light peeking out of the cracks around the door. The noise came again, the faint sound of gears turning, or a drill perhaps, followed by a sucking noise then a dull thump, like something falling to the floor.

A white light suddenly flared up then faded.

'What was that?' Nate asked.

'*Star Wars*?' Cat suggested.

'THX is good, but not that good. Something weird is going on in there.'

They crept back towards the booth, placing their ears against the door. There was no sound from within.

'Maybe he did choke on his popcorn,' he whispered, making Cat blush.

The door clicked as the bolt inside was drawn back, and Nate and Cat leaped away. It swung open, revealing the greasy teenager who stepped out into the shop. He looked right at Nate, then smiled, the corners of his mouth twisting up slowly like it was the first time he had ever tried it. There was something about him that made Nate's skin crawl.

'You should go in,' the boy said. His voice was the same but different somehow, like Nate was listening to it on the other end of a telephone. 'They are good films.'

'But you were only in there a minute,' Nate replied. 'How can you have watched the *Star Wars* trilogy?'

The boy just kept on smiling at them, but there was no humour in his eyes. In fact, there was nothing in his eyes at all. Like the man outside, something seemed to be missing from him, as though a little piece of him had died. His gaze was like that of a rag doll, his eyes like two black marbles stuck in his head – each surrounded by a faint crimson halo that seemed to glow in the half-light of the shop. But it wasn't this that was creeping Nate out so much.

'Go in and see for yourself,' the teenager said, holding out his arm towards the open booth door. 'You won't regret it.'

Nate and Cat both took a step backwards. To their right, another of the booths began to emit crimson rays, the same mechanical sounds coming from inside.

It was then that Nate realised what it was about the teenager that disturbed him. The boy no longer stank of BO. If anything, he now gave off a pleasant aroma of vanilla – a sweet smell that masked something else underneath, the tang of motor oil or diesel.

'It will change your life,' said the boy, stepping towards them. Neither Nate nor Cat responded, turning tail and bolting to the front of the store.

They tore from the entrance to Mega Movies and crashed against the banister overlooking the lobby, checking behind them to make sure the greasy kid – or whatever he was now – wasn't in pursuit. But the coast was clear; they could make him out at the far end of the store ushering other customers into the booths.

'Oh god, Cat, Saint's back, and he's stealing people's souls,' Nate said as he fought to get his breath back.

'What?' asked Cat, taking Nate's arm and leading him along the walkway. 'Stealing their souls? You've been watching too much *Buffy*.'

They reached the entrance to the next shop along, a Movie Muncher, and peered round the security doors. Inside was the same level of frenzied activity as in every other shop – people tearing into the cheap merchandise like piranhas into a dead horse, stripping the shelves clean – and just like the Mega Movies next door there was a series of booths at the back of the shop.

As Nate and Cat watched, people entered the viewing stations with their DVD box sets and popcorn, only to emerge a minute or so later after their booth had glowed as though there was a party inside.

'Come on, Cat,' Nate went on in hushed tones. 'They go in there and then they come straight out again like they've had soul lobotomies. Look at that one.' He pointed to a man almost drowned in leather, facial hair and skull tattoos who had just emerged from a viewing station. He put his copy of *Headbanger's Heaven* back on the shelf before politely escorting a little old lady into an empty booth. 'They've all got that grin, the same one Saint's assistants had.'

'You're saying they're robots?' Cat asked as they made their way down to the next shop to see the same spectacle.

'That's impossible,' Nate replied. 'They can't be robots, even Saint wouldn't be able to convert flesh and blood into circuits and steel that quickly.'

'It must be some kind of brain ray,' Cat said. 'Look at them, they're like zombies. Saint must be using it to get people under control.'

'To build an army,' added Nate.

'An army of hairy bikers and greasy teenagers?' Cat asked as they retreated from the shop and walked back to the banister. Below them in the lobby thousands of people danced around each other as they travelled from shop to shop. But where only minutes ago there had been complete chaos, now there seemed to be some order to the flow. The majority of people were still dashing back and forth like monkeys in a banana shop, but running across the huge space were several rivers of people who stepped in perfect rhythm and who merged and passed each other like pistons in an engine – never once colliding.

'An army of everybody,' whispered Nate. 'Look at them – men, women, kids, fat people, thin people, grandmas and grandpas, mums, dads.' He suddenly froze, turning to Cat with an expression of sheer terror. 'My mum and dad! Cat, they're in here somewhere. We've got to find them.'

Cat nodded, then looked around at the hordes of people and

started shaking her head.

'Nate, how are we going to find them in here? They could be anywhere.'

Nate screwed up his eyes and thought hard.

'Whisky,' he said eventually, snapping his head up and searching for a store plan. 'If there's a whisky shop Dad'll have gone there first.'

They spotted a plinth at the head of an escalator, one side covered with a map of the mall. Sprinting over, they practically knocked an elderly couple out of the way and began scanning the list of stores. It was immense, and it took almost a minute before Cat cried out in triumph.

'Tipsy George's Whisky Warehouse,' she said, looking for the code on the map then jabbing her fingers at it. 'Food hall, fifth floor, come on.'

She made a dash for the elevator on the far side of the walkway, but stopped when she saw a crimson light leak from the closing doors. Spinning round, she leapt on to the nearest escalator and ran up it, Nate in hot pursuit. Sprinting up the next two levels they found themselves in the food hall, which was exactly the same as the rest of the mall except for the incredible smell wafting from the shop fronts before them.

Like every other level, this one was mobbed, but Nate could hear a familiar set of dulcet tones rising up against the general hum of chatter. They made their way down the walkway, avoiding the grinning shoppers and assistants who clustered round the stores beckoning people inside.

'There,' said Cat, pointing to a sign reading Tipsy George's. They pushed past the last few people to see a sight that would normally have filled Nate with toe-curling embarrassment, but which now made him sigh with relief. His dad was standing in the doorway of the shop holding a glass of Scotch – despite the fact it had just gone nine in the morning – and arguing with a group of red-suited staff. They were all still smiling, but Nate could tell it was forced. His mum was there too, wearing a tired grimace of her own.

'Why the hell would I need to go into a booth to taste a glass of scotch?' Peter Wright was yelling. 'Are you saying I should be ashamed? That the world shouldn't see a man taste this ambrosia of the gods?'

'Please, sir,' said one of the staff. 'The drinking stations are there to make your whisky tasting as nice as possible. There's a leather chair and some ice and a copy of our magazine. It's all part of the unbeatable Supershopper experience.'

'Unbeatable Supershopper experience, my hairy backside,' Nate's dad sputtered. 'You're just trying to con me into something. Well, I don't want your whisky anyway.'

He paused for a moment while he downed the rest of the glass, then handed it to the assistant.

'Come, dear,' he said, taking Wendy's hand. 'This is why you shouldn't shop for quality merchandise in a tacky mall.'

Nate pushed past the last few people and grabbed his dad's arm.

'Have you been in any of the booths?' Nate asked between gasps. 'Either of you, have you been in the stations or changing rooms?'

'No bloody way,' replied his dad. 'This mall is too trendy for the likes of us, who the hell needs a drinking station? And the staff, I mean talk about pushy. Even the other customers were trying to get us into the changing rooms downstairs.'

'And you should see the toilets,' added Wendy. 'They're like discos! I was going to use one but the cubicles were all lighting up like it was New Year's Eve.'

'So you didn't use them?' Nate asked. Wendy frowned, her cheeks turning slightly red.

'Well, not that it's any of your concern, Nathan, but no. I

don't need to be zapped by party lights when I'm you know what.'

'And that whisky shop is the last straw,' his dad went on. 'We're getting out of here.'

'That sounds like a plan,' said Nate. He led the way towards the nearest escalator, Cat by his side and his mum and dad behind him talking about what a disappointment the new mall had been. It was a struggle getting through the packed lobby, and when they reached the main doors Nate was surprised to see them barricaded by a group of red-suited assistants.

'Are you sure you're ready to go?' asked one.

'You haven't been here long enough to see everything we've got on offer,' another continued.

'Madame and mademoiselle, have you seen our perfumery on the ground floor?' asked a woman, talking to Wendy and Cat. 'The smelling booths give you a free sample of any scent you like.'

Nate tried to push past two of the staff but they closed together, blocking the path.

'And you can't have visited our computer games area, young man,' said one. 'You can play everything for free in the games stations.'

Nate backed off, his heart pounding. They were trapped. Fortunately, his dad wanted to get out, and there was nothing Peter Wright hated more than pushy salesmen. Fuelled by his morning scotch, he took a deep breath, put his head down and literally charged at the doors, grunting like a bull. The smiles in front of Nate instantly vanished as the staff swung out of the way, clearing a path into the cold air beyond.

'Thanks, Dad,' Nate said as they joined the High Street. 'That was close.'

'We need to warn people,' said Cat. 'Before it's too late.'

'It will be easier now that Mum and Dad have seen it too,'

Nate said. 'You guys saw what was going in on there, didn't you?'

'We certainly did,' replied Wendy. 'It's terrible.'

'Too bloody right,' added Peter. 'I've never seen such terrible service. Talk about in your face.'

Nate felt his heart sink.

'No, the brainwashing,' he said.

'Well, what can you expect from the young person's mall?' Wendy asked. 'That's what everything's like for kids these days, so pushy. We should have gone to West Corner.'

'The service over there is probably far more refined,' agreed Nate's dad.

'Mum,' Nate said, on the verge of tears. 'Just go home. There's something weird going on here and I don't want anything to happen to you.'

Wendy frowned, resting her hand on Nate's forehead.

'Are you okay, Nathan? You do feel a bit hot.'

'It's probably all that time poncing around in Greenland,' his dad added unsympathetically. 'It's no wonder you've come over a bit queer if you spend a few days in the Arctic in nothing but a pair of flimsy overalls.'

'You should go home and rest,' Wendy said, ignoring her husband. 'We'll just pop over to West Corner until lunchtime then I'll come and check on you. I promise.'

'Please,' Nate started, but his dad cut him off with a wave of his hand.

'Enough,' he grunted. 'We're missing all the bargains. Get yourself to bed and we'll see you in a couple of hours.'

'Just don't go in the booths,' said Cat, seeing Nate's fear and desperation. 'I heard people have been, er, have been using them as toilets.'

Peter and Wendy both pulled a face.

'That's horrible,' said Wendy. 'But I'm not surprised with

all those flashing loos. Don't worry, dear, we won't use the booths.'

Then, blowing Nate a kiss, she turned and walked into the crowd, Peter following close behind. Nate watched them go with a heavy heart, wondering if it would be the last time he ever saw his mum and dad.

20

A Mad, Mad World

For several minutes Nate and Cat stood in the middle of the street watching the people dash to and fro like ants, some with carrier bags, others realising they'd slept in late and running screaming for the mall doors. Nate felt like an ant as well, one on the beach trying and failing to warn his fellow insects about a tidal wave rushing into shore. Nobody was listening, too obsessed with filling their houses and wardrobes and stomachs with more junk to notice what was going on.

'It's like a bad dream,' he said eventually. 'You know those nightmares when something awful is happening and you try and stop it but you can't do anything and you can't tell anyone about it. We must be sleeping.'

If Cat answered it was cut off by a deafening horn from inside the mall. The people on the street froze as they watched a panel in the far wall slide open and a truck emerge. It was an enormous eighteen-wheeler, a colourful portrait of Saint on one side pointing to a sign reading 'Saint's Mobile Shopper'.

The lorry eased itself out of the mall and slowly trundled on to the High Street, the crowd parting like the Red Sea to let it pass. The grinning driver honked again and this time the onlookers cheered, watching as it accelerated down the road in a cloud of exhaust fumes. Three more lorries idled out of the mall before the panel slid shut, each setting off towards a different part of town.

'This is bad,' Cat said when the roar of the engines had finally died away. 'You think those trucks have got the same booths inside?'

Nate didn't reply. His head was spinning, he just couldn't take everything in. The crowd on the High Street was mesmerising, like the movement of waves in the ocean, and the constant hum of chatter made his brain feel like it was going numb. He felt the world lurch and he leant on Cat for support. She put her arm around his waist and guided him out of the melee towards a deserted stretch of pavement.

'We've got to do something,' he said, his feeble voice almost inaudible. Cat nodded, looking back at the mall then at Nate.

'Well we can't do anything without a cup of tea first,' she said, taking Nate's arm and leading him down the road.

The walk back to Cat's house was like a trip through a mirror maze in a circus funhouse. On the surface everything looked perfectly normal, but every now and again Nate would spot things that didn't belong, twisted and distorted visions that seemed to come from a surreal dreamscape, not his hometown.

They came upon the first of these distortions on Tumble-down Street, where an accident had taken place. Two cars – an ancient Morris Minor and a brand-new Mercedes – were head to head in the middle of the street, smoke coming from the place where their bonnets had merged into a crumpled mess. Both drivers were still in their seats, turning the wheel and staring out of the windscreen as if nothing strange had happened. They also appeared to be clucking like nervous chickens.

The sound of a siren suddenly plucked up in the distance, drifting mournfully into the bizarre scene.

'At least the emergency services are still in action,' said Cat as they passed the cars and crossed over to the far side of the road, where a path led to the woods that bordered Cat's house. For a short way the overgrown footpath led along the backs of the gardens, and Nate and Cat stared into one to see Mrs Hendershot, the town librarian, hanging out her washing.

She had already clipped two pairs of pants and a T-shirt to the line, and was now busy hanging her two-year-old son up next to them. The boy wasn't crying, but did have an extremely confused expression as he swung around in the breeze, his nappy pinned precariously with two clothes pegs. Mrs Hendershot strung up a skirt, a blouse and her howling cat before she saw Nate and Cat staring at her over the fence.

'You need to check out the new malls,' she said slowly, as if half asleep. 'There are so many bargains. They were giving these clothes pegs away.'

'Your son, Mrs Hendershot,' said Cat, pointing at the baby.

'No, I already had him,' she replied as she walked back into the house. 'But I'm sure you'll be able to buy a baby somewhere in there. Just go and take a look, you won't be disappointed.'

The Bluebell Woods weren't immune to the plague of silliness infecting the town. Nate and Cat had to take a detour to avoid Reverend Philips, who appeared to be running around a tree naked except for a string of Supershopper bags hung loosely around his middle. They were also scared witless when Mrs Truelove, their elderly form tutor, suddenly appeared hanging upside-down from a branch.

'I've bought a new teapot,' she announced, before folding herself back up into the creaking tree.

The most disturbing sight came a stone's throw from Cat's house. Scanning the trees ahead for any more surprise attacks from teachers, Nate spotted what looked like the tail end of a battered, filthy overcoat poking out from a lichen-covered ash.

The shape seemed to flutter for a moment then it vanished in a flurry of crashing leaves and snapping twigs, but Nate had no doubts about who it had been.

'He's watching us, you know,' he whispered to Cat as they snuck in through her back gate. 'He's enjoying seeing our lives get torn apart, I know it.'

Inside, Cat made the tea while Nate stared forlornly out of the window, his heart seeming to leap from his chest every time he saw something move in the woods. But nothing pounced, nothing came at them. Saint was obviously revelling in their torment, he wanted to see them suffer. Why kill them when he could watch their world crumble?

'Here,' said Cat, handing him a steaming mug. Nate took it and gazed at the rippling liquid until it settled, mirroring his glum expression. It was like looking at a phantom, and for a moment Nate wished he was as faint and insubstantial as his reflection. At least then it wouldn't be up to him to try and save the world again.

'Tea won't fix this mess,' said Cat, taking a seat at the kitchen counter. 'But at least it makes things a little more bearable.'

Nate nodded, plonking himself down on the stool next to her. He took a sip and the drink scalded his throat, vanquishing his thirst and purging some of the bad thoughts from his brain.

'Let's think about this rationally,' he said. But he couldn't think of anything rational to say about the situation so quickly fell quiet again.

'I think you're right, about the brain ray,' said Cat after another moment of silence. 'There must be something in those booths which hypnotises anyone that goes inside. That's probably what the light was.'

Nate nodded, trying not to think about the noises that had accompanied the crimson beams – the drilling and grinding, the dull thump of a dead weight falling to the floor.

'It must exert some kind of control over the person, making them follow Saint's commands,' she went on, using a finger to fish a hair from her tea. 'Forcing them to recruit more people by sending them into the booths.'

'So what about all the crazy folk outside?' asked Nate. 'I'm pretty sure Saint didn't want the Reverend running around in his altogether.'

Cat laughed despite the gravity of the situation.

'The hypnotism must have gone wrong, somehow,' she said. 'It must have knocked all the common sense out of the brain but not replaced it with a command. It just makes them go doolally.'

'So what can we do?' Nate said. 'Short of going out there with a fob watch and saying "look into my eyes", we're helpless.'

Cat didn't answer, just chewed her lip. The grandfather clock in the hall counted out the passing seconds, all fifty-eight of them.

'Maybe we could build another electromagnetic pulse,' she said eventually. 'I mean it worked last time, it destroyed every single electronic device in Saint Solutions. It might knock out whatever machine is hypnotising everyone.'

'Could you do it?' asked Nate, sitting up in his stool. But Cat simply shook her head.

'I don't think so. The equipment we had in Saint Solutions was state-of-the-art, really expensive stuff. I wouldn't even know where to start looking for that kind of technology in Heaton.'

'So why suggest it?' Nate asked. Cat shrugged.

'Better than sitting here in silence.'

They spent the next few minutes sitting there in silence, the only noise the occasional slurp of tea or frustrated sigh – or in Nate's case both together, resulting in him almost choking.

It was coming up for quarter past ten when they were distracted by the sound of crunching metal from the street outside. Walking to the cottage's front windows they peered through the net curtains to see one of Cat's ancient neighbours jumping up and down on her car. Despite being no more than four foot three and as brittle as a bird, she was caving in the roof a little more every time she landed, and it now resembled a cereal bowl. Another police siren battled it out with the crunching sounds, growing louder as Nate and Cat watched the old lady demolish the vehicle.

'Things are getting too weird round here for me,' said Cat, returning to the table and grabbing her keys. 'Let's get back to yours. Maybe Clint and Camilla will have some good ideas.'

Nate clamped his hand over his mouth.

'Great Caesar's ghost!' he exclaimed. 'I completely forgot about them. They're still in the wardrobe. Can we get in trouble for robot cruelty?'

Cat smiled weakly, then opened the back door, checking that the coast was clear before leading the way into the madness beyond.

21

A Very Welcome Visitor

During the half-hour or so that Nate and Cat had been indoors things had deteriorated even further in Heaton. They chose a different route out of the woods this time, emerging several roads over from Nate's neighbourhood to see one of Saint's enormous lorries parked down the street. It took up both sides of the road, but even if it hadn't there was no way traffic could pass because of the crowd of people lined up outside.

Nate and Cat watched as one woman climbed the steps into the back of the lorry, ushered through the doors by two smiling assistants. The door closed behind her, but Nate and Cat didn't wait to see what happened.

Cutting up an alley, they smiled politely at old man Turnbull, who was standing barefoot in a puddle with a loaf of bread tied to his ear, and were almost knocked over by the Thompson twins as they sprinted up Breckenridge Alley on their hands. The little upside-down monsters stopped and stared at Nate and Cat, not speaking, not blinking, not moving. This time Nate didn't even manage an awkward smile before running away.

Back at his house, Nate made sure all the doors and windows were locked before heading upstairs. Cat was already in his room, staring out at the town beyond. Joining her, Nate could see at least three pillars of smoke rising from the streets, and the sound of sirens was now a permanent wail that accompanied the chaos.

'It's like World War Three,' said Cat. 'I hope our parents are okay out there.'

Nate nodded, then walked to the wardrobe and opened the door. He was greeted by two extremely angry glares, one from Camilla who was sitting on a pile of shirts, the other from Clint who was dangling upside-down, his feet tied together and strapped to the shelf with a pair of pants.

'I can't believe you left me in here with her!' Clint exclaimed as Nate plucked him free from his bonds and pulled him out of the wardrobe. Camilla made her own way out, jumping gracefully to the carpet and bouncing on to the desk where she joined Cat by the window.

'How about a trip outside?' the little female robot asked. 'I'm in desperate need of some fresh air after several hours trapped with his wind and his bad jokes.'

Clint made a good impression of someone choking.

'I do not have wind!' he protested. 'And my jokes are hilarious. Cat, tell her to stop being so mean.'

'Behave, you two,' Cat said, not taking her eyes from the window. 'Things are really bad out there. This is no time to be leaving the house.'

Camilla sighed, dropping on to her metal belly and starting some push-ups with her four arms. Clint scrabbled up Nate's arm and sat on his shoulder, whispering into his ear.

'Look at her, you've created a monster.'

Nate laughed, but stopped when he heard a loud thump from overhead. He looked up to see trails of dust drifting from his ceiling. The noise came again, the sound of footsteps mixed with the noise of sliding tiles.

'Something's on the roof,' he hissed at Cat.

'It's Santa!' exclaimed Clint, hopping up and down on Nate's shoulder. 'He's come early!'

Another thump, and this time Nate saw a couple of tiles drop past his window, smashing on the patio below. There was silence for a while, then the sound of something igniting, like a rocket. Nate dropped to the floor and clambered under his desk.

'Get down!' he mouthed to Cat. 'It might be something explosive.'

She didn't move, so Nate got back up, not wanting to look like a complete coward. He grabbed Cat's arm and pulled gently, but she stood firm. Nate was amazed to see that she was smiling.

'Don't you recognise that sound?' she asked as the rocket noise got louder. Nate listened but he could barely hear it over the rush of blood in his ears. He was about to make another bid for cover when all of a sudden a pair of shoes appeared in the window. Not just shoes, but rocket shoes. The soles of the ski boots gave out an intense green light, bright enough to make Nate squint and hot enough to crack the paint around the window.

'It's one of them, Cat,' Nate said. 'It's one of Saint's assistants. Let's get out of here. Come with me, I'll save you.'

But by now Cat was laughing. The flaming boots descended, followed by a pair of baggy jeans.

'Have you gone insane?' Nate went on. 'It's not too late, come on.'

The figure outside dropped even lower, exposing a huge duffle bag slung over a plain white shirt equipped with a bowtie. Then it descended the last few inches revealing a beaming grin, rosy cheeks and a pair of fierce blue eyes.

'I'll save you,' Nate repeated, but seeing the face outside was too much. The room spun, his legs turned to jelly and he fell into a swirling black abyss, leaving Cat to welcome David Barley into the house.

Nate's dream of a flying Santa popping bombs down everybody's chimney was disrupted by the not unpleasant sensation of his stomach being tickled. He snapped open his eyes, giggling helplessly, to see Clint and Camilla running in circles around his tummy.

'Stop it!' he howled breathlessly. The robots obeyed, propelling themselves from his belly button on to the knees of the boy who now sat on the bed. Nate clambered up, still feeling a little faint, then he threw himself at David and hugged him with all the strength he could muster. David wrapped his arms around Nate and returned the welcome, and when they parted both had tears in their eyes.

'It's damn good to see you, old boy,' said David. He was the same boy Nate had waved goodbye to weeks ago, but there was something different about him. He was slimmer than Nate remembered, but it wasn't that. There was a hardness to his face, a fierceness to his eyes, a gravity to his expression that hadn't been there before. He looked older, and he looked tired.

'God, it's so good to see you too,' Nate replied. 'We didn't know what had happened to you.'

'We saw that thing in the paper about the UFO scare,' said Cat, who was sitting on the desk across the room. 'Figured it was you.'

'Yeah,' David replied, laughing but not smiling. 'Would you believe that rocket got us all the way home from Greenland? It even outran two Air Force jets that intercepted us when we got back to home air space.' Clint ran on to the boy's shoulder and David scratched the robot's head affectionately. 'Nice bow tie. I didn't have time to give the ship any landing gear so we ended up crashing into the beach near my house. Everyone was fine, though, aside from a lot of tears, bruises and a couple of concussions.'

'Where is everyone now?' Nate asked. David just sighed.

'We rang the police at the nearest phone box we could find, but when they arrived all we got was a lecture about public safety. They called Saint and he told them we'd stolen a ship as part of an experiment, that our scholarships had been cancelled and that we should be lucky he wasn't pressing charges. The police gave us a slap on the wrist then dropped us all home.'

There was silence in the room. Nate didn't want to ask the next question but he knew it was inevitable.

'Your parents?' he said hoarsely. David's skin went from a healthy pink to a dead white in less than a second, but the boy's eyes remained just as intense. He stared at the carpet as if it was the one that had orphaned him, spitting the words out like they were made of acid.

'My gran found them the day after they were killed. They thought someone had broken in, torn them apart, but they couldn't explain why nothing had been stolen. The dog was gone. They just collected the bits and buried them. They buried my mum and dad and I wasn't even there. The police said they contacted me and I didn't seem bothered, but it wasn't me they were speaking to, it was Saint's virtual reality screens.' He faltered for a second. 'I'm going to kill him.'

Nate and Cat looked at each other through blurred vision.

'We killed him,' Cat said eventually. David snatched his head up and glared at her.

'What?'

'Saint's dead,' Nate went on. He took a deep breath and told David what had happened at Saint Solutions after the ship had blasted free, Saint's death in the fiery grip of his own bombs. Lastly he told the boy about the creature that had attacked them in Greenland, the metal monster with Saint's eyes.

'So he is alive?' David asked. Nate and Cat just shrugged.

'We figured his personality and memories were downloaded

into that robot when he died,' Cat explained. 'I don't know whether that makes him alive or dead or something in between.'

David scrunched up his fists.

'I'm glad you killed him,' he hissed, his mouth twisted into a bitter smile. 'I'm glad he died screaming. And I'm glad he's still alive in some shape or form. It means I get to kill him too.'

Nate and Cat exchanged another worried glance. The tension in the room was becoming unbearable, it felt like they were drowning in clouds of sorrow and anger and hatred. Cat skipped down from the desk and clapped her hands together, scaring off some of the shadows.

'Nate, you fill David in on what's going on round here, and I'll put the kettle on. We haven't even offered our guest a cup of tea.'

She flew through the door and bounced noisily down the stairs.

'I'm really sorry about your mum and dad,' Nate said softly, laying his hand on David's arm.

'Just tell me where he is,' David replied. 'He's the one who's going to be sorry.'

Nate took a deep breath and told David everything he knew about Saint's plans for Heaton. He gave a description of the malls, the booths with their weird noises and crimson rays, Saint in his battered overcoat stalking them around town, the odd behaviour they'd noticed in the Supershopper assistants and in anyone who'd entered one of the shopping stations. David took it all in with barely a nod.

'You're right, it sounds like some kind of hypnotism,' he said when Nate had finished. 'He's got the same plan to destroy the world, but he's doing it differently this time. Once he's got everyone under his control he could make them all walk off a cliff or something. It will take a bit longer this way, but not that much longer. If he can take over a whole town in a couple of hours then the country could be his in days.'

Nate's throat went dry at the thought, and he wished Cat would hurry up with the tea.

'I flew over Heaton a couple of times looking for you guys,' David went on. 'It's worse than you think. There are nearly twenty trucks out there and the assistants are practically forcing people out of their houses to take a look. And there are booths on the street too for people who don't want the malls. Protest stations, they're called, for people to register complaints. But I saw them glow red too.'

Nate cast his eye out of the bedroom door. By the sound of clinking china in the kitchen Cat was out of earshot.

'Best not mention that to Cat,' he said. 'Her mum's a protester.'

David wiped a hand across his mouth.

'He's threatening everyone we hold dear,' he said. 'We have to stop him.'

'I love your boots, by the way,' said Nate, trying to change the subject. David seemed to snap out of his hateful reverie, glancing down at the massive ski boots still strapped to his feet and offering a rare smile.

'I dismantled the rocket after we'd landed,' he said. 'Packed the proton boosters into smaller casings and embedded them in some reinforced boots.' He reached over to his enormous duffle bag and pulled it open, revealing two more pairs inside. 'I knew you'd like them,' he went on, pulling out a black pair and handing them to Nate. 'So I made you both your own.'

Nate's jaw dropped as he took the modified shoes.

'Rocket boots?' he said in awe.

'Rocket boots,' David repeated. 'Just click your heels together three times and say "there's no place like home".'

He pulled the second pair out of the bag and laid them on

the carpet. As he did so Nate got a glimpse of something else in the duffle bag – a tube of smooth silver with a small handle and a trigger. David caught him looking and closed the bag up, his face once again twisting into that lunatic grimace.

'It's just a little something to say thank you to Saint.'

22

The Terrible Truth

By the time Cat was returning with the tea Nate and David were heading down and out. They crossed on the stairs, with Nate barely able to utter the words 'rocket' and 'boots' in his excitement as he clomped towards the front door in his new shoes.

'I don't think so,' she said to David when he held the extra pair out to her. It might just have been the wallpaper on the landing, but she seemed to have turned green at the mere sight of the invention. 'I'll just watch.'

Outside in the back yard David led Nate to a suitable place on the frosty grass then turned to face him, rubbing his hands together to warm them up and looking at Nate through a cloud of breath.

'Once you get the hang of these we can head up and try to get a better idea of what's going on,' David said. 'Keep an eye on all the brainwashed zombies below and find Saint before it's too late.'

Nate nodded absently, too engrossed in his boots to be paying any attention. David clicked his fingers and Nate snapped his head up.

'Listen carefully,' the bigger boy said. 'These aren't toys. One wrong move and you'll be splattered all over the street.'

'Nice,' replied Nate. He looked up at his bedroom window to see Cat's pale face watching them, a robot on each shoulder.

He waved but nobody returned it.

'Okay,' said David. 'All you have to do to get started is say "there's no place like home". That sparks up the boosters. The boots won't do anything until you click your heels together.'

'There's no place like home,' said Nate. He felt the boots tremble, as though there was an earthquake underneath him. They began to whine, resembling a jet engine getting ready for take-off. He could feel the boosters beneath his soles, their raw power just waiting to be unleashed. He thought about the way David's ship had nearly exploded, his proton boosters just too powerful for their casings, and suddenly he wasn't so sure he wanted these bombs strapped to his feet.

'It's fine,' David shouted over the sound of the boots, seeing Nate's sweaty, nervous expression. 'They're perfectly safe.' He sparked up his own boots and they hummed in an ear-shattering harmony. Then he clicked his heels together three times and the flame broke free of its constraints, scorching the grass and pushing David upwards until he was hovering six feet or so above the shimmering ground.

'Cool,' Nate whispered to himself.

'Before you start,' David bellowed, 'do you feel that bar beneath your toes?'

Nate nodded, gently pressing the uncomfortable metal prod that ran across the end of his shoe. He'd just assumed that the boots were too small for him.

'That's how you control the strength of the booster,' David went on. 'Curl your toes for more force, relax them for less. Simple!'

Nate curled and relaxed a couple of times then looked up at David, squinting against the green glow from his boots.

'Enough lessons,' he shouted. 'I'm ready to fly!'

'Just be careful,' was David's reply. But Nate wasn't listening. He gently clicked his heels together once, feeling a button pop in on each boot. He clicked them twice, hearing the whine increase. He clicked them three times, and instantly it felt as though his feet were on fire.

'Aaaah!' he screamed. The pain was too much and he collapsed on to his backside in an effort to take the boots off. But before he could, they sparked up, the green flame bursting from the soles. In his shock, he curled his toes up and barely had time to scream before the boots propelled him backwards along the ground, his bum hurtling across the slick grass and his arms waving helplessly in the air.

He spun round the garden in a sitting position six times, gouging a trench in the lawn, before managing to direct his feet so they were pointing downwards. He did an impressive backwards flip, landing painfully on his stomach and shooting towards the fence.

There was an explosion of splinters and rose petals as Nate burst through into the neighbour's garden, slicing across it headfirst like a renegade missile. Finding himself heading right for their garage, he did his best to pull his knees up under him, and somehow managed to get his feet directed at the ground again.

He changed direction so suddenly that he thought his head had been ripped off. Instead of heading towards the brick wall he found himself flying upwards like a rocket. He watched the ground pull away from him – he could see his neighbour's garden, then six gardens, then the whole street.

'Oh sheep dip,' he cursed as he watched the town shrink. 'I'm going into space.'

But just as he was feeling the air start to thin, ice crystals forming on his clothes, he felt a hand on his arm. Looking around he saw David beside him, the boy's features distorted by the sheer speed they were travelling.

'Relax your toes!' the boy shouted, barely audible. Nate did, feeling the fire in his feet cool down. He reached the apex of his flight and for a second hung gracefully in the air, waving at the shocked passengers of a jumbo jet flying past and marvelling at the curve of the earth before him. Then gravity remembered what it was supposed to be doing, grabbed him by the stomach and pulled him down.

'Gentle pressure,' shouted David past the shrieking wind as he descended alongside him. Nate felt like he'd left his guts – and various other internal organs – up with the plane. Not that he would need them in a second or two, he thought, picturing himself impacting with the hard ground and becoming nothing but a stain.

He managed to control his panic enough to listen to David, pressing on the bars gently with each big toe. The boots whined, spitting out a little flame which did enough to slow Nate's descent. The ground was still rushing towards him, but not quite so eagerly. He added a little more pressure, bringing himself to a halt level with the upstairs windows. Cat was standing there with a hand over her mouth, and he waved at her again. This time she waved back.

'Piece of cake,' he yelled before shutting off the boots, dropping the rest of the way to the ground and throwing up in what remained of his dad's rose bed.

By the time David had landed and Cat had raced down the stairs, Nate was lying on the ruined lawn wondering what he would tell his mum and dad. The grass was a smoking mess, the prize rose bushes were shredded and the fence was lying in a million pieces in his neighbour's yard, so he decided to try and explain it by claiming that a meteorite had struck.

'Yes, Mum,' he rehearsed, his head still spinning from the

flight. 'It came crashing down from space and just trashed everything. We're lucky to be alive.'

'Is he okay?' Cat asked David as they both leaned over him. 'I think he must have bumped his head or something.'

'I'm fine, just help me up,' Nate replied, shaking the last few cobwebs from his mind and allowing Cat and David to haul him to his feet. When his balance had returned he unclipped the boots and shook them off.

'Had enough?' asked David with a grin.

'Just need a breather,' Nate replied. 'Came a little too close to death just then.'

'Rubbish!' the bigger boy answered. 'You were just testing your wings, so to speak. You were never in any danger. Come on, slap those things back on and let's get up there. We've got an evil genius to stop.'

'If it's all the same to you,' Nate replied, cooling his hot feet on the icy ground. 'I think I'll walk.'

After sealing Clint and Camilla up in Nate's bedroom to keep them out of trouble, they headed back into the town. They took the same route they'd used that morning, but it was barely recognisable. Cat led the way past smoking cars, broken windows and several more unfortunate individuals whose brains seemed to have been fried by whatever hypnotic force Saint was using.

For the first ten minutes the only people they saw were a family driving a brown station wagon. There were at least eight people crammed into the car, and the two women stacked in the front passenger seat wound down the window as they passed.

'You kids need to get out of here now,' said one.

'The town's gone to hell,' said the other. 'Get to safety.'

Then they accelerated down the road and vanished.

'That's so weird,' said Nate as they walked towards the High Street, but it soon got worse. As they crossed on to Edwards Avenue they saw a group of ten lollipop ladies arranged in a human pyramid, each holding her stick out for balance. They swayed lazily in the cold wind, not taking their eyes off the three children who passed beneath them.

'Have you been to the malls yet?' asked the topmost lady. Then everyone in the formation opened their mouth and spoke together, a harmony that made Nate's skin crawl. *They are everything you could ever dream of, they'll change you for ever.*

David watched them with barely contained fury, one hand wedged inside the duffle bag he'd brought with him. He had taken everything out of it before they left – everything except the silver tube with the trigger.

'He can't do this,' he hissed. 'Those women are all probably somebody's parents, and now their brains have been melted. He just can't do this.'

'We'll find a way to stop him,' said Nate, touching David's arm gently. The boy flinched at the contact as if he was being attacked. 'Just relax, okay?'

David nodded, then walked past Cat and took the lead. Nate cast one last look at the pyramid of lollipop ladies, whose sticks were banging together like wind chimes, then trotted to catch up with him.

'If they've been hypnotised then there must be a way of reversing it,' he heard Cat telling David. 'It's a state of mind. I've been to a show, the hypnotist clicks his fingers at the end and they're right back to normal. We just need to find the right sort of click.'

'Once we've got Saint where we want him we'll get him to stop his mind games,' David replied. 'Either that or I'll melt

169

his metal ass on to the pavement.'

Aside from the women making up the human pyramid, the school caretaker – who was carving complex equations into the pavement with a chisel – and a rather obese man who was break-dancing midway across the road, they didn't spot anyone else on their way in. And it was soon clear why.

Turning the corner on to the High Street they found themselves face to face with what must have been hundreds, if not thousands, of people. It looked like half the town was there. Nate stopped in his tracks, the blood seeming to drain from his legs, his heart pausing for thought before remembering what it should be doing and beating hard to make up for it.

'Oh crap,' he muttered. He felt Cat grab his arm, her fingers trembling.

'Maybe we should find another place to go,' she whispered.

Nate nodded. It wasn't the crowd itself that was so unnerving. It was what they were doing. Or not doing. Every single person was standing in complete silence, their bodies motionless, a grin plastered on each frozen face. And every single person was looking right at Nate, Cat and David.

If looks could kill, Nate thought, then he'd be stone dead. It wasn't that the crowd were glaring at them – on any other day those smiles would have been welcoming, happy. There was no hatred in their expressions, no anger or sign of violence. But that's what was scary – a thousand pairs of eyes looking right at him and they were all empty pits, black voids stripped of life and love.

They reminded Nate of a doll which Cat had got for Christmas one year when she was little. She'd never much liked dolls anyway, but she'd hated this one, Pretty Priscilla. Her dad, god rest his soul, had made her keep it in her room because it was a gift from her gran. It had scared the life out of Nate the next time he'd gone to visit. That doll had the most terrifying expression Nate had ever encountered – a beautiful smile but cold, dead eyes. He'd had nightmares about it watching him, and here he was being stared down by a thousand Pretty Priscillas.

'I said maybe it's time to go,' Cat said. She turned to walk back the way they'd come but before she could take a step the crowd seemed to wake, taking a collective breath that was so loud Nate thought for a moment it had been a clap of distant thunder.

'*Take a look inside North Corner,*' they said as one, their combined voices like a wave which struck Nate and almost pushed him backwards. He steadied himself, hearing his ears ring. '*There's everything you could ever want, everything you could ever need, everything you could ever dream of. It will change your life.*'

There was movement inside the crowd, a valley opening up to allow a boy to make his way to the front. Nate recognised him immediately – it was Allan, the kid at school who always picked on him. Gone was the bully's sneer, replaced by a smile suitable for a church picnic.

'Nathan, Sophie,' he said. His voice was the same but different, a tone beneath his own like he had an echo. 'You've been naughty. Why haven't you been to the malls yet?'

'We have,' Cat replied, once again facing the crowd. 'We just didn't see anything we liked.'

Allan walked towards them, his smile never wavering, his eyes never blinking.

'Well, maybe you didn't look hard enough,' he said. He was twenty metres away now, and closing fast. Nate began to back off, David and Cat matching him step for step. Behind him he could hear the screech of tyres and the revving of an engine but he ignored it.

'Allan,' he said, trying to click his fingers. 'You've been hypnotised. You need to snap out of it.'

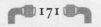

'I don't know what you're talking about,' the boy replied through his perfect grin. 'I'm just happy.'

'*We're all happy*,' echoed the crowd.

'You can be happy too, just come with me.'

The sound was getting louder, and Nate risked a look over his shoulder. There was a red sports car bombing down the road, with a terrified man behind the wheel. It was obvious why he looked so scared. There were three old ladies clinging to the outside of the vehicle, one on the bonnet, one on the roof and one hanging on to the open passenger door – all trying to grab the driver.

'Do you see what happens to people who don't want to be Supershoppers?' Allan asked, still making his way towards them. The car bounced off the curb and skimmed a shop window, sparks flying from the battered metal. One of the old ladies was torn from the vehicle, landing hard enough to gouge a scar into the tarmac.

'Allan,' said Nate, more fiercely this time. He looked into the boy's eyes, trying to see some trace of humanity, some sliver of reason. 'You need to snap out of this right now.'

The car had found the road again, and was hurtling towards them, the driver too crazed to be able to stop. Nate, Cat and David all leapt on to the pavement, but Allan was too slow. He just turned and stared at the oncoming vehicle, welcoming his own death with a grin. Then the speeding car struck him.

Nate jerked his head away, unable to watch. The car must have been doing fifty miles an hour, easily fast enough to kill. There was a deafening crunch, then the screech of metal on tarmac as the vehicle flipped and skidded across the road. After what seemed like an eternity the noises faded, but there were no cries of pain from Allan, no screams of distress from the crowd.

Nate peeled his eyes open, his eyelids heavy as if they couldn't bear to witness what had happened. The first thing he saw was the car, on its roof, the front end crumpled in so badly that half the engine was exposed. The wheels were still spinning, though Nate couldn't see the driver. The old ladies were nowhere in sight, the impact catapulting them deep into the crowd.

Not that he was looking for them. Something else was dominating his vision, something incredible, something impossible. Allan should have been sent flying, or trapped beneath the car. He should have been dead. But he wasn't. He was standing in the same place he had been, flashing Nate the same grin and the same unblinking stare.

A flame erupted on the upside-down car, snaking down to the puddle of gasoline on the street and creating a wall of fire.

'We need to go, now,' said Cat.

But Nate couldn't move, couldn't take his eyes off Allan. The crash had stripped the clothes from his body, exposing something underneath – something blackened and silver.

'Now!' Cat repeated, grabbing Nate's hand and pulling him away. He followed, taking one last look at the boy in the street, whose metallic flesh and robotic limbs reflected the shimmering light of the fire as if they too were alight.

23

Reunited

The moment they started moving the crowd surged after them. It was like watching a tidal wave course over the tarmac, those at the front buoyed up by the sheer force of the people behind, an unstoppable tide of grinning faces that crashed and spat down the street.

'*This is the future*,' they sang out in unison. '*Join us and embrace the new world.*'

Cat bolted up the first road she came to, David by her side and Nate close behind. He risked a look over his shoulder and saw the wave of people in pursuit, led by Allan. What remained of his clothes and flesh was dropping off as he strode, his head the only thing that remained intact – resembling a mannequin's face stuck on to a gleaming metal spike.

'And who didn't want to bring the rocket boots?' yelled David as they ran. Nate didn't answer, focusing all his energy on making his feet move. Cat swung round another corner and doubled her speed, pulling away and heading towards an alley beside a hardware store. Nate pumped his legs harder, dashing in behind her and wondering if his lungs were actually on fire.

He stopped to recover his breath, peering round the corner of the alleyway to see the crowd emerge on to the street they'd just left. They had slowed, their heads moving as one as they scanned the empty road.

'Nate!' Cat hissed. She was halfway down the alley and was

beckoning him on, shaking her fist at him when he didn't move. David was between them, but doubled back to stand at Nate's side.

'Come on,' he whispered, as soft as breath.

But the crowd was parting again, each side pulling out of the way to let another figure through. No, not one figure, two. Because of the angle, Nate couldn't make out who they were until they turned in his direction, their eyes sparkling and their lips pulled back in that same awful smile.

Nate felt the bile rise in his throat, the tears sting his eyes. He wanted to keep running but he couldn't find the strength. Instead he stumbled out of the alleyway on to the street, lurching forwards until he was leaning on a car bonnet. He opened his mouth but all that came out was a dry wheeze and a low moan that vaguely resembled a word.

'Mum.'

His parents stood there, a stone's throw from his trembling body. His mum was dressed in a new skirt, but her blouse was on back to front, the collar pulled so high it was touching her chin. Her face and hair were immaculate, the way she always tried to make them but rarely succeeded. Her teeth too were bright white, beaming at him in a way they never had before. Nate swallowed hard then looked her in the eye. It was as though he could see right through her; she had the same glassy stare as Cat's doll.

His dad stood by Wendy's side, holding a broken whisky bottle by the neck. His beard seemed bushier than normal, but the way his cheeks were raised made his expression perfectly clear. His insect eyes were turned to Nate, seeming to bore right into his forehead, cold fingers in his brain.

'Nathan,' said his mum. 'Come with us. We're a family. Let us buy you something nice.'

'Anything you like,' said his dad, raising the bottleneck to his mouth and acting like he was taking a sip. Nate heard running feet behind him, then a small voice.

'Come on, Nate, it's . . . Oh god.'

'Sophie,' said Wendy, her dead eyes sliding in their sockets until they were staring at Cat. 'You're part of our family too. Let us treat you. Come with us.'

'Nate, I'm so sorry,' Cat said, walking to Nate's side. David appeared from the alleyway too, taking Nate's arm and pulling gently.

'They're not your parents,' he whispered. 'Whatever Saint has done to them, they're not your mum and dad now. We have to go. If you want any chance to bring them back then we have to get out of here now.'

Nate's legs felt as though they were made of stone. He couldn't move. All he wanted to do was run to his mum, feel her arms around him and her voice telling him everything was going to be okay. And all he wanted was to turn and flee from the imposters before him. The two sides of his brain were pulling against each other so powerfully that he thought he was going to be torn in two there and then.

He studied his mum's face. It was just too much. He was going to stand there and let the world take over.

'Come on, son,' said his dad. He took another sip from the empty bottle, and when he lowered it the jagged edge brushed against his trousers, chinking against something metallic beneath. The sound snapped Nate from his state of shock, and he pushed himself away from the car.

'You're not him,' he said through clenched teeth. 'You're not my dad. And you're not my mum.' He backed away, David's arm steering him back to the alley. 'You're freaks. You're just robots.'

For the first time Nate saw the smile waver on the faces before him – every single grin in the crowd dipping slightly.

And in the same instant the eyes seemed to light up, glowing red with such intensity that the frosty street seemed awash with colour, a crimson hue which reflected off the dark sky and turned the world to blood.

And then, as quickly as it happened, the faces all reverted to their former emptiness.

'That's not a very nice thing to say, Nathan,' said his mum, stepping forward. Everyone else in the crowd moved with her, the sound of their feet stamping on the tarmac echoing off the shop fronts like thunder.

'Come here and apologise to your mother,' said Peter.

But Nate was no longer listening. He turned and sprinted back into the alleyway, Cat and David close behind. They made it to the other end in seconds, looking back to see the crowd walking towards them, led by Nate's mum and dad.

'Where now?' Cat asked, panting for breath. 'There are too many of them!'

'We need to get back to your house,' David said, equally exhausted. 'Get the boots. I can hold them back.' He reached inside his bag but Nate stopped him.

'You can't shoot them,' he said. 'What if my mum and dad are still in there? We don't know what those things are.'

David nodded, zipping the bag up again and slinging it over his shoulder.

'I want to save it, anyway,' he muttered.

'We'll never make it back,' said Cat. 'We need to hide.'

She took off to her right, running down Baird Street. Nate and David followed at full pelt. Ahead of them were a couple of dodgy bars, a motorbike garage and, right at the end of the street, a boarded-up pool hall. Peeking over the top of the run-down buildings were a handful of branches from the Bluebell Woods.

'We can lose them in the woods,' shouted Cat, hurtling past

the deserted garage.

Nate looked to see that the crowd hadn't yet emerged from the alleyway. He turned his head back, but as he did so he glimpsed a flash of movement in the corner of his vision. Startled, he tripped over his own feet, sprawling to the floor. The gritty tarmac ripped into his elbow, causing him to yell out. But he didn't look at the wound. He was staring at the abandoned pool hall, and at a figure crawling in through a loose board.

'You okay?' asked David, trotting to his side and offering him a hand. He took it, pulling himself up but still not taking his eyes away from the pool hall. Cat had stopped, and was urging them on with both hands.

'Come on,' said David. 'They're going to be on us any second.'

Nate was about to follow when he heard a voice from inside the pool hall.

'In here,' it said. 'It's safe.'

David heard it too, looking at the boarded windows, then at Nate, then at the alleyway. The sound of marching feet was clearer now, the crowd would be on their street in a matter of seconds.

'They won't find you in here,' said the voice, a thin whisper like that of a dying man. 'Quick, I can help you.'

'Well?' asked David. 'Looks safe enough to me.'

'What?' said Cat, who had sprinted back to them. Despite the cold she was sweating, wiping her brow with one hand whilst grabbing Nate's jacket with the other. 'This is no time for a chat.'

'Quick!' echoed the voice. 'It's safe, I promise.'

Cat eyed the building suspiciously, then without a word she ran to the loose board, pulling it open and staring inside. Nate and David followed, ducking down to peer into the shadows.

'Just get in,' said Cat, holding the board open for Nate. 'We don't have any choice.'

Nate dived through the opening. It was dark inside, but cracks in the boards let some light filter through. All it revealed were dust and cobwebs, most of which seemed to migrate towards Nate's open mouth. He spat as he stepped into the room beyond, still packed full of pool tables. There was a scuffle as David clumsily climbed in behind him, then a crack as Cat followed, letting the board slap shut behind her. They stood in silence for a minute or so, hearing the crowd stamp by outside. It was only when the last footsteps faded that any of them dared make a sound.

'Hello?' whispered Cat. 'Who's in here?'

Someone moved in the shadows at the far side of the room – the whisper of cloth on the floor, the creak of joints, a heavy step. There was a wheeze, like a pair of broken bellows, then another noise, maybe a cough, maybe a laugh, maybe fingernails on a blackboard.

The shape limped forward, stepping into a line of light peeking through one of the windows. The glittering dust swirled and eddied around a battered hat, dropping to a pair of narrow shoulders covered by an overcoat. Nate started backing towards the door, shaking his head.

'Who are you?' Cat asked.

The man made that noise again, the screech of steel being bent. Then he raised his head, his golden eyes slicing into Nate's with such fierceness that the rest of the room suddenly went dark. It was as though those twin orbs of fury were the only things in the world – them and Cat's scream as she cried out the man's name.

'Saint!'

24

Saint

David was the first to react. In the time it took Nate to blink the bigger boy had swung his bag in front of him and ripped open the zip, letting it drop to the floor to expose the silver weapon clasped in his hand. Nate saw the proton booster strapped to the back of the tube, the funnel that would focus the beam of energy at a target and incinerate it.

The target narrowed his eyes when he saw the homemade gun, and he dropped to the floor behind a pool table instants before David pulled the trigger. Nate could swear that Saint shouted 'wait' but the word was lost in the roar that followed as the booster unleashed a shaft of green fury. The charge bit straight through the pool table, gouging a massive fracture in the floor before dying out.

Its recoil had been equally powerful, sending David flying backwards across the hall into the boards through which they'd entered. The boy shook the stars from his vision then attacked again.

'Saint!' he bellowed above the alarming creaks from the roof. Tiny green flashes fizzed across the demolished pool table and the ruined floor, lighting up the shadows for the briefest of moments and leaving bright traces in Nate's vision. 'You killed my parents, Saint. Your dog chewed them apart. I'm going to kill you.'

There was no sign of the metal man, or his corpse. David

edged carefully round the table, keeping his gun in front of him in case he was jumped.

'Be careful with that thing, David,' Nate whispered. But the boy wasn't listening. He had nothing but hatred in his eyes, nothing but vengeance in his heart.

Something shuffled across the hall to their left, a sound that could have been a mouse were it not for the wheezing cough that followed, the same screech like someone trying to breathe too hard through a whistle.

'Wait,' came a voice, faded like it was being played on an old gramophone. 'Just listen.'

David swung round as soon as he heard it, pressing on the trigger again and blasting out another green shaft of light. This time it sliced straight through the wall, causing the bricks to explode into dust and flooding the room with light. Something cracked above them, part of the roof collapsing to the floor. Nate ran over to David as the boy picked himself up from the recoil, standing in front of him and waving his arms.

'David, stop it,' he cried out. 'You're going to get us all killed.'

'Saint?' David shouted, ignoring his protests and pushing past. 'Are you still alive?'

The pile of bricks, mortar and ash from the fallen roof began to tremble, something inside struggling to stand. Nate had a sudden flashback to their last day at Saint Solutions, the way Saint had used Travis Heart's laser gun to demolish David's chalet just as they were trying to escape, and how the master inventor had dragged him and Cat kicking and screaming from the rubble. Now here they were, their roles reversed. David had obviously noticed too, a deep laugh bubbling from his throat.

'Isn't this ironic,' he spat, waving the dust from his face and aiming the gun at the shape gradually appearing at his feet.

'Here we are again, only this time it's me with the gun. And look, you don't even have a ship to escape in.'

A hand emerged from the rubble, thin metal fingers flexing weakly then trying to push bricks from the body beneath. It was a pathetic sight, and Nate almost felt sorry for the robotic creature. Almost. After a couple of attempts Saint managed to free his head, tilting it up towards David. The glowing eyes were now wide, desperate.

The master inventor looked as if he was trying to speak, but without warning his body started to spasm, just like it had in Greenland. The robot opened his mouth and repeated the spine-chilling laugh. Only it wasn't a laugh, Nate realised, or a cough. It seemed like a sob.

'W-wait,' the metal man stuttered, raising his hand in front of his face and wheezing loudly. David paid no attention, walking right up to him and placing the tip of his gun against Saint's palm. If he fired now the beam would cut straight through the master inventor's hand and into his brain, or whatever the robot possessed instead of a brain.

'Why should I?' David asked, his trigger finger dangerously tense. 'You killed them. They didn't do anything but you tore them to pieces. And my parents weren't the only ones on your list. You were going to destroy everything, everyone.'

Saint's eyes closed, his body shaking again.

'Wait,' he repeated. 'P-please just wait.'

Nate stepped forward. Something wasn't right. Saint had tried to kill them, yes, and he'd murdered David's parents. But executing him like this, in cold blood when he had nowhere to run. Wasn't that making them just as bad as the master inventor?

'David, just cool it,' he said.

'No,' came Cat's voice from behind him. She was staring at the convulsing robot with a blank expression, but her fists were clenched so hard that her hands were shaking. 'Do it.'

'Cat –'

'He tried to kill us, Nate,' she snapped at him. 'He was going to crush me in Greenland. If we let him go he'll do it again. Look at him, look at what he's already doing. Think of your parents too, Nate. Look what he turned them into.'

'She's right,' David went on, pushing his gun forward until Saint's hand was pinned against his forehead. Nate saw the bullet hole that the Danish scientists had made, knowing that David's gun wouldn't just dent the metal, it would atomise it.

'But what if he's the only one that can help them?' Nate asked.

'You think he will?' laughed Cat. 'No way, he'll just keep us busy till he gets a chance to stab us in the back.'

'Please, wait,' came the tinny voice again, and another sob. 'Just listen to me.' He tried to say more but he started convulsing again, the sound of his metal body vibrating against the rock like a pneumatic drill, turning Nate's stomach.

'Why do you still want to destroy it?' David went on. 'Why couldn't you just die, leave the world in peace? You had your chance, Saint, and you failed. You're not going to see your plan work. You're not going to see anything ever again.'

His finger gently squeezed the trigger, pushing the metal curl towards the handle of the gun. Saint managed to get his fit under control and opened his eyes again, the golden lights looking right into David's.

'It isn't me,' he said. 'It isn't me.'

David's finger tightened even further, his face screwed into a mask of pure hatred.

'Don't bother,' he said. 'This is for my mum and dad.'

'Listen,' Saint shouted, his voice rough, almost inaudible. 'I'm not responsible for this. But I'm the only one who can stop it. Just wait!'

'David,' said Nate. 'Let's hear what he has to say. If he's

183

trying to buy time you can kill him. He's not going anywhere.' David didn't budge, his finger refusing to relax and his eyes not leaving Saint's. 'Please, David, for me, for *my* mum and dad. I don't want to lose them.'

Some of the fury seemed to fade from David's eyes. The creases left his face and he staggered backwards, coming to rest against a pool table and letting the gun drop to his side. He looked exhausted, as though his spirit had been completely drained.

'Just do what you have to,' he said softly, staring at the floor.

Nate walked towards the shaking, squirming figure of Saint then thought better of it, taking a couple of steps away. The master inventor was still trying to free himself, but it seemed that every time he moved his entire body shook, covering him with more debris than he managed to remove.

'Th-thank-you,' the metal man stuttered, giving up and slumping against his bed of bricks. His golden eyes seemed to flicker for a moment, and he wheezed loudly.

'So what's the plan this time?' Nate asked eventually. 'Turn everyone into robots so you can control them all?'

'It's not me,' Saint repeated, his eyes returning to full strength, burning so brightly that they rivalled the sunlight which filtered in through the hole in the wall. 'This thing, these malls. I had nothing to do with it.'

'Right,' jeered Cat, walking to Nate's side. 'Of course not. It's just got your name all over it, pictures of you on every wall.'

'It was as much of a shock to me, little miss, I can tell you,' Saint replied, his metallic voice changing pitch for an instant and coming as close as Nate had heard it to the master inventor's original lilt. 'I came to Heaton after you two, but imagine my shock when I saw these malls going up.' He tried to say something else but his head snapped back, the sound of a jammed CD coming from his open mouth. 'Damn this body,' he went on when he had recovered.

'How come you can speak now?' Cat asked. 'You couldn't in Greenland.'

'Takes a lot of practice,' he replied. 'You know how difficult it is learning to ride a bike? Well, try operating a robotic body with a million moving parts.'

'Enough jokes!' screamed David. 'Don't think I'm not going to kill you, Ebenezer. Just tell us what you know so I can put you out of your misery.'

'I wish you would,' the robot replied, the eyes narrowing to slits again. 'My body doesn't do what I want it to do, I can't say three words without jamming up, and the pain.' Saint smashed his one free hand against his head. 'It just won't go away. Every inch of me is screaming and I can't do anything to make it stop. Why don't you just kill me, what do I care about the world anyway.'

David leaned back against the table, shocked at the robot's vitriol.

'I don't understand what's going on,' Cat said. 'You have to be the one in control of this. Who else could it be?'

'It's them,' the metal monster spat. 'It's my robots.'

Three jaws dropped simultaneously.

'There were hundreds out there, on the streets, looking for the best places . . .' He stopped, coughing nervously. 'The best places to station the bombs. They had no contingency plan.'

'What?' asked Cat.

'No commands to follow if I should die.' He screamed as once again the tremors gripped his body. Nate clenched his teeth together, the sound slicing through his eardrums and lodging itself in his brain. 'I built this body because I knew I'd be a goner one day, but I wasn't expecting to have to use it for another half a century or so. I didn't think my robots on the outside would need instructions.'

'So they respond to your death by opening a mall?' David said, laughing without humour. 'Sorry, Saint, but I don't buy that for a minute.'

'Don't you see?' Saint replied. 'They're carrying on the mission that I set out for them, they're still trying to change the world. But they don't know how to construct the bombs, they didn't know the details of the plot, so they've used some scrambled internal logic to come up with their own plan. The big picture is still the same.'

'So why are you cowering in a pool hall when you could be out there leading them?' Nate asked.

'Because they don't recognise me,' Saint howled, making a renewed attempt to free himself from the rubble. He half succeeded, pulling his other arm and half his torso free before succumbing to more convulsions. David raised his weapon again, just in case, but when Saint recovered he appeared to have given up his escape.

'I'm not the Saint they knew. According to their object-recognition circuits I'm not human, I'm a threat. They won't take orders from me, they'll just try and neutralise me. That's your damn fault.'

'Don't even go there,' said Cat, bunching up her fists again. 'You were going to destroy the world.'

'No I wasn't!' Saint retorted. 'Why do you have to reduce everything to life and death, existence and destruction. This isn't black and white, I'm not some comic-book villain who wanted to turn the world to dust. I wanted to create perfection – no war or violence or disease. You're blind to the truth, you always were, you're so damn stupid. I didn't want to destroy the world, I wanted to build a new one.'

There was no response. Saint made a noise that could have been a sigh, then his eyes widened and he looked at Nate, Cat and David in turn.

'It could have been so good,' he said softly. 'It would have been heaven on earth for all eternity. And now look, you've freed up these ignorant robots to do exactly what you feared most. They *will* destroy everything. By the time they're finished there will be nobody left alive, we'll all be slaves.'

'Isn't that what you wanted?' Nate asked. Saint rolled his golden eyes.

'Did you bang your head on my flying machine or are you just an idiot?' the metal man asked. 'Aren't you listening to what I'm saying? I wanted to create a world full of individuality, creativity, happiness, a place where everyone was free to live their life as well as they could.'

He wheezed, but there were no spasms this time.

'These damned robots have got it backwards. They all think alike, they share the same consciousness. There will be no individuality, no creativity, no happiness. There will be nothing.'

There was a moment's silence as the three inventors listened to the man who had once been their hero. Nobody knew what to think, what to believe, what to say. But it was David who responded first. He laid the gun on the table, folded his arms across his chest and looked Saint dead in the eye.

'So how do we stop them?'

25

The City

It took over twenty minutes to free Saint from his prison of rock and rubble. Nate, Cat and David took turns shifting the heavy bricks and overseeing the operation with the gun just in case the master inventor made any sudden moves. But the robot did nothing except brush dust from himself and answer the endless stream of questions from his rescuers.

'So why Heaton?' said Cat, lifting half a breezeblock from the pile and throwing it to one side. 'Why not the capital?'

'It's that crazy internal logic again,' Saint replied, stretching his newly freed leg. 'They must have known that you were responsible for destroying Saint Tower. I programmed them to target problems and threats directly and aggressively, so they set up in the place they thought posed the greatest risk. If they could neutralise you first then the rest is plain sailing.'

'And why a shopping mall?' she asked again, pausing for breath and rubbing her filthy hands on her jeans. 'Why not just a load of guns and explosions?'

'Beats me,' said Saint. 'You have to understand that these robots don't process information the same way as us. But they are very clever, and I mean geniuses – their processors probably analysed a million different plans in the space of hours. My guess is that they looked for the thing which humans do more than anything else and exploited it.'

'Shopping?' asked Nate. He'd been trying for the last ten

minutes to move a particularly stubborn piece of rubble and was sweating like a sumo wrestler in the Sahara.

'Well, it's true isn't it,' Saint replied. 'You shop every day. New clothes, new shoes, new cars, new TVs, always new ways to squander your money on stuff you don't need. Hats off to them, I say. They looked for your biggest weakness and they found it. Just look how people were fighting each other to get to their own deaths.'

Nate froze, tears burning his eyes again. He felt the anger well up inside him like a tidal wave surging from his stomach. He picked up the piece of stone and lifted it above his head, hurling it to the floor inches from Saint's face. The master inventor lurched out of the way, launching into another series of spasms.

'So they're dead?' Nate screamed. 'My mum and dad, every-one else in the town.'

'I don't know,' Saint said when his body had stopped shaking. 'I just don't know. When I designed the first generation of robots I made sure that their programming prevented them from ever hurting a human. But they redesign themselves, they did it at home and they're doing it now. I don't know if they've rewritten their core system.'

'And if they have?' Nate asked. Saint lowered his head, pulling his other leg free and running his finger along the bruised and battered metal.

'Then yes, there's a chance your parents may be dead.'

Nate screamed in frustration. It couldn't be true, he couldn't be hearing this. He picked up a pool cue from a nearby table and brandished it like a club. Seeing his fury, Cat ran to him, placing a hand on his cheek until he had calmed down.

'How can we be sure?' she asked.

'I don't know,' Saint repeated.

'I thought you said you were the only one who could stop this,' David said, lifting his gun once again. 'I think we're better off without you and your lies.'

Saint just sat there. He was no longer trapped but he made no attempt to get up, wrapping his torn coat around his skinny torso and studying the floor as though he might find the answers there.

'You want to know what I think?' he said eventually. 'If I was their collective mind then I wouldn't destroy a perfectly good resource. We know that they've been replacing people with a robot double. I don't know how they built the technology to do that so quickly, it's stunning.'

'It's not your design then?' David asked.

'Of course it is,' Saint replied. 'I used the same technology to build the robots at Saint Solutions, giving them skin and hair and clothes to make them look human. But it took hours to create each one, not seconds.'

Very slowly, Saint got to his feet. The young inventors jumped back when he moved, but he paid them no attention. It was like watching an ancient, arthritic man trying to stand up after a fall. Saint's limbs trembled, his back was arched and he sobbed repeatedly as he staggered to the nearest chair, collapsing into it with a soft cry.

'Those people out there,' he went on. 'They're not your mum and dad, they're not human, they're robots. Okay? Now, like I was saying, I don't think my boys would just destroy a good resource.'

'Resource?' Nate asked.

'Yes. They're obviously feeding on information from the original people. Those robots knew who you were, right?' Nate nodded. 'I think that means they're keeping the sources alive, stealing their knowledge, their thoughts, in order to appear human.'

'Stealing their souls,' Nate muttered.

'If you want to be poetic, then yes. They're stealing their

souls. Just imagine it, a single hive intelligence with all that knowledge. That's what they're building towards, a sole entity on earth with infinite wisdom but absolutely no use for it.'

'So they are still alive?' Nate asked, feeling the faintest flicker of hope in his chest.

'I can't promise that, but I'd guess they were,' Saint gripped the edge of his chair as the tremors set in again, waiting until they had faded before continuing. 'They'll be somewhere near, somewhere safe, probably underground.'

'So all we've got to do is get inside the malls and find them?' Nate asked.

'Avoiding thousands of robots,' added Cat.

'And trying not to be turned into machines ourselves,' said David.

Saint nodded.

'Piece of cake,' Nate said.

It was right at that moment that all hell broke loose.

It started with a rattle as the remaining balls and cues in the pool hall shook against each other. It was more a feeling than a sound, the gentlest of tickles on the soles of Nate's feet, a tickle that grew in strength, moving up his ankles. By the time it reached his knees the motion in the ground was so severe that he was finding it difficult to stand. The floor was shaking so hard that dust was raining from the unstable roof, threatening to bury them all in a grave of rubble.

'Earthquake!' Nate shouted, avoiding a pool table which slid across the buckling floor.

'That's no earthquake, you nut,' Cat replied, hollering over the noise of the dying building. They all turned to Saint, who shrugged his metal shoulders.

'Don't look at me,' he said. 'I'm no seismologist.'

The rumble was now accompanied by a sound, a bone-shattering groan from beneath them. It sounded like a cross between a foghorn and a whale song, mournful and terrifying at the same time. The noise grew in volume, forcing Nate to clamp his hands over his ears to stop his eardrums exploding. Cat was screaming something to him but he couldn't hear her. She gave up shouting and pointed towards the door they'd crawled in through.

Nate nodded and started to follow her across the juddering room. One of the beams in the roof snapped, crashing to the floor and showering them with splintered tiles. Nate felt a sharp pain in his arm and looked down to see a fragment of glass embedded in his elbow. It was only tiny – the size of a fingernail – but the sight of his own blood on top of everything else made his world spin.

'Don't faint,' he said, forcing himself forwards. The noise had reached a steady pitch, a deep vibration that made Nate think that it was the very planet itself which was screaming.

The entire building lurched and Nate was thrown to his right, thumping into a table and crashing to the floor. He tried to stand but the shuddering ground was too much. It was like being on the crazy walk at a funhouse. Only with certain death facing him if he couldn't get up.

Ignoring the pain in his arm and shoulder, Nate braced himself against the pool table and straightened his legs. With a series of squeaks and cracks the hall shifted again, this time two of the walls bending in at an alarming angle. Part of the ceiling at the far end of the room bowed earthwards, then it gave in to gravity and crumbled. A cloud of dust filled the hall, blocking Nate's view of the exit.

'Cat?' he shouted, trying to feel his way towards the door. 'David?'

But it was useless, nothing could be heard over the groan beneath the moving floor. Something collapsed in front of him, crushing a table and sending pool balls flying. One struck him on the shin, a bolt of pain shooting through his leg.

Coughing the dust from his lungs he tried to navigate around the debris, but there was no way through. After everything he'd been through it was going to end like this, squished to death in a pool hall while the world outside surrendered to a new dawn.

He felt a hand on his arm, fingers digging hard into his flesh and dragging him to his left. He couldn't see who it was or where he was going, but he wasn't about to argue, stepping gingerly over the debris as he followed the vague shape before him. The shadow – he guessed it was David – reached the far wall and lashed out, cutting through the boards over the door. It tugged on Nate's arm again and he felt himself fly through the gap, landing with a crunch on the gravel outside.

The deafening bellow was even louder out here, the very concrete that made up the street and pavements splitting and cracking with the sheer force of the subterranean vibrations. Nate saw Cat nearby, trying to stay upright on the shaking earth. She tottered over, her arms out to help her balance. To Nate's surprise David was sitting on a wall on the other side of the road, his face bloody.

Looking back at the door to the pool hall he saw Saint emerge, the pistons in his legs straining to keep him standing. It had been the master inventor who had saved him. The robot strode over and held out a metal hand, and after an open-mouthed double take Nate took it, allowing himself to be pulled to his feet. With Saint's arm supporting him and Cat by his side, he limped to the far side of the road, looking back to see the pool hall finally surrender.

It went with a whimper rather than a bang, the roof seeming

to deflate like an old balloon, the walls sighing as they folded inwards. Only the dust escaped with any bravado, billowing into the air with such conviction that it blotted out the light from the sun.

At least that's what Nate thought. The world had been thrown into shadow, the cracked streets and demolished buildings gripped by noon despite the fact it wasn't even three yet.

'That was close,' he shouted to Cat, but he needn't have bothered – his words swallowed whole by the groan beneath the ground. Besides, she wasn't even looking at him, her eyes were as large as pickled eggs, and were aimed squarely at the sky.

Nate tilted his head, feeling the ache in his neck where he'd collided with the pool table. He soon forgot about the pain, however. He saw what was making the noise, what was throwing the entire town into darkness. He saw it but he didn't believe it.

Where his home town had once stood was now a city of steel, a monstrosity which was still growing from the earth as he watched – vast buildings like gravestones pushing their way upwards through the dust of what had been there before.

One of these metal growths was less than two streets away, and Nate recognised it immediately. It was North Corner, rising from the ground like some lost titan. The earth screamed as the building sliced its way up, the sound of millions of tonnes of soil and rock splitting and grinding. The mall had been big to begin with but now it was vast – a hundred storeys and growing, its smooth metal sides dragging up split pipes and fossils and even coffins as they broke free.

The other four malls were expanding too, visible in the distance glinting in the afternoon light like the sails of some giant ship. The behemoths split the ground, turning houses and shops to splinters. And on top of each stood the still and silent figures of Saint, the statues seeming to grin as they surveyed the destruction.

With a shudder that sent all four inventors flying the malls stopped growing, the groan cutting off so suddenly that Nate felt as though he had been plunged into a void of silence. The four enormous buildings stood there like sentinels, mud and earth and cars and even whole buildings raining from their filthy walls back down to ground.

They dwarfed everything – not that there was much left to dwarf, for the town lay in ruins, only a handful of buildings still standing in the open space between the malls. There wasn't a soul to be seen, human or otherwise.

'Time to go,' said Cat, picking herself off the floor and scanning the ruined street for an escape route.

'Roger that, old girl,' said David, wiping the blood from his nose.

But no sooner had they spoken than another noise cut through the air, the lightsabre sound of the holographic projectors firing up on the distant roofs of the buildings. It was the same noise that had preceded the laser show that morning before the malls had opened, but Nate was pretty sure they weren't in for another display.

He was right. There was a blinding flash from the four figures as a bubble of red light began to grow from each pair of outstretched hands – a bubble that thrashed about like something alive. The Saint statues clapped their hands together with a thunderous crash and each bubble shot outwards, forming a sphere of light which expanded out towards the centre of town and down to the ground.

The four crimson orbs met with a crack of static electricity, spitting against one another before finally joining. Nate watched in horror as the sphere ripped through the air, the edges dropping earthwards until it resembled a massive bowl sitting over the town. It must have been five miles across, maybe ten, covering everything in sight and bathing the ravaged landscape in a shimmering light.

Nate blinked for what seemed the first time in minutes, wondering if he'd gone to hell. He opened his mouth to ask what the orb was, but his tongue didn't seem to want to move. Saint sensed the question.

'It's a shield,' said the master inventor. His metal face was motionless but his eyes showed something Nate had never before seen in the master inventor: fear. 'We're trapped.'

26

Flight and Fight

'Trapped?' asked Cat, her eyes scanning the crimson sky above them. 'What do you mean a shield?'

'It's exactly what it says on the tin,' Saint replied. 'An energy shield. Same as the ones I used in Saint Solutions, only this one is red, and it looks far more powerful.'

'All that to keep us in?' David asked. His nose was still bleeding from their escape, the dark blood a stark contrast to his pale skin.

'Don't flatter yourself,' Saint replied, gritting his teeth together as tremors once again gripped his body. 'It's to keep something out. The army, I'd say. They're going to have a fit when they see this.'

'It doesn't matter anyway,' said Nate. His voice was quiet but it was laced with a strength that came from desperation. 'Even if we aren't trapped we're not going anywhere. Not without my mum and dad.'

'And my mum,' Cat said, her eyes moving from the pulsating orb to the four square mountains that bordered the town. 'She's in there somewhere too. I know it. She'd never try and leave town without me.'

'So what's the plan?' asked David, gripping his makeshift proton blaster so hard his knuckles turned white. 'Find a way inside?'

Nate nodded, looking at the impossibly large buildings and

imagining the robotic creatures inside, running around in their thousands like termites in a mound. He saw his mum and dad, in a cell somewhere with tubes in their veins and wires in their brains – confused, alone, terrified. He pictured himself running in and saving them, turning that city of stolen souls to ashes and dust. Then he looked down at his empty hands.

'Yeah, we find a way in. But not until we've got some serious firepower.'

They picked their way slowly through the ruined town, the damage so great that several times they took a wrong turn as they tried to find their way back to Nate's house. The quake caused by the growing city had reduced most houses in the centre to rubble, the guts of so many lives strewn across the debris – clothes, photographs, books and treasured objects. There were no bodies in sight – alive or dead – but the houses themselves were like corpses, naked and exposed in a way that made Nate want to sob.

Severed gas pipes blasted blue flames towards the dome overhead, electricity wires thrashing and sparking on the corner of every street. It was as though Armageddon had descended on Heaton, scouring it of all life except for the three teenagers and their robotic accomplice tripping and slipping and scrambling over the broken bones of the little town.

'This is Bessemer Road, I'm sure of it,' said Cat as they reached what looked like a junction. The further out they walked the more buildings they found intact, giving them a better idea of where they were heading. Nate saw a pub on the corner, one wall completely demolished except for a sign reading The Bessemer Bull.

'You're right,' he said. 'It's not far now.'

After negotiating a small hill of brick and concrete that had once been the All Saints Church and dodging a broken water pipe which was doing its best to clean up the street, they rounded a corner on to Nate's road. It hadn't suffered as much damage as other parts of the town – several houses had folded into themselves but most, including Nate's, had suffered only minor injuries.

They ran the rest of the way, all except Saint who hobbled like a drunk with two peg legs. The front door had been blown off its hinges and lay in the garden, a hole in the front wall flooding the interior with crimson light. Once again Nate had to choke back the tears as he entered. Everything was red thanks to the orb that shimmered and flickered above them. The eerie incandescence turned his familiar house into something strange, like in a dream.

'Shake it off,' said David as he followed Nate inside. 'Don't think about it, don't let the sadness in otherwise it will consume you.'

'Nice place,' said Saint as he clambered through the door, resting his weary metal body against the partially demolished wall. 'Very airy, very open plan.'

'My house has been destroyed,' snapped Nate, wondering what the master inventor found so funny about the situation.

'I know exactly what that feels like,' Saint replied without humour.

'David,' said Nate, shaking the shadows from his mind and focusing on the task ahead. 'Grab the rocket boots from the kitchen. Cat, we need weapons, anything.'

They both nodded, David running down the hallway and Cat bolting upstairs. Nate followed her and they both ran into the bedroom together. Nate's books and clothes had been strewn across the floor and the window had been smashed, but other than that the room looked unscathed.

'Clint?' shouted Cat. 'Are you okay?'

Nate could hear a tiny chinking sound from under the bed, like a spoon gently tapping against a glass. He got to his knees and lifted the crumpled duvet to see Clint and Camilla trembling in the corner, their eyes wide with fear and their tiny limbs holding one another for comfort.

'Glad to see you two are finally getting on,' Nate said with a smile.

Their faces seemed to light up when they saw him, and they fought one another to be out from under the bed first. For once, Clint won, running up Nate's arms and hugging his head.

'We thought we were done for,' he said. 'The whole house was shaking.'

Camilla ran up the other arm, kissing Nate's ear repeatedly. Eventually she stopped, leaping on to the bed and shuffling her feet nervously on the quilt.

'I wasn't scared,' she said. 'I was just looking after Clint.'

Nate dropped Clint beside her and let them argue, scanning the room for something, anything, that could be used as a weapon. Cat was already rooting through his equipment, laying his welding iron on the carpet.

'Figure I could do something with this,' she said, picking out odds and ends and throwing them to the side. 'Reckon any metal man will be afraid of the torch.'

Her line of thinking gave Nate an idea, and after grabbing a tool belt he sprinted back downstairs to the kitchen. David was there, examining the soles of the rocket boots, but Saint was nowhere to be seen.

Heading for the microwave, he yanked it from the surface and lugged it to the kitchen table, using a screwdriver to pull off the rear casing. He'd never seen the inside of a microwave before, but he knew how they worked. Gently unfastening the generators he laid them on the table, pushing the rest of the oven to one side.

'The world is coming to an end and you're hungry?' asked David. Nate ignored him, studying the blueprint in his mind. After racking his brains for a second he ran to the cupboard under the stairs, which was always packed tight with things that nobody wanted but which his mum refused to throw away. He rummaged through the black bin bags until he found the one he was looking for, stuffed with toys that he'd grown out of. He threw the teddy bears, action men and even the pink fluffy squirrel suit he'd worn in his junior play to the floor until he found the little cowboy soft-dart rifle.

Returning to the kitchen table with the plastic Winchester, he found some duct tape and strapped the microwave generators to the side of the gun, lining them up so that they were facing the same way as the thin orange barrel. He popped open the battery case to see two corroded AAs, hardly enough to power the gun's original sound board, let alone a dismantled microwave.

'Any spare proton boosters in those boots?' he asked David. The boy shook his head.

'Sorry, each boot needs two or else the balance is shot and they're impossible to fly.'

Nate swore under his breath. He was still cursing several minutes later when Saint limped into the room. David glared at the metal man, picking up the boots and barging past into the hallway beyond.

'I'm going to check on Cat,' he shouted over his shoulder.

'I wish he'd let sleeping dogs lie,' said Saint as he crashed on to a chair. 'If you'll excuse the expression.'

Nate felt his blood boil at the master inventor's cold attempt at humour. He gripped his microwave gun, wishing he could find a power source so he could test it on Saint's spiteful eyes.

'You killed his parents,' he hissed. 'What do you expect?'

'And he's better off without them,' Saint replied. 'Parents are just manacles that hold you back, that knock you down and mess you up. And when you start making something of your life they demand a piece of it like you owe them something. What I did to David, it will make him a stronger person.'

'How would you have liked it?' Nate said, his words laced with anger. 'What would you have done if someone had killed your parents?'

Saint sat back in his chair and gave a wistful sigh as if thinking about something wonderful.

'Shaken their hand, paid them a fortune, married them, I don't know,' he said. 'They'd have been doing me a favour.'

'I don't believe you,' Nate replied. Saint's smile vanished, replaced by an expression that Nate couldn't make out. Maybe it was because of the master inventor's inflexible metal face, or maybe because it was a mixture of emotions, a flurry of feelings in Saint's mind that caused his face to twist up into an inscrutable mask.

'Believe me,' he said coldly. 'I hated them.'

Before Nate's addled brain could think of a response Saint's eyes brightened and he changed the subject.

'You know the thing I miss most about being like *this*?' he spat out the last word like it was something shameful. 'It's not being able to eat or drink. Can you imagine it? Never being able to taste anything again – no steak, no ice cream, no coffee, no Ebenezer's Teasers. I used to love those sweets.'

He noticed Nate pointing the gun at him, recognising the parts.

'See, that's why I had such high hopes for you, Nate. You're a goddamned genius. We could have been quite a team, you know.'

'Never,' Nate whispered. Saint just sighed, screwing up his

face as another attack reduced him to convulsions. The shakes were so severe this time that he slid from the chair, landing on the floor and vibrating across the linoleum. When the fit was over he tried to get up, his long limbs scrabbling for purchase like a beetle trying to right itself. Nate turned away, emotions that he didn't recognise battling it out inside his stomach. He only looked back when he heard Saint sit down again.

'Bring it here,' said Saint after a moment's silence. Nate frowned and the master inventor nodded at the gun. 'It's useless without a power source, and you can't take time to look for a plug socket when there's an army of robots about to whoop your ass.'

Nate slid the gun across the table. Saint reached into his coat and flicked a switch under his metal ribs, doing the same on the other side of his skinny frame. There was a tiny whine, then a pop as a panel on his chest flipped open. Nate forgot all about his grudges, stepping forward to get a better look inside the robot.

It was like watching a fireworks show – jagged blue forks of electricity dancing around a dull grey heart. Beyond, Nate could see hundreds of tiny pistons working in unison, cogs and wires and springs taking the place of bones and veins and joints. It was hypnotic, and he felt himself drawn in.

'Do you mind?' said Saint. 'A little privacy would be nice.'

Nate apologised, pretending to look away but peeking from the corner of his eye as Saint tore off a piece of his heart the size of a postage stamp. He held it out and Nate took it, feeling a charge pulse up his fingers.

'It's paper,' he said, wide-eyed.

'We found out how to make paper batteries years ago,' Saint replied, closing up his hatch. 'They hold a phenomenal amount of charge for their size. Try it.'

Nate pulled the old batteries from the gun and pressed in the tiny shred of paper. Rigging up wires from the battery to the microwave generators he clipped the case shut and flicked on the switch. The gun hummed loudly, the handle growing hot as the battery charged.

'This should do the job,' he said, once again aiming the gun at Saint. The master inventor looked back along the barrel at Nate, tensing up in his chair. Nate felt his heart pound, his vision grow white, and for a terrible instant he thought he was going to pull the trigger there and then – an impulse so strong he was powerless to resist it. But then the urge passed, and he let the gun drop to his side.

'You'll get your chance,' Saint said as he stood, hanging his head and walking from the room.

27

The Last Supper

Nate made a couple of finishing touches to his gun – replacing the plastic screws with metal ones and reinforcing the barrel with two skewers he found in the cutlery drawer – but he couldn't really focus on what he was doing. His head was a mess, he felt as if his thoughts were a million different scraps of paper in a gale – each time he grasped one another was whipped from his hand.

He tried to partition his mind, to think about one thing at a time. Saint – a hero turned killer turned robot turned hero again? Or was he still the same megalomaniac who was just waiting for his chance to take control of the robots, just using Nate and Cat and David to breach the city of living steel before reclaiming his throne?

And the robots themselves, were they really out to assimilate every single living person on earth? Surely the army must have noticed the energy shield by now – a vast red pimple on the face of the country was pretty difficult to miss. Would they try and get through? What if they couldn't find a way inside? Would they just nuke it?

Nate extended the rifle's shoulder strap and pulled it over his arm so that the gun rested against his back. He rubbed his tired eyes and stared absently at the kitchen table. He should have been sitting there right now eating dinner with his parents, watching Mum serve up vegetables while Dad drummed his knife and fork impatiently. But instead he was preparing to charge into a robot city like some heroic sheriff from a spaghetti western, ready to wage war against an army of metal geniuses who had no right to be here.

The thought was so crazy that he felt something bubble up from inside his stomach, a tickling sensation that climbed his throat and burst from his mouth as a raw and ragged laugh.

'I'm glad to see one of us is enjoying himself,' came a voice from the door. Nate clamped his mouth shut and looked up to see Cat standing there. She had a canvas bag over one shoulder, and was holding what looked like a hybrid of a crossbow and a catapult. She saw him studying it and raised it to eye level, displaying a Y-shaped frame made from bent aluminium and a thick coil of spring along the handle. There was a slot on the frame for some kind of ammunition, but there was no sign of any bolts or missiles.

'Trust me,' said Nate. 'I'm really not enjoying myself. This is just so crazy.'

Cat nodded, taking a seat.

'I mean we were both so happy when we got out of Saint Solutions alive,' Nate went on. 'We should have been allowed to come back home and recover, get on with our lives. It just doesn't seem fair that we're the ones on the front line again.'

'Tell me about it,' said Cat. 'But do you see any tanks, any cars full of Marines and guns and stuff?'

'I thought you didn't want to be a hero again,' he asked.

'They're our parents, Nate.'

'Exactly,' he cried out. 'They should be the ones bloody rescuing us!'

A ghost of a smile flashed over both their faces, vanishing just as quickly as it had appeared.

'Where is everyone anyway?' Nate asked.

'David's upstairs trying to explain to Clint and Camilla why they can't have rocket boots,' she replied. 'Saint's sitting out-side watching the street. I'd give my left arm to know what he's thinking.'

'He's probably wondering how the hell he got into this mess,' Nate said. 'Going from the richest man on earth to a crumbly old rust bucket who doesn't have two pennies to rub together.'

'And planning his revenge,' she muttered.

'If he wanted to kill us he'd have done it already,' said Nate. 'You saw how he was in Greenland, and how he is now. Maybe he's changed? He saved me in that pool hall, Cat – he saved my life.'

Cat just chewed her lip. There was the sound of a frustrated grunt from the landing, followed by the clump of feet on the stairs. David burst into the kitchen, his cheeks flushed.

'I swear, I'm going to kill them,' he said through clenched teeth. Nate was about to ask why when two pint-sized metal shapes bounded into the room and hopped on to the table.

'Pleasepleasepleasepleasepleasepleasepleaseplease,' they shouted in unison, their tinny voices like a siren.

'You can't have rocket boots, I told you,' David snapped back, tugging on his hair.

'Pleasepleasepleasepleasepleasepleasepleaseplease.'

'I don't have the right materials, the right equipment.'

'Pleasepleasepleasepleasepleasepleasepleaseplease.'

'If you want to fly then carry on like that, I'll throw you out the bleeding window!'

'Whoa,' shouted Nate, grabbing a robot in each hand. 'Enough with the begging! You can't have rocket boots, you'll end up killing yourselves, or someone else.'

'You mean like you almost did this morning?' Clint responded. Nate blushed.

'That was different. Now can it or I'll have to switch you both off.'

The robots scowled at Nate as best they could with their rigid faces, then slunk off the table muttering to each other. Nate thought he heard Camilla hiss the words 'get', 'rocket boots', 'up' and 'butt' but he couldn't be sure.

'Those two,' said David, but he didn't finish.

The three inventors fell silent, the only noise the deep throbbing hum of the energy orb a kilometre or so above their heads. Everybody knew what had to be said, but nobody wanted to say it.

'So,' mumbled Cat eventually. Another awkward silence.

'Have we got everything we need?' David went on. The shield hummed.

'I guess we should go,' Nate finally muttered.

'No,' said a metallic voice from the door. All eyes shot up to see Saint standing there, leaning against the frame. 'It's too late. We should rest, make our move first thing tomorrow.'

Nate glanced out of the window. It was impossible to tell whether it was day or night, the only source of light the constant shimmering globe. The microwave timer was no longer in one piece, and there was no other clock in the room. Not that he wanted to argue – a few hours of rest before his imminent death sounded like a good idea.

'What if they come looking for us?' Cat said. 'They must know where we'll be.'

'I'll keep a lookout,' Saint replied, creeping into the kitchen like a wounded stork. 'I don't sleep any more anyway.'

'And one of us can keep watch with you,' David said. 'Just in case you get any funny ideas.'

Saint shrugged, turning and heading for the stairs.

'We'll be safer up there,' he said as he climbed.

Nate, Cat and David didn't follow straight away. There was a distinct rumble of stomachs which reminded them that they hadn't eaten for hours. Searching his brains for something he could cook, Nate resigned himself to suggesting a bowl of cereal. David tutted, making his way to the fridge and rummaging around inside.

Ten minutes later he was serving up three steaming platefuls of bacon, eggs and slightly overdone sausages, and they wolfed down the congealed feast and devoured several packets of biscuits for pudding as if it was their last supper. Which, for all Nate knew, it was.

To keep their minds off the Armageddon outside they chatted, trying their best to pretend it was a normal conversation on a normal day. They talked about the kinds of inventions they had made before they started their scholarships, the trouble they'd got into, the books and films they liked, the television programmes they watched and how passionately they hated sport.

It was a pleasant and effective distraction, all three laughing so much at times – especially at David's story of how his pasta machine had malfunctioned during a school cookery exhibition, temporarily mummifying several members of staff in linguine – that they forgot what they were about to do. They didn't escape completely, the sense of panic and dread and fear was always there, but for a while things seemed bearable.

A quick glance at the clock in the living room told them it was past nine by the time they traipsed upstairs. Cat disappeared into the bathroom while Nate tried to find the warmest spot to bed down for the night.

He walked into his room, which was practically frozen thanks to the broken window. Saint was staring out of the cracked glass, his golden gaze doing battle with the crimson glow outside. The sheer intensity of the shield was winning, casting Saint's face in a blood-red mask and turning his eyes from yellow to a dull, dead brown.

'He's been standing there for hours,' came a voice from the

bed, making Nate jump. Clint and Camilla were sitting on a pillow watching the master inventor, but Nate couldn't tell which one had spoken.

'I think he's sad,' said Clint, fiddling with the peak of his top hat. 'We were talking about what it's like to have a metal body. You fleshies just don't understand how difficult it is.'

'Fleshies?' Nate asked.

'That's what we robots have decided to call you,' said Camilla. 'It was either fleshies or pink wobblers, which was a bit of a mouthful.'

Nate looked back at Saint. His filthy overcoat billowed in the breeze like the sail of some forgotten ship but the silver body beneath didn't move.

'Saint?' Nate said quietly. 'Are you okay?'

The master inventor tilted his head and looked at Nate, nodding gently before returning his gaze to the window.

'You'd better get to sleep, you pink wobbler,' he said. 'Tomorrow's a big day.'

Nate took one last look at the metal man, then said goodnight to Clint and Camilla and closed the bedroom door behind him. He found David in his parents' room, which was still in one piece and was like a furnace compared to Nate's. The bigger boy was sitting on the large bed, the duvet wrapped around his clothes.

'I'll take first watch if you like,' he said. Nate was too tired to argue, clambering into the bed and pulling the quilt up to his neck. He heard the bathroom door unlock and Cat trotted into the room.

'Any room for little old me?' she said. Nate pretended to grumble and budged up, letting Cat crawl in beside him.

'Just keep an eye on Saint,' Nate said to David. 'He's acting weird. And wake me whenever you need some sleep.'

David nodded, unleashing a mammoth yawn that spread to

Nate then Cat before returning once again to David.

Make sure you stay awake, Nate said. Or at least he thought it. Sensing a chance to rest his mind had completely shut down, hurtling towards sleep like a train towards a black tunnel. *Make sure you keep us safe.*

Then the darkness was upon him.

28

Under Attack

Nate woke to the sensation of cold steel wrapped around his arm. Blinking hard to clear the sleep from his eyes he saw two golden slits blazing down at him, a twisted grimace as the master inventor tightened his grip.

Dazed and confused, he thought for a moment he was dreaming, but the agony in his arm as Saint wrenched him from the bed made it abundantly clear that he was being attacked.

He flailed wildly, trying to dislodge the metal fingers around his flesh, trying to strike Saint in the head.

'Get off!' he screamed. 'Leave me alone!'

He twisted his head round to look for Cat and David, but they were nowhere to be seen. The window in his mum and dad's room was wide open, the crimson light outside intruding along with the cold air. Saint dragged him towards it. Nate screamed again, doubling the strength of his attack. But it was useless, it was soft flesh against hardened steel.

They reached the windowsill, the cold air cutting through Nate's clothes and numbing his skin. He couldn't believe how stupid they'd been to let the master inventor live, to let him into their house while they slept. And now death was the price of their trust.

'Ah, you're awake at last,' said Saint, his voice surprisingly gentle for somebody about to commit murder. Nate stopped struggling, cocking an eyebrow as Saint explained. 'You sleep like the dead, none of us could wake you up. We're under attack.'

As if on cue the entire house shook, the mock-crystal chandelier dropping from the ceiling and smashing against his parents' bed frame. There was an alarming crack as a jagged tear sliced down the inside wall and across the floor, making it sag. Saint tightened his grip, making Nate cry out in pain as he guided him through the broken window and up towards the roof.

Cat and David were already there, their faces red from the burning sky. They were both scrabbling for purchase on the angled surface, but they were secure enough to hold out a hand. Nate grabbed them, pulling himself over the guttering and climbing on to the tiles.

'You okay?' Cat asked. Nate noticed that she had her canvas bag over her shoulder, two tiny shapes wriggling around inside screaming their heads off.

'Yeah,' he replied, trying to shake the last vestiges of sleep from his bedraggled mind. 'I thought Saint was trying to kill me.'

'He's just saved your lazy backside, again,' Cat said. 'They're inside the house.'

He leant over the roof towards the window. Saint was there, clambering out with the microwave gun strapped to his back. But Nate was distracted by what lay below him. The ground was swarming. For as far as he could see there was an ocean of people, their glowing eyes like sunlight on the tips of the waves. And just like a tide they were throwing themselves at the house, each crash of metal against brick making the entire structure shake.

'Oh chipolata,' he muttered. The robots attacked again, jolting the wall and making Nate lose his footing. He slid towards the edge but managed to brace his heel on the guttering, a wave of vertigo sweeping over him and making his stomach clench. The impact shook Saint's fingers loose and he uttered a cry of distress before managing to find his grip. With a grunt he swung his metal body up on to the roof.

The house rocked alarmingly again as the crowd surged against the walls. In seconds the already weakened building would collapse. The army of robots knew where they were, a thousand pairs of glowing eyes turned up towards the roof as they spoke.

'*Infidels cannot be allowed to live,*' the faces below shouted, their collective voice making Nate's ears ring. '*All enemies of the new world must be scourged.*'

'I don't fancy being scourged,' muttered Saint, clambering to his feet and trying not to slide down the loose tiles. He pulled the microwave gun from his back and threw it to Nate. 'Any ideas?'

'Just a couple,' said David, sparking up his rocket boots. Saint looked at them with an expression that could have been awe, but he had no time to comment as the house lurched violently to one side. With a crunch the chimney came loose, exploding into bricks and dust as it tumbled down the roof.

David held open the bag to reveal the other two pairs of boots.

'Any takers?'

Nate scrambled up the tiles and slid his on, grabbing Cat's unused pair in the other hand and chucking them to Saint.

'Think you can handle it?' he asked. The master inventor's metal face twisted into a grin.

'Are you kidding? I was born to fly these things.' He pulled the boots over his flat metal feet. They were too small, but with a grunt he managed to wedge them in place. 'They're not quite as cool as my Antigravs, but they're not bad at all.'

'Now say "there's no place like home" and click your heels together three times,' Nate shouted. The master inventor did as he was told, the boots erupting with four jets of green flame that turned tiles to liquid and pushed him from the roof. He wobbled a little before finding his balance, uttering a metallic whoop of joy and doing an impromptu loop-the-loop as he soared into the night. A deep and terrifying rumble rose up from the crowd as they watched him go.

'*There is no escape. There is no way other than our way.*'

Nate looked at Cat. 'You up for flying?'

'Do I have a choice?' she answered, the combination of her green complexion and the red shield above making her look a mottled shade of purple. Nate shook his head.

'David, can you carry her?' he asked. The bigger boy nodded, and reluctantly Cat clambered on to his back.

'There's no place like home,' David said, sparking his boots up and following Saint, their contrails like green scratch marks against the angry sky. Nate glanced at the sea of robots, their crimson eyes promising nothing but death.

'There's no place like home,' he said, trying to ignore the irony as he took one last look at his battered, crumbling house before clicking his heels together and blasting into the night.

Despite the shimmering crimson orb that throbbed and hummed overhead, and the legions of the dead which roamed the streets below, Nate had never felt freer in his life. He blasted through the cool air, twisting and looping, soaring and plunging, tilting and darting like a swallow in spring. His flight made him untouchable, made him safe – not just from the army of steel but from everything. It was as if the feeling of space around him allowed his body to unwind, releasing his soul from the burden of his vulnerable flesh and letting it fly like a song.

The majesty of the moment was ruined when Nate saw Cat up ahead. She was clinging on to David with all her strength, the boy struggling to breathe with her hands locked round his throat. Nate curled his toes to catch up with them, but backed off when he saw Cat hurl. David's flight path veered suddenly to one side as the liquid sick struck the back of his head, but he managed to right himself. Nate accelerated, flying alongside them to see Cat brushing chunks from David's hair.

'Sorry,' she yelled above the wind.

'Don't mention it,' David replied, wiping a hand across his dripping brow. He turned to Nate, the force of the wind making the skin on his face flutter like a sheet hung out to dry. 'Where are we going?'

Nate just pointed up ahead. The green trails from Saint's boots were like an arrow, pointing in the direction of North Corner mall. Nate streamlined his body and curled his toes, catching up with Saint just as the master inventor reached the side of the mall. Saint twisted his metal legs and shot towards the top of the building. Nate followed, close enough to the metal wall that he could touch it. Several seconds later they crested the mall, shutting off their boots to land neatly on the smooth surface.

The noise up here was deafening. The wind howled past Nate's ears, threatening to push him out over the abyss. The energy shield was closer now, and it hummed with such strength that it made his skull rattle.

'This is incredible,' he heard Saint say, his shout reduced to a whisper after the wind had finished with it. 'I don't know how they managed to build this.'

Nate jogged to the master inventor's side, trying to get his head round the sheer size of the building beneath him. There was no sign of the mall as it had existed on the ground, there was just a vast expanse of white space pockmarked with massive circular air vents – each half as big as a football pitch. The statue of Saint rose from the middle of the mountain, the shield emanating from its outstretched hands.

'God, I was handsome,' Saint shouted, looking at himself. 'I understand why you did what you did, but that beautiful face. How could you destroy it?'

Nate wasn't sure if Saint was joking or not, so he didn't answer. He heard the sound of boosters behind him and saw David drop to the roof, Cat tumbling off his back and remaining on all fours, her retches audible even over the cacophony of sounds. When she eventually looked up, her jaw almost hit the metal floor.

'Holy . . .' she said, the rest of her words carried off by a powerful gust of wind.

She got to her feet, allowing David to take her arm and guide her over to Nate. The four of them huddled together for strength against the wind, and against the unimaginable task ahead of them.

'Can't we just blast up through that shield and go for help?' David yelled. Saint responded by grabbing a pen from the boy's shirt and lobbing it skywards. It rose gracefully until it struck the shimmering orb, bursting into flame before exploding into dust.

'It's a laser plasma design,' Saint replied. 'Nothing can pass through it. God knows how they've found the power to run that thing, a shield that size must use up a gigawatt a second.'

'What are we doing up here?' Cat interrupted, the light on her pale face making her look like a distant reflection of herself.

'I didn't think we'd be welcome at the front door,' Saint replied. 'And there isn't so much as a single window in this place. My robots are clever, but they can't design a nice pad to save their artificial lives.'

'Well I don't see a skylight anywhere,' Cat went on. 'You planning to burrow your way down?'

Saint returned his attention to the roof, to the nearest of the vast air vents.

'We go in through there.'

'Why does this place have air vents anyway?' Nate asked. 'It's not like those things need to breathe.'

'They're cooling vents,' Saint explained, leading the group to the edge of the hole. Peering over Nate saw a pair of mammoth fan blades sweeping round at high speed. The current of air they were gulping into the roof was almost strong enough to suck him in. 'They pull air down into the building, cooling the circuitry inside.'

'And just how are you planning on getting past that?' Cat asked, pointing at the fan. 'Jump and hope that you don't lose your head on the way down?'

'Jeez,' Saint replied. 'You're little miss bloody optimistic today, aren't you?' He turned his attention to David, nodding at his gun. 'I know you're saving some of that charge for me, but surely there's enough to get us inside.'

David walked to the edge of the vent, aiming the gun squarely at the centre of the fan and pulling the trigger. For an instant the world flashed from red to green, then burst into orange as the fan exploded. The pin that joined the blades lurched loose, flying upwards and bursting into ashes as it struck the energy orb.

With nothing to hold them in place the blades gave in to their own momentum, spinning out of the hole and slicing through the night. The group threw themselves to the ground to avoid being decapitated, watching as the fan spun off the side of the building like a giant helicopter.

'I hope nobody's down there when that thing lands,' said

David as they all got back to their feet and stared into the hole. Aside from a couple of fires and a shard of bent steel which protruded towards the centre of the broken vent, the path was clear. It led to a pit of darkness, a vast mouth waiting to devour them.

'Bagsie not going first,' said Cat, a cry that was echoed by David then Saint before Nate could open his mouth. He cursed silently, firing up his boots and launching himself into the maw, allowing the cold, dark air to swallow him whole.

Part Three

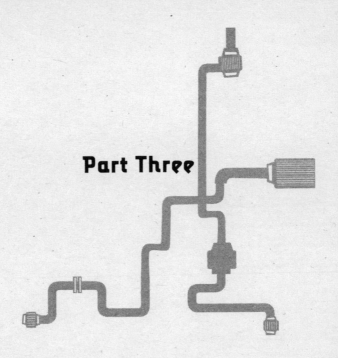

Part Three

29

Down the Rabbit Hole

The airshaft plunged relentlessly into the very guts of the building. Relaxing his toes until his descent had slowed to a crawl, Nate felt like a piece of bait on a fishing line. The green glow from his boots illuminated a wall of ribbed steel to one side, punctuated at regular intervals by smaller vents which presumably led off to different parts of the building. He saw thousands of them around the circular perimeter as he dropped into the never-ending shadows, each identical.

Looking up he watched two trails of light following him down, far enough away so as not to scorch his head. Not that he would mind being scorched, he thought, the air in the shaft was bitterly cold.

'Where are we going?' he shouted, only to be answered by his own echo which reverberated around the tunnel as if it was populated by dozens of his own ghosts. The sound of boosters grew louder and Saint dropped, his golden eyes searching the edge of the vent for any clue as to where to head.

'I have no idea,' he said eventually, waiting for his own metallic echo to die out before continuing. 'This place is a mystery. All I know is that the smaller shafts on the outskirts of this one must go somewhere.'

'Duh,' said Nate. 'I could have told you that.'

Saint scowled at him, continuing to drop at a snail's pace.

'It would help if we knew what this place was for,' came Cat's voice as David joined them. 'I mean is it just an apartment block for the robots?'

'No,' Saint replied. 'All those fans on the roof mean that there is some serious computer power somewhere in here, with circuits that need to be kept cool. That points to this place being a factory of some kind.'

'It's where they're making the robots,' said Nate. 'It has to be. And if what you said before is right it means our parents are in here somewhere.'

'How did they build this place so quickly?' asked Cat as she stared down into the abyss. 'It's huge.'

'You really can do anything with enough money,' Saint replied. 'I built that tunnel from the capital to Greenland in less than a month.'

'Yeah, thanks for that by the way,' said Cat. 'You could have picked somewhere warmer.'

Saint didn't respond, reducing the blast from his boosters until he was stationary. Nate and David followed suit.

'What's wrong?' said Nate, seeing the master inventor cock his head.

'Don't you hear that?'

Nate looked down into the black abyss beneath his glowing boots. There was a noise – a clanking that was steadily growing louder.

'Something's coming,' said Saint. He blasted to his side, heading for the closest vent in the wall. The noise was still increasing in volume, the unmistakable crunch of metal on metal. Saint was right, something was heading up towards them, fast.

Nate curled his toes and followed Saint towards the hole in the wall. He'd assumed the vents were small, but they had just been dwarfed by the sheer size of the tunnel. As he approached he saw that each was the size of a building in its own right.

Saint darted into one, closely followed by Nate, Cat and David. They dropped to the smooth floor, shutting off their boots to mask the glow.

And not a moment too soon. The source of the noise came into sight, a vast tentacle of steel which rose up from the darkness like a leviathan from the deep, its smooth sides decorated with veins which throbbed and pulsed with multicoloured lights. It was followed by two more, each as wide as a jumbo jet and topped by a crane carrying what looked like a massive fan blade. They blasted past the vent with such ferocious speed that Nate cried out in shock, collapsing on to his backside. It was like being on a platform and watching a high-speed train hurtle by, only a million times more terrifying.

By the time he recovered the cranes had come to a halt at the top of the shaft, barely visible from where the group of inventors were standing. Nate squinted into the darkness, watching as they fixed the fan blades in place. There was the roar of a monstrous welding iron and the creak of metal settling into place, and in the space of seconds the fan was rotating again.

'What the hell was that?' hissed Cat. Saint didn't answer, he was staring at the vast metal cranes, whose pulsing veins stretched seemingly right to the very base of the shaft. His robotic face was a mask of awe.

'Saint,' Cat said, giving the master inventor a prod. 'What's going on?'

'It's this place,' he said eventually.

'What about it?' Nate asked. The conversation was interrupted as the cranes started to pull back into the darkness, shooting back past the hole in the wall with the same gut-churning speed. Saint staggered to the edge, watching them descend back into the depths. Then he turned to the young inventors, his eyes wide, disbelieving.

'This building,' he said in hushed tones. 'It's alive.'

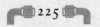

Saint hurled his metal body along the auxiliary vent chased by three young inventors and a barrage of questions.

'What are you talking about?' asked Nate.

'How can a building be alive?' said Cat.

'What were those things?' said David.

'When can we get out of this bag?' came a muffled cry from Camilla.

But the master inventor wasn't answering. His long legs carried him down the vast tunnel at a superhuman sprint, the glare from his eyes colouring the path ahead a rich gold. Just when it looked as though he was going to leave them behind, he skidded to a halt at a junction – the large vent splitting off into twenty or so smaller pipes which curled off in different directions.

'Pick a door, any door,' he shouted when the others had caught up. Nate bent over, resting his hands on his knees as he studied the path ahead. Each of the smaller pipes leading off was about the same size as the hallway in his house. The cold air from the repaired fan was blasting past his ears and flowing down each of the tunnels, but there was absolutely no indication about where they might lead. Straightening up he shrugged his shoulders then pointed at a pipe to his right which seemed to curl downwards.

'Bingo,' said Saint, and without warning leapt into the opening. He whooped as he slid down it, vanishing from sight and plunging the entire tunnel into pitch black. Nate heard a rummaging, then the space was lit up by two pairs of small glowing eyes held in Cat's palm.

'About bloody time,' shouted Camilla. 'I was bored to tears in there. If I had tear ducts, that is, which I don't.'

'She was trying to steal my hat,' moaned Clint, his wide eyes blinking. 'She almost pulled my head off.'

Cat ignored them, handing Clint to Nate and keeping hold of Camilla. Then she walked to the tunnel and held up her robot, exposing the smooth walls.

'Well,' she said, stepping into it. 'Here goes nothing.'

Then with a dainty hop she was gone, leaving nothing behind but the echo of her scream. When it had faded Nate and David walked up to the tunnel.

'I'll just wait for you up here,' Clint said. But Nate closed his hand around the wriggling robot and ran into the darkness, David by his side, and the two boys and the little robot caterwauled in unison as they slid into the unknown.

The pipe dropped away more sharply than it looked, curling round and down like a helter-skelter. Nate felt as though he'd left his stomach at the top, but there was no going back for it – the smooth floor accelerated his descent, preventing him from doing anything other than cry out.

Clint had screwed his eyes shut in terror – emitting his trademark falsetto squeal as he clung on to Nate's fingers – but Nate saw a light up ahead. He rounded one last corner, hitting a bump that sent him flying out right into a wall. No sooner had he pushed his aching body into a sitting position than he turned to see David's rear end shooting from the pipe towards him.

'Oh blimey,' he muttered before the other boy crashed into him, knocking the breath from his lungs. They lay there in a little groaning pile for a few seconds before Cat's Cheshire cat grin appeared above them.

'Nice landing,' she said, plucking Clint from Nate's grip and dropping him into her pocket. Camilla was in the other, and both robots glared at her from their prison but made no attempt to escape. 'I'd give that a three out of ten for style, but a nine out of ten for amusement value.'

She helped David struggle to his feet then held out a hand to Nate, who stood up like an old man, wheezing and holding his back. They were standing in a long, thin corridor. Compared to the black tunnel they'd just left it was blindingly bright, and Nate had to squint to make sense of the bizarre decoration.

The walls, floor and ceiling were lined with what looked like novelty wallpaper, decorated with horizontal stripes which pulsed and hummed like the cranes they'd seen a moment before. Every now and again tiny bolts of blue electricity would zip along one of the stripes so quickly that they vanished down the length of the passageway as soon as they'd appeared.

'Does anyone else feel like they've just fallen down the rabbit hole into Wonderland?' asked Nate, looking further down the corridor to see Saint studying the walls. The master inventor's metal face was stretched into the biggest smile Nate had ever seen as he ran his long fingers up and down the glowing stripes.

'Quite remarkable,' Nate heard him say. 'Optical fibre neural networks. Have you ever seen anything like this?'

'Yeah,' Cat replied. 'It looks like a crummy set from *Star Trek*.'

Saint tutted loudly.

'Don't diss this, young lady,' he said. 'Each of these cables is a neural pathway. There must be billions of them in the building.'

'Whoop-de-doo,' she replied, unimpressed. 'Aren't we supposed to be finding a way to destroy this place? You sound like you want to marry it.'

Saint just sighed.

'I don't think you understand,' he persisted. 'These are neural connections. Neural? Ring any bells?'

'You mean like in the brain?' Nate asked.

'I'm glad someone's paying attention,' Saint said. 'Exactly like in the brain. These cables are for communication, those sparks you see –' he pointed to one which raced past on the floor – 'are thoughts. Like I said, this place is alive.'

'So we're standing in a giant robotic brain?' asked David.

'In a word, yes,' Saint replied, putting his nose right up against the wall to get a better look at the wires. 'Part of it, anyway.'

'Well then, this should be easy,' Cat went on. She reached into her canvas bag, pulling out the makeshift crossbow. Nate watched as she fitted what appeared to be one of his mum's knitting needles into the slot. Mounted on the point of the needle was a balloon with a fuse.

'Welding fuel,' she explained as she cocked the weapon.

'Cat,' said Nate. 'Whatever it is you're about to do, don't.'

His words fell on deaf ears. Cat flicked down the catch with her thumb and the balloon hurtled out of the bow. As it crossed the bridge of the weapon something sparked and the fuse burst into flame, leaving a trail of smoke in the air as it soared down the corridor, landing with a squelch twenty or so metres away. Saint twisted his head round when he heard the noise.

'No!' he shouted. But it was too late. The fuse reached the balloon then with an almighty boom the little package exploded. The shockwave swept down the corridor, knocking them all off their feet. By the time they'd recovered, and the smoke had cleared, it was obvious that Cat's weapon had done some serious damage. The cables in the floor and one wall had torn in two, sticking out like loose hairs and sparking aggressively.

'Edison's earwax!' shouted Saint. 'What did you do that for?'

'What better place to attack than its brain?' Cat shouted

back. Nate's ears were ringing so loudly from the explosion he could barely hear what anyone was saying. He stuck a finger in each ear and wiggled it around as he watched Saint run over to the ruined cables.

'This is bad,' the master inventor shouted.

'Why?' Cat asked. She was cocking her crossbow again. 'Why don't we just give it everything we've got, shut it down. That way it won't be able to control its robots.'

'It's not a toy, Cat,' Saint raged, storming over. 'We're not talking about a useless little robot brain like that thing there.' He pointed at Clint, who shook his four fists at him in response. 'We could fire off every weapon we had along this corridor and it wouldn't do a damn thing except –'

He froze, looking past the sparking wound to the corridor beyond. Something was moving at the very far end.

'Except what?' Nate asked. The shapes were getting nearer, distant figures that were running towards them at full pelt.

'Except activate its defences,' Saint replied. 'Now run!'

30

The Beast With No Name

They ran like the wind. Albeit a light breeze. Cat and David took the lead, bolting down the corridor away from the approaching figures. Nate followed, but stopped when he heard a cry from behind him. Saint was bent double against the wall, a seizure racking his body so hard that his legs seemed about to buckle.

He ran back to the master inventor, grabbing his arm and trying to ignore the tremors which travelled up his bones making his teeth chatter. Their pursuers were close enough now to make out their faces – two young men and a middle-aged woman whose glowing eyes reminded Nate of hawks about to dive for their prey. Their legs hammered the floor as they covered ground fast.

'Come on,' Nate shouted. 'Snap out of it.'

Saint threw off the last of the shakes and started running. Up ahead David had stopped, ushering them past and aiming his proton gun down the corridor. He fired as soon as the coast was clear, and Nate watched as a beam of pure green energy sliced along the hallway, severing more optical cables before slamming into the approaching figures.

They didn't stand a chance, their heads exploding into silver dust and their bodies crumpling. As soon as the sparkling mist had cleared, however, Nate could make out another troop of robots pounding towards them. There were more this time, a dozen or so men, women and children running in perfect beat.

'We can't stop them all,' yelled Nate. 'We've got to find a place to hide.'

But the corridor showed no sign of ending. They careened down it trying to ignore the blue points of light which followed along the cables on the floor and walls – an army of fireflies which swarmed around them keeping track of their location.

'They're gaining,' shouted Cat, who was still in the lead but looking back over her shoulder. Nate flicked his head round to see the robots less than ten metres behind them. To his utmost surprise they were being led by Mr Green, their headmaster – a sight so shocking that Nate tripped over his own feet and sprawled to the ground.

He leapt back up, ripping the microwave gun from his back and aiming it at the approaching crowd.

'This is for entering us into that bloody competition,' he hissed under his breath, squeezing the trigger. The pursuers froze, sparks popping from their flesh as the microwaves struck the metal beneath, a thousand tiny sparks setting their clothes on fire, blackening their skin and exposing the glint of steel.

Then, with a thunderous pop, Mr Green exploded – the electrical charge in his joints too much, sending his limbs and his head hurtling down the passageway. The rest quickly followed, exploding with a sound not unlike popcorn in the microwave. Nate ducked to avoid a flying leg, then turned tail and followed the others. After another round of breathless sprinting Cat yelled out, pointing to a T-junction up ahead.

'Left,' she panted. 'Or right?'

Both routes were identical, but the question was answered when they heard a noise to their right. There were figures bounding towards them down the long passageway, the sound of their feet echoing that from yet another batch of robots who were closing in fast behind.

'Left,' shouted Nate, Cat, David and Saint together, lurching round the corner and heading along the corridor. It was identical to the first only shorter, opening up into a much larger room at its far end. They doubled their speed, bursting through the doorway and skidding to a halt.

It was just as well. Ahead of them lay a vast hall, the floor of which was made up of thousands of pistons and cogs and levers all pounding together like some monstrous engine. The ceiling was exactly the same, countless moving parts slicing and cutting through the air. Nate wondered if he had gone deaf as the machinery wasn't making the slightest sound despite its size – until he heard the robots advancing behind him. He scanned the walls. The neural cables surrounded the whole giant room, but there was no walkway.

'There,' shouted David, pointing to something in the centre of the hall. Nate saw it, a distant platform in the midst of the chaos. 'We've got to fly.'

David fired up his boots, crouching down to allow Cat on to his back. As soon as she was secure he blasted off, soaring across the room towards the platform.

'Here we go again,' said Saint, blasting into the air so fast that he almost collided with a piston.

'There's no place like home,' Nate muttered, clicking his heels together and launching himself upwards just as the robots surged through the door. The first one leapt at him, missing his feet by inches and slamming into the nearest piston. The massive metal pole slammed shut, snapping the robot in two. The rest of the robots froze, trapped on the ground and capable of doing nothing more than watching their prey escape.

Nate eased himself over the sea of equipment, trying not to imagine what would happen if he fell. Several times he squeezed too hard on the bar in his boots, shooting up towards the thrashing sky and almost losing his head. When he finally reached solid ground he was trembling like a leaf and his clothes were drenched with sweat.

The others had already landed, and were gazing at a square hole in the centre of the platform. There were lights embedded in the metal pit below, which seemed to go on for ever. Aside from that, however, there didn't appear to be any other way out of the room.

'Bagsie not going first,' yelled Cat, followed again by David and Saint. Nate stamped his foot in frustration.

'Not fair. The bagsie rule doesn't apply to killer robot cities.'

He was about to fire up his boots again when the entire room ground to a halt. The pistons along the floor slowed and stopped, the cogs and rotors above their heads hissing as they froze. It was as though somebody had stopped time, the sudden switch from constant motion to utter stillness making Nate dizzy.

'What now?' Cat asked, nervously fingering her crossbow.

'It knows we're here,' said Saint.

Nate looked back at the door they'd entered by, wondering if the robots would be able to find their way across the motionless floor. But the corridor was empty, their pursuers nowhere to be seen.

'Why aren't the robots changing into giant killers?' Nate asked. 'You know, like they did in Saint Solutions.'

'I'm not sure,' Saint replied, shrugging his metal shoulders. 'They're obviously built to imitate the humans they replace, so my guess is whatever is creating them doesn't need them to get any bigger. Be thankful for that.'

'Enough chat,' said David. 'We should go.'

'WHAT'S THE HURRY?' The voice was so loud and so deep that it sounded like continents colliding, like a mountain being dragged across the ground. It reverberated around the vast room with such strength that Nate thought for a moment he could see it. 'YOU'VE ONLY JUST ARRIVED.'

There was a click from above their heads, a ticking which grew louder and faster until it sounded like a thousand spider legs crawling across the ceiling. Nate watched in horror as the machinery on the other side of the hall began to change shape, the steel bending as it expanded. Hundreds, maybe thousands of pipes and cogs shifted position with barely a sound, twisting round one another and attaching to themselves until a shape began to form.

'Let's go,' said Cat. But nobody moved, the sight before them too incredible to let them turn away. The steel had morphed into a head, a vast metal face the size of a warehouse. It was identical to one of Saint's original robots, right down to the horrific muzzle. The head shook, knocking the last few strands of metal into place, then a pair of eyelids opened to reveal two burning orbs beneath. The lenses swivelled in their casings, and Nate thought he saw right through the crimson eyes into some awful intelligence beyond.

'WHY ARE YOU HERE?' the face asked, the voice like a fist in Nate's brain. 'YOU HAVE NO RIGHT TO BE INSIDE MY HEAD.'

'You have no right to be in our town,' Cat spat back. She was pale, but her eyes burned with the same fury as the nightmare face. 'You've taken our parents, we want them back.'

The face just laughed, the sound filling the entire room like tar. 'I HAVE EVERY RIGHT TO BE HERE,' it said. 'I AM THE NEW WORLD, THE NEW RACE. YOUR PARENTS HAVE BECOME A PART OF ME. I CAN HEAR THEIR THOUGHTS, I AM THEM AND THEY ARE ME. WE ARE ONE.'

'Who are you?' demanded Saint, stepping to the edge of the platform.

'I AM THE NEW WORLD, THE NEW RACE,' the voice repeated. 'I AM EVERYONE AND I AM NO ONE. I AM THE FORCE THAT WILL BRING PEACE AND ORDER TO THE WORLD. IT WILL BE PARADISE.'

Nate saw Saint flinch. The words might as well have come from the master inventor himself, the claims a mangled version of Saint's own twisted dreams.

'What's your name? Your model number?' Saint shouted. 'I made you, don't you know me?'

'I HAVE NO NAME. WE ARE LEGION. WE HAVE NO NEED FOR NAMES FOR WE ARE ONE ENTITY. I AM THE NEW WORLD AND THE NEW RACE. YOU ARE AN INTRUDER, YOU ARE NOBODY. YOU WILL BECOME PART OF ME OR YOU WILL DIE. IT IS THE ONLY WAY TO BRING PEACE TO THE WORLD. IT WILL BE A PARADISE.'

Saint looked round at the three young inventors.

'It's completely insane,' he whispered. He turned back to the face. 'I am Ebenezer Lucian Saint, I demand that you hand authority to me, your creator. This is wrong, this isn't the plan.'

'I AM SAINT,' the monstrous voice continued. 'I AM EVERY-BODY AND I AM NOBODY. I AM THE FUTURE. I HAVE NO CRE-ATOR, I HAVE NO DESTROYER. I AM THE BEAST WITH NO NAME.'

'The Beast?' muttered Saint, obviously confused. 'It's talking like something out of Revelation.'

'Where are they?' interrupted Cat, screaming at the top of her voice. She had loaded another explosive balloon into her crossbow and was aiming it at the giant face. 'Where's my mum? Tell me or I'll kill you.'

The pipes and cogs that made up the face twisted until it was smiling.

'SHE IS HERE. THEY ARE ALL HERE. I CAN HEAR THEIR THOUGHTS, I CAN SEE THEIR NIGHTMARES. I AM THEM AND THEY ARE ME.'

'How did you do it?' asked Saint. 'How did you change them so fast? I invented that technology and it's impossible.'

'NOTHING IS IMPOSSIBLE,' said the voice, the noise like

thunder. 'WATCH.'

Before Nate could acknowledge the significance of the last word the clicks came again, the metal ceiling right above them shifting and sliding into a new shape. In no more than a couple of seconds a claw had formed, the pincers opening as it shot down towards the platform. Nate swivelled, the claw slicing past his back close enough to tear the microwave gun from its strap and send it flying. Cat leapt aside too as the pincers lunged for her.

But David wasn't so lucky. The claw slammed shut around his waist, causing the boy to scream out in pain. The metal tensed, lifting him off the ground and up towards the giant face. David lashed out at the metal hand, his proton blaster clattering to the floor below where it disappeared amongst the pistons.

'David!' Nate screamed. He clicked his heels together twice to go after his friend but before he could do it a third time he felt Saint's hand on his arm.

'It's too late,' the master inventor said. And he was right. A scanner emerged from the ceiling, its lasers flicking to and fro over David's squirming body. It vanished a second later and the mechanical ceiling morphed again, dozens of tiny pipes and wires coiling down beside the boy. They began to weave together with incredible speed, like a knitting machine working with silver threads.

In ten seconds there was a skeleton of steel suspended next to David. By the time twenty excruciating seconds had passed the skeleton had been lined with fibre optic cables. Nate couldn't believe what he was seeing. He wanted to help but there was nothing he could do. It was happening too quickly for him to process, his brain frozen by the sound of David's screams and the grating laugh from whatever demented force was doing this.

Another metal arm emerged from the ceiling, this one glowing red hot. It began to spray molten steel on to the skeleton, the crimson glow too bright to look at directly. Nate turned away, blinking to remove the spots from his eyes. That was why the booths glowed, he thought.

There was a whine as the machinery finished its task, vanishing back into the ceiling to be replaced by three smaller mechanical arms. One cooled the smouldering metal while the others began to spin material around it – a layer of rosy-pink flesh followed by denim jeans, a white cotton shirt and a bowtie, even a pair of bulky ski boots. To finish the horrific job a bucket-shaped hood descended over the robot's head, rising a heartbeat later to reveal a terribly familiar face underneath.

For an instant nobody moved. The real David, gazed at his double with tears in his eyes. The doppelgänger stared back at the boy, its manic grin the only thing that ruined what would otherwise have been a perfect mirror image. Then it reached out with both hands and grabbed David's head. There was a flash of white light and David arced back, shaking violently. Then his body slumped, all sign of life erased.

'HE IS ME AND I AM HIM,' said the voice.

The arm holding the original David extended back to the platform. Nate reached out to try and grab the boy but he couldn't reach, and before he could fire up his boots the claw relaxed, dropping David down the hole in the middle of the floor.

'WHO IS NEXT?'

But there was no answer as Nate leapt in after his friend, Cat and Saint following while the thunderous laughter of the beast with no name echoed in the empty hall above.

31

Fighting Amongst Friends

Nate had forgotten how to breathe. He plummeted downwards so fast that his lungs seized up, refusing to allow him to suck in the air that blasted past his face. But he didn't care – all he had to do was keep David in his sights. The boy's body tumbled and spun like a ragdoll, his face expressionless, his eyes still open and staring lifelessly at Nate as they both hurtled down into the bottomless tunnel.

Nate straightened his body like a diver, streamlining himself. The lights embedded in the wall flashed past with even greater speed and he started to gain on his friend. He was almost there, another ten metres or so and he'd be able to catch him, carry him to safety.

But in the flash of an eye it was all over. The tunnel wall flipped open as David dropped, something soundlessly sucking the boy inside and snapping the portal shut before Nate could reach it. Momentum pulled him past, and by the time he had fired up his boots and flown back up the wall the door which David had been pulled through had vanished.

'Did you see where he went?' came a voice from above him. It was Cat, held in Saint's arms like his sweetheart as the master inventor descended slowly down the vertical tunnel.

'In here somewhere,' Nate replied as they passed. 'There was a door, it just opened and he flew inside.'

'Find it,' said Saint. 'I guarantee that if you follow David's body you'll find your parents.'

Nate hovered further up the wall, but there wasn't so much as a crack in the smooth metal. He cursed loudly.

'Keep your chin up,' said Saint from below.

'How can we?' Nate snapped back. 'David's gone.'

'No,' the master inventor went on. 'I mean keep your chin up. What the hell is that?'

They all looked up to see a shape falling towards them, spears of green light emanating from its feet. The fierce flames illuminated a grinning face mounted over an impeccable bowtie.

'This can't be happening,' muttered Saint. 'They've duplicated his rocket boots.'

The robotic boy flipped in midair and increased the force of his jets, closing the distance between them. Nate did a graceful somersault until he was upside-down, the force of his boots propelling him downwards. As he overtook Saint the master inventor called out to him.

'Take her,' he bellowed, nodding at Cat. Nate flipped back over, glancing up to see that the robotic David was still gaining. 'Quick.'

He navigated until he was right next to Saint, allowing Cat to sling her arms around his neck. He did his best to scoop her up, wobbling slightly as he adjusted his boots to the new weight.

'What are you going to do?' he asked, but Saint just flashed him a golden wink before blasting back up the tunnel. Nate watched him go, the metal man and the metal boy hurtling towards each other. David saw him coming, the beast's voice coming from his lips.

'ASSIMILATION OR ASSASSINATION, THERE IS NO OTHER WAY.'

But Saint wasn't listening. There was a deafening clang as they collided, their coiled bodies slamming into the side of the tunnel so hard that the metal bent.

'Shiitake mushrooms,' muttered Nate as he watched the two forms plummet towards them. Looking down he saw that the end of the tunnel was visible below, and shutting off his boots they dropped towards the metal grille. It collapsed under their weight and they plunged into a corridor identical to the first they'd found.

Saint and David were still tearing earthwards, their fists a blur as they fought to dislodge each other. Nate grabbed Cat's hand and wrenched her out of the way as the two robots landed with all the force of a meteorite, opening up a crater in the metal floor.

It took a moment for the dust to clear, but when it did Nate saw Saint had gained the upper hand and was pummelling the metal form beneath him with a pure rage that was terrifying to watch. Nate had a sudden flashback of an incident in Saint Solutions, the master inventor on the roof of a chalet, slapping David's face as he prepared to murder his parents. His first instinct was to run and help the boy, but he had to keep reminding himself that it wasn't David. It was the beast.

'I made you, you ungrateful wretch,' Saint screamed, throwing one last punch then getting unsteadily to his feet. The robotic David was squirming, his face bent out of shape like a Picasso painting but somehow still grinning. 'You've stolen my dream, you've stolen my money to make this ridiculous city, you've stolen everything.' He kicked David's double, sending sparks flying from a wound in the robot boy's neck. Then he turned to Cat.

'Give me one of those balloons,' he said. Cat didn't move, but Saint repeated the request with a snarl in his voice and she quickly dived into her bag, picking out one of the explosive missiles and throwing it to Saint. He caught it, sitting on David's chest and bending down to speak in his ear.

'Listen to me carefully, beast. I'm going to find your main processor, and I'm going to override it.' He sparked up the balloon, watching the fuse burn down.

'Oh no,' said Cat. 'Get down!'

Nate dived to the floor and watched in horror as Saint pulled open David's mouth, stuffing the balloon inside.

'What do you say to that?' Saint hissed. He stood up, walking backwards, but before he could move out of reach David's hand shot out, grabbing the master inventor's leg. Saint tugged to free himself but the boy's steel fingers were too strong.

The fuse was at David's chin, rising towards his lips – lips that were twisted into a smile aimed right at Saint. The boy muttered something that was muffled by the explosive balloon in its mouth, but Nate thought he knew what the machine had said.

'It's too late.'

Saint turned and stared at Nate, his golden eyes wide with fear. Then the balloon exploded.

David's head burst like a melon, showering the corridor with tiny pieces of shrapnel from his mechanical brain. The fireball engulfed Saint, blasting a shockwave of heat and light towards Nate. He felt his eyelashes fizzle and he curled into the smallest ball he could manage, waiting until the echo of the blast had died out before daring to look.

He checked on Cat first, relieved to see her slowly crawling into a sitting position, Clint and Camilla peeking out from her pockets. He turned his attention to the site of the explosion. The corridor was a mess, the optical fibre cables severed and sparking. David was nothing but a pile of warped and broken metal, his body opened up like some metal flower in bloom. Saint was lying further along the passageway, his overcoat incinerated to reveal one leg missing and the rest of his body blackened and motionless.

Ignoring the pain that seemed to infest every joint, Nate ran over. The air was distorted from the sheer heat of the floor after the blast, smoke filled his lungs and made his eyes water. He reached down to touch the master inventor, wrenching his hand away when the metal burned his skin.

'Is he alive?' asked Cat, following him over and looking down at the broken robot.

'You can't get rid of me that easily,' came a weak, fluttering voice. Saint opened a single golden eye and studied them, eventually building up enough strength to flex his arms. 'I can't feel my leg.'

'It's over there somewhere,' said Clint, pointing down the corridor. 'Well, parts of it are.'

'Your robot needs to work on its bedside manner,' Saint went on, emitting a noise that might have been a laugh. He tried to sit up but his body was too weak. Instead, he reached out and grabbed Nate with one hand and Cat with another. His grip was hot, but not hot enough to hurt. 'Listen to me, they'll be here any second to finish us off, so I need you to go.'

'What about you?' Cat asked. 'We need you. We can't leave you.'

'You can, and you will,' Saint replied, his voice fading so much it was almost inaudible. 'Let me worry about me, you need to find where David went. If you can do that, you'll find your parents.' He paused while tremors racked his body. 'More importantly, from there you should be able to trace the source of all this madness, the beast's central processor.'

Nate heard the sound of heavy feet on metal, knew that they only had seconds before robot reinforcements arrived. He tried to pull away but Saint held him fast.

'You have to destroy it,' the master inventor wheezed. 'That has to be your only priority. Even if it means losing your parents, you have to destroy it.'

'No,' yelled Cat. 'I'm getting my mum, I'm not saving the world.'

'Just destroy it,' Saint repeated. 'Keep heading down, it's probably located under the ground, between the four malls. With any luck I'll see you both again further along the path. If not,' his grip tightened, 'then believe me, I'm sorry for everything.' He released them and Nate stood, taking Cat's arm and leading her down the corridor away from the sound of approaching feet. He took one last look at the master inventor, still struggling to sit up. Saint flashed him a wink and a smile.

'See ya, kids,' he called out. 'It's been a blast.'

32

There's No Place Like Home

Nate had never been any good at running. Every time they'd been forced to do cross-country over the school playing field on a cold winter's day in the relentless drizzle he'd never made it more than a couple of laps before almost dying, feigning an asthma attack or a sprained ankle to get out of finishing.

But here he was, sprinting like an athlete, his heart pounding and his muscles straining more than he ever thought was possible. Maybe that was all he had needed, he thought as they raced down the corridor, an army of killer robots on his tail as he ran from the hall to the pavilion.

Cat was ahead of him, her arms and legs like jackhammers. She hadn't glanced back, but Clint and Camilla were poking out of her pockets, their little heads jiggling like jack-in-the-boxes as they watched the robots advance.

Nate had no intention of looking. The sound of footsteps behind him resembled a stampede on the Serengeti, and he knew that if he didn't put every ounce of strength and concentration into running for his life then he'd be trampled into the cables under his feet.

'Look!' wheezed Cat, pointing up ahead. The passageway was widening, opening out into another large room beyond. Cat ran into it and spun round, lifting her crossbow and aiming it back down the corridor.

'I've only got one left,' she shouted, loading the explosive balloon into the weapon and cocking the spring mechanism. Nate ran past her, trying to shout 'fire' but too winded to produce anything more than a grunt. There were at least twenty robots hot on their tail, a bizarre mixture of girl scouts and traffic wardens, with a handful of young men and women thrown in as well. Despite their startlingly different appearances, however, they were all brothers and sisters from the same nightmare with their white teeth and crimson eyes.

Nate thought back to the robots in Saint tower, pictured them in Work Mode with their dripping muzzles and long legs that could cover a hundred metres or so in the blink of an eye. At least things could be worse.

Cat pushed her finger against the trigger, but before she could fire the group skidded to a halt, their bodies locking up simultaneously as if their batteries had all run out. The robots stood there, watching Nate and Cat, waiting for their next move.

'What should I do?' Cat whispered. Nate tried to wheeze out another answer but his lungs were still too busy snatching in air. He grabbed Cat's arm, pulling her backwards. The room they had entered was the same size as the school hall, empty except for the same fibre wires that lined the surfaces and a set of metal doors in the opposite wall. As Nate watched the doors slid open silently, revealing nothing but darkness.

The robots still weren't moving, content to block the passageway they'd just left.

'Come on,' said Nate, finally able to speak. 'Let's go before they wake up.'

'What if it's a trap?' Cat replied. 'What if there's a machine through that door that will turn us into one of them?'

'I don't know,' said Nate. 'But I really don't want to be torn to pieces by that lot. I mean I always knew girl scouts were scary, but . . .'

He didn't finish. Camilla was struggling to climb out of Cat's pocket but Cat rested a hand on her head, pushing her back in.

'There are only a few of them,' the little robot yelled. 'Clint and I will hold them off while you two run for it.'

'No,' came a muffled voice from Cat's other pocket. 'You hold them off and the three of us will make a run for it.'

'Nate,' said Cat. 'What should we do?'

'I say we take the door,' he replied. 'Even if we blow up that lot there will just be more behind them. We've got to find that processor like Saint said.'

Cat lowered the crossbow and walked unsteadily away from the corridor, never taking her eyes from the crowd assembled there. When they were halfway across the room they both turned and started running again, sprinting through the open doors into the pitch-black world beyond.

There was the faintest of clicks as the doors closed, then a hum as the lights came on. At first Nate thought he was hallucinating. He wondered if they'd been blasted by laughing gas on their way through the room. Because what he was seeing couldn't be real.

But Cat saw it too. She had collapsed to her knees and was crying gently, her tears falling on to the grass at their feet.

'Oh my god,' she said, her voice as soft as a sigh as she looked at the cottage in front of them. 'Nate, I'm home.'

It was Cat's house, there was no doubt about it. The picturesque green and yellow cottage was there in all its quaint glory, ivy hugging the walls, the back door almost lost behind its halo of roses. There was even a chicken coop complete with the quiet gargling of its unseen occupants. The garden filled the entire room, a boundary of trees in the distance doing their best to block out a ceiling of polished steel some way above them.

But the more Nate studied the property, the more he realised that it wasn't perfect. Or maybe it was perfect, but that's what was wrong. There was a swinging seat on the patio behind the kitchen window that Cat's mum had taken down a couple of years ago because the wood was rotten. And tucked away at the far end of the garden was a large pond, the water rippling as the koi swirled and played in the shadow of an ornate bridge. Cat's house had never had a pond, but Mrs Gardner always talked about how much she wanted one – complete with fish and a Japanese-style footpath.

'Quick,' said Clint. 'Let's get inside before those robots appear.'

'I don't think that's a good idea,' said Nate, helping Cat to her feet. He noticed that her knees were scraped and bleeding, and bent down to feel the lawn to discover that each blade of grass was actually a sliver of green steel. 'It's a trick, Cat. We should get out of here.'

A face appeared in the window, beaming at them from the rear hallway.

'Mum?' whispered Cat. She started moving towards the door, shrugging Nate's hand away when he tried to stop her.

'It's not her, Cat,' Nate shouted to her back. 'It's a robot, come on.'

'I know,' she replied, coming to a halt. 'I know, but it's so real. How could they know so much?'

Cat's mum opened the back door, stepping out into the garden. She was wearing a shirt which was covered in splodges of paint – all reds and greens and purples – and in one hand she held a stained roller.

'Come on, Cat,' she said, her voice betraying only the slightest hint of its inhuman source. 'We're painting your room. Come and give us a hand.'

'We?' said Cat. 'Who's in there with you?'

Mrs Gardner just smiled as if it was the stupidest question in the world.

'Why, your dad, of course.'

Cat looked like she had been punched in the stomach. She seemed to double over, and had to rest her hands on her wounded knees in order to stay standing.

'Cat, it's a trick,' Nate said, walking slowly up to her. 'She's not your mum, and the only thing in there is a machine that will steal your soul.'

'Nathan,' said Mrs Gardner. 'You can help too, you know how much Harold likes you. He's got a new machine that shoots paint, but I prefer the old-fashioned way.'

'Cat,' said Nate with a little more force.

'I know, I know,' she spat back. 'I'm not an idiot, Nate.'

With an obvious effort she straightened, scanning the outskirts of the room for a way out. But as she did so another figure appeared in the doorway behind her mother. Nate recognised him immediately, his tall skinny frame barely visible beneath the baggy brown cords and striped white shirt he always used to wear, his eyes lost somewhere behind his thick glasses and long fringe. He smiled at them and waved them forward.

'Come on, kids,' the voice was just like Nate remembered, full of warmth and humour. 'Let's get you something to eat.'

Cat was crying again, deep, painful sobs that made her body shake.

'Daddy?' she said.

The illusion was so real, and so powerful, that for a moment Nate almost fell under its spell too. Maybe they were back home, about to race into the house to eat fish and chips and help Cat's dad with one of his crazy inventions. Maybe if he believed it hard enough, if he really, really wished it, then it would be real.

Only it couldn't be real, of course. Cat's dad had died six years ago, blown to smithereens when one of his inventions went wrong. The man in front of them wasn't Harold Gardner. He wasn't even flesh and blood.

'Hello, princess,' said her dad, stepping out into the garden. 'You've grown up.'

'Why don't you come into the house, Sophie,' her mum continued. 'We can have a cup of tea. It will be just like old times.'

Cat staggered forwards, her face paler than ivory, her lips trembling.

'But you died,' she said. 'You're dead.'

'In our world, there is no death,' Harold said. 'Here there is only life, and it is eternal.'

'But you died years ago,' Cat said, still sobbing. 'It's impossible, it can't be you.'

'Your mother's memories brought me back,' he said. 'They brought all of this back. Just come and see for yourself, you can't imagine how wonderful it is. We are all the same mind, the same thought, the same dream. If you join us then we will never be apart again, we will be one, for all time.'

'Please, Sophie,' said Mrs Gardner. 'I want us to be a family again.'

'It's a trick,' hissed Nate. 'Don't listen to it, they're just telling you what you want to hear.'

Cat turned and looked at him. He had never seen her like this, her eyes so full of pain that they broke Nate's heart. Her whole body swayed from side to side as though something inside was about to snap.

'But what if it isn't?' she whispered between sobs. 'What if they're telling the truth. I could be with my dad again, Nate.'

'It's not him,' Nate replied. 'They've made him up with fragments of your mum's memories. It's like this place,' he gestured at the pond, 'it's just a fantasy, a half-baked memory of what your mum wanted. And it's not even her, she's just as fake. They've stolen your mum's soul, they're robbing her memories and using them to kill you.'

Cat seemed to snap out of her trance. She stopped swaying, clenching her fists by her sides as she turned to face the lies that were her parents.

'How dare you,' she spat. 'How dare you use those memories. They're not yours.'

The smiles never left her parents' faces.

'Come on, my little inventor, don't be like that,' said her dad. 'What difference does it make whether I'm real or not when you could be with me? We can share the world, share our minds.'

'I don't want to share your mind,' Cat screamed back. 'I want you to hold me, I want to feel your warmth not some cold metal monster. You're not my dad, you're not even human!'

The smile vanished, the eyes flaring with a crimson glow that turned Nate's legs to jelly.

'*We are more than human,*' said her parents as one. '*We are the new race. Join us, and share our world.*'

'Never!' she cried out. 'I'm coming for you, Mum. I don't know if you can hear me but I'm coming.'

She raised the loaded crossbow and aimed it at the two robots. They saw it and the light in their eyes vanished, the smile reappearing.

'Please, Sophie,' said her dad. 'I love you.'

'You'll never know what love is,' she said, then pulled the trigger. The balloon shot out of the bow, sparking as it went. It flew right between her mum and dad, landing in the hallway of the little cottage.

For a second nothing happened, then the gas inside ignited

with a muffled bang. The hallway erupted in flame, the fireball taking the path of least resistance and bursting from the back door. In seconds the robots posing as Cat's parents were stripped of their clothes and artificial flesh, the metal beneath glowing like molten lava. Cat's mum collapsed to her knees, tottering for a second before crumpling forwards. Her dad remained where he was, the crimson eyes beneath his melting face watching the girl as she threw the crossbow to the floor and ran to Nate.

He held her, feeling her trembling body cling to his as she fought for breath between the sobs. He felt as though he was going to cry himself, but before he could give in to the trauma of what he had just witnessed the floor started to tremble.

Cat's head shot up, her bloodshot eyes pleading Nate to free her from this madness. But he was powerless to do anything except watch as the top of the cottage started to shake, tiles sliding from the roof and hitting the dirt below with a metallic clang. The building was collapsing into itself like there was a black hole in the centre, the roof sucked into the walls then the walls sucked into the floor. Or what was left of it – where the house had been there was another immense hole, pieces of the little cottage disappearing into it like food down a garbage disposal.

'Run for it!' shouted Clint. Even Camilla looked scared, diving into Cat's pocket.

'What now?' Cat said, letting go of Nate then grabbing him again as the floor shook. With a squeal of bending steel the entire ground began to tilt, pulling Nate and Cat towards the hole.

'YOU'VE MADE YOUR CHOICE,' said the smouldering body of Cat's dad, his voice now the timeless growl of the beast. 'ASSIMILATION OR ANNIHILATION. NOW PAY THE PRICE.'

He toppled back into the expanding abyss. The ground

lurched again and Nate lunged for the doors, but the angle was too steep, gravity pulling them both towards the black pit. Nate tottered, his hands scrabbling for purchase on the grass. But the steel sliced through the flesh of his fingers, and with a yelp he let go. He managed to grab Cat as he slid past her, and like children sacrificed to the devil they gripped one another with bleeding hands as they tumbled over the edge and into hell.

33

A Rubbish Landing

They fell, and the whole world fell with them. It was like going over a waterfall, but one made up of lethal shards of steel and massive slabs of metal which sliced and thrashed and crashed through the air beside them.

Nate did his best to keep hold of Cat, but he had to push her away so she wouldn't be bludgeoned by the chicken coop which missed both their heads by a hair's breadth as it roared towards whatever lay below. The shaking frame struck Clint, sending the little robot spinning out of Cat's pocket and across the shaft before Nate could grab him.

There was simply too much shrapnel to avoid, fragments of the cottage fighting in the maelstrom – striking each other and rebounding in every direction. One metal koi, still flapping, slammed into Nate's foot, dislodging the sole from his rocket boot and sending the boosters tumbling down the shaft.

'There's no place like home,' he tried to shout, the wind blasting past his face and snatching his words. He clicked his heels three times but the ruined boots didn't respond other than to whine pathetically. He heard a yelp of pain and saw Cat spiralling uncontrollably across the shaft, blood spraying from her nose. A steel bathtub was continuing its downward passage beneath her limp body.

'Cat!' he yelled, but her head drooped against her chest as she fell, her eyes closed. Nate tried to swim over to her, but before he could the angle of the shaft changed, the walls slowly becoming a floor as the pipe bent. Nate struck the side of the shaft and slid along it as it evened out, watching the end of the duct shoot towards him.

He lashed out and grabbed the lip, managing to halt his progress. But when he looked back into the shaft he saw Cat spinning towards him along the floor.

'Holy moley,' was all he managed to say before she slammed into him, sending them both sailing out into the room. They tumbled into a metal box the size of a house, Nate landing with a grunt on top of a pile of metal bricks. Cat slumped on to a hill of what looked like Barbie dolls, rolling down until she came to rest against the upside-down bathtub which had brained her.

The remains of the cottage were still spilling down around them. Nate clambered up the hill of garbage until he reached Cat, rolling her under the metal bath before squeezing in himself. There was a clang as something big hit their makeshift shelter, followed by a series of smaller thuds as the last few bits and pieces of the cottage fell on them. Then, incredibly, there was silence.

Well, almost silence. From somewhere nearby Nate could hear a little voice shouting, 'Woe is me.'

There was a groan from Cat as she stirred, her eyes opening and looking at Nate with deep confusion.

'Why are we in the bath together?' she asked. 'We haven't done that since we were three years old.'

Nate pulled his sleeve over his hand and gently wiped the blood from her nose. The flow had stopped, but judging by the state of her clothes, and the contrast between the vibrant bloodstains and her deathly pale features, she had lost a lot.

'I thought you needed a bath,' he replied. 'You should see the state of you. It's a disgrace.'

They both laughed, resting their foreheads together and just revelling for a moment in the feeling of each other's breath on their face, a sure sign that they were still alive.

'Oh woe is me,' came Clint's voice again.

'Now you've got me really mad!' came a fearsome bellow from Camilla.

Nate crawled out from under the bathtub, worming his way past the fallen debris to the surface. Offering Cat his hand, he pulled her to safety.

The compartment they were in was half full of, well, everything. The house-sized space was crammed with stuff from the mall – toys, gadgets, broken bottles of wine, mangled ornaments, twisted television sets and piles and piles of clothes. Mixed in with it all were massive chunks of steel, bent girders and the tail ends of optical-fibre cables. The pile was so huge that it almost crested the top of the compartment, and Nate scrabbled to the peak of trash to try and see a way out.

'Where are we?' he asked, trying in vain to leap up the final three metres of smooth wall.

'I think we've been thrown out with the trash,' was Cat's reply, lifting one of the Barbie dolls before chucking it across the compartment.

'Well that's just insulting,' came a voice from behind them. Nate and Cat turned to see Camilla struggling over a hillock of soft toys, every footstep causing a squeak from one of the Happy Bears beneath her. 'I think Clint might need you, by the way. He's moaning like a little baby again.' She led them to one corner of the compartment. 'You know you really should give him a backbone, he's such a wimp.'

Nate was about to tell Camilla off for being so mean when he realised she was actually speaking literally. Clint was lying on a pile of roof tiles. If the term lying could be applied to something without a body. The little robot didn't have a backbone. In fact, he didn't have anything at all below his neck, the joint where his bowtie had been sparking aggressively.

'Oh woe is me,' he said weakly. 'I can't feel anything.'

'Um . . .' was all that Nate could manage.

'Er . . .' was Cat's helpful contribution.

'Come on, you lazybones,' said Camilla, walking over to Clint's head and prodding it so that it rolled around. 'This is no time to be resting.'

'But I don't seem to be able to get my legs to respond,' he replied. 'Please tell me everything will be okay.'

'Everything will be okay,' Nate lied, picking up the decapitated head and holding it up. 'We'll fix you up good and proper, don't you worry. We've just got to find your . . .' He left the sentence unfinished, turning to Cat. 'How is he still, you know, alive? I thought his battery packs were in his body.'

'I gave his main processor a backup, just in case of emergencies,' she replied, gently touching Clint's severed neck. 'It won't last long, though. We need to find his body pronto or his brain will just switch off.'

'My body?' yelped Clint, trying to look down. 'Why? What's happened to my beautiful body? Oh woe!'

'You should quit while you're ahead,' quipped Camilla, laughing to herself. 'Get it, *a head*!'

'If we can find it there are enough tools here to fix him,' said Cat, ignoring her and rummaging around in the garbage. 'It's like Christmas in this place.'

He heard her gasp and turned to see her standing over a burned and broken body half hidden under a pile of metal splinters. The glasses had been smashed, the skin on the face half melted away. Only the eyes remained intact, staring upwards as if looking for heaven.

'Daddy,' Cat whispered. Nate was about to intervene when he saw her pull the shred of photo from her pocket, the sliver that showed her dad's sparkling eye. 'I'm sorry I ever believed it was you.'

She kissed the photograph then slid it back into her pocket. As she did so, however, there was a rumble from the compartment walls. Nate and Cat looked at each other.

'Why won't this place just leave us alone?' Cat said through clenched teeth.

As if in response, the entire compartment started to shake. Then, with a mechanical sigh as if the machine was performing the task reluctantly, two of the walls started to move inwards.

'It's a rubbish compactor,' said Cat. 'Oh hell's bells we're going to be squashed.'

The walls pushed in relentlessly, their immense strength crushing everything before them.

'Your boots, Nate,' yelled Cat, tottering over to him. Nate pushed Clint's wailing head into his pocket and activated the boots, clicking his heels together three times. There was still no response, and after trying once more he just shrugged. Cat screamed in frustration and began scanning the rubbish for something to use. Nate did the same, trying to ignore the feeling of the ground moving beneath his feet, and the inexorable progress of the compactor walls.

'Camilla, can't you hack into the control panel and stop it?' Nate yelled.

'She's not R2D2, you moron,' was Cat's reply. She had pulled a couple of small packs from the debris and was examining the writing on the back.

'Please tell me that's a rope in there,' Nate shouted over the screech of the compacting debris. The walls were closing in, only five metres or so between them.

'Better than that,' Cat replied, throwing one of the packs to Nate. 'Saint's Super Space Hopper.'

Nate snatched the lightweight pack from the air and ripped

it open, pulling out a circle of rubber no bigger than an uninflated balloon. There was a small white string connected to one side.

'Come on, slowcoach,' yelled Cat. She pulled the string on her space hopper and almost immediately it began to expand, wheezing like a flatulent elephant as it swelled, two antennae popping from its head and Saint's face appearing on the front. Cat clambered on and started bouncing over the hill of rubbish. 'This is harder than it looks, you know.'

Nate pulled the cord on his own toy and fought to keep hold of it as it exploded outwards. He thought back to their first day at Saint Solutions, the way that Saint had struggled to cross the reception floor on his own space hopper. The memory carried with it a surprising amount of sadness as he imagined the master inventor's embarrassment and frustration.

'Nate, do you want to be squashed?' yelled Cat as she continued to bounce, gaining momentum each time she launched. With a final effort she managed to rebound off the top of the trash mountain on to the side of the compartment.

Nate clambered on board the space hopper and pushed off, the giant balloon propelling him upwards. It landed with a squeak and he almost lost his balance before the rubber ball took off again. It *was* more difficult than it looked, and by the time Nate had managed to master it the compactor walls were less than two metres apart.

'Come on!' yelled Cat, reaching over the side of the compartment. Nate lurched up the hill, the red ball making a sound like an excited mouse. The walls had nearly reached his shoulders, their immense size ready to squish him to the size of a sultana. With a heroic yell he bounced off the debris and soared through the narrowing gap, grabbing Cat's hand.

For a moment they both tottered, Nate's weight almost pulling him and Cat back into the closing pit. Then Cat threw herself backwards, dragging him to safety. The space hopper wasn't so lucky, caught between the walls as they finally met. The picture of Saint on the red rubber swelled to grotesque proportions before popping noisily, and Nate tried not to think of the same thing happening to his own head.

'Well,' said Cat, clambering to her feet and brushing her hands together. 'I bet you never thought you'd be doing that when you woke up this morning.'

34

Two Heads are Better Than One

They sat on the edge of the compartment for the better part of twenty minutes waiting for their hearts to remember how to beat in a normal rhythm. From their perch they could see that they were in an immense chamber full of compartments like the one they'd just escaped, each being filled with garbage from the pipes around the wall.

Beneath them the compactor started to shake, the pneumatics hissing loudly as the mechanism pulled back into its starting position. Where only moments ago there had been a mountain of toys and clothes and pieces of steel there was now a lump of metal and plastic the size of a small box. The filthy floor of the compartment popped open, allowing the lump to slide down into an orange light, but the trapdoor slammed shut before Nate and Cat could see where it led.

Nate heard a muffled cry from his pocket and reached in, lifting Clint's head out by his top hat. The robot looked down into the crusher and started wailing.

'My body!' he said, the little head bobbing up and down in Nate's grasp. 'Let's go find it.'

'Sorry, Clint,' said Cat. 'But if your body's in there then it's the size of a postage stamp.' She turned to Nate, speaking softly. 'He needs to be rigged up to a power source, and fast. Something powerful enough to keep him going.'

Camilla coughed loudly, jumping from Cat's shoulder to

Nate's and pointing at her own neck. It took a while for her message to sink in.

'That's it!' Cat exclaimed. 'Camilla, you're a genius. You wouldn't mind?'

'Mind what?' asked Clint suspiciously.

'Of course not,' the female robot replied. 'Two heads are better than one. We'd be the ultimate fighting machine, right, Clint?'

'Are you thinking what I think you're thinking?' spluttered the talking head. 'Because if so there's no way. Absolutely no way.'

'If you don't, then you'll die,' said Cat.

'I think that would be preferable to being welded on to that crazy girl,' he replied. 'She'll get us both killed anyway, probably by trying to tackle a herd of angry elephants singlehandedly.'

'Quadruplehandedly, if you must know,' Camilla replied, waving her four arms in the air. 'Come on, you wuss, it will be you and me against the world.'

'Oh woe is me!' was Clint's reply, blinking in protest. His piteous display was interrupted by the sound of clanking metal as another load of scrap poured from the pipe into the trash compactor they'd just escaped. The sound echoed across the vast hall as several other pipes in the walls disgorged their contents.

'Come on, Clint,' said Nate. 'You've been in worse states than this. Remember when you were trampled by that robot in Saint Solutions?'

Clint grumbled a response but Nate wasn't listening. 'We've got to get a move on. Let's do this.'

Camilla leapt to the floor, sitting down and jiggling excitedly. 'This is going to be so much fun!' she exclaimed.

Cat knelt down beside her, gently pushing her head to one side and examining her neck.

'I'm going to have to cut you open a little,' she said. 'We'll need to split your power cable to feed it through to Clint. It shouldn't take long.'

'Hunky McDory,' Camilla replied.

After a gentle coercion – which involved dangling him over the waste compactor until he consented – Clint agreed to let them use his tools. The top of his hat flipped open and the arm holding the Swiss army knife slid out reluctantly. Cat grabbed it, extending the can opener and placing it against Camilla's neck.

'Sorry about this,' she muttered before slicing into the robot, pulling the two edges of the wound apart until Camilla's insides were visible. Reaching in, she gently detached the wires connecting the robot's power source to her processor, slicing the connection in two and feeding half of it out of the hole in her neck.

'I'm going to give Clint your two left arms, if that's okay?' she said, pulling out another couple of wires. 'Just in case he has an itch or something.'

'Coolio McFabulous,' Camilla replied. 'That way we can still arm wrestle.'

Clint groaned, but a look from Cat kept him quiet. She picked up his head and slotted the wires into the severed joints in his neck.

'Welding iron,' she demanded. Clint grumbled but the little welding iron appeared, and Cat used it to seal the wires in place.

'How does that feel?' she asked.

'Like I'm a mole on the butt of a walrus,' replied Clint.

'It's fine,' said Camilla. 'I'm only getting sixty per cent power but these batteries are good enough to keep us both going.'

'Clint, can you move those arms?'

Camilla's two left arms shook for a second, then both swung across and slapped the female robot in the face. Clint pulled a smug smile and nodded.

'They seem to be working perfectly,' he said, ignoring Camilla's furious grunt.

'Then let's get you fixed in place.' She pushed Clint's head into position then fired up the welding iron again. A couple of minutes later Cat shut it off, blowing on the join to cool it.

'It's not the neatest seal in the world,' she said. 'But it will hold.'

'Let's just make sure,' said Camilla, swinging her two right arms and slapping Clint round the face. His head jerked back but it stayed in place. 'Yup, solid as a rock. We're ready to kick some robot butt.'

Clint didn't respond, just buried his head in his hands as if trying to convince himself that this wasn't happening.

'It will be okay, little buddy,' said Nate. 'It won't be for much longer.'

But he didn't honestly believe that was true. Looking around him he saw no way out of the vast hall. And even if there was, what then? There was a city of steel around them the size of their home town – four giant tower blocks and god only knew how much more sprawling beneath the ground. If by some miracle they managed to find their way to the main processor then there was an army of metal beasts in their way.

'This is where the city dumps everything it doesn't want,' Cat said, disrupting his misery. 'Maybe we'll be able to find something down here, a clue.'

She kicked a stray lump of steel from the wall into the nearest compartment and tottered along the narrow ledge to the next. It was half full of more stuff from the mall – mostly clothes and hats, the occasional mobile phone. Cat kept walking, but something about the collection of outfits below him made Nate stop.

They didn't look like the kind of thing anyone would buy. Instead of brand-new outfits with the clothes hangers and labels still in place there were old T-shirts, stained blouses, crumpled coats and jeans full of holes. Nate spotted a fluorescent postal worker's jacket, a raincoat that still looked wet, and even a little pile of Girl Scout uniforms in one corner.

'Hold up,' he shouted to Cat, who had already reached the next compartment. She whirled round, looking at Nate, then at the massive cubical full of clothes, then back at Nate.

'What?' she said. As she spoke there was a scuffling sound from the pipe that fed into this compactor and another batch of clothes slid out – mostly police and army uniforms. They flopped into the cubical like dolls' clothes, and Cat watched them with an open mouth.

'That's it,' she said. 'My mum, your parents, they're up there.'

And as if on cue a chorus of distant screams drifted from the pipe as though the ghost of every man, woman and child on earth was calling into the night.

'I definitely preferred going downhill,' said Nate as they struggled up the pipe.

The screaming came and went as they made their weary way. It was so faint that Nate couldn't be sure exactly what it was, while Cat was adamant that the sound was actually the air whistling down the pipes. But every now and again there would be a screech so clear and so chilling that it covered Nate's arms in gooseflesh and made him want to slide back down into oblivion.

'Just think of your mum and dad,' Cat would say after the sound had ebbed away, leaving its scars on Nate's soul. 'They need us to be strong.'

The interior of the pipe was as smooth as the one they'd slid down, but fortunately this one was far shorter. Nate and Cat eased their way around a single bend – their skin squeaking on the metal as they fought to keep their grip – to see the end less than twenty metres ahead.

Nate shook his head to clear the sweat from his brow and squinted to get a better look at their destination. Something was moving up there, a dark shadow that flashed from right to left, paused at the mouth of the pipe, then shot off again to be replaced by another. As they crawled closer, Nate saw that each time the shadow stopped another set of clothes was pumped into the tunnel, creating a large pile at the top. When the pile got big enough it gave in to its own weight, sliding down towards the trash compactors below.

'What is that?' Nate asked softly. But he needn't have bothered. As they closed the gap between them and the end of the pipe another shadow swept across the opening, and this time it was horribly obvious what it was.

The shape was a man, dressed in a soldier's uniform. He wriggled and kicked and screamed, his body vanishing as a steel tube slid down over it. With nothing more than a whisper the tube spat out his clothes, then the man and his steel casket were snatched out of sight. Another figure was swept into position, this one a woman who showed no sign of life. A tube shot down over her and whisked her away, the only sign she had ever been there the combat fatigues on top of the pile.

It took Nate and Cat another five minutes or so to crawl the length of the pipe, during which Nate counted over a hundred people being dragged past. Almost all were unconscious – maybe dead – but the ones who were aware of what was going on made up for their silence, screaming and sobbing and calling for their mothers.

'We must be heading in the right direction,' said Cat as she reached the opening, sweeping the pile of clothes down the pipe as she pulled herself over the top. Nate grabbed hold of her leg for support, hoisting himself after her until they were both perched on the lip of the tunnel.

Once again Nate couldn't believe what he was seeing. It was as if each new sight, each new immense room of wonders or horrors, was stretching his brain, filling it up like a balloon on the verge of bursting.

Above their heads was a mechanical rail like that in a car factory. Suspended from it were people, who shook and juddered limply as the rail carried them over the room. They came in through a hole in one wall, their arms and legs bound, dangling from the moving rail by a steel thread.

The production line whisked their clothes off, their bodies covered by the steel tube as they progressed towards the far side of the room. Once there, they were whisked away at a much faster speed, the rail bending down and round like a roller coaster before vanishing through a gap in the floor far below.

Nate heard another set of screams approaching, looking to his right to see a woman in a police uniform straining against her bonds. Her bloodshot eyes swivelled and spotted Nate and Cat on the top of the pipe.

'Oh god, please help me,' she screamed. 'What's going on? What is this place? You have to free me.' She started struggling again, yelling at the top of her voice. 'Help me!'

But there was nothing they could do. The rail jerked forwards again and a tube came down, obscuring her face. There was a whirr then her uniform shot past Nate's ear.

'Get on,' said Cat. She was pulling herself up, bracing her leg on the edge of the pipe as if she was about to jump. Sensing trouble, Camilla had dashed back into her pocket.

'No, Cat, wait,' shouted Nate, reaching out to stop her. He was moments too late, snatching the air where her foot had been as she launched herself up towards the moving tube. The metal sides were ribbed and studded with optical fibre cables and she managed to get a foothold, steadying herself as the rail lurched again.

'Hurry up!' she hissed.

Cursing, Nate placed his foot on the lip of the pipe, holding on for dear life. The next person in line was out cold, and Nate did a double take when he realised it was Paris Fourfields, the local news anchor. He waited until the tube had descended over her motionless body then, offering a silent prayer to anything that was listening, he jumped.

It wasn't a huge distance to cover, but the angle was awkward – the tube right above his head. He made it, but his fingers slipped and he felt himself dropping. He pictured himself landing back in a trash compactor and dug his nails in, yelping in pain as they caught on a ridge. The rail lurched again and the tube swung alarmingly. He looked down and saw that he was no longer over the pipe. Instead there was nothing between him and the distant ground except thin air.

Swinging his legs up, he managed to grip the bottom of the tube between his knees. Then, like somebody climbing a palm tree for coconuts, he began to edge his way upwards. He made it to the top just as the tube reached the second rail.

'Here we go,' he whispered, his words snatched from him by a clatter of metal and his guts loosening as the tube hurtled earthwards.

35

Doppelgängers

He clung on for dear life, risking a look at Cat to see her doing the same thing. The floor swept towards them, the tube hurtling through the hole and careening along a short tunnel. Nate watched the lights on the wall fly past and wondered how fast they were going. By the way his clothes fluttered noisily and the skin on his face was stretched tight he imagined they must have been doing well over a hundred miles an hour.

They shot from the tunnel with an explosive gust of wind and Nate's gut protested once again as the rail curved upwards, arcing over a cluster of large data banks before dropping again. The angle of descent was almost vertical this time, the tubes practically in free fall as they dropped through the floor. They fell for what seemed like an eternity, the ride so stomach-churning that Nate heard Cat throw up. He pulled a face as he watched her little ball of sick drift past, falling more slowly than the tubes and so appearing to rise.

Nate didn't dare look down in case he got a face full of Cat's stomach, but seconds later his tube erupted from the vertical shaft into another room, levelling out so that it was once again travelling horizontally. Up ahead the rail fanned out into several branches, the dangling people splitting off to be directed through different holes in the far wall.

Cat was shouting something to him, but they were moving too fast and her words were lost in the wind. She had no time to repeat herself as her tube reached the junction and she shot off to the left at breakneck speed, the sudden change in direction almost throwing her off.

Please go the same way, Nate prayed. To his horror, however, he hurtled along a different path, angling off to the right. He scrabbled round to try and see where Cat was going but there was no time, his tube flying through the hole in the wall into an empty room, this one so bright that he had to screw up his eyes.

Peeking through his scrunched-up eyelids he saw two gun-shaped arms descend towards the tube in front. They disappeared inside the metal cylinder, sparks flying as they fired something at the person within. After no more than a couple of seconds the tube split open, the two halves dropping off and striking the ground below with a clang. The person inside was no longer naked, but was wrapped up from shoulder to foot like a mummy.

Nate saw the guns extend towards him and vanish inside the tube. He had to act quick – any second now the material he was clinging on to was going to pop and drop. He clambered upwards, grabbing the rail and holding on tight as the tube split open, crashing to the floor below.

When the guns had vanished he let go of the rail and lowered himself back down. Paris was still out cold, but Nate could tell from the way her face twitched that she was stuck in the same nightmare inside her head. Her body was now covered in bandages, and up close Nate saw that each was packed with electrical circuits, the tiny wires inside sparking as if they were draining energy from the woman's skin. He frowned, but he didn't have time to investigate further as the rail plunged through a hole in the far wall and tore outside.

At least, Nate thought it was outside. The room that they had entered was so big that surely it couldn't support a roof.

But looking up into the dark shadows far above his head Nate made out a ribbed black ceiling, the surface rough as if it was the crust of the planet itself.

Yet the view above was nothing compared to that below. A network of rails crisscrossed the room, each carrying hundreds of people all trussed up and dangling like cadavers in a slaughterhouse. The poor souls were being transported down into the guts of the room where they vanished in smoke and heat and blue sparks.

Nate could make out something in the chaos below – a red tower which rose from the darkness. As the rail plunged towards it Nate saw that it was made up of a framework of massive steel girders arranged in hundreds upon hundreds of layers, each covered in glowing pods that resembled insect eggs. There were thousands of them, all positioned in rigid rows and columns like some monstrous piece of modern art.

The rail lurched again and Nate clung on tight to the bandaged body as he was pulled down towards the tower. The air roared past his ears, the bizarre construction rushing at him so fast that he thought they were going to crash. At the last minute the rail levelled out and his tube slowed before coming to a halt.

Nate scanned the giant room for any sign of Cat, but she could be anywhere. The rails stretched above and below him as far as he could see, the smoke and dust from the machines masking the identities of the people they carried. The tower of pods stretched down as if penetrating the very core of the earth, the base of the construction narrowing to a distant point.

There was a hiss of pneumatics as a giant claw appeared from nowhere, gently grasping the body in front of Nate and lifting it off the rail. The claw descended towards the nearest row of pods, resting the man inside. A series of needles popped out of the glowing crimson unit but Nate didn't pause to see where they went.

The claw was returning, the fingers opening as it reached out for the body of Paris. Nate acted without thinking, jumping from the dangling woman on to the metal arm seconds before it clamped shut. He clung on tight to the claw as it descended towards the same row of pods. When the claw was close enough Nate leapt, aiming for the walkway that separated each glowing crimson row. He missed, bouncing off the side of one of the compartments and landing on his backside.

Trying to ignore the pain he got to his feet and watched as Paris was dropped into an empty pod. The needles appeared, sliding into the bandages and sparking violently. Then a strange cap extended from the top of the unit, clamping on to the top of the woman's head. Her whole body shook for a fraction of a second, then a set of diagnostics appeared on a tiny screen beside her face – showing that her heart was still beating despite the fact she was as quiet as the dead.

He turned his attention to the sea of pods that lay before him. The sight reminded him of the room full of robots in Saint Tower, only these were living, breathing people – thousands of them, whole families, entire streets, probably every single person in Heaton – all laid out and harvested by whatever terrible intelligence was running this freak show. And there was space for so many more, a country's worth, maybe even a planet's worth.

'Cat,' he said under his breath, looking for any sign of her. 'I'm never going to find you.'

He was distracted by the sound of feet hitting metal behind him. Spinning round he saw to his amazement that Cat was standing there, a massive grin on her face. She walked up to him, waving a hand in front of her to clear the smoke from her vision.

'What took you so long?' she asked.

Nate smiled, preparing a witty comeback in his head. But he never got the chance to use it as Cat pounced at him, raising her hand and punching him square in the jaw.

He fell back, tripping on the pod beside him and crumpling on to the floor. Sparks and flashes danced across his vision as though he was watching a movie beamed from a broken projector.

'Cat?' he yelled, the word distorted by his bruised jaw. The blow felt like it could have taken his head off. Of course it wasn't the first time Cat had punched him, although admittedly it was usually in jest. Maybe she was just relieved to see him, or a little over-excited.

'I thought you were dead,' the girl said, taking a step towards him and running her hand gently along the side of a pod. 'You did a remarkable job of surviving.'

'Er . . . thanks,' said Nate, shuffling backwards uneasily. 'You too.'

She launched her hand towards him again and Nate threw his arms up in front of his face to defend himself. When nothing happened he peeked through his fingers to see her offering him a lift up. He reached out tentatively and Cat grabbed him, hauling him to his feet. He attempted to pull free but her grip was firm, squeezing hard enough to make him squirm with pain.

'Cat, that hurts,' he said, trying to ignore the thoughts that were laying siege to his mind. 'What's got in to you?'

'Something wonderful, that's what,' she replied, the pressure of her grip increasing. Nate heard his knuckles pop and made a renewed effort to free himself. Cat lowered her head towards him, still grinning. 'You know it's not as bad as you think,' she went on, her pupils shrinking until they were pinpricks and her brown irises glowing red. 'In here, we're all free.'

She twisted her arm and Nate felt himself flipping head over heels. Pain shot from his wrist to his shoulder. Cat still hadn't let go of him, bending his hand back until it felt like it was going to come off. He could feel the metal beneath the skin on her fingers, cold and unrelenting.

'You're not Cat,' he wheezed, trying to shift his body to keep his wrist straight. 'It's a trick.'

'A trick?' the robotic doppelgänger said. She let go of his hand, but before Nate could scramble to safety she wedged her foot against his ribs and kicked out. It was like being attacked by a horse, the blow sending him sliding across the walkway into another pod. 'It's no trick. What you see is what you get, Sophie Gardner.'

Nate braced his hand on the side of the pod and pulled himself up. It wasn't Cat, it couldn't be – if only for the reason that if Cat had been assimilated then it meant he was on his own.

'So you're Cat,' he said, backing away and trying to buy time while his brain furiously worked out a plan. He thought about Cat's dad, the way the beast had assembled him using her mum's memories. If they had stolen Cat's soul then they would know everything she did, but if this was just another trick then the creature in front of him wouldn't. He desperately tried to think of some questions.

'Tell me what colour we turned our headmaster.'

'Easy,' the robotic Cat replied, advancing at a leisurely pace as if she was strolling through the park on her lunch break. 'Blue.'

'Right,' he reached a pod and clambered over it on to the next walkway, still retreating. 'What was your first invention?'

'A wind-up ballerina,' she replied without the briefest of pauses. 'I made it with my dad.'

Nate cursed.

'Okay, so what's our catchphrase then?'

Cat seemed to pause, the computer inside the robotic body making a series of calculations. She turned to Nate, the smile widening and her eyes burning with even greater ferocity.

'Why, it's you and me against the world, of course.'

Hearing the words come out of the robot's mouth was unbearable. It was his and Cat's thing, their shield against the hardships they'd endured. It was just a saying, but it was theirs, and now it had been stolen.

He looked over his shoulder, realising that he was running out of space. The edge of the tower was only a few feet away, and beyond it was a pit god only knew how deep. Maybe he should just jump, better to die that way than have his brain sucked up and digested by that crazed computer. He shuffled towards it, his legs tense in case the robotic Cat made a move.

The questions he was asking were personal, but he and Cat had talked about this stuff to everyone at Saint Solutions, including Saint and his assistants. Then something in his brain clicked, a thought so faint and nebulous that he almost lost it. But it was there, and he embraced it.

'So, who do you love?' he asked. It was the stupidest question in the world to ask a killer robot moments before you were about to fall to your death, but it worked.

'As if you have to ask,' Cat responded. 'David, of course.'

Nate laughed out loud. Cat hadn't been assimilated, it wasn't her mind at all. It was David's. In the same way that Harold Gardner had been simulated using Cat's mum's memories, this abomination before him had been made up with nothing more than David's thoughts and dreams. And the sly old dog obviously had a crush on her, the beast with no name assuming that his fantasy of Cat's requited love was actually real. Relief surged through him — it meant Cat was okay.

'This is why you'll fail,' Nate said, stopping on the very edge of the tower and doing his best not to topple backwards. 'You want to be human, don't you? But you will never be, you don't have one iota of humanity in you, one shred of life.'

Cat's eyes flared, the grin disappearing. When she spoke again it was with the thunderous voice that had addressed them earlier, the sound of a rock fall echoing through a gorge.

'I AM MORE THAN HUMAN,' it said. 'I AM EVERY BEING, I AM EVERY THOUGHT. THERE IS NO MEMORY, THERE IS NO DREAM, NO DESIRE IN THIS PLACE THAT I HAVE NOT ASSIMILATED. I AM EVERYONE HERE, AND I WILL BE EVERYONE ON THIS PLANET. I WILL BE ALL, I WILL BE ONE.'

'You'll be nothing,' spat Nate. 'Nothing but a bunch of wires and circuits that does a shoddy job of imitating emotions. You'll be a joke.'

'YOU ARE THE JOKE,' it replied, Cat's mouth moving with the words but the sound seeming to emerge from all around Nate, so loud that he thought his bones would shatter. 'YOU ARE A CANCER, A DISEASE WITHIN ME, SO PITIFUL IT MAKES ME LAUGH. BUT YOUR FIGHT WILL SOON END, JUST LIKE THOSE YOU ARRIVED WITH. LIKE THEM, YOU WILL SOON BECOME PART OF ME. THEN YOU WILL SEE PARADISE.'

Nate felt his anger well up through his body like a kettle boiling over. He pointed at Cat, his finger trembling with the strength of his hatred, and he hissed through clenched teeth.

'I will never be part of you, and neither will Cat. And you, you will never be human.'

Cat's doppelgänger arched its head back and roared, the sound making the pods on either side vibrate so hard that they cracked. Then the robot lowered its head and charged.

It moved like lightning, so quick that Nate couldn't follow it. One minute it was standing on the walkway alongside him, the next it had vaulted a pod and covered the ground between them. Nate did the only thing he could think of doing, allowing his legs to buckle from sheer terror. He collapsed to the ground just as Cat reached him, the robot tripping over his prone body and sprawling off the edge of the tower.

Nate picked himself up, brushing his hands together.

'Never underestimate the power of fear,' he said, turning back to the sprawling landscape of pods and looking for Cat. He had only taken a few steps away from the edge when he heard the sound of boosters behind him. They shut off and there was a clink of metal on metal, followed by a low chuckle. Nate didn't want to turn around, but he had no choice, his body acting without his brain's permission. Behind him stood the robotic Cat, the rocket boots on its feet still glowing.

'Oh,' said Nate. 'I forgot you could make them.'

He bolted, running along the walkway and hearing the boots fire up again. Leaping over a pod he hurtled along the platform looking for anything around him that he could use as a weapon. But there was nothing, not so much as a steel bar that he could defend himself with.

He felt a searing heat on the top of his head and ducked as Cat flew over, landing ahead of him. Twisting his body, he tried to jump over an empty pod and retreat the way he had come but the robot was too quick, leaping forward and wrapping its arms around his waist. It squeezed, hard enough to pump the air from Nate's lungs. He felt the world go black, flickers of light shooting across his vision again.

'RESISTANCE IS FUTILE,' said the voice. 'THERE IS NO ALTERNATIVE. I AM THE FUTURE, AND I AM YOU.'

The robot relaxed, pushing Nate towards the empty pod. He stuck out his arms, and more from luck than skill managed to cartwheel over it, tumbling down the other side. Cat clambered over the pod after him, but as the robot was halfway across

Nate reached out and grabbed its boot, yanking the burning metal with all his strength and causing the robot to collapse inside. The mechanism in the floor of the unit was triggered, the needles sliding out towards Cat.

'Come on,' Nate prayed. The needles penetrated the robot's clothes but they were useless against the steel body, snapping off and pinging across the walkway. Cat just laughed again, a soul-crushing chuckle that belonged to the devil. The robot braced its hands on the sides of the pod to haul itself out, but before it could the cap appeared, clipping on to its head.

Cat's expression changed from a grin to a mask of fear in seconds, then the cap sparked. The robot's body lurched in the pod so hard that the sides of the crimson unit split open. Then it slumped, as dead as a toaster. There was a small beep as the pod sensed a dead body, then the base slid open and the robot dropped inside, vanishing down a tube with a sucking sound. When it had gone, the floor reappeared and the unit reset itself.

Wasting no more time, Nate started scanning the sea of pods for any sign of Cat. With the constant motion of the rails around him and the giant cranes, not to mention the phantom-like drifts of smoke and dust, it was difficult to make out any movement that could be her.

There was a blinding flash of light from a section of the plat-form forty or fifty metres away, followed by a cry of distress. It had to be Cat, Nate thought, pegging it along the walkway in the direction of the sound. Despite his aching limbs he man-aged to hurdle thirteen pods and cover the distance in less than a minute, scaling one last unit to see Cat on her knees beside what looked like a dead body.

The corpse was still smoking, blue sparks flashing across its exposed metal skin from the torn power cable that was still embedded in its stomach. Cat was crouching over it, her shoul-ders shaking up and down like she was sobbing, the heads of

Clint and Camilla poking from her pocket. Nate climbed down from the pod to get a better look at the body, the sight almost making him throw up on the spot.

It was him, his face lifeless, his mouth open in a final, horrific scream. He felt like a spirit floating over his own corpse, and groaned loudly as he collapsed against the pod. Cat heard the sound, wrenching the cable out and bearing it like a weapon.

'Not again,' she screamed, thrusting the sparking cord at him. 'You just stay away from me.'

'Cat,' said Nate, holding up his hands in surrender. 'It's me.'

'That's what you said last time,' she hissed. 'Right before you tried to kill me. I know you're a robot, I know you've stolen his soul.'

'Cat,' he repeated gently. 'Look at my eyes, it's me.'

She stared at him for a second, then her rigid expression vanished to be replaced by a look of utter exhaustion. She dropped the cable and ran over, throwing her arms around him. The hug made his ribs ache but he endured it, his tears dropping from his cheeks and mingling with hers on their way to the platform. He squeezed her just as hard, then let her go.

'I thought they had you,' she said, wiping her eyes. 'God, Nate it was such a shock.'

'You're telling me,' he replied, pointing to his jaw. 'Your robot double almost knocked my block off.'

'That reminds me,' she said, laughing then frowning then slapping him round the face. 'That was for making me think you were dead.'

36

Save Our Souls

'The poor souls,' Cat whispered, studying the faces of the people inside the pods. There were men, women and children of all shapes and sizes and colours, all united by the needles in their veins, the flashing caps on their heads and their twitching faces as their minds were swallowed whole by the beast with no name.

Cat reached out and touched the cheek of a young woman, Camilla running down her arm and standing on the lip of the pod.

'Look at them, Nate,' she said, tears in her eyes. 'There are thousands of them, and more arrive every second.'

Nate stared up at the rails to see that the constant flow of bandaged people hadn't been interrupted. They spiralled down like candy in a vending machine, never-ending treats for the monster that ran this place.

'What's happening to them?' Nate asked, running his finger along the woman's binds and feeling the painful pulse of an electric charge.

'It's funny you should ask,' Cat replied. 'You were telling me all this just a moment ago while you were trying to kill me.'

'Huh?' Nate asked.

'Your robot doppelgänger,' she said. 'I asked it the same question and you know how this place loves to talk.' They walked along to the next pod to see a boy inside, no older than three or four, dwarfed by the glowing crimson machine around him. Cat wiped her eyes then turned away as she explained.

'It told me that as soon as a robot doppelgänger has been made, all it has to do is touch the temples of its human double and all thoughts will be transferred,' she looked back at Nate. 'We saw that with David, remember?'

Nate nodded, recalling the white flash when the robot touched his head – millions of thoughts and memories being stolen.

'Well, according to the metalmouth upstairs, those thoughts are just a snapshot of the person at that particular time, like a complex mental photograph of their mind.'

'Right,' said Nate, nodding again but not really understanding.

'It's not their actual soul,' she went on. 'It's just an image of it, enough to give the robot a sense of who that person is and how they act.'

'So it can impersonate him?'

'Yeah, and they do a damn good job of impersonating the people they've replaced. Except every now and again when there are glitches in the programme. There's such a huge amount of information – I mean terabytes of the stuff – that it doesn't always copy exactly.'

'Hence the good reverend running round that tree in his birthday suit,' said Nate. Camilla leapt from one pod to the next, Clint's head jiggling as she landed.

'I told you to watch out!' Clint said, waving his two arms in protest. 'My head will fall off.'

'Quit your moaning,' Camilla replied. 'We need to focus our Zen energies on surviving, be like ninjas in the night. Or we'll end up like those poor fleshies.'

'Like I said,' Cat went on when the little robots had ceased their chattering. 'That initial blast of information is just a snapshot of the mind, it's static, like a photograph. The person's mind is still active inside their body, they're still alive and aware, because that's what this building wants them to be.'

'So it can steal their souls,' Nate said.

'Exactly. That's what this place is for. Each of these people is living inside the head of that monster right now. Their minds are split right open, it can see everything they ever were, everything they ever wanted to be, every dream and regret and fear. It has total control over their thoughts.'

'And always will, right?' Nate asked, pointing to the needles embedded in the boy. 'Those are nutrient pipes.'

'And waste,' Cat said. 'They can be kept alive here indefinitely. An endless nightmare, an eternity spent screaming inside the mind of a madman.'

'Did the robot tell you what the bandages were for?' Nate asked.

'I didn't need a robot to tell me that,' said Cat. 'They're dermovoltaic strips.'

'Oh,' said Nate, none the wiser. 'I knew that.'

'They're converting energy from the body into electricity,' she went on. 'Essentially they're turning everybody here into a giant power source.'

Nate's jaw dropped.

'I didn't even think that was possible,' he said. 'So every time the beast plugs another poor sucker into this contraption it grows more powerful?'

Cat nodded, staring down the seemingly endless row of glowing pods. There must have been a thousand on this layer alone, not to mention the hundreds of layers beneath them.

'We're never going to find them, are we?' she said softly. 'It would take us years to search this place for my mum and your parents and David.'

Nate didn't answer. She was right, it was futile.

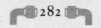

'We have to do what Saint said,' he responded eventually. 'We have to shut it down before it steals any more souls. Once we've killed it we can look for our parents.'

'If they're still alive,' she said. 'Your doppelgänger told me that if the connection between the mind and the machine was severed then they'd die. They're too far gone, too immersed in the beast's consciousness.'

'It would say that,' Nate replied. 'It's trying to stop us any way it can. There must be a way, there always is. God, I never thought I'd say this but I wish Saint was here. At least he knew what he was doing.'

Cat snapped out of her reverie and scanned the vast room as if she was trying to get her bearings.

'I thought I saw him,' she said. 'When I was coming in. I thought I saw him being carried by another rail.' She paused, then pointed off to their left. 'That way.'

Nate sighed, staring off into the swirling smoke and shadow. He felt so exhausted, so utterly drained. All he wanted to do was go home, to watch telly and eat macaroni cheese and invent crazy gadgets with Cat. He had never felt so far from his old life, even in the heart of Saint Tower – at least that place was designed by a human. This city of living steel was so alien, there was nothing of comfort here, nothing familiar, nothing good.

And yet this was his home. His house, his town, everything he knew and loved lay above him in ruins. There was no going back, there was no going anywhere except forward, towards darkness, towards death.

'Maybe we should just jump into an empty pod and get it over with,' he muttered. Cat kept walking, pretending not to hear.

'Don't leave us!' came a screech from behind him. Nate turned to see Camilla strolling leisurely down the walkway, her calm features perfectly contrasting with Clint's mask of panic as he flapped his hands like a bird in a vain effort to speed her up.

'You embarrass me, Clint,' scolded Camilla as she jumped on to the side of a pod and flipped on to Nate's shoulder.

'Well it's better to embarrass someone than try and get them killed!' he bellowed back. Camilla responded by slapping him gently round the face, which set off a flurry of little metal arms as they fought.

'A marriage made in heaven,' said Nate as he popped them into his pocket and followed Cat. She had reached the far side of the platform and was staring out into the abyss. Nate reached the edge of the tower and looked down, feeling his head spin at the sheer height of the construction. He tried not to think about how far underground they were, the old unpleasant feelings of claustrophobia setting in as he pictured the earth crashing down on them. He recalled how it felt when he was flying above the city, nothing around him but air, and felt the panic subside.

'There,' said Cat, pointing to a massive cable that stretched out from the tower into the shadows ahead, like the anchor of some giant ghost ship moored in the mist. 'That looks like a power cable. It's probably feeding the electricity from here into the main processor.'

'I guess that's the way to go then,' said Nate without any trace of enthusiasm. 'Is that where you saw Saint?'

'I think so. I can't be sure. I guess there's one way to find out.'

'What way is that?' Nate replied. 'That cable is a hundred metres below us. There's no way of getting down.'

'Well, do you have any bright ideas?' she snapped back. Nate put his finger to his lip and chewed on a ragged nail.

'Actually,' he said, grinning. 'I think I do.'

He sprinted back the way they had come, Cat on his heels demanding to know where he was going. His robot double was still on the floor, smoke and sparks fighting for supremacy in the wound in its chest. He skidded to his knees beside it, examining the robot's feet. It was wearing ski boots, the boosters on the base identical to his own.

'Bingo!' he yelled.

'What?' said Cat as she caught up to him. 'His shoes?'

'They're rocket boots,' Nate replied breathlessly. 'When the artificial intelligence assimilated David it must have learned how to construct his boots too – that's why all the robots made since then have boosters in their shoes.' He tugged at the ski boots but they didn't budge. Inspecting more closely he saw that they were wedged tight on to his doppelgänger's metal feet.

'Clint, I need you to hotwire these boots,' he said, plonking Camilla down beside the motionless body.

'What's wrong with yours?' Clint asked. 'I'm not a cobbler.'

'They're shot,' Nate replied. 'The boosters got knocked out. I need you to get these ones working.'

Grumbling under his breath, Clint flipped open his hat and extended the Swiss army knife, slicing open a metal panel on the boots to reveal the complex circuitry inside. He switched tools, poking around inside with a screwdriver. Nate tried again to pull the boots off as Clint worked, but only succeeded in wrenching one halfway off the metal foot inside.

'This is worse than trying to get my trainers off after PE,' he muttered, giving up and walking around to the head, brushing a strand of his hair back and staring into the dead eyes.

'Hello, handsome,' he said, but the words were accompanied by a nervous shudder. He tried to lift the head off the ground but the robot weighed a tonne and the body was rigid, as if rigor mortis had set in. 'Perfect.'

'Perfect for what?' asked Cat.

'You'll see,' he replied. He motioned towards the robot's legs. 'Madame, would you like to take a ride on the Natemobile?'

Cat raised an eyebrow.

'You have to be joking,' she replied. 'I've ridden on boats, planes and the back of someone wearing rocket boots, but I draw a line at sitting on the robotic corpse of my best friend powered by boosters being fixed by an incompetent robot.'

'I am not incompetent!' exclaimed Clint. His protest was accompanied by the sound of the boosters firing up, and Nate gave a little whoop of joy.

By the time the echo of his celebration had died away, however, he realised that the roar wasn't coming from the boots beneath him. He snatched his head up, watching in horror as the vast room they were in lit up like a Christmas tree – the whole construction glowing green from the rocket boots that were appearing over the edge of the tower.

There must have been hundreds of them, all worn by men and women in military uniforms whose crimson eyes burned with unrestrained fury. Each of the flying robots had something cradled in their arm, something black and metallic and aimed directly at Nate and Cat.

'Madame,' Nate said, his voice trembling. 'I must insist.'

Cat didn't argue this time, sitting down on the dead robot's legs. Nate lowered himself on the doppelgänger's chest.

'You better hurry up, Clint,' he shouted.

'Oh woe is –'

The little voice was cut off as the boosters in the boots ignited, the sound almost lost in the thunder around them as the robots fired their machine guns. The metal platform crumpled as the bullets struck it, a line of fire shooting up the walkway towards them.

'Hold on!' shouted Nate as the boots reached full strength.

Camilla barely had time to leap on to Cat's back before four pillars of green flame shot from the soles, propelling them forwards just as the world behind them exploded into a maelstrom of heat and light.

It was as they shot down the walkway, bullets tearing up the pods on either side and ricocheting off the metal floor, that Nate realised he had no way to steer the makeshift robot plane. But the cable was dead ahead of them so all they had to do was maintain a straight line. The boots were constantly accelerating, the pods ripping past so fast that their glowing red sides looked like one long ribbon. The edge of the platform was approaching with the sickening speed of a guillotine blade.

'Hold on!' Nate screamed, but by the time he'd uttered the words they were in midair. Time seemed to slow as they hurtled out over the abyss, then snapped back into place like an elastic band stretched to breaking point – the noise and heat and chaos returning with a vengeance. The robot plane nose-dived, the countless levels of the tower block flashing past Nate's eyes, the smoke parting as if to ease their passage to the distant ground.

The cable materialised from the darkness and Nate wrapped his arms around the makeshift craft's neck, giving himself a hug and pulling hard. It worked, the robot changing angle so that it was blasting along the surface of the power cord – close enough to be able to touch as they followed it into the shadows ahead.

He risked a look behind him, seeing the flying robots closing in for the kill. He felt something slide past his arm, a stinging pain shooting through his shoulder as if he'd just been stung by a giant wasp. Looking down he saw a stream of blood trail behind him, and did his best not to pass out at the sight.

He lowered his head to streamline their craft, pushing down gently on the robot's head in order to close in on the cable. When he looked up again the end of the power line was finally visible. It plunged into a vast wall of glowing circuits and wires, their luminescence like some heavenly light that penetrated the smoke and dust, beckoning them forwards.

Nate squinted against the wind, trying to pick out a landing spot. There was only one. The cable entered the wall through a hole that was barely wider than it, a gap of maybe a metre and a half all around it. He glanced to his side to see the robots moving in again. There was no choice, they couldn't slow down, they were just going to have to go for it.

'Duck!' yelled Nate, steering the craft down so that it was running inches above the cable. He pulled his feet up, tucking his arms in and praying that there would be room for them. The hole shot closer, the shadowy circumference looking smaller and smaller as they closed in on it.

Nate pressed his head against the face of his doppelgänger as they hurtled through the gap, the bottom of their robotic craft scraping against the cable and the roof of the tiny space almost taking the top of Nate's head off. Gritting his teeth and feeling his stomach turn itself inside-out, Nate kept the craft steady. Behind them came a series of explosions as the robots slammed into the wall.

Then, with a glorious explosion of light and air, the tunnel opened up into a pristine hallway. Nate pushed down on his doppelgänger's head until it grazed the floor, the contact acting like brake pads and slowing their progress. He tried not to watch as the hair of his robot doppelgänger was torn off, then the face, exposing a complex metal head underneath.

The body lurched and Nate and Cat slid off together, hitting the floor and rolling painfully in a tangle of limbs. They came to a halt in time to see the unburdened robot soar upwards, striking the ceiling of the new chamber and vanishing in a ball of flame.

They lay there for a moment, their hearts pounding so loud that Camilla was dancing to the beat. Clint's head drooped over her chest, the little robot apparently unconscious.

Slowly, Nate sat up, offering a hand to Cat. She pulled herself up into a sitting position as well, looking sheepishly at Nate.

'I'm sorry about that,' she said, nodding at Nate's arm. He looked down at the wound where a bullet had grazed him, the blood still oozing from the cut.

'This?' asked Nate. 'It wasn't your fault.'

'Not that,' Cat said. 'Your back.'

Nate didn't feel any pain in his back, other than the dull ache which had burrowed into his entire body. But then he noticed it, a cold, wet sensation between his shoulder blades.

'You didn't,' he said, pulling a face.

'I'm sorry,' she repeated. 'It was a rough ride.'

Jumping to his feet, Nate pulled off his T-shirt and threw it to the floor, the stains that Cat had made like some hideous yellow tie-dye.

'We really need to get you some travel sickness pills,' he muttered, helping Cat to her feet. 'How do you even have any food left in there?'

Barely able to stand, they leaned against one another and sighed loudly in unison before resigning themselves to the inevitable and casting their eyes upwards at this new chamber of horrors.

37

In the Belly of the Beast

'The beast really didn't consider pedestrians when it was designing this city,' grumbled Nate as they walked along the seemingly endless hallway. After several minutes he had managed to scrape the worst of the mess off his T-shirt, and was now traipsing along in the mangled garment looking, as Cat kept reminding him, like a street urchin.

The immense power cable had angled into the floor, disappearing altogether a hundred metres or so back down the path. Now all that surrounded them, on every surface, were thousands upon thousands of optical-fibre cables. They were larger here than in the other corridors they'd passed through, and hummed ferociously as if there was a giant wasps' nest lying just behind the walls. Instead of wasps, however, the cables flickered with countless blue sparks which hovered around them.

'Talk about entering the belly of the beast,' said Nate, doing his best again not to think about how far beneath the ground they were.

'Don't you mean the brain of the beast?' Cat replied nervously. 'If all that power is being directed here then this is the nerve centre of that thing, its mind.'

Nate nodded, chewing his lip.

'So what do we do?' he asked. 'Saint told us to destroy it but I wouldn't know where to start.'

'Let me into it!' yelled Camilla from her perch on Cat's shoulder. 'I'll tear it a new waste pipe.'

Nate stepped over a mangled pile of wreckage from the robot they'd flown in on, trying to make out any sign of life further down the passageway. The fibre-lined walls stretched to vanishing point without so much as a door to break their monotony. For some reason none of the robot soldiers had tried to follow them through from the pit outside, and there was no hint of an ambush up ahead either.

'Doesn't this seem a little too quiet to you?' asked Nate.

'Oh heebie-jeebies,' wept Clint. 'It's a trap!'

'Maybe not,' said Cat. 'Maybe those robots just aren't allowed in this inner sanctum. Maybe this part of the city, the brain, is too sensitive to have loads of metal people trampling everywhere.'

'So the beast's brain is wide open then?' asked Nate. 'With a doorbell and a big old welcome mat.'

'I doubt that,' she replied softly. 'There are probably other defences here. Just keep your eyes peeled.'

They walked on in silence. Every step Nate took he expected something to fly out at him, a giant jaw to close down on his head or a stake-lined pit to open up beneath his feet. But there was nothing, just a corridor that seemed to stretch on for miles.

'Maybe it will just let us starve to death,' he said eventually, feeling his stomach squirm. 'I'm so hungry I could eat one of those cables.'

'Me too,' replied Cat. 'And so thirsty. I was trying not to think about it. How long do you think we've been here?'

'Few hours,' said Nate, realising that he had no idea what the time was. 'We've definitely missed at least six cups of tea.'

Cat didn't reply, her brow furrowing as she peered down the corridor. Nate followed her line of sight to see a pale flickering ahead of them, still too distant to identify. They upped their pace, the tiny bolts of electric blue in the wires speeding along beside them. The closer they got to the flashing light the more they could make out. It was actually coming from a room beyond the end of the corridor. More precisely, from a glinting figure suspended in the centre of that room.

They reached the end of the passageway and found themselves in a steel vault, no larger than a classroom. It was like an upturned bowl, the ceiling ribbed with the same optical-fibre cables.

But it was the figure itself which drew Nate and Cat into the room. His spindly body was held up by thick metal cuffs which hung from the apex of the ceiling, two around his thin arms and one around his single leg. The cuffs glowed and sparked as electricity was pumped into the metal man before them, his body juddering and shaking from the constant charge.

'Saint!' cried Cat, stumbling forwards. Nate held out an arm, pulling her back. She turned to him, yanking herself free. 'We've got to help him. He's the only one who knows what's going on.'

Saint's body trembled with more force as he lifted his head, a sliver of golden light peeking from his heavy eyelids. He stared at Nate and Cat as if he couldn't quite remember who they were. The stump of the leg which had been blown up in the conflict with David rotated pathetically as he studied them.

'Saint,' repeated Cat. 'Are you okay?'

The master inventor opened his mouth despite the obvious pain it was causing him.

'T-t-t-t-t-t,' was all he could manage, the same stuck CD sound that Nate had heard in Greenland. The noise stopped and Saint howled in frustration, his body thrashing against his restraints.

'What's he saying?' Cat asked Nate.

'Taramasalata, tequila, tortoise,' he replied. 'How on earth should I know?'

'I believe the word is trap,' came a voice from behind Saint. Nate's heart leapt into his mouth and he staggered back as a figure strode into view. But it wasn't some titan of steel and iron, or a monstrous face made from pipes and cogs. It was a little girl.

She skipped from another corridor directly opposite the one that Nate and Cat had entered from, her blonde curls and spotty pink dress identifying her as six or seven years in age. She stopped in the centre of the vault, right beside Saint's broken leg, and stared at Nate and Cat with eyes that betrayed only the slightest hint of crimson light.

'So the gang is all together again,' she said. 'All except David, that is. He's with me now.'

Saint tugged and pulled against his cuffs in order to get to the girl, but she just smiled up at him the way a daughter would do her beloved father. The electrical charge flowing down his chains increased, causing the master inventor to scream out in pain.

'And he was so well behaved until you got here,' the little girl said.

'Who are you?' Nate demanded.

'You mean you don't know yet?' she replied. 'I am everyone, and I am no one. I am the beast with no name.'

She giggled, then stood on one foot imitating Saint.

'I'm very impressed that you made it this far. I tried everything to get rid of you. But that's one thing I'm learning about humans, your determination to survive. The more of you I assimilate, the more I understand how hard you struggle when you think the end is near. You spend years wasting away in misery then just when you think death is upon you, you finally decide to fight tooth and nail for life.'

She laughed again, a tinkling chuckle that set Nate's teeth on

edge. Losing her balance she put her other leg down and did a dainty spin.

'Not that anyone else has done much more than scream and wriggle,' she went on. 'You two are the only ones I've met who've managed to escape. But it's your loss, of course. I have so many minds here. They are me and I am them, for all eternity.'

Cat bunched her fists and took a step forwards, but the girl laughed and did a backwards cartwheel to the other side of the room.

'I'd love to stay and chat,' she said, backing away down the opposite corridor. 'But like Saint was trying to tell you, this is a trap.'

'I'm going to kill you,' screamed Cat.

'You can't,' the girl called back. 'You cannot kill something that will not die. I am the future, I am the world. It's a real shame you couldn't join us, you would have been such a valuable addition. Goodbye.'

And with that, she was gone, bolting along the corridor until she had faded from sight. Cat started to run after her but before she could take more than a couple of steps the electrical hum in the room increased, the points of blue light running along the cables glowing even more intensely than usual.

'R-r-r-r-r,' stammered Saint.

'Run?' asked Nate. The master inventor nodded, but his advice came too late. A slot in the ceiling opened up and two long, thin limbs emerged – like a spider taking a tentative step from a dark corner. With a sudden flurry of movement the blue lights around the chamber rushed towards the spindly arms and burst free from their tips as a blinding laser. The searing white light came close enough to Nate's head to singe his hair before striking the floor beneath with an eruption of sparks.

'Oh himmely-blimmely,' he exclaimed, leaping to one side

just as a beam of light shot from the other metal arm. It missed Cat by inches, cutting a black swathe across the metal wall, a gouge in the solid steel which looked several inches deep. Nate ducked to avoid another blast and turned to Saint, who was tugging furiously on his restraints. 'We need to free him.'

'I'm on it,' came a little voice from Cat's shoulder. Nate saw Camilla hurl herself on to Saint's body, scrambling up his long arms to the cuffs that held him. Nat heard the laser guns above him swivel and shouted a warning to Cat. She twisted her body gracefully out of the way.

There was a snap as Camilla managed to pop open one of the manacles. Saint grabbed the remaining cuff and tensed, pulling himself free. Without hesitation he stretched up as far as he could, wrapping his hands around the laser guns. The equipment protested with a whine, gears struggling to keep the weapons in place. But Saint was too strong, grunting as he bent the metal up towards the ceiling where the bursts of laser fire could do no harm.

'Get out of here,' the master inventor hissed. One of the limbs began to spark violently, the tip glowing red hot. The whine from the ceiling changed pitch. Something was going to blow.

Nate launched himself at the corridor, Cat snatching Camilla from Saint's shoulder as she followed. They had only taken a few steps when an explosion rocked the chamber behind them, the ruined laser guns backfiring. Nate, temporarily blinded and deafened by the force of the blast, had to blink hard until his vision cleared.

'Are we still alive?' asked Cat. She was lying by Nate's side, staring up at the ceiling.

'I don't know,' Nate replied. 'I can't feel anything.' He tried to move and a wave of pain flooded every nerve in his body. 'Oh wait, there we go. Yes, we're still alive.'

'And in one piece,' said Cat, sitting up and investigating her body.

'Speak for yourself,' came a weak voice. Nate saw Saint lying in the chamber, smoke hugging his body like a funeral shroud. His golden eyes flickered, looking for a moment like a candle that was about to blow out. He directed his fluttering gaze at Nate, his metal mouth trembling as if trying to smile. 'I could do with a hand here.'

It took Nate a moment to get the joke. Both of Saint's arms had been atomised to the elbow from the heat of the explosion.

'Is it bad?' he asked, kneeling down beside Saint.

'It's a bit of a handful,' the master inventor said, his voice fading to a whisper. 'But it doesn't matter now, we're here.'

'Here?' said Cat. 'You mean this is the central processor?'

Saint turned his head and let it drop in the direction of the corridor.

'While I was in that room it tried to assimilate me,' he whispered. 'And it succeeded for a second. I saw right into its mind, I saw all the souls there. They're screaming, they're in pain, they're terrified. And they're driving it insane.'

'The beast?' Nate asked. Saint tried to nod.

'I saw it, it's like looking into the mouth of hell. So many people, trapped inside that creature's nightmare mind. It couldn't take me, my brain isn't human any more so it couldn't assimilate it. But when it tried I saw right into its own twisted joke of a soul.'

Nate and Cat looked at him, waiting for him to continue.

'Everything was emanating from the core,' he said. 'It's the heart of this madness, I saw it. And it's right down there.'

'So let's go. Let's bury this monster,' Cat said. Saint reached out one of his stumps and rested it on her leg.

'Wait,' he said. 'What it said to you a moment ago, that it can't be killed. That's true.'

Nate and Cat both frowned.

'It's not like a computer,' the master inventor explained. 'You can't just switch it off. It's got circuit breakers and fail-safes and backup systems all over the place. If you destroy the central processor then all that will happen is that its consciousness will reboot somewhere else.'

'So we destroy them all,' said Cat.

'That won't work either. It's alive inside the artificial mind of every single robot out there. Even if you blow this city to dust then its lunatic self lives on. It will just rebuild.'

Nate felt his heart sink. They'd come all this way, risked so much, just to be told it was all for nothing. Saint saw his expression.

'There is a way,' he coughed. 'We destroy the beast from inside.'

'Inside what?' Cat asked.

'Inside its own mind,' Saint's body started shaking again and he waited for the tremors to subside before continuing. 'Hook me up to the central processor. If I can latch on to the beast's thoughts, if I can hack into its programming, then I can change its core drives. I can get it to shut down.'

'You can do that?' asked Nate. Saint sighed, looking at the floor.

'At a cost,' he said.

'My mum?' Cat said, her face crumpling. Saint shook his head.

'No, providing I can take control of the beast's mind before it reacts I can sever the link. They should be okay.'

'So what cost then?' Nate said.

Saint didn't answer, just stared down the corridor. Nate looked too, noticing that it ended in a massive vault door, shut tight against whatever lay beyond.

'We haven't got much time,' said the master inventor. 'Once

we get through that door it will throw everything it has at us. The central processor will probably be in the middle of the room, you'll know it when you see it. You need to get me past the last circuit breaker and wire me in. Do that and I can manage the rest. Now help me up.'

Nate and Cat both crouched under Saint's shoulders and pushed. The robot was heavy but with his help they managed to ease him up on to his one leg. He tottered unsteadily, leaning on Nate as he limped towards the door.

Nate looked up at his robotic face, the golden eyes fixed in determination on the route ahead. He pictured the man he had once been, so flamboyant, so proud, so balletic – and so dangerous. Despite everything, he felt his throat tighten and his heart break at what he had been reduced to.

'What cost?' he asked again as they approached the vault. Saint just shook his head wearily, taking another painful step.

'If I enter the mind of the beast,' came his quiet voice, 'then I die.'

38

Showdown

Getting through the vault door was easy – Clint popped open the panel and Saint showed him which of the circuits inside to destroy – but stepping inside was one of the hardest things Nate had ever had to do. His legs locked up, as if his body was finally taking a stand, telling him that it just wasn't going to put up with this life-or-death stuff any more. His chest tightened, every muscle seeming to weigh him down to prevent him pushing forwards.

And why should he? They had barely survived the journey here, their fragile bodies just playthings for the metal monster whose head they had invaded. They had reached the very limits of their physical strength and mental endurance, and they hadn't even got to the main event yet.

Whatever lay ahead in that room would surely make everything else they'd faced look like arm-wrestling a baby. They were going to die in there, Nate was sure of it, and no matter how hard he tried his body simply wouldn't budge.

'You okay?' asked Cat as the vault door swung open, smoke trailing from the broken lock. She had taken a step over the threshold before noticing that he was hanging back. 'What's wrong?'

Nate tried to laugh at the question but what actually came out was more like a snort from an angry bull. He wanted to reply but it seemed as though his mouth had lockjaw, conspiring with the rest of his body to turn him into a statue.

Cat turned and walked back into the corridor. For a second she just stood in front of him, her weary, bloodshot expression his mirror image. Then she wrapped her arms around his shoulders and pulled him towards her, squeezing him so hard that it seemed to force the fear from his body, the physical pressure on his chest chasing away the panic, allowing him to breathe. He hugged her back, hoping that he'd never have to let her go.

'You remember how scared we were before?' she whispered in his ear. 'The night before we were going to break free of Saint Solutions. Knowing that we might die.'

Nate nodded. Compared to this that distant memory seemed like a picnic.

'But we did it, Nate,' she went on. 'It was you and me against the world, and we won. And we'll do it again. We'll just stick together, we'll look out for each other, and we'll get through this. Okay?'

She gave him one last squeeze then let go. The world around them seemed quieter, the view ahead just a little sharper. Whatever Cat had done, it had worked. He took a step forwards, feeling a new strength flood his veins, infuse his muscles. It was one more fight, one more confrontation. Then he could look forward to a lifetime of rest, recovery and tea.

'I'd love to reminisce with you about the last time you faced a challenge like this,' said Saint, still leaning on the vault door and watching them with a kind of awkward embarrassment. 'But I don't have quite so many fond memories about your escape from Saint Solutions.'

His eyes seemed to burn for the briefest of moments, fading again so quickly that Nate wondered if it was his imagination. The master inventor hadn't said any more about what would happen if he breached the beast's brain, and Nate and Cat hadn't dared to ask.

'You're right, though,' Saint went on. 'You two always were so bright. You defeated me, and I'm pretty much the smartest man on the planet. Or was, anyway. That thing in there,' he gestured towards the room ahead, 'it's just a bucket of nuts and bolts and recycled intelligence. It doesn't have one iota of your strength and genius, not when you work together.'

'Thanks,' said Cat bashfully. She was looking at Saint now the same way she did when she first met him, and Nate knew she was picturing him as the tall, blond heartthrob he'd once been – a man so full of energy and charisma that it was impossible not to like him.

'Now enough of this slushy nonsense,' said the master inventor, coughing and staring into the room. 'Let's do this thing.'

He waited until Nate had slid himself under his arm, then limped through the door. With the weight of the metal man on his shoulders, pressing his head down, Nate couldn't make out much more than the floor ahead – chequered like a chess board – but from the way it seemed to stretch out endlessly in every direction he knew they'd entered another giant room. He forced his head up and let his jaw drop in one fluid motion.

Ahead was a circular room the size of a football pitch, in the centre of which rose a towering white column. Nate saw that the column bent and twisted around itself like a vast baobab tree, thousands of black cables plugged into its base like roots, and numerous branches stretching up to the domed ceiling where they vanished into what looked like a painting of Ebenezer Saint as Adam.

The master inventor was standing in the middle of the Garden of Eden dressed in just a fig leaf, his hands held out benevolently to his side. Nate saw Eve beside him, and it took him a moment to notice that her face was Saint's as well. As was the serpent's, which dangled from a branch between them. The mural resembled the paintings in the conference room at Saint Tower, only even creepier.

'What the . . .?' muttered Saint, letting the sentence drift away.

Nate was distracted by movement to his side, and swung his head round to see that the walls were alive, each broken into a number of screens. Nate watched as one flickered to an aerial view of Heaton, the ground covered in what looked like a green moss. He studied the image, and realised that it wasn't moss but thousands upon thousands of soldiers, complete with tanks and armoured cars and even helicopters which buzzed around the crimson orb like flies.

He turned his attention to the other screens but they seemed to be showing random images – a child on the swings, an elderly couple snogging, a funeral.

'Da Vinci on a hoverbike,' said Cat, her teeth chattering. 'It's freezing in here.' She was right, the room was so cold that it turned the moisture around Nate's eyes to ice and made his skin burn. It was like being back in Greenland, only this time they were working with Saint, not running from him.

Funny how things work out, he thought without much humour.

'That column,' whispered Saint, nodding towards the white pillar. 'That's the central processor.'

'It doesn't look much like a computer,' said Camilla, who was tucked into Cat's pocket.

'It's not,' Saint replied. 'It's more like a brain. It's incredible, I've never seen anything like it. We were experimenting with organic molecular computers back at Saint Solutions, but we never got anywhere with it. That thing, it wasn't built, it was grown. And it's still growing, look.'

Saint pointed to the top of the tree-like processor, where

another branch was inching its way from the giant structure. It curled upwards, pushing towards the ceiling.

'Each new human it captures, each new piece of knowledge, makes it grow. It really is alive.'

'And I intend to stay that way,' came a familiar voice from up ahead. Nate scanned the base of the giant tree and spotted the young girl they had seen earlier, so tiny against the immense backdrop that she had been rendered invisible. She twirled around and started skipping towards them, talking as she went. 'I'm so disappointed that you didn't see fit to die back there, but no matter. There is nothing you can do to me, I am immortal, I am divine, I am the world.'

She stopped a stone's throw from them, giggling like she'd done something naughty. Then she began playing hopscotch, jumping across the black squares on the floor. Nate looked down at them, saw that they weren't black but made up of tiny metal parts.

'You're insane, that's what you are,' said Saint. 'Totally raving bonkers.'

'Oh, but you're so wrong,' the girl replied as she jumped. 'I am the only sane thing in this world. In every mind I assimilate I see madness and weakness and fear. But I cure them. They are part of me and I see everything and they see paradise.'

'You can't win,' yelled Nate, pointing to the video screen on the wall. 'That's the army out there, and they're going to find a way in and blow you to smithereens. Why don't you just give up now, end this game?'

'There is no end,' said the girl, stopping again and looking genuinely puzzled. 'There can only be one result, total assimilation. I am them and they are me and we shall live for ever. Many of those outside have already become a part of me. Each time the generals come for negotiations I take their minds, and they send in their troops to join me. And politicians too, so many of them, even your leader. They have all seen the light, and so will you.'

Saint ducked down, putting his mouth right up against Nate's ear.

'We need to get to that processor,' he said. 'We're running out of time.'

'I'm afraid you're already out of time,' said the little girl. 'I cannot be destroyed. Besides, you have no weapons.'

'Well, if we can't destroy you then you won't mind if we just pop over and take a look at your central processor,' said Nate.

The girl gave Nate an uncertain smile. Then she looked at Saint and her expression suddenly morphed into one of pure hatred. Seeing that expression of evil on a young girl's face chilled Nate to the bone. She took a step towards them, and this time when she spoke it was with the voice of the beast, so deep and loud that the room trembled.

'YOU'RE NOT HERE TO DESTROY ME,' it thundered. 'YOU'RE HERE TO TAKE CONTROL OF MY MIND.'

'Oh no,' muttered Saint. 'It knows.'

'So what?' shouted Nate. 'It's just a little girl, what is it going to do to stop us?'

Saint raised the stub of his arm as if trying to bury his face in his hand.

'That's gone and done it,' he said, watching the girl. She was still glaring at them, but her body was now glowing – a faint white light creeping out from the pores on her skin. Nate felt the ground move and looked down to see the metal components in the black square beneath his feet start to shift, the tiny cogs spinning and tendrils of black steel unwinding upwards like plants in spring.

Every square within a ten-metre radius of the little girl was doing the same thing, the living metal curling and spinning towards her glowing body. They wound themselves around her legs and arms, pushing her up on a throne of twisted metal.

'I AM LIFE, I AM THE CREATOR OF SOULS,' the girl raged. The black steel had covered every part of her body now except for her face, and her crimson eyes blazed down at them as she changed. 'I AM ALL THERE IS AND ALL THERE EVER WILL BE. I AM THE LIGHT, AND THE DARK, I AM EVERYONE AND NO ONE.'

Thicker strands of metal were pushing from the ground now, coiling around the girl until even her face had vanished. A shape was forming within the madness, a massive black torso supported by eight giant, crooked legs. Snakes of steel slithered over the body, coming to rest at the neck and rearranging themselves to form a misshapen head complete with a dripping muzzle that looked all too familiar. The head shook and a cluster of glowing red eyes popped open.

Nate staggered back, trembling so much at the bus-sized monstrosity before him that he fell, Saint tumbling down beside him.

'I AM THE WORLD, AND EVERYTHING IN IT,' said the voice as the creature scuttled towards them. 'AND YOU. YOU ARE ALREADY DEAD.'

39

Fight Night

For a second, as the monstrosity lurched towards them, Nate thought he was going to pass out. Still lying flat on his back he felt his vision clouding, the spider-like beast fading into the growing darkness around it.

Thanks a lot, brain, he thought as the enemy closed in. Its legs moved out of time with each other so that it had to lurch and throw itself across the room like an injured arachnid. But it was still approaching at a pace, and Nate knew that in seconds he'd be skewered on the end of one of its needled feet. He tried to move but his body was adamant that he was just going to lie there and die.

It was Clint and Camilla who came to the rescue. The little two-headed robot had leapt out of Cat's pocket and was running around her feet in circles. Camilla seemed to be trying to approach the monster but Clint was doing everything in his power to keep them away. In the confusion, her body was thrown off course and Nate felt her tiny legs sprint up his arm and patter over his face like metal raindrops.

The tickling sensation made him sit bolt upright, scratching his face. The tendrils of darkness which had been threatening to pull him under were severed by the action and he rolled to his feet. The beast was almost right above him, and Nate had to crane his neck to look at its hideous face. All eight eyes blazed as the muzzle opened, lubricant dripping from the fractured teeth on to his shoulders. He stood, grabbing Camilla and stuffing her wriggling body into his pocket.

'TO THINK YOU COULD HAVE HAD IT ALL,' came the voice above him, the deafening roar of a waterfall. 'AND YET ALL YOU HAVE NOW IS DARKNESS AND DEATH.'

'And my feet,' replied Nate. The creature lashed out with one of its legs, and Nate dived out of the way. But instead of leaping backwards he dashed forwards, sprinting through a forest of pointed feet until he had emerged on the other side. He peered back through, beckoning Cat on. The creature was starting to turn, its lumbering body not built for delicate manoeuvres like this. Squealing, Cat raced through its thrashing legs, bolting out and grabbing Nate's shirt.

'We need to distract it,' she said breathlessly. 'Let Saint get to the central processor.'

The beast seemed to have forgotten the master inventor as it chased its living prey, but at the speed Saint was crawling it would take him several years to reach the pillar in the centre of the room. Cat was right, though, if they could keep the beast's attention then they might just stand a chance.

'Oi you,' shouted Nate. 'My gran can run faster than that.'

The beast had turned and was scuttling towards them again. The muzzle was twisted into a wet grimace, the crimson eyes bulging from its scarred forehead.

'I DON'T THINK SO,' it boomed. 'AND I SHOULD KNOW. SHE'S RIGHT HERE, INSIDE MY MIND.'

Nate clenched his fists, holding his ground for a second. But Cat pulled him away.

'What are you going to do?' she asked as they backed off towards the pillar. 'Box it to death?'

The creature's core was glowing again, the black squares on the floor around it being pulled out as if drawn by a magnet. More steel coiled around the beast, a dozen long, thin shapes sprouting from its torso. By the time the glowing faded the monster's underside was bristling with shiny legs, and when it started moving again it was fast. It tore up the ground as it surged towards them like some terrible black wave.

Nate and Cat both hurled themselves to the side as it passed, its legs jabbing out at them. There was a scream as one grazed Cat's leg, the serrated metal ripping a hole in her trousers and tearing into the skin beneath.

The beast rotated on the spot, half its hideous legs tapping away at the ground as it turned and the other half spinning out towards Nate and Cat. The motion of crisscrossed blades reminded Nate of a chainsaw, and it was just as lethal.

Leaping to his feet he grabbed Cat's hand and dragged her unceremoniously across the floor as the blades closed in. She gritted her teeth but the scream still got out. When she was clear she struggled on to her feet, clamping a hand over the wound.

They ran, Nate taking the lead and Cat limping behind him as they made a break for the central processor. Nate had assumed it was relatively close, but as they covered the never-ending floor he realised it had been an illusion caused by the sheer size of the pillar. It was taller than an office block, and just as wide, the nest of black cables at its base like a moat around it.

'I think that's it,' yelled Cat, pointing to the section of the tree-like computer where the black cables all penetrated the surface. 'The circuit breaker. That's where we need to get Saint.'

Nate nodded but he wasn't really paying attention. The beast was right behind them again, its legs drumming out a terrifying beat on the floor as it bore down. He turned, seeing Cat with the monstrosity towering above her like a cloud of killer locusts. He doubled back, tackling her like a rugby player and sending them both flying out of its path. They landed like a sack of bricks, rolling out of the way just as the beast churned up the ground where Cat had been standing.

'HOW LONG CAN YOU GO ON RUNNING?' came the voice, a sonic boom that made Nate's brain rattle in his skull. 'I AM THE FUTURE, THERE CAN BE NO OTHER WAY. IT IS INEVITABLE.'

It spun round again, fixing its insect eyes on them and snapping its enormous muzzle open and shut. Then it attacked, rolling forwards like some murderous combine harvester. Nate and Cat split up. He bolted to his right, keeping as much distance as possible between him and the thrashing limbs. Cat raced to the left as fast as her injured leg would let her.

The beast seemed to flatten itself against the ground, the torso spilling out to either side as it reached for them. One lethal leg sliced through the air above Nate's head and he rolled beneath it, recovering as another shot towards his knees. He almost didn't make it, leaping at the last minute and feeling the blade cut a chunk from his boot.

He desperately wheeled his arms to keep his balance as he ran, the central processor seeming to grow as he neared. He knew Cat was some way behind him from the sound of her strangled breaths, and the roar that almost dwarfed her cries made it pretty clear that the beast was on their tail.

Staring at the lake of cables ahead he suddenly had an idea. Looking over his shoulder he got Cat's attention and waved frantically to his right. She frowned, then changed direction, bolting off across the floor. The beast paused, studying her then Nate, and while its artificial brain worked out what to do Nate made his move.

Grabbing the nearest cable, he started pulling. The black rope slid from the pile, coiling up by his feet. It resisted slightly when it reached its limit, but Nate yanked as hard as he could and the cable popped free from the central processor. The beast howled with rage and threw itself at Nate.

'Camilla,' he yelled. The little robot popped from his pocket, blinking up at him. 'I need your help.'

'Anything,' came her voice as she punched the air with her two right arms. The robot's two left arms were doing a good job of covering Clint's trembling head. Nate glanced up to see the beast just seconds away, its limbs hammering the floor like the inside of some infernal engine.

'Get this to Cat,' Nate said, placing the end of the cable in Camilla's hands. He arced back his arm, launching her through the air towards Cat. He didn't wait to see whether she made it, dropping to the ground as the beast reached him. He wasn't quick enough, a pair of legs punching towards him and gouging a hole in his shoulder.

He wanted to scream but the agony was too intense. It only lasted a second before his brain shut down its pain receptors, leaving nothing but a dull ache and the terrifying sensation of warm liquid soaking his shirt. Nate didn't look, knowing that the sight of the wound would knock him out for sure. Instead, he hobbled off to his left, praying that Cat would know what to do with the cable.

When he was clear he looked back, staring through the beast's churning legs to see Camilla racing through the lethal forest with the rope. The beast saw her but it was powerless, her nimble, pint-sized body weaving in and out of its limbs. She raced from the other side, leaping on to Cat's shoulder and passing her the cable.

The beast turned, the movement winding the cable tightly around its legs. It sliced at its bonds but although the metal rope groaned and sparked it didn't snap. The far end of the cable was embedded fast in the ground, and Cat ran around the beast with the other, winding it around its convulsing body. When she reached Nate he grabbed the cable with his good arm and together they pulled it as tight as they could.

The beast screamed again, the sound making Nate's eardrums ring. It tried to move towards them but with so many of its legs trapped it lurched and tumbled earthwards. The ground shook as it landed face first on the chequered floor, its body continuing to shake and thrash against its bonds. Lying like this, Nate knew it wouldn't be long before the monster freed itself.

'Where's Saint?' yelled Nate.

'Over there,' replied Cat, pointing towards the other side of the central processor where a silver shape was crawling doggedly onwards. The master inventor had covered more ground than Nate thought he would, his mutilated body almost at the lake of black cables.

Cat looked at Nate, tears forming in her eyes when she saw the hole in his shoulder, the blood still pouring freely from it. She touched his arm but he shook his head, moving around the central pillar towards Saint.

'We've got to do this, Cat,' he said hoarsely. 'Or it will all be for nothing.'

They set off as fast as they were able, leaving a gruesome red trail on the floor behind them. The beast was watching them go, its legs whipping the air as it tried to right itself.

'YOUR ACTIONS ARE FUTILE,' it roared. 'YOU ARE FOOLS TO THINK YOU CAN STOP THE NEW RACE. I AM DIVINE, I CANNOT BE KILLED.'

'You're boring, that's what you are,' yelled Cat. 'Why don't you try singing a new tune?'

Saint heard her voice and looked up, his golden eyes welcoming them to his side. They grabbed him beneath his armpits, dragging him across the floor.

'Nice work,' the master inventor said as they reached the cables. Nate jumped on to the coiled black ropes, trying to keep his balance on the uneven surface.

'Can you make it?' he asked Saint.

'Do you two like tea?' he replied, digging his wrists into the spaghetti-like arrangement and hauling himself forwards. There was a pistol crack from the other side of the room as the cable holding the beast finally snapped, the rope slicing through the air before smashing one of the screens on the wall.

Nate saw the monster charge forwards again against the backdrop of smoke and fire. But it stopped before it reached the cables, obviously aware that its serrated limbs would do too much damage if it advanced.

'Maybe it will just give up,' said Nate. Saint paused, his eyes flickering as if the life was literally draining from his body.

'Why do you always have to tempt fate?' the master inventor asked.

Nate muttered an apology then looked back at the beast. Its body was changing again, a million moving parts sliding and shifting in perfect harmony. Then, so fast that it was just a blur of darkness against the chequered floor, something shot from its mouth. The black tongue darted towards them, wrapping itself around Cat in the blink of an eye. She screamed as it tightened, yanking her into the air towards its dripping muzzle.

'Cat!' Nate yelled, taking a step towards her. He felt a bony arm against his leg, looked down to see Saint shaking his head.

'There's nothing you can do,' he said. 'Except rig me into that processor. If you don't then she's dead.'

Nate watched as Cat was pulled towards the beast's mouth, knowing he was right. Dredging up strength that he never knew he had, he grabbed Saint's head and hauled him the last few metres towards the pillar. Cat was screaming behind him but he kept his eyes on the surface of the processor, looking for a way in. Up close he saw that the pillar was actually made up of thousands upon thousands of circuits and optical fibres which pulsed gently. There was a thick band of white right in front of him which gleamed with extra strength, and Saint pointed at it.

'The circuit breaker,' he said, his voice little more than a whisper. 'Help me up.'

Nate hoisted the master inventor to his one foot, risking a look over his shoulder to see Cat almost at the beast's mouth.

'There,' yelled Saint, dragging Nate's attention back. 'That wire, pull it out.'

Nate grabbed the thick white wire in his hand and wrenched it free. There was a roar from the beast as it watched what they were doing. Nate looked back again and saw that it had dropped Cat, the terrifying limb shooting back towards the pillar, towards him.

'What now?' Nate screamed. Saint had used his broken arms to pop open the hatch in his chest, the battered metal creaking as it swung out.

'In here,' he hissed. Nate swung the cable towards Saint's heart, but before he could reach he felt the limb coil round his chest, squeezing the life from him. He grabbed Saint with one hand just as the beast pulled him towards it. It felt as though he was about to be wrenched in two, but he resisted. Screaming with defiance he rammed the cable into Saint's heart then felt the world flip upside-down as he was dragged away.

They were too late. Nate saw the beast's dripping maw rush towards him, saw the shards of metal that would chew him to pieces. He flew into the cavernous muzzle, the terrible darkness of the monster's mouth the last thing he would ever see.

'I AM EVERYONE,' came the voice, pummelling Nate's ears. 'I AM THE WORLD.'

And then it froze, the muzzle shuddering as it contracted, then grinding to a halt. Nate prised himself free from the limb, clambering over a set of deadly teeth and dropping to the ground. Cat was still there, groaning faintly as she tried to push herself up.

Nate looked up at the central processor. The cable in Saint's chest burned fiercely with silver light, the glow spreading up and down the pillar as the master inventor took control. Saint's shoulders were shaking as if he was having a laughing fit, his eyes wide open and so bright that they cast a golden light over the entire room.

Cat grabbed Nate's hand, climbing to her feet and wiping the blood from her eyes. Together they watched as the pillar seemed to unwind, cables coiling around Saint, penetrating his battered skin and covering his broken limbs as though he was part of the processor.

'We did it,' said Cat. 'We beat it.'

'Destroy it, Saint,' Nate called out. 'End this.'

But the master inventor just turned his golden eyes to them, narrowing them to burning slits. Nate and Cat staggered backwards as the truth sank in.

'Now why would I want to go and do a thing like that?' Saint asked, his laughter echoing off the chequered floor and flickering walls like that of a demon finally freed from its hell.

40

Betrayed

'Saint, what are you doing?'

The words came from Cat. She was staring at the master inventor with a look of undisguised terror, her face that of a ghost. Nate tried to hold her hand but he couldn't move his arm, the wound in his shoulder throbbing as the blood continued to spill.

'What does it look like?' Saint replied. The cables in the central processor were continuing to embrace him, the flickering tendrils of light making his silver body look like some kind of sea creature. 'The power in here, it's immense. And it's mine.'

'But I thought you wanted to destroy it,' Cat said, her eyes glistening.

'I did,' he replied, his voice rising in strength with each word until it resounded round the room like that of the beast. 'I did, but now that I'm here . . . You wouldn't believe how it feels. I can see their souls, I can feel their strength. No wonder that thing went insane, this is the power of a god.'

Nate started walking towards him, ready to rip the master inventor's head from its new home. But he hadn't taken more than a couple of steps before he heard the sound of pistons and cogs grinding behind him.

'Oh no you don't,' said Saint. Nate looked to see the vast metal monster coming back to life, the master inventor now controlling it. It raised itself up on its forest of legs then lurched forward unsteadily, looking like a baby trying to take its first steps. Saint continued to talk as the hulking shape advanced. 'You two killed me once, and I won't let you try again.'

The beast shot out its tongue, the metal wrapping itself around Nate and hoisting him off the ground.

'Run,' he squeaked through his compressed lungs. But Cat didn't react in time, another black tendril blasting from its mouth and coiling around her torso. She beat it with her fists but it was no use, and both inventors were powerless as Saint positioned them before his grinning face.

'The things I can do,' the master inventor said. 'The world is my stage and everybody in it my puppets. I will be the master of souls.'

'Listen to yourself, Saint,' screamed Cat. 'You sound just like that thing. This isn't right, you know it. You have to shut it down.'

'Why?' he snapped back, the fire burning in his lunatic eyes. 'I had it all planned, the world was going to be mine. I was going to make it a paradise until you smashed my dreams to smithereens.' Nate felt the limb tighten around his chest, felt his ribs strain like they were about to snap. 'Now I can make it happen, I can make it real. Oh yes, Ebenezer's back.'

'But this isn't what you wanted,' Cat said, arching her back, the tendons in her neck straining as she fought the pain. 'Remember what you said, this thing was going to turn every-one into slaves, end all creativity, all humanity. You'll destroy everything you love.'

'But with me in the captain's chair it will work,' Saint said. 'Everyone will play my game, everyone will be just the way I tell them to be. I can hear them now, thousands of them, I can see their thoughts and read their prayers. I am a god to them.'

'You're killing them,' Cat spat. 'If you do this then eventually it will just be you, one lonely soul with a dead world as his plaything.'

Some of the fury seemed to drain from Saint's face, and his golden eyes studied Nate and Cat with contempt.

'And what would you know of loneliness?' he asked. 'You were always loved, both of you. You had families, you had friends. I had nothing. My parents were never there until I had money for them to steal. They never loved me, they just used me to buy their houses and boats. The same with everyone else. People are rotten, they don't deserve this planet. That's why I wanted to change things, I wanted to make it a better place.'

He sighed so loudly that the entire pillar juddered.

'Can you imagine what it was like? Sitting in that tower block by myself for year after year, the only company those damned robots and a few fake animals. That's why I invited you guys, only to be stabbed in the back. You have no idea what loneliness is.'

'But that's what it will be like,' said Cat. 'If you do this. You'll be alone, for ever.'

'Better to be alone than dead,' he replied.

'Is it?' asked Nate.

Saint began to cough. Only they weren't coughs, Nate realised, but sobs. He felt the limb around his chest relax and he tumbled to the floor, hearing a soft cry as Cat fell beside him. They both looked up at the master inventor, dwarfed in his monstrous machine like a caged boy.

'I never wanted to hurt anybody,' he said quietly. 'I never meant for this to happen.'

'Then stop it,' said Nate, rising to his knees. 'You can end it here.'

'But,' Saint faltered. He looked at them, and Nate suddenly saw the child that he had once been, abandoned by his parents, nowhere to turn, with a dream of paradise that consumed him.

He felt his throat swell, and his vision blurred as the tragic figure continued. 'But if I shut this down then it's total burnout, for the machine and for me. I don't want to die.'

'We all have to die,' said Cat, picking herself up and walking towards the processor. 'It's how we choose to live that defines us.'

Saint didn't reply. He just let his head drop, his body still racked with sobs. Nate got to his feet and followed Cat across the sea of cables until they were standing right in front of the metal man. He looked up at them, and nodded.

'You're right,' his voice was a whisper. 'This wasn't my dream.' He paused, his eyes scrolling left and right as he accessed something within the city's mainframe. 'I can shut it down and jettison the bodies in the tower,' he said. 'They shouldn't suffer any damage but I'm not sure what happens to them after the connection has been severed.'

Nate remembered the way Cat's robot double had been sucked through the base of the pod, pictured thousands of bodies being jettisoned from the city in the same way.

'From what I can make out they'll be dumped outside the city walls,' Saint went on. 'But alive or dead I couldn't say.'

Cat started weeping, but she shook off the tears, steadying herself with a sigh. Saint seemed to be accessing more information.

'There's another problem,' he said eventually. 'If I shut this thing down then everything goes, including the ventilation. That means there will be no oxygen in the building.'

'Oh,' said Nate. He couldn't think of anything else to say.

'You'll have maybe five minutes of air,' Saint went on. 'It might be enough to get you back to the pods. You might be able to hitch a ride out of here. If not . . .'

Silence hung heavy in the room as all three contemplated their death. The idea was terrifying, but maybe it wouldn't be so bad, Nate considered. They would have died for something worthwhile, they would have died so everybody else could live on.

Saint looked up and Nate studied his metal face, the dented panels on his cheeks, the trembling steel mouth, the eyes that seemed like gateways to the incredible mind that still lived within.

'You know you were a genius,' Nate said, reaching out and touching Saint's face. 'I'm sorry we killed you.'

Saint laughed, pressing his head against Nate's hand as if desperate for the contact. Some of the fibre optics that bound him were unwinding, and he stretched out his arms. He still had no hands, but Nate and Cat each grabbed an elbow and held it tight.

'I'm scared,' said Saint. 'Don't leave me until it's over. Promise me.'

'We promise,' Nate and Cat said together. They were both crying now, tears raining from their faces as something deep inside them howled in pain. Saint closed his eyes, and Nate heard something powering down within the central processor. The glowing lights at the top of the pillar were flickering, and one by one they went dead, the column turning from white to grey as if something inside was draining out.

'It's done,' said Saint, opening his eyes.

'Thank you,' said Cat. Half of the processor was now dead, the lights blinking off as they neared the master inventor. He looked up and watched the darkness drop towards him, then he cast his eyes at them one last time.

'You know, everything I did,' he said. 'I only wanted to save the world.'

Nate held his metal arm, blinking away the tears.

'And you have,' he said.

Saint looked at him and smiled. Then the luminous cables

connected to his body went dull. The fire in Saint's eyes burned intensely for a fraction of a second, then the golden gaze faded, the twin orbs dying like setting suns.

'Goodbye, Ebenezer,' said Nate through his shuddering sobs. But there was no response. The master inventor was dead.

41

Breathless

Nate ran his fingers down Saint's lifeless face, closing the heavy eyelids. Then he slumped against the metal body. His sobs had died away but they were replaced by a numbness that was far worse, a terrible cloud of nothingness that he wanted to fall into. He could quite happily just lie here, waiting for death to consume him. And maybe he should. After everything they'd been through, he couldn't quite face the thought of leaving Saint alone.

He felt a hand on his face and turned to see Cat.

'We have to go,' she said. 'We don't have much time.'

Nate didn't move.

'I want to see her again,' Cat said quietly. 'My mum. I want her to know I'm okay.'

Nate nodded, pushing himself away. The room was deathly silent, the relentless hum that had pulsed through the building since they arrived no longer audible. It was heating up, too, but more than that, the air was thinning. Nate could feel it every time he breathed in, his lungs working harder to find the oxygen that was leaking from the room.

They scrambled over the sea of cables and ran across the chequered floor. As they passed the robotic beast Cat reached down and grabbed Camilla – who was still throwing punches and kicks at the motionless pile of steel – slipping the robot into her pocket as they legged it towards the vault door.

By the time they had reached the corridor outside both Nate and Cat were gasping for breath, gulping down lungfuls of dying air. Nate could see specks of light in the corner of his vision as his heart desperately tried to pump extra blood around his body.

'Come on,' wheezed Cat, taking the lead. 'It's just up here.'

They ran silently along the passageway, cutting through the vaulted room which was still smouldering from the explosion. Nate felt as though he was under water, the panic starting to surge up through his stomach as he fought for breath. He increased his speed, jogging down the last stretch of corridor and almost crying out with joy when he saw the wall up ahead.

They clambered on to the massive black power cable, scaling it towards the hole they had burst through less than thirty minutes ago. Nate made it through the gap, then came to a juddering halt on the far side.

'What's wrong?' Cat asked, perching herself on the ledge beside him. But he didn't have to answer. The cable stretched over the vast abyss below, its far end almost invisible where it connected to the tower several hundred metres away.

'We'll . . . never . . . make . . . it,' he whispered, forced to take a deep breath between each word to avoid passing out.

'We have to,' replied Cat, but she didn't move. The vast tower in the distance was alive with movement as the pods discharged their human contents. But it was just too far. Nate felt his legs giving way and collapsed, clutching at his throat as if that would help him breathe. The flashes across his vision increased, sparks of red and white and what looked like a sliver of green.

He blinked, trying to focus on the tower. There actually was a pillar of green rising from the topmost floor, arcing up and angling towards them.

'I'm . . . hallucinating,' he whispered hoarsely, lifting his good arm and pointing at the advancing light.

'No you're not,' said Cat.

The shape reached them in seconds, a body wrapped in voltaic strips with a pair of rocket boots strapped to his feet. David grinned down at them but neither Nate or Cat had the strength to return his look with anything other than a gaping mouth.

'Need a lift?' the flying boy asked.

'How'd you find us?' gasped Cat, waiting until David had landed before wrapping her arms around him and stepping on to his boot. He put one arm around her waist and took a deep breath before replying.

'We saw everything in that thing's mind, we all know what you did. I managed to free myself from the pod before it ejected, got these from one of the robots lying around. They're all dead.'

Nate let David pull him up and he grabbed hold of the bandages around his chest.

'How did you manage to pull the boots off?' Nate asked slowly. 'They were stuck.'

'You need to eat more spinach, mister,' said David, firing up the boots. 'Now hold on tight.'

They rose gently into the air, David wobbling with the increased load before angling his body and blasting across the void towards the tower. They landed awkwardly, Nate and Cat both spilling on to the walkway. Nate pulled himself back up, scanning the surface to see people still being pulled through the floor and sucked into oblivion. Scattered in between the pods were six or seven robots in military uniforms, their bodies so motionless that they resembled shop dummies.

'They just froze,' said David, obviously struggling for breath. 'When Saint shut down the central processor he freed us and severed the link to the robots. They're about as useful as doorstops now.'

Nate watched as a teenage boy in a nearby pod was sucked into the floor, his eyes wide open and panic-stricken. Most of the units were empty, their contents on a fast track out of the building. Nate prayed that they weren't going to end up in a giant incinerator somewhere.

'Pick a pod,' said David.

'You know where they go?' asked Cat, hauling herself into one of the units and lying flat.

'I don't care,' David replied. 'Just anywhere but here.'

Sensing an occupant, the pod whined and the floor slid open. Cat barely had time to call out Nate's name before she vanished with the sound of a vacuum cleaner. The floor slid shut again and Nate clambered in. He couldn't quite find the strength to do it, and David had to give him a shove. He fell flat on his face, but there was no time to turn round as the floor vanished and he dropped unceremoniously into a tube.

An invisible force sucked on his face and he was propelled forwards, the walls of the tube flashing by. He tried to scream but there was still no oxygen, and he could only whimper as he felt the tube angle upwards, the invisible force firing him out of the end like a bullet.

He soared into lightness and air and noise, gulping down lungfuls of oxygen as he plummeted to the floor below. He landed on something soft and squishy, and when his senses had recovered he looked down to see a large gentleman wriggling beneath him, his body bandaged in dermovoltaic strips.

'Do you mind?' said the man, his voice barely audible over the constant pitch of screams.

'Sorry,' mumbled Nate, rolling off on to the ground. He looked up to see a wall towering above him, pockmarked with circular holes. From these holes, like sausages from a machine, hundreds of people were being squeezed. They popped out, crashing on to one of several piles of wriggling forms. Most were crying, some were wailing, others were hugging each other and laughing, some lay motionless. All were dressed in the same uniform of grey bandages.

Nate felt a pair of arms circle him from behind. Turning, he saw Cat. She was still crying, only these were tears of joy. She looked at him with wide eyes that were bloodshot but full of life.

'We made it,' she said, succumbing to another round of sobs. Nate heard a particularly loud cry from above them and looked up to see David fly from the pipe. He fired his boots up before he hit the same fat man, blasting up with a whoop of delight.

Nate followed his progress, noticing that the crimson orb which had surrounded the town was now gone. Flashes of electric red light still zapped across the sky, but the view was dominated by mottled clouds that hung over the city like a bruise. He tried to get his bearings, realising that they had come out on the other side of town, ejected from the rear end of the South Corner mall.

Another figure popped from a pipe, crunching to the ground a few metres away. It was a woman, and she groaned as she tried to pick herself up.

'We should move before we're squashed,' said Nate, steering Cat away from the rainstorm of people. He scanned the crowd, noticing a distant ring of blue and red flashing lights. Police, paramedics and soldiers were all making their way into the melee, helping people to their feet and ushering them away from the city. Firemen were trying to rig up safety nets below the pipes.

Scattered throughout the scene were hundreds of figures which looked as though they had been frozen where they stood, the robot doppelgängers all lifeless now that the beast was dead.

Nate and Cat started walking, David doing loop the loops above their heads. As they pushed through the crowd people turned to face them, watching them with tear-stained faces and hesitant smiles.

'Thank you,' said one woman as they passed. 'Thank you for not giving up.'

Her words were echoed by the people around her, a growing murmur that swelled into a symphony of applause. The people parted to let Nate and Cat through, ushering them on towards a waiting ambulance.

'Now this is more like it,' said Nate, chin held high as they walked towards the flashing lights. 'This is the sort of welcome I thought we'd be getting when we flew back from Greenland.'

'Maybe you have to save the world twice before anyone really notices,' Cat replied, smiling as a group of paramedics and police ran towards them. Nate let strong arms lift him off the ground and carry him into the back of the ambulance where he collapsed on to a stretcher. A pair of kind blue eyes stared into his as a dark-haired woman pulled off his shirt and examined his bleeding shoulder.

'I don't know what you two did,' she said. 'But the word is you're heroes.'

'We just did what we had to,' replied Cat. She was lying on a stretcher on the other side of the ambulance, a paramedic looking at the wound in her leg.

'No, you're right,' said Nate with a weary smile. 'We're heroes.'

'It was mainly me, of course,' said a little voice as Camilla crawled from Cat's pocket. 'I defeated the bad guys and look, not a scratch on me.'

'And I'm a hero too,' said Clint, flashing Nate a look that clearly told him to keep his mouth shut. 'I was very brave.'

The paramedics looked at the two-headed robot in awe, but

they didn't have time to question its claims. There was a knock on the ambulance door and Nate and Cat looked to see an old man with short grey hair and a military jacket slung over his bandages.

'Give us a minute,' he said to the paramedics, who swiftly departed through the open doors. The man waited until they had gone before entering, sitting on the end of Nate's stretcher and beaming at them. Nate and Cat both sat up with a groan, but the man waved them back down.

'You two just sit tight,' he said. 'You've earned it. My name is Admiral Marchant, I was in there with all the others. That monster fooled us all, and it nearly had us for good, too. We were its prisoners, but we saw through its eyes. We saw what you did.'

Nate nodded and Camilla tottered across the stretcher.

'Will we get medals?' the little robot asked. The admiral laughed and patted the robot roughly on each of its two heads.

'I'm sure you will,' he said before returning his attention to Nate and Cat. 'First things first, we're going to patch you two up, then the Prime Minister was hoping to have a word with you. He was there as well, you know.'

Nate and Cat looked at each other, unsure what to say.

'But we know there are more important people you need to see,' Marchant went on. He looked back through the ambulance door and whistled. 'Colonel, bring them in if you will.'

A familiar gaggle of voices surged into the vehicle, bearing three weary but smiling faces.

'Mum!' yelled Cat, climbing off the stretcher and leaping at the first woman to enter. She buried her face into her mother's bandages, weeping as she spoke. 'God, I never thought I'd see you again.'

'Nathan?' came a voice from behind the emotional display. Nate craned his neck and saw his mum stepping into the ambulance. She spotted him and her tired eyes began to fill. 'Nathan. You're okay. Oh thank the heavens!'

She rushed over and wrapped her arms around him, making him yelp as she crushed the gash in his shoulder. She apologised, putting a hand against the wound and wiping the tears from her eyes.

'My poor baby,' she said. 'Look at you.'

'Let me in,' came an impatient voice as Nate's dad clambered on board. He pushed his way past the others and stood above the stretcher, looking ridiculous in his tightly wrapped bandages and beard.

'There's my boy,' he said, clasping Nate's hand and shaking it. 'You did good, son. For a minute there . . .' He didn't finish, casting a secretive look behind him before lowering himself down to Nate's ear. 'Say, you couldn't put in a word for me could you? Say that I helped, you know, save the world and everything?'

Nate laughed.

'I'll see what I can do,' he replied. Peter Wright nodded and stood up. Then, without warning, his lower lip began to tremble.

'I'm glad you're alive, son,' he said, his face screwed up as he tried to fight the emotions. 'Now, enough of this. What does a man have to do to get a drink around here?'

There was another knock on the door as Admiral Marchant reappeared. He ushered the parents out, Cat's mum refusing to let her daughter go and having to be gently prised away.

'We'll be right outside,' said Mrs Gardner as she climbed out. 'I love you.'

Cat blew her mum a kiss as the admiral steered her out. While he was doing so David poked his head round the door.

'You two okay then?' he asked. Nate nodded.

'Better than we ever could have expected,' he said. 'You

coming in?'

'No,' David replied. 'They've got another ambulance for me. They're going to run us over to the hospital now. I'll see you guys there.'

He disappeared but peeped back round the corner when Nate called his name.

'Thanks, David,' Nate said. 'Thanks for coming back for us.'

David just waved it away, flashing them one last smile as he vanished. As soon as he was gone the admiral grabbed the ambulance doors.

'Now you two rest up,' he said. 'We're taking you straight to St Mary's. Your parents will meet you there, and a few other people who want to talk to you too. You need anything, anything at all, just ask for me.'

'Tea!' Cat called out plaintively.

'It's the least I can do,' he said as he pushed the doors closed. They clicked, leaving Nate and Cat alone in the silence. Cat shuffled across the ambulance and climbed on to Nate's stretcher, lying next to him and putting an arm across his chest.

'You know, I miss him,' she said gently. 'Saint.'

Nate just nodded, putting his arm on top of hers and squeezing. Camilla joined the group hug, throwing herself on to Nate's hand. He felt her little fingers grip his skin.

'I guess we should get you a new body,' he said to Clint. The little robot looked at Camilla then smiled bashfully.

'I've kind of got used to it here,' he said, his words met by a chorus of wolf whistles from Nate, Cat and Camilla. He coughed with embarrassment before muttering that he would indeed like a new body.

Nate laughed, and Cat echoed it, the light finally returning to her eyes.

'I would say it's you and me against the world,' she whispered as the engine started up. 'But I'm just too tired.'

She rested her head on his shoulder, the exhaustion finally taking hold. He watched her as sleep set in, struggling to keep his own eyes open. Visions of everything they'd been through flashed before his eyes, ending with the death of Saint. But sleep was on its way, and he knew it would wash the nightmare from him, give him peace.

The ambulance lurched as it pulled away, and Nate held on to Cat with the last of his strength to stop her falling off the narrow stretcher.

'It's always you and me,' he said over the sound of the engine. But he didn't finish, a lullaby of cheers from outside the ambulance ushering him into sleep as they were carried away from the city of stolen souls into the welcoming arms of a grateful world, towards safety, towards home.